A Late Flooding Thaw

Gary Guinn

For Larry and Reba — With best wishes for good friends — hope it's a good read —

Gary 7/10/05

**MOON▲LAKE
PUBLISHING COMPANY**
SILOAM SPRINGS, ARKANSAS

MOON♠LAKE
PUBLISHING COMPANY
14213 Lake Forrest Heights
Siloam Springs, AR 72761

A Late Flooding Thaw. Copyright © 2005 by Gary Guinn. All rights reserved. No part of this book may be reproduced in any form or by any electronic or mechanical means, including information storage and retrieval systems, without permission in writing from the publisher, except by a reviewer, who may quote brief passages in a review. Any members of educational institutions wishing to photocopy part or all of the work for classroom use, or publishers who would like to obtain permission to include the work in an anthology, should send their inquiries to Moon Lake Publishing Co., 14213 Lake Forrest Heights, Siloam Springs, AR 72761.

Printed in the United States of America

Design by Joel Armstrong
Cover photos: Schrader Photo Archive/Arkansas History Commission

Library of Congress Cataloging-in-Publication Data
Guinn, Gary
    A Late Flooding Thaw / Gary Guinn
       p. cm.
    ISBN 0-9755950-2-4

1. Young women—Arkansas—Fiction
2. Family—Arkansas—Fiction
3. Christian fiction, American

PS3557.U36L3 2005
813.54 G948   2005107679

10 9 8 7 6 5 4 3 2
First Edition

Acknowledgments

I am grateful to many people for their help with this novel. Chiefly I am indebted to Lake Knight and Lou Combs for going with me to Delaney and reliving their past, telling the stories about what it was like to grow up there. My apologies to all those living who remember Delaney as it was during its heyday. The Delaney of this novel is a place of imagination, a fiction, and any resemblance to real people or events is purely coincidental and unintended.

The good people at Shiloh Museum were kind enough to find photographs and first-hand accounts of life in the Ozarks at the turn of the century. The University of Arkansas library provided microfilm of *The Fayetteville Democrat* for the period covered in the novel.

Many people offered helpful responses to the manuscript of the novel. Some years ago, at the Port Townsend Writers' Conference, with only the early chapters in rough form, Alan Cheuse told me it was worth doing. During the following years, I spent three summers at the Sewanee Writers Conference. From the time at Sewanee, I want to especially thank Ellen Douglas and James Gordon Bennett for insightful critique and encouragement; and thanks to Alice McDermott for encouraging me to bring Purity onto center stage. Thanks to those captive audiences in the Honors Composition classes at John Brown University and the other students at JBU who listened patiently at various readings.

And my deepest thanks to three people who had a profound influence on this work. Kathi Appelt, a writer of beautiful children's books whom I first met at Port Townsend, read the manuscript in its early drafts and edited with patience, toughness, and kindness. The remaining weaknesses in the book are a result of my stubbornness in spite of her advice. Roger Hart, a writer of wonderful short stories, whom I met at Sewanee and who has become a very close friend, read the manuscript and gave constant encouragement and hope. And finally, my wife, Mary Ann, read every chapter as it came off the printer and convinced me she liked every one of them. Sweet talker.

Chapters from this work appeared, in slightly altered form, in *The Rockford Review, Words,* and *Arkansas Literary Forum.*

In memory of Lake Knight, who died before the novel was published.

Glimmerings are what the soul's composed of.
Fogged-up challenges, far conscience-glitters
And hang-dog, half-truth earnests of true love.
And a whole late-flooding thaw of ancestors.

                    Seamus Heaney
                    Station Island

Part I

The Refiner's Fire

1

July 1898
Delaney

THE SUNLIGHT LIFTED FROM THE HILLS, and a white moon hung over the river. Dusk gathered with the mists in the fields, and the dark shapes of sycamore and cottonwood thrust up along the river bank. The soft lights of the lamps of Delaney were scattered like fireflies in the valley.

Walter Bass leaned forward from the doorway of the toolshed and listened. The faint sounds of a piano and a tambourine drifted up the valley through the night, softened by the thick oak foliage, the humid air, the drone of crickets and tree frogs. He stared hard down the hillside through the trees and imagined a train of worshipers filing through the woods, weaving up the rocky footpath, shadowy forms like ghosts in the moonlight. The singing and the notes from the piano and the ring of the tambourine rose and fell with the sounds of the night.

Walter stepped to the edge of the porch and wedged the empty whiskey glass under one arm and the newspaper under the other and struggled with the buttons of his fly. In the dark his water thudded in the dust below the porch. The insect sounds echoed around him. Behind him in the doorway of the shed, an oil lamp lit the clutter. Light and shadows merged in the boxes, chains, and tools. A woodstove stood potbellied in the center of the room, the foot of a rough-board bunk just visible, a blanket rumpled and pushed over the edge.

When he buttoned his fly, the tumbler slipped from under his arm, bounced on the wooden decking at his feet, and dropped into the dark with the hollow sound of glass on a layer of old leaves.

He raised the newspaper close to his face and squinted. Lieutenant Colonel Theodore Roosevelt and the war in Cuba commanded the front page. The nation vibrated with the energy of conquest. But the faint patriotism and thoughts of enlisting that had stirred in him in the early weeks of the war had faded, and Walter had wearied of the news. The only vibration in Delaney was the uneven rhythm from the dark woods.

He closed his eyes and breathed deep. Tall and thin, his face narrow, canine, he felt his awkwardness like a blanket draped over him. He thought of the women of Delaney–the mothers, the daughters–that slept behind closed doors and curtained windows. He remembered his mother's hands skitting like water bugs across the surfaces of the world, never resting, and the eyes of Naomi, his brother's wife, following him, her soft moans in the night beyond the thin bedroom wall. The voice of Purity Morrison, quiet in the aisle of the mercantile, having waited so long, insisting that she could not wait forever.

The whiskey had not erased the image of Emma standing naked in the creek, looking up at him. Her round face. The gray eyes beneath her dark eyebrows, daring him. The full lower lip.

Wheelin Combs had told him at the mill that Emma would be at the revival.

The whisper of the music from the church drifted up to him, and he held his breath and listened. Listened for Emma's voice, willed it to separate itself from all the rest and drift up to him over the trees.

He turned back to the shed, reached out to the door frame on both sides to steady himself as he entered. A cricket chirped from the shelves. Walter sprawled face down on the wooden bunk against the wall and drifted halfway into sleep, but his eyes ached, and he pushed himself up onto his elbows. He got up slowly, brushed his hair back out of his eyes. His feet dragged as he moved out onto the platform. He took the steps down the end of the platform carefully, dragging one hand down the wall of the shed.

The well from the old house stood halfway between the shed and the dark scar of the tumbled rocks of the old foundation. The orange whorls of sparks that had spiraled upward when the house burned had carried the ghost of his mother, Lilly Bass, sucked her anger upward into the night sky, her hands quiet, stilled at last. The filament of memory stretched like a spider's web, shifted in the wind, tenuous, uncertain. He stepped onto the concrete slab of the well and reached for the pump handle, leaning on the nozzle, the metal cool and wet with dew. When the water pulsed from the nozzle, he cupped his hands full and splashed his face, then sucked up a mouthful and rinsed his mouth.

The fog rose in the valley. Delaney, the railroad, and the

river sank into it, the lights fading. A crow's call echoed up to him. A bobwhite whistled from somewhere in the mist. The night sounds dimmed until only scattered insects sang. The music from the church drifted up again, muffled in the fog, and he imagined the building lit up, the people singing.

He could be there in a few minutes. The music stopped. He picked up the battered bucket that lay beside the pump, hung it on the nozzle, and levered the pump handle. In the valley, in the moonlight, the upper story of the hotel floated like a barge on the surface of the mist. He lifted the bucket and poured the water over his head and sputtered in the chill of it. He shook his head and bent to refill the bucket.

2

Two Days Later
Purity Morrison

A MAN WAITING TO HANG might change places with me. I don't know anyone else who would. I am no better than an indentured servant. Washing dirty diapers, scrubbing kitchen floors, cooking and cleaning for thirteen people ages one to forty-five who don't know the meaning of the words "thank you."

My future looks like a narrow gully that gets narrower the farther ahead I look, until it turns into a dark hole that just drops off into nowhere. For example, it takes two good-sized chickens to make a meal. Wring their necks, scald them, pluck the feathers, gut them, piece them, fry them up. Takes the good part of an afternoon. It wouldn't be so bad if I was getting some help, but Sissy, who is twenty, thinks her one duty in life is to play with the little ones. She's getting married in the fall, and it goes without saying that I'm real happy for her, but people say that if the younger sister marries first, there is an old maid in the offing. And that's me.

Then there is Moria Lynn, who is fifteen and seems to have Mama's blessing to spend every daylight hour helping Mama with the two littlest boys. And Sarah June and Tennessee and Mary Grace are old enough they ought to be learning what housework is like, but they have the knack of disappearing except at meals, and Mama does nothing about it, and I do not have time to go chasing them down.

Meanwhile, Mama herself sits on the sofa nursing babies and resting her eyes like she was the Queen of Sheba. Her only purpose in life is to produce a baby every other year.

Day before yesterday, when I just happened to mention to Moria Lynn that it would not hurt her delicate looks to give me a hand in the kitchen, Mama had the nerve to say, "Purity, if you don't rein in that sharp tongue of yours, it will poison the well, and not a man in all of Delaney will want to drink."

I could feel the tears rising in my eyes and so I just turned and left the room without saying anything. It always comes down to that in Mama's mind—who would ever marry me the way I am? Twenty-six years old, the oldest of eleven children, still living at home.

Maybe Walter Bass might.

If anybody in Delaney has a claim on Walter Bass, it's me. Not that anybody does have a claim on him. Not that anybody in Delaney would ever want to claim any of the Basses. When the preacher Cravens' niece Naomi ran off and married Walter's older brother Henry a few years ago, nobody could believe their eyes and ears. But then Naomi is not from Delaney and doesn't understand the situation. She has tried to act like a normal person since her and Henry built that two-story house on the edge of town, but she is a marked woman.

Most people think Walter Bass is not quite right. He is so shy he can hardly talk to a member of the opposite sex. But that never stopped him from looking, and I saw the way he looked at me plenty of times, like some hillbilly standing at a store window.

Mama says any woman worth her salt ignores men's eyes. That is easy for Mama to say. She was married at fifteen. But in my situation I find it harder and harder to ignore Walter's eyes. One day last week I told Walter straight out when I saw him at the mercantile and we were alone in the aisle by the far wall and he was standing there looking at the chewing tobacco, too shy as always to say anything to me, and so I did all the talking. I told him that I'd seen the way he looked at me and that if he had anything to say, go ahead and say it because I was listening. I was giving him his chance because he obviously needed help.

I don't know how I could have been any plainer. He just stood there as still as could be, looking at the tobacco on the shelf. Big plugs of Duke's Mixture right there at eye level. His Adam's apple, the size of a black walnut, moved up and down one time, and the artery in his neck beat steady. I pulled one of my braids around and played with the gray cotton bow at the end, waiting for him to talk. Gray goes real nice with the red of my hair. Not that Walter noticed. He wouldn't even look at me.

Two aisles over, by the counter, Mama was telling Mr. Roberts about Billy, the baby, getting diarrhea because Mama's milk is so rich, like a jersey cow. We could hear every word she was saying. Could hear Pauline Roberts sweeping in the next aisle, the broom straw sighing on the wood floor. A wagon moved past the front door of the mercantile, the horses' hooves clumping on the rocky dirt and the wagon tack jingling.

Walter's head is thin, and his nose and his narrow-set eyes make people think of a dog. And he kind of slumps, like he's trying not to be taller than the people around him. Doesn't want to be noticed.

His straight hair hung down across his forehead into his eyes. Some people call him homely, but I've heard girls talking, and there's something about Walter Bass. His brother Henry has a mean streak that scares me to death, but Walter is quiet and seems lost, and I always want to touch him. I don't know if it's what you feel for a stray dog with droopy eyes or what. But it's something.

And he can't even talk to a woman.

"I can't wait forever," I said, and after standing there for a minute, playing with that gray cotton bow in my hair and listening to Mama go on about Billy's diarrhea, and then noticing that the broom straw was about to turn the corner at the far end of our aisle, I walked off and left Walter standing there staring at the tobacco.

If Mama knew I'd even talked to him, she'd be so ashamed of me. But I've wondered ever since that day if what I said to him was true, that part about not being able to wait forever.

I have never thought I was pretty, but me being the oldest of eleven children in a strict church-going family and seldom setting foot in town has surely been a hindrance to most of the men around here. Not that I would have most of the men around here.

When the Basses first came here, back before the railroad, they were the dirt poorest people I have ever known of, and they kept to their ragged selves on that blistered hilltop back up Delaney Creek not far from the Sinclair place. They raised a few hogs and a little corn. About all that would grow on that hillside. Walter only came to school about half the time. Henry even less. Walter was looking at me even then.

Othell Martin, a deacon in the church, called the Basses hillbilly trash, people whose sole purpose in the world is to exercise the generosity of the rest of us. And Delaney is a generous place. There were food baskets left at the Bass doorstep at Thanksgiving and hand-me-down clothes and toys at Christmas.

Virgil Bass fixed fence for Daddy for about a week one summer, but he came to work drunk one day and Daddy sent him home before lunch. Then some of Daddy's tools turned up missing and Virgil left Daddy's new come-along lying on the ground down by the south corner one night after stretching wire all day, and so Daddy let him go. Daddy is particular about his tools, and he was proud of that come-along. The next week somebody set fire to the chicken coop, which is right next to the hay barn. The dog barking woke Daddy up, or the barn might have burned down.

The people around here didn't like it one bit when the Basses took over Uncle Mose Joiner's sawmill ten years ago. Daddy says where would people as poor as the Basses get the money? And it was awful convenient that Uncle Mose had that stroke six months after Virgil started working for him. Foul play, Daddy says. Clear as crystal. Uncle Mose was awful well-liked by everybody in this valley, but he couldn't talk, or write, or nothing after the stroke, or whatever it was, and so there was no way in this world to prove Virgil had done anything. And Virgil Bass was smarter than a snake, and the next thing anybody knew, he had a contract with the railroad selling them cross ties.

Well, night before last, we got the surprise of our life. The thirteenth night of a two-week Holy Ghost revival at the Word of Holiness Church. We had seen signs and wonders right from the start—lots of people slain in the spirit, speaking in tongues. A good revival, but the last thing any of us ever expected to see was Walter Bass come sneaking into a holiness meeting and get the spirit. The only thing that would surprise me more would be his brother Henry coming with him. Now that would be a miracle.

I didn't even know Walter Bass had come in the door until after he got struck down. I was on the other side of the room, ministering to Magin Wilson in the laying on of hands, praise Jesus. The Spirit was moving. When Walter went down, word spread across that sanctuary like a brush-fire in a stiff wind, and you could see everyone craning their necks and looking. Of course I would be the last one to hear.

I tried to get over there as fast as I could, but by the time I worked my way over to where folks had been praying over Walter, they were helping him up off the floor. I picked up his hat and handed it to him when he first stood up. I was going to give him a big hug and welcome him into the Kingdom as soon as he looked at me. The Bible says to greet one another with a holy kiss. I could feel my whole life about to turn. It crossed my mind that he may have come there looking for me, after what I said to him last week in the mercantile. But he didn't even notice me. Emma Sinclair, the princess of Delaney, twenty years old, and an only child by the way, led him over to the wall where he could get his feet back under himself.

I'm beginning to believe it is not my sharp tongue, like Mama says, that will keep me at home, but dumb blind luck. The circumstances of my life conspire against me. How can you fight that? I am not yet prepared to say it is Providence.

I just can't help thinking that if only I could have been the one to pray Walter through, the clouds might have parted over this gully I call a life. I don't know.

But Emma Sinclair, she wouldn't give Walter Bass the time of day.

3

The Next Day
Naomi Bass

I DON'T BELONG HERE. It didn't take me long to figure that out when I arrived ten years ago at the age of thirteen. But I thought marrying Henry Bass would change everything. I was right. It changed everything.

I'm an educated woman. I read Latin, have in fact read Vergil's *Aeneid* in Latin. My father, the Right Reverend Jeremiah Stotts of the Lion's Presbyterian Church in Fayetteville, in his infinite wisdom never allowed me to attend school, but taught me at home with a combination of strict discipline and grim determination. Mama was dead by then.

Lucky Mama.

And the good people of Delaney, none of whom as far as I can tell read a word of Latin, treat me like someone who was just released from a mental hospital. They are polite, but watchful.

They cannot fathom how any woman in her right mind, let alone an educated woman, could run away from the security of her uncle's house, the house of the Reverend Isaac Samuel Cravens of the Riverside Church of Christ in

Delaney, to marry Henry Bass. But then neither have they plumbed the depths of life in the house of Isaac Samuel Cravens. The Bible reading and prayer before we could touch our food, the sermon on holy living and the dangers of unbridled passions while we ate. My cousins, Elisha and Samuel, smirking over their milk at me.

The people of Delaney never had to lie in bed after dinner and try to breathe as I did whenever Isaac Samuel Cravens prayed over me, gripped my hands and pressed them to my chest, pressed the air out of me as he called on the Lord to gird up my loins and lead me in the paths of righteousness. Hunched down over me, his eyes wedged shut, his nose thick and porous, his beard shifting with the movement of his chin, he breathed heavily, his breath greasy. His nostrils flared with each breath. I was afraid to turn my face away.

My father sent me to live with the Cravenses four years after Mama died. Three years later I bolted with Henry. Like Queen Dido in the *Aeneid,* I spurned public opinion and the will of God and fell into the arms of my Aeneas. I thought anything would be better than Isaac Samuel Cravens. That was seven years ago. I was sixteen. What did I know?

Before Henry and I ran off and got married, I had heard all the talk about the Bass family, but I thought Henry was what I was looking for, someone who didn't give a tinker's damn about what anyone else expected. And I thought at the time that I could love anything my uncle hated. I had never even met Henry's family before he brought me home with him, and I'm sure from their reactions that he had never even mentioned me. We were standing in the living room of the Bass house in the late afternoon when Virgil Bass came in mad enough to fight because Henry had not come in to work that day. When Virgil saw me, he stopped short, stood there staring with those rheumy eyes, brown and yellow stains at the corners of his mouth and down his beard. He said, "Who the hell is that?"

My blood turned to sludge and my knees almost buckled, but I kept the smile on my face. With Lilly, Henry's mother, sitting in a rocker staring at my feet, her hands fluttering over the knitting in her lap, I began to see the real potential of my new life.

When Henry told Virgil I was his wife, Virgil made a "hmph" sound in his throat and shifted a wad of tobacco to the other side of his mouth and said, "I might have known." And he pulled a pint whiskey bottle out of his hip pocket and walked out of the room unscrewing the lid.

Living with the Basses was like living in a snake pit. Virgil drank himself into a coma every night sitting there looking at his glass. Smelled like old piss and stale tobacco. He got to a point, before he passed out, like a snake coiled and ready to strike. Henry and Walter stayed out of the way, but Lilly seemed to want to provoke him. And she got bit more often than not.

Then one evening Virgil didn't come home. I lived there only three weeks before he left. But it was a long three weeks. Henry and Walter said he left the mill in the middle of the afternoon to go to town. That was seven years ago, and nobody has heard from him since.

Lilly had a sharp nose with a high ridge to it, and her eyes were close set, like Walter's. Her eyebrows were thick and untrimmed and gave her a wild look, especially since her hair was never more than halfway tied back and loose strands hung about her face. She barely had any lips, and she kept her mouth pulled in a tight line, even when she spoke, which may be why I could seldom understand her. I think she was trying to hide her teeth. But the most striking thing about her appearance was her ears. They would have been large on a man's head. On hers they were enormous. Any other woman would have kept them hidden with her hair, but Lilly seemed indifferent to them. It's no wonder people in Delaney thought she was a witch.

Her face was all deep wrinkles, and she stooped. The veins coiled thick and blue all over the back of her hands like a nest of water moccasins, and no matter how hard she tried to subdue those hands, they were moiling every second of the day.

She couldn't leave Henry and Walter alone, especially Walter. Both men tensed up when she reached for them to button the top button on their shirts or push the hair back off their foreheads. Grown men. It seemed like when they got close to her she couldn't keep her hands off of them, but somehow couldn't ever quite get hold of them either. Those hands of hers skipped around over Henry and Walter like water bugs on a pond.

Yesterday morning Aunt Rose Eltha Belle Cravens, Isaac Samuel's wife and my father's sister, came by for a cup of coffee. I was standing at the sink drying the last of the breakfast dishes, looking out the back window, when she got here. The hills were dusty green in the July sun. The dirt road alongside the White River trailed away into the trees, and the sun glinted on the railroad tracks running north toward Fayetteville.

Aunt Rose drops in every Monday morning full of all the latest gossip. Yesterday, she acted like a cat on a porch rail watching a bird in the grass. I was the bird, and I resigned myself to wait for Aunt Rose to spring.

While I put the dishes into the cupboard, Aunt Rose drank her coffee. She raised her eyebrows, looked down at her cup and said, in that nonchalant tone some people use when they begin to serve up a story about someone else, that she had heard over at the mercantile that Olivia Farley had a crush on Walter Bass. Olivia thought Walter was dark and mysterious, the strong silent type. Aunt Rose couldn't believe it. Walter Bass. She just couldn't see it. Walter reminded her of a wolf. Gave her the creeps. A little too much like his mother, she thought.

The fact that Walter was my brother-in-law and that the conversation might make me uncomfortable or even angry did not seem to occur to her.

She puckered up her lips and said, "Course, we all know how young women are attracted to the forbidden fruit. What was it Emily Dickinson said? Heaven is what I cannot reach?" Then she smiled and breathed a sigh of satisfaction.

Aunt Rose always sounds as if she is preaching a sermon or trying to imitate John Wesley or some other eighteenth-century divine. Or her husband, Isaac Samuel. And she likes nothing better than to quote a little inspirational poetry. I am always tempted to give it back to her in Latin, but never do.

I draped the limp dishrag across the faucet and watched a hawk drop into the thick fescue in the field behind the yard. It rose again, beating the air, wing feathers splayed, something small and dark in its talons. I told her that I doubted if Olivia Farley was the only girl in town that had her eye on Walter Bass, but that most of them had more sense than to tell anyone about it. And the hawk climbed across my reflection in the windowpane and glided into the woods on the hillside beyond the field.

I turned back to her. "I guess that's what attracted me to Henry, Aunt Rose. The forbidden fruit. The mystique of the outcast."

One afternoon while Henry and I were still living at the Bass house, Walter helped me with the wash. It was a Sunday and the mill was closed, but Henry was down at the mill tinkering around anyway. When Virgil ran off, Henry didn't miss a beat. Started bossing everybody around as if Virgil had never existed. It was just like him. And Wheelin Coombs and Ewing McCracken and Isham Birkes fell right in step, probably glad to get Virgil off their backs. And Walter never said a word that I could tell. Quiet as ever. I never asked him about it.

So Henry was fixing himself an office at the far end of the loading dock. And Walter was hanging around the house, sitting out back on the porch steps, leaning back and whittling a hickory stick, the curled shavings scattering on his jeans and on the steps in front of him. When I started the fire under the kettle in the yard, he folded the blade of his knife and put it in his pocket and came over to help me, brushing the shavings off his legs.

It was August, and right at a hundred degrees by the thermometer under the shade of the eave. The heat around the fire and the boiling water was intense, and I unbuttoned the top few buttons of my blouse because I couldn't stand to have it clear up to my neck. And as Walter and I stood, each holding the opposite end of a pair of work pants, steaming from the kettle, and twisted them to wring out the rinse water, he looked at my open blouse, stared at it, and when he looked up and saw that I saw, he looked down quickly. But when he looked up at me again, I felt like I did when Henry would reach out and pull me to him. But not quite like that either. It was something else.

I often wondered what Walter thought about me and Henry. Walter slept on a mat in the living room and could probably hear everything that happened the other side of that flimsy wall at night. He never said anything, of course. People around here think Walter is stupid just because he is a Bass and because he is so shy and seldom speaks. When that old house burned down three years after Henry and I had moved, rumors flew all over the place. Rumors about what Walter might have done. His living alone in the shed afterward and drinking so much didn't help matters. Living on beans from a can and Old Longhorn whiskey. He is thinner and more hollow cheeked now. Hardly ever comes to town.

But I understand the attraction Olivia Farley felt.

Of course, I wouldn't have told Aunt Rose any of this as she sat there sipping her coffee. She looked up at me and hesitated, her mouth just opening to speak, then looked down at her cup, her face set in the look of saintly compassion that makes me angry. Then she said, "Isaac Samuel and I pray for you and Henry every day of our lives, Naomi, asking God to bring you into His fold."

In the first place, Henry and I have no desire to be in any fold that was left in the charge of Isaac Samuel Cravens. And in the second place, I knew exactly what Isaac Samuel really prayed. That God would strike me and Henry down with an iron fist and thoroughly humble us before He brought us in. Isaac Samuel hasn't spoken to me since I eloped with Henry. Seven years. The Right Reverend Cravens' forgiveness and reconciliation will come only after God has rendered justice to the reverend's wounded pride.

"Well, after this weekend," Aunt Rose said, her head a little turned, the corners of her mouth pulling down, looking at me with the inspired expectation that I knew would lead to the real gossip, "our prayers don't seem so far out of reach."

She paused to revel for a moment in the silence, but I didn't give her any encouragement.

"If it can happen to your brother-in-law, after all," she said, "surely it can happen to anybody."

My mouth must have dropped open. Aunt Rose breathed deep with satisfaction. I said, "Did you just say that Walter Bass got religion this weekend?"

"Oh, dear me," she leaned forward again, "not just religion, holiness religion. Can you believe that a person as low as Walter Bass would even get close enough to a church to hear the word of the Lord by accident, let alone walk right into the middle of a holiness revival and, as those people so quaintly put it, get 'struck down' by the Holy Ghost and 'come through'?"

My face must have been something to see. "Walter got the spirit in a holiness revival?" I said and leaned back against the sink.

"I know just how you feel," she said. "I swear I could hardly believe my own ears when I heard it. It was just pure good fortune that I stopped in at Roberts' Mercantile on my way over here this morning. Two or three of the sisters from the Word of Holiness Church were there with Pauline Roberts, telling it. Miriam Martin and Rachel Hogan and one of the Simpson girls I think. They were all there last night and saw it happen."

Aunt Rose watched me. On the far wall, the curling brown vines climbed in parallel lines in the wallpaper, and I tried to imagine Walter being "struck down" by the spirit. I could not even picture him in the church, let alone getting religion.

"Well," Aunt Rose said, and she pulled in a quick breath

for emphasis, "you know what shameless gossips Miriam Martin and Rachel Hogan are. I swear it made me blush to hear the way they went on about it. Well, according to them, they had a full house last night at that revival meeting. Must have been sixty or seventy people, they said. A little tight for all the jumping and shouting, wouldn't you say?"

She covered her mouth with her hand, then dropped her hand to her chin and said, "I ought to be ashamed of myself for talking like that, I know it. Sometimes I just wonder if I was really cut out to be a preacher's wife." She smiled a covert little smile at me, as if we were sharing the joke, the stark impossibility of her not being cut out to be a preacher's wife.

I walked over to the stove just so I wouldn't stand there looking like a goose. I got the coffee pot, refilled Aunt Rose's cup, and put the pot back on the stove.

I stood there at the stove for a second and tried again to picture Walter Bass going into the Word of Holiness Church. What could have made him go there? What was he looking for? I remembered his eyes when he looked at me that day in the heat. It wasn't really surprising. That soft emptiness of his that had kept him so quiet since the fire, living alone in the tool shed at the mill. Something, or somebody, was bound to draw him out.

But a holiness revival?

"You were about to tell me about Walter's conversion," I said as I returned to the table and sat down.

"Well, I must say," Rose said, and then paused to sip her coffee. She took her time. It's an irritating habit she has when she knows you want to hear what she has to say. It makes me want to swear.

She dragged the moment on as long as possible. "Our holiness friends get carried away with more than their emotions at times," she said. "The stories they are spreading about what happened at that church last night are enough to make a good woman... Well, Isaac Samuel has always said about them 'In for a penny, in for a pound,' so I shouldn't be surprised at the excess of their imagination." She stopped and breathed deeply, taking her time, and took another drink of her coffee. Then she looked at the kitchen window and shook her head, pushing her bottom lip out.

I wanted to scream at her, but I said as calmly as I could, "But what exactly are they saying about Walter's conversion?"

She waited with a frustrating confidence, feeling for the perfect moment to speak. "One of those women," she said and stopped again. "You know, I think she used to be a Simpson and might have married one of the Miller's from down Delaney Creek."

She looked thoughtful. "I know you're going to think I'm making this up," she said, "because I'd think the same thing, I'm sure, if I was you and it was you sitting here telling this to me, but I'm telling you just like she told it to Pauline Roberts. She said that the dark specter of the devil himself swept up out of Walter Bass and around that room like a whirlwind, and that the very earth groaned under the building and light suffused the room, those were her very words, suffused the room as if a thousand prisms were scattered around the walls."

Rose's eyes widened as she spoke, and she moved her face a little closer to me and waited for a reaction to what she had said. I had to lean back in my chair, and put my hand over my mouth, and try not to laugh at the dramatics, try to appear shocked. Aunt Rose seemed satisfied and continued, "Well, Rachel Hogan, who was part of the laying on of hands, which is itself a sort of a strange thing to do, don't you think? Rachel swears, and says that the others who laid on hands, every one of them, swear as well, that the spirit leapt upon them like Saint Elmo's fire—her words, not mine, Saint Elmo's fire." She stopped again and watched me.

I imagined Aunt Rose standing in the circle of women at Roberts' Mercantile, eyes wide, devouring every word and gesture. But I still could not imagine, no matter how hard I tried, Walter Bass struck down by the spirit, or the charged hands of those holiness women laid on him.

The dark specter of the devil rising out of Walter Bass. It was just what the people of Delaney would want to hear. Just what they would find easy to believe about a Bass.

Aunt Rose nodded and said "Hard to figure, isn't it? Nobody doubts that a mighty work was done, but there is some debate, seems to me, about whose work it was."

She stood up as if she had just pronounced the latest meeting of the Women's Temperance Society adjourned and was picking up a placard and headed for a march.

"I promised Charlotte James I would stop by this morning," she said, "and so I'll be on my way."

She took both our cups to the sink and emptied them and put them on the counter.

"Thanks for the coffee," she said, and she held out her hand to me.

We gripped hands for just a moment and smiled, me lost in the image of Walter Bass shimmering in Saint Elmo's fire, her glowing with success. She walked out of the room, a woman with a mission.

I had the crazy thought that I might go out to the mill and ask Henry what time he would be coming home. I wanted to see Walter, to see if he was changed by the laying on of hands, by the exorcism. To see what was left after the devil had shaken him and God's house to the very foundations. But it was a crazy idea. I had never gone to the mill to ask Henry about anything.

I washed the two cups that waited on the counter and went outside to build the fire under the kettle and start the laundry by myself. Another Monday ritual. Aunt Rose in the morning, laundry in the afternoon.

As I placed the kindling around the base of the kettle, I tried again to imagine Walter on the floor of The Word of Holiness Church in the grip of the holiness women. And the strangest image came to mind. Women draped like the worshipers of some primitive god, Bacchanalian revelers preparing to tear their male victim to pieces, bent over Walter. In their eyes the abandon of religious fervor. In Walter's eyes, abject fear.

When the specter of the devil began to rise from him

like a tiny whirlwind, I shook the image from my head and went to get the matches.

4

August
Purity Morrison

THE WILL OF GOD IS A HARD THING. Jesus commands us to take up our cross and follow him. Of course, the way I see it, he could mean almost anything by that. He doesn't exactly say what our cross is. Just says we each have one. Could be anything.

I can't help but wonder sometimes what Jesus would have said if he'd been a woman like me, twenty-six years old and living at home with no prospects on the horizon.

Friday at the cannery I burned myself on the soldering iron. Sunny Barton and I were closing the cans of applesauce. I had been sitting there closing those cans, thinking about Walter Bass, which I have been doing a lot lately, and listening to Sunny talk, which I do a lot every day because she has a lot to say. And I had just opened my mouth to tell Sunny about that time I had talked to Walter Bass in the mercantile, the time he wouldn't answer me, and then about him getting struck down in the church and me just missing the chance to pray him through. And maybe, if I got the nerve, I would ask her what a girl in my position could do. Sunny has had plenty of experience.

That's when I burned myself on the soldering iron. I was just running a bead around the top of that can when I looked up at Sunny because she stopped to take a breath and I opened my mouth and that's when it happened. I blistered my thumb real good. And I guess it's a good thing I did, because today, Monday, I heard the news about Walter Bass. There are some things a person just cannot be ready for. You could have knocked me over with a feather.

It's hardly been a month since he was struck down by the Holy Ghost at the church, and now this. And to think I might have been the one that prayed him through. I was just that close. It has to be providence. Things like this don't just happen.

I was coring the apples at the cannery this morning when I heard. I had told Lester Matlock that I was not going to close cans any more, not the way I blistered my thumb on Friday. I have only been working at the cannery for three weeks, and I could tell that Lester wasn't too happy about me being choosey that way. But this is the first time Daddy has ever let me work somewhere besides the farm, and I've never used a soldering iron before, and I can't be going home with my hands burned so bad that I can't do the housework. It would be the end of any chance for me to work outside the home.

Daddy is a man of strong opinion. He says a woman's place is in the home, not in the cannery. Doesn't matter how many women in Delaney, married and single, work at the cannery during the summer. It is a disgrace to the family for me to work there. The only work any woman in his family has ever done outside the house is hoeing the garden and picking the orchard and stuffing the sausage when he slaughters a hog every autumn.

Modern ways are not God's ways. He quotes chapter and verse, and what can I say? But I finally wore him down. I was a challenge to his theology. And finally, I think he began to see that the cannery might be my only chance. And besides, Moria Lynn and Sarah June, who is eleven, are old enough to do some of the housework while I'm gone.

I think Daddy feels guilty. He sold the right-of-way to the railroad eleven years ago, and I've heard him say a hundred times, if I've heard him say it once, that selling that right-of-way was the sorriest thing he ever did. He says that Delaney is no longer any fit place to raise up children. That would, of course, be a concern to him, since he has eleven of them, but I'll say here what I would never tell Daddy to his face. And it's the truth. I was a fifteen-year-old girl eleven years ago who had spent her whole life up 'til then washing clothes and cooking and taking care of little brothers and sisters on the farm, and I saw that railroad as the hand of God. It was deliverance. I would never have known anything else in the world but dirty diapers and dust balls and mashed potatoes if it hadn't have been for that train.

And the hotel and the stores and the sawmills and all the rest of it have opened my eyes to what's possible in the world beyond the White River Valley. Delaney is like a beehive now and the coming and the going never seems to stop, and the honey from that hive is something I would never have tasted otherwise. And if the laying bare of the hardwood forest is the price of it, so be it.

Even now, working five and a half days every week, I sometimes feel the hand of time tighten its fingers around my throat, and I fear that I will never escape my father's house. I do not want to risk my freedom by trying to learn how to use a soldering iron.

Coring apples, on the other hand, is something I could do with my eyes closed. I've cored enough apples in my life to feed the city of Fayetteville. Every fall since I was thirteen, Mama and I have harvested apples from July 'til October, peeling and coring and canning until I could do it in my sleep. Give me a good sharp paring knife, and I can keep up with any woman here.

But I have to admit that it's a wonder I didn't slice my thumb off this morning when Truly Greenway shared the news about Walter.

There were at least a dozen of us on the coring line this morning. Letty Oatman and Imogene Farley were just across the table from Truly and me, and we were having a good time talking as we worked. I feel a real burden for these women.

Letty has to work at the cannery because Elias doesn't make any money laying stone, partly because he drinks more homemade whiskey than he sells on the side. And who wants someone laying stone for them while he's under the weather? Imogene, on the other hand, works just to get away from Mel, and I can't see that anybody blames her for that. But Truly is the one I feel most sorry for. Her husband, Tobias, is about as nice a man as you would ever want to meet, but since he lost his right arm at the mill, he hasn't been the same. Their ten-year-old takes care of the two little ones while Truly works. It would just scare me to death to leave my kids that way, but they need the money.

Well, anyway, this morning was going real good. Sitting with the other women, coring apples, talking. Away from the heat of those firepots that make soldering such a miserable job. And then Truly Greenway dropped the bombshell.

"I had an interesting conversation with Martha Sinclair after church last night," she says. Truly's voice is the oddest thing I've ever heard. I swear it sounds like she has a scarf around her neck tied so tight she can't breathe.

Letty and Imogene and I nodded and smiled, not looking up from the apples we were coring. We get paid by the bucket.

"I believe Martha was about to cry," Truly said, "though she was trying real hard to smile like she really was pleased to be telling me about it." Truly's voice can be irritating under the best of conditions, but when you're trying to hear her over the noise of a cannery, it's hard to be patient.

But Letty Oatman, who is the picture of patience, says, "Not like Martha. She having trouble at home?"

By that time, Letty and Imogene and I were all looking at Truly, who was still coring an apple. When she finished it, she dropped it into her bucket and wiped the peelings and core off the table, between the two of us, and watched them drop through the slots in the floor. She picked up another apple, but before she started on it she said, "Well, you'd think that having an only daughter get engaged to be married would be a thing to rejoice over, wouldn't you?"

For about two heartbeats the steam hissed from those big cooking vats and the chains rattled on the hoists while the three of us looked at Truly.

"Emma Sinclair is getting married?" Imogene said. She wiped her hands on her apron and said, "Well, I swan!" She chuckled and shook her head and picked up another apple and started peeling it.

Steel wheels rumbled on the concrete floor as Lester Matlock pulled a dolly loaded with crates full of cans from over by the front door where three women were pasting on labels. The lids of the cans in the crates stacked over by the loading dock door were popping as they cooled like twenty-two rifles shooting.

Letty just stared at the open front doors with this awful look on her face.

"Oh my God," she said.

"Why Letty Oatman, what's the matter with you," Imogene said, not looking up from the apple she was coring.

Letty didn't say nothing. Just put her hand over her mouth and kept looking toward the front doors.

Imogene and Truly looked from her to the open doors and then back at her, waiting. But I knew exactly what Letty was thinking. For a few seconds, which seemed like forever, the cannery got quiet. It was one of those times when, in a place like that, all the different noises stop at once, and then start back up one at a time, and if you notice it you get this creepy feeling like something weird has happened.

I had already guessed what Letty was thinking, but I

couldn't make myself say it, and my stomach got queasy. The hogs were snuffling through all the scraps just below our feet, under the cannery. And for just a breath or two the rotted apple peelings and cores smelled sickly sweet, mixed with the stench of the muck wallowed up by the hogs.

"Oh my God," Letty said again with her hand still over her mouth so that the words were muffled. Then she said, "Poor Martha," and she picked up an apple and started coring it, but real slow and thoughtful.

Imogene was fit to be tied, and she said, "Letty Oatman, what in the hell are you talking about? Poor Martha what?"

Imogene Farley is the only woman that I hear cussing at the cannery. If you live with a man like Mel Farley for very long, I guess things like that are bound to rub off on you.

"Well, what do you think I'm talking about?" Letty said. "Where have you been, woman? Haven't you heard anything at all about Walter Bass going up to the Sinclairs every night the past couple of weeks?"

"Oh my God," Imogene said, and she looked over at Truly.

Truly looked at Imogene, then at Letty, then at me, a smug look on her face.

"Letty's right," she said and nodded her head as if it was the most significant thing in the world.

Like I said, her voice is irritating under the best of circumstances. Right then I wanted to wrench her neck so that it wouldn't ever bother anybody again.

But I picked up another apple and started peeling it and said, "A person with their eyes open and any sense at all would have expected it."

Imogene looked over at me and shook her head and said, "Well, I just swan, that's all."

I could feel my face burning, starting in my neck and working its way up to my cheeks, and I was sure it was turning red, and so I put down the apple and wiped my face on my sleeve. The heat from the cooking vats keeps the cannery hotter than a brooder house, even with all the doors open. There was not even a hint of a breeze this morning, so you can imagine what it was like.

The hogs snuffled through the scraps, grunting beneath our feet. Truly and Letty and Imogene started coring apples again. One of the women pasting on labels over by the front doors laughed real loud, and there was a big hiss of steam, and the chains rattled as they lifted the lids on the cooking vats.

Miles Beach, Mason Combs, and Enos Waite were loading cans into crates and carrying the loaded crates back to the dock beside the tracks. Just carrying them back there without using a cart or anything. Showing off. None of them were wearing shirts.

Walter Bass was going to marry Emma Sinclair. Who says lightening never strikes twice in the same spot? First Henry and Naomi. Now Walter and Emma. The Basses' revenge on Delaney.

The day I cornered Walter Bass in the mercantile, his eyes looked like the eyes of an animal caught in a trap. Tense. Not looking at me. Ready to spring if I touched him. Knowing there was no escape. And the last words I said to him, that I couldn't wait forever, came back to me. I couldn't quite get my breath.

I was that close to being the one who prayed him through that night in the church. The laying on of hands is a powerful thing. When a woman prays a man through by the laying on of hands, there is something that happens between them that can't be explained.

I was in the Spirit that night. Things would be different now if I had got to Walter before Emma Sinclair did.

Maybe this is the cross that I have to bear. To come so close, yet miss the mark.

5

The Same Day
Naomi Bass

IT WAS NEARLY NOON, and I had given up on Aunt Rose coming by for Monday morning coffee. Uncle Isaac Samuel sometimes puts her to work on church business, insisting she do it on Monday morning, knowing she can't come see me if she does. He has the mind of a six year old.

Really, I was relieved. I didn't feel up to being Aunt Rose's gossip, and I wanted to get the kitchen floor scrubbed. But when she knocked and walked in the front door and called my name, I was glad to get up off my hands and knees and lay the brush down.

She swept into the room like a hawk landing on a window ledge, and she didn't waste a breath.

"I'm so glad you're here," she said. "I was afraid you would give up on me and go off on some errand."

"I'll heat the coffee," I said.

"Oh, yes, do," she said. "I need something to settle my nerves."

I stirred the coals in the firebox and laid on a couple of pieces of wood and blew until the flames started.

Meanwhile, Aunt Rose was running at the mouth. "I almost ran over here," she said. "You're scrubbing your floor. I'd stay and help, but I only have time for a quick cup of coffee. I need to get over to Charlotte James' to see what she knows."

Aunt Rose can change directions in a conversation quicker than a chicken chasing a grasshopper.

I said, "I'm glad you interrupted the scrubbing. What's the big news?"

She looked right at me, and her eyes narrowed. "Naomi Lee Bass, have you been keeping something from me?"

For just a second I had the crazy idea she thought I was pregnant, and my stomach jumped, and I said, "What in the world are you talking about?"

"Sit down," she said.

I was curious. I had never seen Aunt Rose go straight for the finish line before.

She was still looking straight at me. "If it weren't so tragic, I'd laugh," she said.

I wondered who had run off with somebody else's wife. "Rose," I said, "what has happened?"

She walked over to the cupboard and took down two cups, and as she was walking over to the stove, she said, "Walter Bass has outdone himself this time."

As usual, she talked about Walter as if he weren't my brother-in-law but just another mutual acquaintance in town. I tried to imagine who he might have killed that would be funny if it weren't so tragic.

"What?" I said. "What did Walter do?"

She poured the coffee and brought the cups to the table.

"Sit down," she said. "Believe me, you are going to need to be sitting when I tell you this."

I sat down.

"Rose," I said. "What did he do?"

"If you are as innocent as you act," she said, "I don't know where to start."

She put two big teaspoons of sugar in her coffee and stirred it in. She turned her head a little to the side, keeping her eyes on me, and said, "Who is the absolute last person in this town that you would pick to marry Walter Bass?"

My coffee cup stopped halfway to my mouth. I'll never forget the look on her face. She was like a dog about to lunge at a rabbit, her body tense and leaning toward me, her eyes boring into my face.

I don't know how long I stared at her with my coffee cup slowly moving down in front of me. It seemed like forever, with pictures running through my mind of Walter at the Bass house reading the paper, on the front porch in the evenings looking off down the valley at Delaney, twisting the other end of a steaming pair of work pants in the back yard, looking at my open blouse, lying on the floor of the Word of Holiness Church, the hands of the holiness women pressing down on him.

So that was the big news. Walter was getting married. The impossible was happening.

"Well," Rose said, "who?"

"Who?" I said, and my voice sounded like I was trying to swallow crackers.

"Well, if you'd been keeping your ear close to the ground, like me, you might have known who he's been courting these three weeks past, since he got religion."

I was the rabbit, trapped in the shallow burrow between the roots of a great sweet gum tree, and she was the hungry dog standing over me. I was frozen, waiting for her to pounce. Maybe it wasn't true. Maybe I misunderstood what she was saying.

She pushed her lips tight together for a second, then said, "What would you say if I told you it was Emma Sinclair?"

I felt cold, and goose bumps ran up my arms. I don't know why. Emma Sinclair accepting Walter.

"I thought that might set you back," Rose said. "Emma Sinclair is the prettiest girl in town, and Walter Bass is, well, I just don't see how it could happen."

She took a drink of coffee and leaned back in her chair. The way she kept looking at me, I must have been a sight to see. I was holding my coffee cup in my lap. I put it on the table. A blue jay out back screeched at something, its voice harsh, and a crow somewhere beyond the back fence cawed. Emma is pretty alright. And most people would not call Walter handsome. But I wasn't surprised she accepted him. I remembered the day he was helping me with the laundry and looked at me the way he did.

When I didn't say anything, Rose hesitated, fingered the handle of her coffee cup, looked down into it. And I knew that something else was coming. Maybe it was the way she worked her lips. She looked up at me and said, "Naomi, I know Isaac Samuel sometimes seems hard, the way he doesn't speak to you and all."

So typical of her, that jump to some totally unrelated topic as if it were the next logical thing to say.

Then she did it. She said, "It's the same with your daddy. Now don't shut me out. I know this is an unpleasant subject for you, but it's no use pretending it's not there. Jeremiah is your daddy, but please remember he is my brother; I've known him all my life, and I tell you he's a saint if ever there was one on this earth."

My father a saint. The Right Reverend Jeremiah Stotts, of The Lion's Presbyterian Church in Fayetteville, canonized right there at the kitchen table. I could not think of a thing to say to that. I had spent four years at the master's feet, getting a better education than my brothers got in the public school. But he never let me forget that the only purpose of all those lessons was to discipline my idle female mind and keep me out of the way of temptation. The Old Testament prophets, the letters of the Apostle Paul, *The Meditations* of Marcus Aurelius.

He was very big on *The Meditations,* and he required me to take the popular English version of George Long and translate it into Latin. He seemed to feel a perverse pleasure in the fact that I was translating into good Latin the one work that Marcus Aurelius, a brilliant Roman emperor, had written in corrupt Greek. I, on the other hand, found comfort in knowing that the Christians in Rome suffered their worst persecutions under Marcus Aurelius. But, though I kicked against the goads and hated Aurelius at first, I grew to love *The Meditations,* their bleak stoicism. And in recent years I've thought of that grim old emperor trying to keep a disintegrating Roman empire in check, and I've felt a certain sympathy. There are meditations that come back to me now as a comfort. Like when he said, "In a word, your life is short." That's a comfort. Or when he said time is like a river, a violent stream. There's a truth.

Father finally gave up on me and sent me to live with Aunt Rose Eltha, the wife of the Right Reverend Isaac Samuel Cravens, of the Riverside Church of Christ in Delaney. From the frying pan into the fire.

Aunt Rose slid her coffee cup away from her and folded her hands. I wanted more than anything not to talk to her about my father. I wanted to reach down and get the scrub brush and say, sorry but I've got to get back to this floor. But I resigned myself to the inevitable. The pious zeal rose in her face, her back straightening and her chin lifting higher.

She pushed on. "Naomi, you have to humble yourself before your daddy and confess your sin against him."

Humble myself before my daddy. As if he hadn't humbled me enough those four long years after Mama died. Sitting there looking past me at the wall behind me, a look of tired disapproval in his eyes, with his little starched white collar and his close-cut black beard, his hands folded in front of him. When I finished reciting, he would look down at his hands, never at me, and assign another reading.

Rose's head tilted slowly back, her eyes still fixed on mine, until I felt that she was sighting me down the straight line of her nose. "If you would do that," she said, "I know he would forgive you and raise you up from the dust and ashes of your shame and restore you to your rightful place." She sounded just like Isaac Samuel preaching a sermon.

I saw my father again in the raised pulpit of the Lion's Presbyterian Church. The church was austere. He was austere. The dust and ashes of my shame. What could Rose Eltha Belle Cravens possibly know about my shame?

Aunt Rose's face softened a little. "It was hard on Jeremiah after your mama died," she said.

I wanted to say, "Not as hard as it was on Mama before she died."

"It was a blessing," Rose said, setting her cup down in the saucer, the corners of her mouth turned down slightly, again in the smile of a suffering saint, "when he sent you to stay with us. Isaac Samuel and I felt a real calling to raise you up in the nurture and admonition of the Lord."

I remembered when she met me at the train station, straight backed, chin high, looking down her nose, her black-gloved hands together at her abdomen holding a small black bag, her hair covered by a black scarf, a black shawl draped around her shoulders. Isaac Samuel was a dark figure beside her. All I can remember about him that day is his thick beard. And the two boys, Elisha and Samuel, five and three years old, standing there looking at me as if I were a trained monkey on a string.

I stood there on the loading dock, holding my bag and looking at the severe woman in front of me, one of Mama's songs running through my mind. Ring around the rosie, pocket full of posie, ashes, ashes, all fall down.

Ashes to ashes, and dust to dust. Marcus Aurelius was right. "Soon," he says, "very soon, thou wilt be ashes."

The silence lengthened in the kitchen. The hollow tap, tap, tap of a woodpecker came from the walnut tree outside the back door, and Rose's smile melted away. "Isaac Samuel was humiliated," she said, "when you ran off with Henry."

Her eyes shifted and she stared down at the table in front of her and slumped as if she was sleepy. "And telling your daddy," she said and blinked and turned her head a little to one side, as if a gnat was pestering her, "was more than I could do." She paused, then added, "Isaac Samuel took it on himself to tell Jeremiah."

I did not want to hear this. I wanted to walk out, go upstairs, leave Aunt Rose mumbling to an empty room. But I sat there, feeling too tired even to get up and move.

Rose touched her shawl, moved it aimlessly. "Jeremiah looked away when Isaac Samuel told him, his face turned to stone like the statue of the confederate dead at the cemetery in Fayetteville."

I forced the composed expression on my face. The pious resignation returned to hers, the gradual thrust of her mouth, the sympathy tendered there.

"The words your father spoke at that time," she said as her back slowly straightened again, "were awful, and I felt like the daughters of Zion when the prophets spoke the judgments of God on a rebellious nation." She was preaching again, the words, of course, straight from Uncle Isaac Samuel.

I could almost see her standing in the pulpit. She said, "I will never forget the righteous indignation in his eyes as he pronounced the curse, calling on Jehovah as his witness before the sin of his daughter, declaring her—declaring you—anathema and forever no part of him or his seed."

Every detail, her eyes wide, her mouth curving down in a perfect arc, the tilt of her head, the lean of her rigid body toward me—even the sweep of the coffee cup from the saucer to her lips and back again—asserted an unbearable purity of motive that made me sick. But I sat in silence, without moving, and waited.

"Naomi, dear," Rose's tone of voice perfectly matched her face and movement, "if nothing else will convince you of your need to turn back while there's still time," she hesitated again, glanced down, perfectly timed, then looked back at me and said "surely you can see that your own barren womb is a curse from the Lord, visited on you to save your soul, to lead you back to Him."

My reaction was visceral—a shiver, a shrinking in the abdomen, a ringing in the ears. Seven years. Henry and I had been married for seven years. A nice round biblical number. The famine in Egypt lasted seven years, in which everything fruitful withered away.

Aunt Rose rushed on. "I swear every time I see Catherine Morrison and her eleven kids being herded around this town, I ache for you, thinking to myself that if you would just humble yourself before the Lord and your father Jeremiah that your quiver would surely be filled to overflowing. For surely the

Lord in his grace and mercy looks down on the two of you and yearns for you like the shepherd yearned for the one lost sheep, not caring for the ninety and nine which were safe in the fold."

That was all I could take. I pushed my chair back from the table, stood and walked to the sink, where I picked up the dishrag and began to wipe the metal. I scrubbed, the roaring in my ears making it impossible to think. I felt the zeal of Aunt Rose's eyes on the back of my neck.

After a long minute, during which the only sound was the soft rasp of the dishrag on the metal of the sink, Rose broke the silence. "I've said too much. Lord knows I speak sometimes before I think, but sometimes we quench the Spirit if we hesitate, and maybe it's not always bad to speak freely."

I kept rubbing the bottom of the sink. The air hung thick around us.

Rose stood up and pulled the black shawl together in front of her. "I didn't want to hurt you, only to help," she said.

The words hung for a moment in the soft, rasping silence and faded away.

"You'll forgive me. I know you will," she said.

The wisp of the dishrag sounded hollow in the sink.

"You know," she said, "that Isaac Samuel and I will pray for you both."

She turned and started for the door. I scrubbed at the sink, stared down into it.

When I heard the door close behind Aunt Rose, I stopped scrubbing the sink and looked up into my reflection in the window in front of me. The sky above the hills was gray. I was gray. I thought of Walter Bass in the little church, struck down and held by the agitated hands of the Pentecostal women. And I thought maybe my barrenness wasn't a curse.

Seven years of famine.

When Henry and I eloped, the town acted like it was trying to swallow dry bread crust. It was a scandal. Rose Eltha Belle Cravens' niece had run off with a Bass. But like all scandals, it had, after a time, to be swallowed. And Henry built the house, bought a nice buggy, and went about the business of running the mill. At the end of that first year we attended the annual Christmas tree celebration at the schoolhouse. Just about everybody in town came to it.

We had just moved into our new house. We went to the party as a lark, because we didn't care what people thought, and we didn't care about the foolish gifts that hung for everyone on the tree. And I laughed when they gave me—I remember exactly where it was hanging, on one of the lowest branches—the traditional gag gift for newlywed couples. A diaper with our names printed on it.

Seven years.

Yesterday morning, Sunday, he rose before dawn, just as he does now every morning of every week. And I—just as I do every morning—rose before him, heated his water for shaving, cooked his breakfast, put it on the table for him, ate alone after he was gone.

I looked into the eyes of my reflection in the gray window, a plain, thick woman, with eyes too small. I could leave him. Women do that. But what good would I be? Where would I go? Back to Fayetteville, where I was anathema and no part of my father's seed? Back to the house of my uncle Isaac Samuel Cravens, where he might pray that the Lord would gird up my loins? I could catch the train to Fayetteville, make a connection to Kansas City, lose myself in all those people.

The world beyond the White River, beyond the Ozark hills, fell away from me like a black void, empty of warmth, filled with a multitude of voices, none of them familiar, none of them knowing my name.

And now Walter was going to marry Emma Sinclair. She had plucked the forbidden fruit. I wondered if her eyes would be opened.

The daughters of Zion. I knew the scripture Aunt Rose had referred to. For we have wept on the banks of the rivers of Babylon, it says, and they that carried us away captive required of us a song, and they that wasted us required of us mirth, saying sing us one of the songs of Zion. But how shall we sing the Lord's song in a foreign land?

A beautiful passage.

As I stood looking out the window, the damp dishrag in my hand, my stomach tightened and I fought down the urge to laugh. The songs of Zion sung in a foreign land.

I thought of my old nemesis, Marcus Aurelius, and his meditations.

Time is indeed like a river. A violent stream. But altogether the interval is small. And consider, says the old stoic, with how much trouble, and with what sort of people, and in what a feeble body that interval is passed. And do not consider life a thing of any value.

I picked up my scrub brush from the floor, dipped it in the bucket and got down on my hands and knees and started scrubbing the floor again. The brush made a wet chugging sound like a train picking up steam.

6

September
Emma

WHEN I WAS BAD, Mama would say, "Emma, if you dine with the devil, bring a long-handled spoon." Then Mama would use a long handled spoon to drive the devil out. The welts on the backs of my legs were the tracks he left behind. I grew up knowing if we missed a service at the Word of Holiness Church the devil was waiting with talons like a hawk to drop us into the fiery furnace. Daddy was a deacon. Every time the church doors opened, we were there. Sunday morning, Sunday night, Wednesday night prayer meeting. The devil was a handy man to have around.

During summer revivals, Brother Leery breathed fire and brimstone two hours a night for two weeks. And every night the altar call droned on and on, as Brother Leery stood on the dais like a fighting cock, head thrust forward, eyes bulging, praying in the spirit to break the grip of the white knuckles hanging on to the pews, to pry them loose and bring them down the aisle weeping, all the fight gone. He welcomed the lost sheep into the fold, washed in the blood of the lamb.

Daddy would smile, Mama cry with joy. I stood between

them scratching the back of the pew with my fingernail, scolding the weak-livered sinner who had held out for nine verses but caved in on the tenth. The confession and baptism would take at least half an hour. The bullfrogs called from the White River just beyond the cottonwoods outside the open window. Henry and Walter Bass might be out there on the river with their daddy, noodling for catfish under the full moon. I envied the Basses. They had never set foot in a church.

The Basses lived up Delaney Creek from our farm. Virgil Bass rode a bony old mule past the house now and then on his way to town. Sometimes that mule pulled a wagon, though I don't know how it could, and maybe the two boys would be in the back, dirt-faced, staring at the house.

When I got old enough to go off with the dog and look for crawdads in the creek, Mama and Daddy reminded me, time after time, to stay away from the Basses. Not even to speak to them. The devil was lurking. And, of course, I did what I was told. And the Basses kept to themselves.

But when I turned twelve a seed sprouted inside me, and its tendrils fed on my unruly blood, angry at Mama and Daddy and their rules and the Word of Holiness Church. More than once I wandered up the creek as far as the Bass house, watched for signs of those two boys. From behind a black willow I watched them split wood, slop the sorry hogs penned up by the shed, torment the old bloodhound tied to the front porch. I waited with flushed face for them to come find me in the woods.

Then one day late that summer I waded up the creek with the dog, looking for crawdads, and came to a pool in a bend in the creek, washed out in a big rain that spring. Tree roots twisted and coiled in on themselves from the high bank on the other side at the elbow of the bend. Daddy would have called it snaky. Mama had forbidden me to go swimming by myself. I pulled off my shirt and jeans and left them on the bank and went in.

I walked out into that pool, bare to the sun. I was getting breasts, but Mama wouldn't hear of me wearing a brassiere. And she refused to say a word to me about the dark triangle of hair that was growing at the very center of me, making me a woman whether Mama liked it or not.

The sun had never felt so good on my back as it did when I walked into the creek, and the spring-fed water seemed to finger-walk up my thighs.

As I swam around that pool, I had the feeling I could do anything I wanted, anything in the world. No matter what Mama and Daddy said.

Then the dog barked behind me, and I looked up on the bank on the steep side opposite my clothes, and Walter Bass was standing half behind a sycamore trunk watching me. He wore a pair of ragged jeans, out at the knees, held up by a pair of suspenders over his skinny shoulders. His hair fell down over his forehead, covering one eye. He was maybe fifteen at the time.

For years afterward, my stomach rose when I remembered it. I stood up in the pool, with the water coming just up over my navel, and my first thought was not that I should cover myself. It was don't scare him off. Don't do anything to scare him off.

My heart was beating fast, but I let my hands float out to

my sides and spoke to him as calm as I could, like we were standing in the schoolyard.

"Water's cool," I said.

He was staring at my chest when I spoke, and he looked up at me. I thought I was going to lose him, thought he was going to turn and run.

"I'm Emma," I said, and I moved the water with my hands.

He didn't say anything. The low rumble of the dog growling came from the bank behind me.

I wanted him to get in the creek with me. I was close to a Bass, talking to a Bass. Had a chance to swim naked with him in broad daylight. But he stood there dumb and not moving.

I had no idea what to do next, what to say. "Suit yourself," I said. "Come in if you want." And I turned and swam back across the pool to the gravel bar on the far side, my stomach turning flips and my heart beating hard, the sun warm on my back.

When I neared the gravel bar and could reach the bottom with my hands, I turned around, squatting in the shallows. He was not there. I looked up and down the far bank. My face burned, and I pulled a rock from the bottom of the creek and threw it at the sycamore tree.

"All right, then," I yelled, "see if I ever speak to you again." And I threw another rock at the tree.

And then something moved off to my left, and he stepped out from behind a big black willow. He looked like an animal with its leg in a trap, and without thinking I stood up. The dog barked once, whined, and went silent. The water came up to my knees. I stood in the bright sunlight, dripping, a rock in each hand. A squirrel chattered from the woods behind him. He looked all the way down me and back up and then reached up to his suspenders like he was going to drop those jeans and walk into the water. The blood beat loud in my ears, and I felt dizzy.

He took a deep breath and backed away in slow, short steps. I wanted to say something, anything to keep him there.

"Come back here, now!" I said, the voice of Mama yelling at the dog.

His steps quickened and I knew I had lost him, and I threw one rock and then the other at him as he disappeared up the bank toward his house. I sat back down in the shallow water with my fists pushed into my eyes. I had bared myself to the devil and a Bass, and even the Bass would have nothing to do with me. My face burned and my stomach shriveled up inside me. But I had lost more than the Bass, something that I couldn't put a word to. It hummed like a mosquito at my ear. Invisible, persistent, threatening. I heard Brother Leery's deep voice booming from the pulpit, "The soul that sinneth shall die! And the wickedness of the wicked shall be upon him!" I beat the water with my fists and crossed my arms to cover my breasts.

When I got home, my hair was wet and smelled like creek water, and Mama asked me what I had been doing. I lied the first thing that came to my mind. I told her I had fallen in the creek grabbing for a crawdad.

She felt of my blouse and said, "Your clothes are dry. How could you have fallen in?"

I looked at my feet, my chest burning, tears welling up, and said nothing.

"Emma," Mama said, "you're lying to me."

We stood there in the silence, and I squinted back the tears, wanting to tell her everything, to drive home the truth like a nail. She didn't go get her long-handled spoon. She just looked out the window and took a breath.

And that day began the long trial between my mother and myself. The years of not quite saying everything, but of saying just enough, of letting what was left unsaid lacerate the heart. The years of patient martyrdom that no relationship can survive.

Not long after that day, my first menstruation seemed like a sign to me, the pain and the blood another kind of loss, mortal and warm and accusing. A loss about which Mama could not speak. I could not hide it, and when she looked at the stains, her face tightened into a look I had not seen there before. And I went down the aisle on the first night of summer revival at the Word of Holiness Church, on the first verse of the invitation hymn, and was met by Brother Leery. I began to speak in tongues and was washed in the blood of the Lamb, but I could not forget how easily my own unruly blood had betrayed me. I said long prayers in the dark on my knees on the hardwood floor.

And that fall the Basses took over Mose Joiner's saw mill and moved into the house up by the mill. For the next eight years, I avoided Walter Bass and carried my secret shame like a cross.

And then a few weeks ago, the next-to-last night of the summer meetings, Brother Leery was preaching Holy Ghost revival. He was strong in the Word, and we were all in the Spirit. The house was full, and I was standing as usual against the wall up near the front on the left, at the end of the pew where Mama and Daddy always sat. We were singing "Have a Little Talk with Jesus," clapping, having a good time when Walter Bass slipped in the back door and slid up against the wall and lifted off his hat and held it down in front of him, his black hair falling down over his forehead.

He looked scared, like he wanted to run, and I was suddenly back in that cold creek water eight years earlier, and I shivered and crossed my arms over my breasts. Nobody at the back of the sanctuary even noticed him come in.

As far as all of those people were concerned, Walter Bass and I had nothing in common. They knew the Basses were trouble. My daddy owns 600 acres of the best bottomland in Madison County, and he is a pillar in the Word of Holiness Church. And, of course, I was washed in the blood of the Lamb.

After Walter stood against that back wall for a minute, he started up the narrow left aisle, working his way in my direction.

I couldn't quite get my breath, thinking Oh, God, he is going to expose me in front of the church. The people along the wall and at the ends of the pews stared at him as he passed, turning their heads to whisper to each other without taking their eyes off him. A Bass in church was something to see. He turned sideways to slide past people, his hat still held in both hands down in front of him.

A shout sounded from the other side of the sanctuary, and Magin Wilson, who has been resisting the Spirit for as long as I've known him, jumped up from the front pew. Magin is one of those boys that everybody likes but nobody thinks will amount to anything. Never stays at one job more than six months. With Otis Hogan playing the piano not ten feet from him and Otis's wife, Rachel, pounding the tambourine against her hip, Magin stood there, swaying just a little, as if he was alone in a quiet room listening to the sound of footsteps coming down the hall.

People backed away to give him a little space. Magin went rigid with his arms straight out to the sides, the notes from the piano and the sharp beats of the tambourine holding him up. Then his chin jerked down to his chest and he hunched over and then straightened up and twisted like a colt under its first saddle.

But it was too late to throw off the Holy Ghost. At the shouts of hallelujah and praise Jesus from the people around him, Magin dropped to the floor like someone had knocked the wind out of him, and Purity Morrison slipped out of the end of the second pew and she and Thelma Rich knelt beside him for the laying on of hands.

Just then one of the Hogan girls stood up and stepped into the center aisle and began to minister in the speaking of tongues. Walter had stopped, maybe ten feet from me in that side aisle, and had turned and looked at what was happening like he had stumbled onto a nest of snakes. He was struggling, breathing hard.

And he turned and looked right at me, his hair falling across his forehead, his blue eyes fearful, and he blinked hard like he was having trouble seeing me. The hair stood up on my neck and arms, and I felt naked, just like I was standing in front of him in the creek. He was still holding his hat with both hands, but he dropped it and took a step toward me and stumbled and fell face down and didn't move.

Several of the people around him stepped away like they didn't want any part of this one, but Pauline Roberts and Tobias Greenway, with his empty right sleeve pinned up to his shoulder, knelt and began to pray, though they did not touch him. I moved to him and knelt beside him and reached out and laid my hand on his back and began to pray in the spirit.

But when I touched him, I saw him again standing on the creek bank above me, looking down, his jeans ragged. And then he turned over, slow, like he was waking up, and I wanted to hide my face before he looked at me.

The narrow aisle was crowded with the three of us praying over him and people craning their necks to see, and I smelled the sweet stench of alcohol on his breath. Everyone knew the Basses were alcoholics. I laid my right hand on his chest and stretched my left hand up to the Lord and prayed for his release, asking Jesus to plunge him in that fountain filled with blood drawn from Immanuel's veins and wash his sins away.

Then it happened. The power of the Lord ran through me with a shock that I thought would rend me in two like a bolt of lightning boils the sap and explodes the trunk of a tree. I opened my mouth thinking I would speak in tongues, but I cried out, "Who may abide the day of his coming? And who shall stand when he appeareth? For he is like a refiner's fire." But I felt like it was me on fire.

And when I called on the Name of Jesus for the baptism of fire, it seemed like the heat burned down through my arms and my hands 'til the cloth of Walter's shirt on his chest would wilt under it and his skin would be singed. The Lord was burning away my shame, redeeming it in an act of grace, the redemption of a lost soul, the very soul that knew my secret.

He cried out, looking up at me, and he crossed over the dark gulf, I know he did, his life shifting on that great fulcrum, dying to his old self and rising a new creature, in his eyes a look of wonder and dizzy relief. I helped him stand up, somebody handed him his hat, and he followed me over to my place at the wall. He stood beside me. My knees were weak. I was crying and smiling.

But it was not that simple. Things never are in Delaney. He was a Bass.

The day after he was struck down at the revival, he found me in the mercantile and walked up to me and said "Emma" and smiled. The mercantile got as quiet as a henhouse at midnight, and everyone looked every way but at Walter and me. But they were listening. Pauline Roberts and her husband, Bill, had been at the service the night before. My stomach was jumping, and I made myself breathe slow and easy.

I said "Walter" and turned away and walked down the second aisle toward the toiletries. I stopped in front of the bath oils and examined one of the bottles and glanced back at him, but he was gone.

When Mama and Daddy and I went to services that night, the last night of revival, he was leaning against the wall up there in that left aisle, waiting, where I was supposed to stand. Mama and Daddy went right to their usual pew, and I went to the wall beside Walter. I could feel everyone on that side of the sanctuary staring at us.

Mama looked up at me and then at Walter and then back at me, and her lips pushed together and then relaxed as she looked away. And two or three times during the service she did it again. Looked at Walter, then looked at me. Looked away real quick when I looked at her.

I did not speak to Walter during the service, did not even look at him, though I felt him looking at me, and I sometimes smelled his shaving soap. He tried to sing a little of "I Have Found a Friend in Jesus," but the hymns were all unfamiliar to him. And after the service there was an awkward moment before Mama called me over to where she and Miriam Martin were talking.

Then the next day, Walter came out of Job Delight's store as I walked by, and he called my name. Right there on the street, "Emma," he says, real loud. Lester Givens, sitting in front of the mercantile across the square, lowered his newspaper and stared at us over the top of it. And Job stood there in the window behind the counter, wiping his hands on his white apron, and watched us, a half smile on his greasy lips.

Walter asked me, without any small talk, right there on the street, if he could come to my house that evening. I couldn't breathe slow enough, and I had the feeling I was in trouble. I said yes, remembering Mama's face when she looked at us the night before in church.

When I walked into the living room, Mama looked up from cutting out a pattern and said, "Well, how was your afternoon?"

"Walter Bass is coming over to see me tonight," I said. There just wasn't any easy way to break the news.

"What do you mean?" she said.

"He saw me on the street," I said. "He asked if he could come and see me after dinner. I told him he could."

She went back to cutting, and the silence got heavy. "On the street," she said and glanced up at me. She was cutting the material slow and exact, concentrating on the line, but her lips were working. "He drinks," she said. "They all drink."

"Mama," I said, but she cut me off.

"Everybody in Delaney knows that Virgil Bass beat his wife." She stopped cutting and looked up at me, the scissors still straddling the cloth.

Not many people in Delaney had ever even seen Lilly Bass before she died, but everyone in town knew that she never showed her face because of what Virgil did to it. Mama was convinced of the truth of it all. The drinking, the violence, the insanity that she was sure ran in the Bass family.

Mama started cutting again and opened her mouth to say something else, but she quit cutting and started to cry in that way she has, working her lips around as she talks, her watery eyes looking away from me.

I wanted to tell her that I had stood naked in front of Walter Bass and invited him into the water, and it had taken him eight years to decide.

Mama started cutting the material again, the muffled scritch of the scissors the only sound. "Your father won't allow it," she said.

I pictured Daddy standing on the porch and threatening Walter when he tried to come in, and it felt like a lead weight slid into my stomach.

"Walter got saved," I said. "He won't be drinking any more."

She made this little snorting sound and opened her mouth like she was going to say something, but thought better of it.

Around town, the news of Walter being struck down by the Holy Ghost was a big surprise. Nobody in his right mind would have expected a Bass to get saved. But Walter's conversion was eclipsed by the rumor that he was coming to my house every night, the house of Ben Sinclair, who owned just about all the good bottomland between Delaney and Crosses. When Walter had stood beside me at church in full view of everyone, people had taken the charitable view that I was encouraging a new convert. But when he started coming to our house, the attitudes evolved.

Whenever I walked into the mercantile, people said "Hey, Emma," and then their conversation died, and they stood there with a smile that lasted too long. And they watched me as I did my shopping, as if word had gotten out that I had a cancer and they were looking for the symptoms. Always the silence while I pulled a pound of coffee from the shelves here, a sack of flour there. People watching, waiting.

At home, Mama and Daddy were polite to Walter, which was more than I thought possible. Daddy talked to him about the lumber business. Mama was quiet. Walter and I sat on the porch every evening after Mama and Daddy went inside, and we listened to the cicadas. Walter didn't say much, especially when we were alone. And the first time he reached out and took my hand, I swear the heat of some dim, flickering thing, buried under years of living as a Bass, flared up in him.

Mama fretted and picked at me. But Daddy was so quiet that I began to wish he would lose his temper and yell a little, or threaten to lock me up in the cellar. But he just sat by himself in the evenings, reading or looking at the fire. I was being courted by a Bass, and people around town, at the mercantile and the train depot and Solomon's Café, were treating Daddy the same way they treated me. The smiles, the silence. He didn't have to tell me. I knew.

He never said a word to me about Walter until Mama brought me in to him one evening.

"Ben Sinclair," she said, "you have got to talk some sense into your daughter." She pushed me a little toward him.

Daddy put down his pipe and closed his book and stared down at his hands and didn't say anything for a minute. Mama stood there with her handkerchief in her hand, working her lips like she was trying hard not to speak for him, her eyes red and puffy.

Mama and me were getting uncomfortable when Daddy finally said, "Martha, you know I've always trusted Emma, and she's never once disappointed me. I think I'll trust her on this one." That was it. That was all he said. Then he gave me, just for a second, one of those clear, steady kind of looks, but not long enough for me to be sure what his eyes were saying before he turned away, and he picked up his book and opened it again.

I was crying and Mama was crying, but for different reasons.

So a month later Walter and I married, and it was a full house. Some people, I know, came to the wedding out of curiosity. Some out of spite. Some just to gossip. They came for the same reason they went to circus side shows. It started slow, people trying not to stare, watching Walter and me like we were exotic animals brought to town for only one day. But sometimes a wedding has a power all its own. And for just a little while when the service was over, people looked at Walter and me like we were something new in creation. Like the resurrection wasn't so far-fetched after all. Like all the good they had believed about people all their lives, out of stubborn habit and in spite of all the evidence to the contrary, might just be true.

With one exception. Like a prisoner of war, Mama stood when the congregation stood, and she sat when the congregation sat, like she was shackled to my father's left arm, all the while staring straight ahead, past Brother Leery sitting on the dais, through the back wall of the baptistery and into the dark woods beyond.

Earlier that morning, when I was dressing, Mama had made one last attempt, had sat and watched, drying her eyes with a handkerchief, sniffling, begging me not to go through with it. I had no bridesmaids because there was nobody Walter wanted to stand beside him as best man. Not even his brother Henry. So we were going to stand alone.

"What kind of a wedding is that?" Mama said. "None of your friends will even stand with you."

"I didn't ask them, Mama. They understand."

"What do they understand, Emma? What?" She blew her nose and folded the handkerchief. "Do they understand that my only daughter is marrying a man that nobody in Delaney will stand with, because they are afraid they will have to hold him up so he can say 'I do'?"

"He hasn't had a drink since he was struck down, Mama." Again I had the urge to tell her about standing naked in front of Walter eight years earlier, about inviting him into the water like the whore of Babylon. But I also wanted to tell her to get out and let me at least enjoy putting on my dress.

"He was never an alcoholic, Mama," I said. "He drank because of people who never gave him a chance. People like you."

I was sorry as soon as I said it. "Mama," I said, "I didn't mean to say that. I just—"

"I see he's turned you against me," she said and stood up. "How am I supposed to feel about that?"

What could I say? None of this really mattered by then. In a little while Walter and I would be married. I just wanted to enjoy putting on my wedding dress. She left the room, and the door shut with a quiet click.

I turned to the mirror and set the veil on my head and slid the bobby pins in place. As I pulled the veil down over my face, it was like closing the window on the noise outside. Peace and quiet. I could breathe easy again.

Mama insisted that when Brother Leery asked "Who gives this woman?" that Daddy say "I do," rather than "Her mother and I do." I wondered whether Walter noticed the missing words. Her mother and I. When Daddy said it, I glanced through the veil at Walter. His blue eyes were steady on Brother Leery.

After the wedding we ran down the long double row of well wishers showering us with handfuls of grain and climbed into the wagon, grain bouncing off the seat and spreading on the floor. Daddy was there to hug me and help me up and pat Walter on the back as he climbed in. I didn't see Mama.

7

The Same Night
Henry Bass

I DID NOT WANT TO GO INTO THAT CHURCH for the shouting and drooling that bunch of hypocrites was bound to work up to. The red sun was dropping into the treetops on the other side of the river. It was late. I was thirsty. I was going home.

A gray-bearded scarecrow stood on the church porch ringing a bell. Brother Leery, they call him. Damn him and his bell both. My buggy was tied at the edge of the grove, easy to get out, and I looked for Naomi in the crowd of people drifting toward the building. She was leaning back against a walnut tree not far from me, her eyes fixed on me. We were both over dressed for this crowd. She had pinned her hair in a knot on top of her head. Her shirtwaist was cinched up so tight I didn't see how she could breathe. Big, puffy sleeves. The latest thing.

I walked over to her, glad that we could get away. "Let's go," I said as I stopped in front of her.

She didn't say anything, and I could see it would not be easy after all. She looked toward the front porch of the church house.

"Your precious whiskey can wait," she said, almost a whisper. "It's your brother's wedding. It's been a pleasant day."

It had not been a pleasant day. My feet were tired. I had listened to small talk from people I did not want to be with. I had watched a horseshoe game, a foot race, and croquet. I had looked twice through the weekly newspaper, read all the latest news from the war in Cuba. I knew exactly how many officers and men were killed and wounded to date. It was not really much of a war. In the heat and humidity I had stood around in my coat, vest, and white shirt. I had chewed about all the Duke's Mixture I could chew in one day. I wondered how in the hell this whole thing had ever happened.

"I do not intend to go in there like some braying jackass," I said.

"Well, don't then," she said and pushed herself away from the tree. "Stand out here by yourself if you like, but I'm going in." She walked past me.

I felt my face flush as I looked at the walnut tree where she had stood. It was useless to argue. My stomach hurt. It wasn't right.

I headed for the front porch of the building.

Naomi stood at the foot of the steps talking to Hiram Wesley's wife, Dora, patting her on the arm, her handbag swinging from her wrist. The look on her face was smug, some private thing between women. I wanted to go to the church porch, get Naomi by the arm, and drag her to the buggy. I wanted to go home, I was thirsty, the wedding was over.

Walter had made a complete damn fool of himself over a woman he had no business being with in the first place. Ben Sinclair and his holier-than-thou wife and daughter put on airs.

Martha Sinclair takes every chance to tell you her family was from Old Virginia. As if anybody gives a tinker's damn. They purchase lumber as if they are doing a man a favor.

And now Walter was joining the family.

I walked over to Naomi and Dora. They stopped talking and looked up at me as I approached. Naomi's face was empty. Dora smiled.

"Evening, Mr. Bass," Dora said. "You coming in for the blessing?"

I wondered what Naomi had said to her.

"Guess so," I said and nodded to her and turned to Naomi, whose eyes told me nothing. Dora Wesley excused herself and joined Hiram going into the building. Neither me nor Naomi even looked at her when she left.

"Can we at least sit in the back, so we can get away if this foolishness lasts too long?" I said, keeping my voice low.

Naomi waited before answering, nodded and smiled to two or three people who passed.

"Why not?" she said and slipped her hand into the crook of my arm. As we started up the steps, she lifted her skirt out of the way with her free hand, tilted her head just a little away from me, made it all seem natural.

As the people came into the building, their voices got quiet. Some of the older women had already sat down up near the front, and they rocked back and forth, fanning themselves. Gradually the pews filled with men, women, and children.

As me and Naomi stood just inside the door, looking at the pews, I felt like a rabbit caught in an open field, tense, ready to bolt at the first sign of a dog sniffling in the grass. Emma and Walter were standing in the center aisle beside one of the front pews. Ben Sinclair talked to Walter, who looked like a man standing in the middle of a sewing bee. And that was just where Walter belonged, messing with a bunch of women. Walter's hand rested easy on the end of the pew. He seemed at home in that place. But his eyes glanced to one side, then the other, like a damn weasel.

At some signal that I did not see, the people sat down, and me and Naomi moved to an open space at the end of a back pew. The rustling and the whispering stopped, and it seemed like even the children knew what was about to happen. I was damned if I could see it. Someone coughed and a cow bawled in the distance.

Up on a platform, old Leery sat in a big oak chair that looked like a damn throne, the seat upholstered in red leather. His left arm lay on the armrest with his Bible open in his hand, and he leaned his forehead into the palm of his right hand. It was a pose, if I ever saw one. His eyes were closed and his lips were moving. A regular holy man.

Then Otis Hogan, who's got the brains of a hog, started playing the piano and singing "Bringing in the Sheaves." I'd be embarrassed to sing if my voice was as high as his, but everyone joined in, standing and clapping. Me and Naomi looked at each other, then stood; our hands stayed on the pew in front of us. Rachel Hogan's fat face lit up, and she banged a tambourine on her big hips and shouted "Yes, Lord!"

It was all a lot more than I had planned on, and when the

volume kept going up, it started feeling crowded to me. I was more than ready to climb in the buggy and go home. But Naomi stood on her tiptoes, looking over the heads of the people in front of us toward the front of the room, smiling as if she were watching children play. I gripped the pew to keep from walking out and leaving her.

Old Leery walked up to a podium, and people shouted "Hallelujah!" and "Praise the Lord!" all over the room, but the music kept going for a while with Leery standing there clapping his hands and nodding his head. When Otis Hogan finally quit playing, there was a big sigh it seemed like, with people saying "Yes!" and "Praise you Jesus!" and there was clapping and shuffling and the creaking of the pews as everybody sat down. All over the room heads rocked back and forth, looking at the preacher.

Old Leery started slow and level, and he built up to a big show. And he ended every sentence with this big loud "Yes!" stretching it into two parts every time he said it, until I was about ready to go up there and choke him. Fans fluttered, and heads rocked back and forth, and people shouted "Amen!" prodding the old fart on.

It was disgusting. That old man extended one arm up in the air, his wrist bent, his fingers crooked like he gripped an apple he was about to throw. Reminded me of Virgil in the firelight of the front room of that stinking old house down by the mill, with his head face-down on the table, an empty bottle beside his outstretched arm, his fingers curled around a shot glass. When the preacher lifted his head toward the ceiling and prayed, I could see Virgil lifting his head up off the table and looking over at Mama. Her standing there wide-eyed, waiting, and the rocking chair still rocking back and forth behind her.

The people in the church started singing again, "All hail the power of Jesus' name, let angels prostrate fall." I didn't know about the angels, but I was about to fall. I had had enough of that stuff. Walter and Emma sat together on the front pew. She still wore the wedding veil pulled back over her head, but she had changed into a blouse and skirt instead of the wedding dress. Walter slapped his hand on his thigh in time with the singing, getting carried away with his own little vision of the glory about to come, no doubt.

They were snugged right up against each other. It made me sick, and I had to fight back the urge to laugh. That wall-eyed calf was scared of what was waiting for him outside those walls. Scared to death. The poor son of a bitch would be worse than worthless to little Emma that night.

As worthless as he was the night at the roadhouse.

Now there's a night I'll never forget. The yellow light through the curtains of the open window of the room at the back of the roadhouse, the soft laughter of Pearl Bear from inside. I leaned against a tree outside, listening, drunk, imagining Pearl's long black hair hanging down as she leaned forward, the hair brushing Walter's chest. One of the horses chuffed in the dark behind me. The trip to the roadhouse was my gift to Walter, who was too damn shy to do it for himself. It was Walter's fifteenth birthday. Pearl was doing it as a favor to me, taking care of the kid brother.

When we were leaving the house to go down there, Mama hung on every word I said about needing to go to town, and her hands fluttered around Walter, brushing back his hair, straightening his shirt, always about to land, like moths at the globe of a lamp.

Somehow nothing could ever be simple in our house, and I could see trouble coming. The bravado Walter showed when I first told him the plan melted under Mama's assault, the spark in his eyes faded, even the smile was snuffed out. I finally took him by the arm and dragged him out the door, but as I did I felt the resistance.

After three or four beers at the roadhouse, Walter's face flushed and the smile came back. But when he reached for his glass, his hand shook. Walter's fear of women was a joke. It was pitiful. His innocence was embarrassing. And the problem would never go away if I didn't start somewhere, so I talked to Pearl. And I brought Walter to the roadhouse. I slapped him on the shoulder and took him around to the back and handed him through the door to Pearl with her long black hair and her dusky eyes. And he hesitated, reached out to the door frame, looked at me, before Pearl took his hand and pulled him in.

And then it got too quiet in there. I pushed myself away from the tree and walked closer to the window and listened. The curtains parted and Pearl stuck her head into the window and looked at me with this damn smile. "Better come get your lover boy," she said, and there was something about the way she said it that made me want to ask what was wrong. But I went to the door and opened it and went in.

Walter sat on the bed to the left of the door, dressed and staring at the floor. Pearl stood by the window over to the right, buttoning her blouse. She shrugged at me, then looked over at Walter.

"What?" I said. "What's going on?"

"Maybe he's just not ready," she said.

I felt the color rise in my cheeks. I was a fool to try and take Walter there. It was a mess, and Walter was hopeless. He had failed me again. Just like at the railroad tracks when we were kids. The time we were going to run away. The time his eyes got real big as we stood beside the tracks, the freight train rolling past. The time he stood there and cried, the tears running down his cheeks, and I knew he was going to run, and there wasn't anything I could say to stop him. And so once again, standing there in Pearl's room, with her smirking, there was nothing to say, nothing to do.

That wedding service went on for over an hour. The moon was high, and my jaw muscles were tightening. Finally, that old crow Leery stood up on that platform and looked out over everybody.

"Now, Brothers and Sisters," he said, "it's time we ushered these two young people out that door and into holy matrimony." Then he added something about the Holy Ghost and tongues of fire and the glory of the Lord.

It was all I could do to keep from laughing, but amen's came from around the room. Then Leery looked down at

Walter and Emma.

"Will the newlyweds please rise?" he said.

Walter and Emma stood, their hands held tight between them.

"Their wagon is ready outside the door." The old man's voice was friendly, and he muddled on about the Lord leaving the earth and having a lot of mansions in the sky. It was rich, I can tell you. Then he said, "Brothers and Sisters, the church is the bride of Christ, and our prayer is that Walter and Emma enter into it with power and with thanksgiving."

Well, I hated to disappoint the old man, but I wouldn't have bet on there being much power in Walter's entering in.

Right about then Emma turned toward Walter and looked up at him. Naomi had turned toward me, that same way seven years earlier. Where the hell do they learn that shy little angle of the head? As we stood in the parlor of the justice of the peace down in St. Paul, man and wife, Naomi looked up to kiss me with a smile that I could swear was mocking me.

All the braying asses at the Word of Holiness Church stood and moved toward the doors in the rear of the building. They shook Walter's hand and slapped his back and some of them even smiled. The women hugged Emma and kissed her and whispered into her ear. Some of the old hens were weeping, probably at Emma's innocence, soon to be lost. Some of them looked like the gorge was rising in their throats.

Walter and Emma were jostled along toward the door, then hurried on out to the wagon through the cheers and the shower of grain that pelted them from all sides and rattled on the porch and steps. Ben Sinclair was crying like an old woman himself when he hugged his daughter one last time and helped her up into the wagon.

Walter fumbled with the wagon lines in the light of several lanterns held up in the crowd. Someone yelled, "Ease up, Walter, it'll wait a minute" and a rush of laughter ran through the people, and Walter tried to smile, like an idiot. Then he released the wagon brake, and dropped the lines altogether, grabbing them just before they slipped down between the horses, who lurched forward, then stopped with a jerk as he grabbed up the lines again. Everyone laughed.

"Hey, Walter," the same voice yelled, "want me to drive ya'll on home? Might could even stay for a cup of coffee if you like."

The laughter was louder then, and someone else yelled, "Shut up, Tom, or they'll never get on the road."

Emma's veil slipped down over her face when the wagon lurched, and she pushed it back and laughed herself. She reached out and touched Walter's arm.

And I felt Naomi's arm resting in the crook of my own. When I turned, she looked up at me, a smile still on her lips. But the smile dropped and her eyes narrowed. She turned her face away and drew her hand from my arm. "I think we can go now," she said. "You've been a good boy, Henry. But I'm sure you're thirsty." I felt like someone had landed a surprise punch to my stomach. She turned her head a little back toward me and looked at me from the corners of her eyes.

When Walter and Emma were finally gone, and the buggies

started pulling out onto the lane, I stood in the dark of the grove of trees and smoked a cigar and waited for Naomi, who was hanging around at the near corner of the building and talking with Martha Sinclair. Ben Sinclair stood alone in the moonlight at the foot of the steps and looked down the empty dirt road.

I was thirsty. My hand trembled when I lifted the cigar to my mouth. Naomi and Martha Sinclair kissed each other on the cheek and said goodbye, and Naomi started for the buggy. She was humming real soft and slipping her hands into white gloves that shined in the moonlight.

8

Later That Night
Emma

A LITTLE BEFORE MIDNIGHT, we rolled to a stop in front of our house. The moon was cream-colored in the ragged branches of the red oak by the road, and moonlit limbs reached off into black shadows in the woods. The gravel under the wheels popped and crunched.

Walter set the brake, dropped the lines over the handle and climbed down. He lifted me to the ground like he thought I would break, and stood beside me. He didn't say anything, just put his hands in his pockets and stared like he was inspecting the house.

The house had belonged to Grandaddy Sinclair, and my Uncle Beau and Aunt Jean had lived there until Uncle Beau was killed in a riding accident. I spent part of each summer with Uncle Beau and Aunt Jean. Walter didn't like the idea of us moving in there, but I finally talked him into it. He wanted to wait until we found a place of our own, but I wouldn't hear of it. It was our only disagreement. I wouldn't call it a fight. But it was hard for him to move into the old house.

I knew what the problem was. Everyone had always

called that house the old Sinclair place. It would never be called the Bass place. No matter how long we lived in it. And then our moving in there seemed like charity to Walter. That old problem between the Basses and Delaney.

The moon lit the house, the yard, the rail fence down the side of the yard, the shed at the end of the lane.

"Walter," I said, "better take care of the horses." I squeezed his arm.

He looked down at his feet, then back at the house. He cleared his throat. "Okay," he said, "I will. I'll take them around to the barn."

He walked the horses and wagon down the side lane. The horses hooves and the wagon wheels were muffled on the dirt and grass, and the harnesses jangled in the slow rhythm of the horses walking.

A thin edge of shadow marked each shake shingle of the roof of the house and each rock of the chimney. The porch lay in partial moonlight, a swing at one end, two straight-backed cane chairs at the other. Halfway up the screen door the shadow of the porch roof cut across the front of the house. Hollyhocks clustered at the end of the porch, nearly as tall as a man, their red blooms gray in the moonlight.

I heard Walter's steps before he came around the corner of the house. The shadow of his hat fell across his face as he approached me, and when he stopped in front of me, he drew in a breath and released it.

I reached out and touched his chest. His belly trembled, and he clenched his jaw, but the trembling did not stop. I slipped my arm around his waist and he put his arm around my shoulders, and we went up the two rock steps to the porch. Our heads and shoulders were in the darkness of the shadow of the porch roof, and Walter turned back toward the road. The woods vibrated with the rising and falling sounds of tree frogs and crickets, the voices distinct and insistent, independent of each other, like the singing in the Word of Holiness Church.

I went to one of the two cane chairs against the house, sat and loosened the laces down my shoes, pulled them off, set them aside, and returned to Walter, who stood still, staring out across the gray road into the darkness of the woods.

Just beyond the road, the hillside dropped off into a gully, and the tin roof of a small chicken house showed in the moonlight, level with the road. The trees that surrounded it rose up in a tangle of shadow and gray leaves. A narrow gap opened in the tall grass at the side of the road, the top of the path that cut an angle down the hillside to the door of the coop. I had bought the chickens from Purity, who lives just down the road, and they roosted there below the embankment.

"What are you thinking?" I said.

When he answered, his voice began in a dry whisper, and he stopped to clear it before going on. "About us," he said. "About me even being here. In this house." He stopped, then added, "I don't know."

I reached out again and touched him. His shirt was damp. His hands hung loose at his sides.

About two weeks after the revival, Walter and I had sat together on the porch at my parents' house, listening to the night sounds. And they all stopped at once, one second the woods ringing with the loud wailing, rising and falling, and the next second silence. And I knew it was a sign. And so I waited in the silence, barely breathing, for the word to come. The soft light through the window lay on the sharp lines of his face and the frayed edges of his shirt collar.

And he said will you marry me, and I thought I hadn't heard him right and I asked him what he'd said. He looked out into the dark and swallowed, his Adam's apple moving in the light, and he said, like he was talking to himself, that he would hate living without me, but that he knew better than to think he could live with me. And the tree frogs and cicadas and crickets all began again, first one, then another, until the whole multitude of them sang in the darkness.

It was a sign. I said yes.

And so, in the moonlight, on the porch of our new home, I knelt down and began to unlace his shoes. The smell of fresh polish rose from the shoes, and I pulled the waxy laces loose.

"Step out of them, Walter," I said. And when I lightly gripped his leg behind the knee to help bend and lift it, he shuddered.

I laid the shoes aside, and when I stood, I was close to him. As a young girl, I curried DeSoto, our big bay horse, every day, my face flush against his side, breathing his pungent warmth, one hand on his belly, the other pulling the comb down across his flank. Once Dr. Blake, as he wrapped plaster gauze around my broken foot, said, "You got to stand back from that horse, Emma."

The faint odor of shaving soap came to me from Walter's

face in the darkness, and I reached up and lifted off his hat, laid it in the chair behind me, and lifted off my veil and put it beside the hat. I took his arm in mine and led him through the door into the small front room.

Through the window to our right, the moonlight made a rectangle on the floor. Pausing to let our eyes adjust, we breathed the sweet smell from years of burning hickory and oak, sunk into the fabric and wood of the room. Aunt Jean had left the furniture and took the kids back to her family in Kansas City. The house was just as it had been when she and Uncle Beau lived there. Under the window a worn sofa rose from the linoleum on dark wooden legs. I lay there summer afternoons as a girl and read the tales of Camelot. The forbidden love of Lancelot and Guinevere. To the right of the sofa, in the corner of the room, stood a small table, and just beside us, to our right, the dark outline of Aunt Jean's rocker showed in the window that looked back out onto the front porch. In the middle of the room, like a dark and human outline, rose Uncle Beau's pot-bellied stove with its pipe reaching straight up through the ceiling.

To our left, the door to our bedroom stood open. Straight ahead, a door led into a small dining room, with a table and four chairs, and an open hutch that contained Aunt Jean's dishes, the floral pattern I loved. They were my dishes now. To the left of the dining room another bedroom, the room where I slept with all the cousins when I stayed here, and beyond the dining room the small kitchen, mostly counters and cupboards, a stove and an icebox. A deep sink hung from the wall in front of a small window, beside it a butcher block on short square legs where Aunt Jean had made pies and let me roll out the dough with her big rolling pin. I knew every inch of this house, all of it familiar, comfortable. The old Sinclair place.

Walter shifted his weight from one foot to the other. I leaned forward a little and looked past him at the dark opening into the bedroom. "Walter?" I said.

He leaned back the tiniest bit. But I squeezed his arm, and we turned into the door. I nudged him forward, and his hands moved out to the door frames, his fingertips touching the wood, holding him back, and he looked over his shoulder at me, then at the pot bellied stove, then through the door to the dining room at the hutch and the dishes. He looked down at me, into one of my eyes and then the other. I was holding my breath, and I made myself breathe out and smile, and it came out like one of those little breath laughs people do when they are afraid. Then he lowered his hands to his sides, and we stepped across the threshold into the bedroom.

The dark outline of the foot of the bed showed in the window on the far wall. In the darkness to the right, at the head of the bed, was a table with a lamp, and against the wall to the right of the door, hidden by the open door itself, stood the chest of drawers. This was Uncle Beau and Aunt Jean's room.

When Walter and I first looked at the house and I told him this had been my aunt and uncle's room and I wanted it to be ours, he was quiet for a minute and then said, "Couldn't we sleep in that middle bedroom?" But I told him how all the good light and the nice breeze came with this corner room and how I had always dreamed as a little girl of it being my room someday. He didn't say anything else, just nodded his head.

When we moved toward the bed, his arm pulled back, barely noticeable, and we stopped and stood in the darkness. And all of Delaney crowded between us. Mama pleaded with me to come to my senses and looked at me from the corners of her eyes, crying, betrayed. The men in the mercantile looked at each other and smiled, secretive. The women in the church whispered to each other, and Daddy stood there silent.

And for the first time since that night on the porch when I said yes, a cold ripple rose and tightened in my throat. I couldn't swallow. In the romances of the Round Table, Guinevere was the queen, and she lost everything. Camelot was destroyed. I pushed my face against Walter's arm and breathed deep, the warm odor of sweat and shaving soap.

When we reached the bed, he turned and sat on the edge near the foot. I pulled down the light summer bedspread and fluffed the feather pillows.

When I touched the bedding, I shivered. I closed my eyes and folded my arms and rubbed them to take off the chill.

Walter was quiet. I lifted his chin, and my hand moved over the surface of his face, the high ridge of his nose, and I began to unbutton my blouse. His face was smooth and warm, and when my hand passed over his mouth, he tried to kiss my palm.

With both my hands, I pulled his face to mine, brushed back his hair, and kissed his forehead, his eyes, the high cheek bones. I slid his suspenders off his shoulders, then unbuttoned his shirt and pushed it back and down and pulled it off one arm at a time.

In the faint light, I ran my hand slow through the thin hair of his chest and down across his stomach. I reached out to his waist, struggled with the buttons. I could hear his breathing like the slow movement of sandpaper on wood.

I knelt and removed his damp cotton socks, catching the warm odor that rose from them. When I sat on the edge of the bed and pulled off my stockings, I closed my eyes and imagined the piano and the singing and the hallelujahs rising up through the warm summer air.

Walter let out a slow sigh, and he said, his voice low, rising out of the darkness, "Emma?" And I knew that was the question, and I was the only one who could answer it. And the answer was a treasure hidden in a field, a pearl of great price, for which I would give everything. Delaney, my friends, Mama and Daddy—I would ransom them all to possess it.

And then the voices of all my accusers were silent. Mama and Brother Leery and the women at church. And the silence of Daddy and the silence in the mercantile and the silence years ago that hung between Walter and me as the water moved slowly past my knees was filled with the voice that was older than guilt or sin, older than silence. The voice of the blood.

"Yes," I said, and I reached across the darkness to him.

9

The Next Morning

WHEN WALTER WOKE, the sun was just climbing above the trees across the road. It filled the window off the porch, and the sheet that lay over him and Emma seemed to light up the room.

A mockingbird whistled outside the window. A squirrel chattered from across the road. The cracked and faded paper on the ceiling above him spread like the skin of an old hand. When he closed his eyes, he could smell the sheets, smell Emma.

She lay facing away from him. Her bare shoulder rose through her long hair, which covered part of the pillow and trailed down under the sheet, and her breathing moved the sheet up and down. He moved his face into her hair and breathed.

He had never believed that this would happen. He had been sure that he would never be able to live with a woman this way. When Henry brought Naomi to the Bass house to live while the two of them had built their own house, Walter lay on the mat in the living room at night and listened, still as a dog pointing on a bird in the grass. Every night he heard the movement from the other side of the wall in their bedroom. Heard Naomi's low laughter. And he barely breathed so that he could hear every sound.

The closest he had ever been to a woman was the time Henry had taken him to Pearl Bear.

The image of Emma standing in the creek had tormented him for eight years. The way she looked straight at him and said "Suit yourself. Come in if you like." He heard that voice, almost pulling him down off the bank, every night as he lay down to sleep. "Come in if you like," she said, standing there, dripping, the water only up to her knees, a rock in each hand.

So when Henry and Naomi groaned in the next room, or Naomi sounded as if all the air were being squeezed out of her, and then it got so quiet he could hear himself taking deep breaths, he felt as if he were standing on the edge of a bluff high over the river looking straight out into empty space, with Emma down below, calling. As if he were going to lose his balance and fall. He tried to picture Naomi lying on the other side of that wall, but all he could see was Emma standing in the water.

And he was sure it would never happen to him.

When he was twelve, Miles Beach paid Henrietta Shumate a nickel to flirt with him at school. Then Miles bet her another nickel she couldn't make Walter talk. She took the bet and approached Walter at lunch, sitting down next to him in the grass under the ash tree south of the schoolhouse. He didn't know the others were watching. Miles knew what he was doing. Henrietta lost the nickel back to him.

Her voice was like a cat purring. She opened her lunch box, scooted close to Walter, so close their knees touched, and she stared at him, gauging his response, then pushed her lips out as if she were trying to decide something. She broke open a blueberry muffin and held out half of it to him.

But he could not talk. He could only breathe slow and easy and fumble with the cornbread in his lap. He could not even offer her some water. She tried to talk to him until Miss Tweedy rang the bell. Then Henrietta's face reddened and she stuck out her tongue at him and slammed the lid on her lunch box. Miles and the others laughed.

It was always that way for Walter with women. Virgil had always said he was just too stupid to know a good offer when he got one.

But later, when the offers came, one way or another, he knew them well enough, but it was always the same. Something seized in his chest, in his throat, and his head rang like the school bell and he had to concentrate on breathing. Women were always disappointed. Pleasant Tweedy, when she stood beside his desk, a book open in her hand, waiting for him to answer a simple question, waiting longer than when she asked anyone else, as if his failure had a special quality to it. Jake Morrison's daughter Purity, who came with her father to the mill and watched Walter while she waited, caught his eye and smiled. And finally she caught him in the back aisle of the mercantile and spoke to him. And he could only concentrate, breathe steadily.

But worse than all the others was the roadhouse. The way Pearl Bear looked at him when she unbuttoned her blouse. The way she took his hand and put it on her breast, warm and soft, and kissed him and slid her other hand up his leg. He reached out with his other hand, and just as he touched her, he thought of Emma standing in the creek, looking up at him, her eyes saying get in the pool with me, a rock in each hand. And so with both his hands on Pearl's breasts and her pulling at his belt, he went cold inside and pulled back.

And she said "What?" And he couldn't speak. She chewed on the inside of her mouth, her dark brown eyes, almost black, puzzled. She looked over at the door, still chewing on her mouth, and he knew she was trying to decide about Henry, and she sat on the bed up against him. But too late. He was breathing slow and steady, and nothing she did made any difference.

But the first morning of his married life, lying in the bed beside Emma, his hands still felt the shape of Emma's breasts, his mouth her mouth opening in a kiss.

He slipped out from under the sheet. Emma sighed and moved in her sleep. He put on his shorts and pants and grabbed his socks and walked out to the front porch, pulling his suspenders up over his shoulders. The sun was bright, the morning warming up quick. Emma's shoes and his boots lay beside the chair to the left of the door, one of his boots over on its side, the other leaning over against it. In the chair his hat and her veil. He picked up the veil and felt the gauzy material, then laid it in the second chair and put his hat on and pushed it to the back of his head. He sat in the chair and put on his boots, then stood and walked down the steps into the front yard.

He and Emma had two days together before he had to go back to work on Monday. On Sunday he would go to church for the first time as a married man, sit in the pew beside his wife.

The farm lay along the crest of a long ridge a mile south

of Delaney, a hundred acres, only twenty of it cleared for pasture, the rest wooded gully and hilltop. Walter liked it that way. He had never lived on a farm, and he did not know much about farming. When he was little, Lilly kept a goat for milk and raised a patch of garden, mostly weeds, on the sloping ground behind the house. But he had always liked the rough hillsides covered with oak and hickory, the pitched landscape, steep and rocky places.

The road from Delaney south to Patrick, Combs, St. Paul, and Pettigrew ran through the farm and in front of the house. Across the road from the house, the hillside dropped off into a large section of wooded gully. Just to the north of the house five acres of field opened up and ran along the road for two hundred yards or so, bordered on the far north end by woods.

On the roof of the house, the moss spread across the shake shingles at the north end, thickest at the chimney. The night the old house at the mill burned, Walter had been drunk. He sat in the dirt in front of the house as the fire from the fireplace lit the doorway with a pale light that made the skin on his arms hum. He sat and listened, sure that there was no escape, that there could never, ever be any escape from Lilly. She was sprawled face down on the floor by the table, and he listened for the sounds of her coming after him. But only the faint cracking and popping of the fire came from the cabin, at times like the fluttering of moths, or of Lilly's hands, and the tree frogs droned in the woods behind him.

In the morning sunlight, with Emma asleep in the bedroom, the thought of Lilly was like a fist in his stomach. He sucked in the cool air and walked around the side of the house.

Behind the house, the land dropped off into a steeply wooded gully. On a sloping stretch of backyard an old well and a shed stood at the lip of the gully. The wood at the base of the well housing was weathered gray, in some places nearly black. The old shed at the gully's edge stood at a slant, though the oak studs were nearly as hard as the rock that showed through the ground around the base of it. Its tin roof was rusted. Beyond the shed squatted a small outhouse with a large flat stone in front of the door for a step, the door open to the dark inside.

The old chain rattled as he cranked the bucket down into the dark well. The bucket splashed in the water. When it rose up out of the darkness, he pulled it to him and set it on the lip of the well and laid his hat beside it. He splashed cold water on his face and neck and ran his hands through his hair to pull it away from his eyes. The grass on the hillside below him was wet with dew. The bobwhite whistled, the mockingbird chattered, and the cardinal called, insistent.

He wiped his hands on his pant leg. The sun broke just over the crest of the roof and seemed to ignite the dark outline of the house. A chill slid up his back. When the old house at the mill burned as he stood and watched, the curling tongues of flame had created their own wind, and he had felt a flood of relief, even joy, at the thought of Lilly's hands wilting, turning to ash.

It was a refiner's fire. When the roof collapsed, a riot of gold fire erupted into the gray morning sky, and he thought she was finally gone, swept upward in the rushing wind, freed from the darkness of her life.

The piercing whistle of the cardinal sounded again, and he turned back to the well and picked up his hat. Lilly had been gone three years. The last shreds of her, what little still lurked in his unguarded moments, had been whisked away on the porch at Emma's house when he asked her to marry him and she said yes and turned to him and touched his cheek before opening the screen door and slipping into the house without saying anything else.

The cardinal called again from behind him, and he put his hat on, went to the outhouse and relieved himself, then set out down the hillside toward the bottom of the gully.

On the slope to his left, the old orchard grew unpruned and choked with Johnson grass, the early apples rotting on the ground. Below the orchard, at the bottom of the gully, the barn grew out of the hillside, crouched like an old troll huddled against the slope, shabby, waiting. The metal roof on the uphill side, only a few feet off the ground, needed nailing down. The native stone wall on the downhill side, a gaping crack at the near corner, rose nearly twice a man's height. The hay loft door above it hung helter-skelter across the opening on one hinge.

Beyond the barn, at the bottom of the gully, the woods grew thick. An open passage, fenced on both sides, cut through the woods up the opposite hillside, for the moving of cattle, leading to fifteen acres of rolling, open pasture on the hilltop above. The trees had grown up against the fence so that the bark had overlapped the wires. As he started up the other side of the gully, walking along the fence line, a pair of fat gray squirrels barked and chattered at each other as they ran down the long limb of a white oak and disappeared around the trunk.

When he moved from the early morning shadows on the hillside out into the bright sunlight at the top, he stopped to catch his breath. The field was bright with the sun on the dew. Emma had said yes. She had said I do. At the church Walter had fallen, and she had lifted him up. Brother Leery preached every Sunday about a kingdom of light and fire.

Across the gully, the sun glinted on the wet grass of the yard and the orchard, and on the roof of the house, so that he had to squint. Emma was sleeping there, and the sheet was rising and falling with her breathing, her hair spread on the pillow. The curse of Virgil and Lilly Bass was gone, had been washed away forever in the baptism of water and of fire and of the Holy Ghost. In the words Yes and I do. He was sure of it. He started back down the hill, into the shrinking shadow of the gully, toward the house on the other side.

Part II

The Owl Called Softly

10

June 1903
Purity Morrison

THE BIBLE SAYS TO COUNT IT ALL JOY, my brethren, when you meet various trials. But I just wonder sometimes. Have you ever stopped to think about what that means exactly? Mama always said that suffering draws you closer to Jesus, and I believe that. But I just can't help thinking that a person is crazy, in a way, to be happy about troubles.

When Emma came by this afternoon, I was doing what I am always doing of a Saturday afternoon. Taking care of Jackson Lee. He is the latest, and Mama says the last. An even dozen. Mama says she has traded fertility for female problems. She's taking Dr. Dromgoole's English Female Bitters to try and get regulated, but Dr. Blake has told her that she is through being pregnant. I can't believe she doesn't have a party and celebrate. Too much of a good thing.

Jackson Lee is nearly two years old, and he is spoiled rotten. Sarah June, who was number six, takes care of him during the week while I'm working at the cannery, but you can't expect a sixteen-year-old to be any good at discipline. Sissy was different. She was number three, after Horace, and she was much better with the little ones than Sarah June will ever be. That is, she was before she got married and left to start her own family.

So now on the weekends I do what I can, but I'm afraid Jackson Lee is a lost cause.

When Emma got here, I dumped the blocks out on the living room floor for Billy Boy and Jackson Lee to play with. Those blocks are real cute. Daddy made them out of wood scraps, and Sissy painted faces on them; it was probably twelve years ago. The faces are all but worn off now, but Billy Boy and Jackson Lee will stack them up and knock them down for hours.

Anyway, I was just thinking yesterday that some girls when they get married, they start playing house. You know what I mean? Acting like a married woman overnight. Like it was the only natural thing they were ever born to do. It makes me want to laugh. Give them a year or two and most of them will have a different look about them. I've had time to observe.

Then there's Emma. After five years of marriage to Walter Bass, she is the same as ever, like a low fire burning in a wood stove. You can still see the glow through all the creosote that's fogged up the glass on the door. It's been that way from day one. No airs. None of this look at me, the first married woman to walk the face of the earth.

Five years.

I was not prepared to "count it all joy" when Walter and Emma moved into the old Sinclair place right next door. And of course, there is no such thing as living next door to Emma and not being her best friend. It can't be done. It's not in her nature.

I've never told a soul about me and Walter. Especially not

Emma. About the fact that I all but proposed to him in the mercantile that time. Or about me being one minute too late when he was struck down by the Holy Ghost at the revival and became like a child lost in the woods and ready to run into the first arms that opened to him. I mean since it was Emma's open arms and all, it's a little awkward.

It's just that Emma is so damned pretty. Excuse my language. You can't peel and core with Imogene Farley for five years and not pick up a word or two.

Pretty is not really the word I want. She is more than that. Not like those women in the magazines down at Roberts' Mercantile. I don't mean that. Nothing fancy. You just can't stop looking at her face is all. I've seen grown men who meet Emma for the first time stand there and stare, which is rude, of course, but they can't help it.

She could have had any man she wanted. Really. Any man in Delaney.

I'm thirty-one years old, and it wouldn't be exactly right to say that I'm keeping my trousseau fresh. But then I haven't given it away yet either. Walter Bass is not the only man in Delaney. Isham Birkes for instance. Shave and a haircut and Isham would clean up fine.

People can be really thoughtless, can't they? Every now and then someone will use the words "old maid" when I'm in the room, not even thinking that I'm standing there, thirty-one years old and still living at home. It's not aimed at me, you know, but when I hear them say it, it's like I just swallowed cotton, and I know my face gets red. I just know it. I can feel it getting hot. Old maid.

She could have had any man she wanted. With a snap of her finger.

If only Walter had said something, anything, that day in the mercantile. A girl can only do so much.

Or if I'd noticed when he came into the revival that night, I could have gone to him straight away, since it's a fact nobody else would. And I'd have been there to pray him through when the Spirit struck him down. A lot of good it did me to pray over Magin Wilson.

Emma tells me things. That's what best friends do, isn't it? Little things about Walter. Personal stuff. The face he makes when he brushes his teeth. How he's ticklish in the small of his back. And I wonder sometimes, you know, what it would be like, me and Walter.

And Emma, well, sugar wouldn't melt, as the saying goes. Like it never occurred to her that I might have a problem with all that. And everyone needs someone to talk to, I guess. Emma's no different. A friend has got no choice but to listen, really. And I did feel just awful after both of her miscarriages.

Truth is, Emma is the only person in Delaney who doesn't make me feel like an old maid. You know what I mean? Like that might never even have occurred to her.

When I was growing up, I hated Emma. She was an only child. Not a single sibling to watch over all day. Never spent a single afternoon of her life washing diapers. Go to every dance. Be in every school play. Not a care in the world. Darling of all the grown-ups in Delaney. The perfect child. I have never, not once in all my life, heard anyone say anything bad about Emma.

It took me a while, but now I like being with her.

Mama scrunches her face up like a great big raisin every time she takes a dose of Doctor Dromgoole's. Sits there with her eyes closed for about a minute like she's asleep.

She was forty-seven years old when she had Jackson Lee. Aunt Mary said it was scandalous.

Being the first born, I have done my part in the birthing of the other eleven. In fact, it's no secret in Delaney that I delivered Samuel, the seventh one, all by myself before Faith McCormick, the midwife, even got there. Not that I had any choice in the matter.

But Jesus I sat there holding Samuel still wet and puckered, the cord still dangling down to Mama, and I swear it was like he was mine. I had this tingling in my breasts like I was starting to make milk. I was so sure right then that it would soon be me having babies of my own. I was seventeen.

That was a long time ago.

Anyway, I thought that at least after Mama had Jackson Lee I was through being that oldest Morrison girl who still delivered her Mama's babies. The last two or three deliveries had got harder and harder. For me, not for Mama. Mama could drop babies easier than an old dog. But people at the mercantile asked me about the new baby every time, how the birthing went, how Mama was. All the while that "poor Purity" look in their eyes. They never said anything directly, but I could see it. The old maid sister-mother. That's what they were thinking.

It didn't make things any easier when Sissy had her first one. She was barely eighteen and had been married less than a year. I was twenty-three. And of course I was there to help with the delivery. It was the cutest little baby girl you ever saw. Blue eyes, good Lord, and a head of black hair I couldn't believe. That was just six months after Mama had Billy Boy, her eleventh. Mama and Sissy pregnant at the same time, having babies almost right on top of each other.

That's when I practically asked Walter Bass to marry me right there in the far aisle of Roberts Mercantile.

Of course, Sissy has had three more to Mama's one since then.

So yesterday Emma comes walking right into my house, without knocking of course. She knew I'd be there since the cannery is only running two or three days a week. We are between green beans and apples, and they just blow the steam whistle to call us in to work when they get a load of tomatoes.

Emma asked me if I would take her to see Hamilton Blake. Emma's one honest-to-god failing in my way of looking at things is she refuses to drive a buggy. It's not natural. Walter keeps that old buckboard wagon and has tried to get her to keep a buggy, but she won't do it. Now why is that? If I didn't know Emma so well, I'd think she was putting on airs, having people drive her everywhere like that.

Well, of course the first thing I wanted to know was what was the matter, was she sick or what? And she says oh of course not, she's not sick exactly. Then she tells me, with that little girl embarrassed look, that she has missed her monthlies.

Missed her monthlies, and she wants me to take her to see Hamilton Blake. Does that beat all? It just seems to me that a person with Emma's brains could figure that one out without going to see a doctor.

I don't know. Maybe it's the two miscarriages. Maybe she needs someone to tell her out loud that it will be alright this time. As if anybody could. We had a cup of coffee and I finished up the kitchen. Mama came in for a few minutes to chat, but she had to go lie down. Two years and she's still gray around the gills. Myself, I think it's the Doctor Dromgoole's, which she takes religiously. Face like a big raisin three times a day. I didn't say anything to her about Emma, only that we were going to town for a little bit.

Emma is too small to be having babies. There's just no use dancing around the fact. I could give him a better baby. I have a good strong pelvis and enough breast to make milk, like Mama. I could make a dozen babies and never miss a lick. But Emma is frail. Those miscarriages for instance. We all have our cross to bear.

Sometimes when I see Walter and Emma together I want to laugh. Last week, for instance, when I was snapping beans with Emma, Walter came home from work for lunch, which he does sometimes. They've been married five years now. You would think the puppy love would have worn off, but it hasn't. In fact, puppy is a good description of Walter about half the time. And most of the time he acts like he wants to play fetch-the-stick.

How happy can they be, really, with him that way? It's not natural.

I have a reputation down at the cannery for being the best

woman with a paring knife that has ever worked there, and since we get paid by the bucket, I can look forward to a little extra money when the apples get ripe. Pauline Roberts showed me a real nice gingham blouse she got down at the mercantile last Tuesday. It would show my red hair to advantage.

Pauline has some real nice yellow ribbon on sale. It would be the perfect touch with that gingham blouse and my hair.

11

September
Henry Bass

EACH TIME I BRING THE AX DOWN and the red oak wood pops open like a ripe melon and the chunks fall off the sides of the block, I think of Walter. Sweat drips off the end of my nose and my eyes sting and my shirt sticks to my back. The sun, rust colored, touches the hilltop off the meadow's edge.

Naomi is sitting at the kitchen table looking at her hands. She's been there since Emma left. Over an hour. Hasn't done a thing about supper, and it's almost dark.

Emma's always coming and going. That's natural. She's Walter's wife, and Walter is my brother. I should have seen it coming. Emma has shared the pregnancy with Naomi—the sickness, the movement in her belly. And something in Naomi's eyes, in the quick way she looks at me and then away, and in the way her smile wavers and fades, makes my stomach turn. We've been married a long time. A breeder of horses would have sold the mare—or the stud—at auction long ago.

Jake Morrison is a son of a bitch.

Every time Jake Morrison comes to town, he brings his whole family, twelve kids, the oldest one a daughter, thirty years old I reckon and still living at home, the youngest still a toddler. Seems like I've never known his wife, Kate, when she wasn't pregnant. Can't even imagine her without a great big belly like a melon under her dress, sticking out from the shawl that drops down off her shoulders and lies along both sides of it.

I cross the street to avoid them whenever I can. But there is no escape from a family of fourteen when they come pouring into a store and disperse down all the aisles. Even if Jake or Kate don't see me, one of the children is sure to sing out "Mornin' Mr. Bass," and then Kate will swoop down on me with that missionary smile dripping with compassion and stand there bouncing the latest shoat on her shoulder and ask after Naomi, that damning hopeful note in her voice as she looks at me with her face turned slightly to one side.

And something turns in my belly, and I want to say, "Since Naomi and I haven't slept in the same bed for a very long time, you might as well stop asking." I want to see the smile drop off her face at the words, the infant suspended in her mute surprise. But instead I say, "Oh fine, we're both fine. And your family? All well I hope." And I get away as quick I can and slip out the door cursing the casual fertility of people like the Morrisons.

The high whistle of the train comes from south of town, the low rumble of the engines straining at the grade. It's running late. When Walter and I were kids, we planned to run away. Stood by the track out on the grade up Piggot's Hill and counted the cars that creaked and groaned past us. The flat cars were loaded with ties and posts, the box cars half empty, crates of canned goods and tools. They moved so slow we could have swung up onto them at a walk, but we stood and watched as they slipped by.

We had jumped the train before, rode a mile or so, just for fun. But this time, when it would have made all the difference in the world, Walter folded. Turned and ran. Right before he ran, I smiled at him, my heart beating so fast I thought it would come out of my throat. But I knew as soon as I saw his face. He wouldn't hardly look at me, wouldn't look at the train. Just stood there with his hands together in front of him, eyes on the cross ties at his feet. I knew it was over. Knew it was no use to say anything. But I said it anyway. Come on Walter, let's go, I said.

We'd had enough of Virgil and Mama. I was sick of her whimpering, of her taking it the way she did, her poor-baby hands fluttering around my face when Virgil was through with me, and her cooing over Walter in the rocker as he cried. It was her that Walter couldn't leave. He was running back to her instead of getting on the train. A mama's boy.

So I stood there and watched the cars go by. And in the heavy smell of creosote, diesel, and hot metal, the ground vibrating under me, our clothes in a gunny sack in my hand, I reached out and touched each car, the warm moving metal of it. The hot air, stirred by their passing, was hard to breathe. I could see myself grabbing a handle, stepping up onto a rung. The air would be cool there.

When the last car passed and I thought, in that sudden open space and quieting sound, that I could still run and catch the train, but didn't, and knew in my stomach that I wouldn't, I think I finally knew what it meant to be a Bass in Delaney. And I picked up rocks from the rail bed and threw them at the last car as it moved away. As many rocks as I could throw while it was still in range, and then some more, into the emptiness, the silence it left behind.

When I walked through the kitchen a while ago, Emma was wearing her maternity dress, six months pregnant. She's so little it don't look like much, but it's there, the swelling pushing out the cloth enough to see. They were drinking coffee. I must have stared because Emma giggled like a little girl who's wearing a new dress to the end-of-school exercises. And the look on her face, a little shy, like she was trying not to look so satisfied.

"Emma," I said and nodded, "nice to see you." Nice to see you. That swelling in your belly is a loaded shotgun in my face. There's nothing I can do, nothing I can say to Naomi, nothing that will make her belly swell that way. There's nothing I can do. I left them there and came out back and started splitting wood, not bothering to change clothes.

When Emma left, they came out the back door. Maybe she wanted to see me stare again. But when she said I'll see you later Henry, I didn't look up, just said yep sure and split another piece of wood. Naomi went right back into the kitchen.

Then I looked. Emma walked around the side of the house and out to the road. Like a little porcelain figure. Straight, breakable.

I went up on the porch to the screen door. Naomi sat at the table like an old, old woman propped up in the corner waiting to die. I opened my mouth to say her name. Naomi. She told me, a long time ago, her name is Hebrew. Means "my pleasantness." More of her daddy's worthless learning. But it stuck down in my throat, and my belly seized up like I was trying not to laugh. Or maybe my belly was swelling, pushing out my shirt like Emma's dress. I imagined myself with Kate Morrison, my shawl hanging down the sides of my belly. Kate smiles that sheepish smile and pats her belly and looks at me with a little nod like I'm supposed to pat mine too.

I bit down hard there at the door and pushed my lips together, but I laughed, a little laugh that barely snorted, and Naomi didn't move.

Emma walked away, humming a low hum, like the last train car rolling down the track. The last car, loaded, heavy, leaving.

Splitting the wood helps. Thinking of Walter as I swing the ax helps. The ax pops through with a "chuck." A gnarled and knotty piece refuses to split, grabs the ax head, and I have to swing the whole thing up over my head and down onto the block with a heavy "clump" three times to make it yield. I think of Walter, standing by the tracks, head down, not getting on the train. I bring the stubborn lump of wood down, forcing a groan up from my belly, and the ax pushes farther in. The wood splits and falls away, and the pieces hang together by a spindly string of heartwood stretched across the block. Sweat stings my eyes. I taste the salt of it on my lips. I raise the ax and bring it down one last time, putting my weight into it, and snap the heartwood like a match and bury the ax head deep in the chopping block.

12

A Few Minutes Later
Naomi

LIFE RUNS LIKE AN UNDERGROUND SPRING moving through the earth, purifying itself, rising to the surface now and then, just as it's rising now in Emma's body.

I should have started supper an hour ago, but the sun is setting behind the hills and the dark is rising around me. My chest is thick as mud. My arms and legs are heavy. When Emma left, I felt so tired I couldn't walk. Thought I would sit for a minute, but now I can't make myself move.

The fly crawling across the table toward my hand is more alive than I am.

A minute ago, the ax stopped splitting wood. Henry's boots sounded on the porch, and I thought he would come in. I wanted him to, wanted him to come in and pull me up out of this chair. When we first got married, he was strong.

Childish, sitting here holding my breath.

The sound of his boots stopped at the door. I opened my mouth to say his name, but couldn't. And he laughed before he turned away.

13

November
Emma

I HADN'T MUCH MORE THAN cast on the stitches to start the booty when I dropped a stitch and had to tear it out. I should have known better than to try and knit the booties myself. Mama's the one who does the needlework in our family. It's one of those skills she tried to teach me at the wrong time in my life, when I was too busy grooming DeSoto or following Papa around the farm.

The fine yarn just made it harder. Mama would have scoffed to hear me say that. She had made the baby quilt that was draped across the chair next to me, the little red dutch girls beautiful in the sunlight. She wanted a granddaughter.

I put the yarn and needles on the chair by the quilt and just sat and rocked. The next day was Thanksgiving. It was one of those warm and sunny November days, Indian summer, that are so sweet after three or four weeks of cold, and when we know the cold that is coming the next three months.

The pregnancy was like a holiday for Walter. At first he was scared of it, but like Mama told me, he just needed a little time to get used to the idea. We had been trying to have a baby for nearly five years. I guess maybe we were beginning to think it wasn't going to happen.

And Walter hadn't seen much of what a father was supposed to be, and he was scared to death of what he didn't know. It was the same way when we first got married. He didn't know much about being a husband. Mama told me that was no surprise. She didn't know any man who did.

But the pregnancy was different. When I started showing, he could not stop looking at my stomach. The first time I wore a maternity dress, you'd have thought I was some stranger he was meeting for the first time. And when we lay down in bed at night and I put his hand on me to feel the first movements, his eyes got as big as a child's watching an egg hatch. All of this made the pregnancy like one long birthday party for me. I didn't mind the tiredness or the backache. The women at church made over me like I was the first one it ever happened to.

It would be a Christmas baby.

If it was a boy, I wanted to name him Walter Benjamin after Walter and Daddy. If it was a girl, I wanted to name her Martha Emmaline after Mama and me. Walter didn't want to name the baby after himself, but his name would have been a gift to the child.

14

December
Doctor Blake

I'M GLAD THAT'S OVER. Never thought I'd feel that way about delivering one of Emma's babies. But I can't overlook the fact that I delivered Virgil Bass's grandson.

When Virgil and Lilly Bass first rattled into town on what was left of a wagon pulled by a half-dead mule, Lilly was pregnant with Henry. Maybe thirty-five years ago. I was a young doctor out to save the world, and when I saw how big Lilly was and figured she was about to be delivered, I went out to that shack they'd moved into on the hilltop north of town, bare knob broken by a few scrub oak. Virgil met me as I stepped out of the buggy. Didn't even invite me onto the front porch.

When I held out my hand and told him who I was, he just turned his head and spit tobacco juice into the dirt.

"I can see what you are by your pretty little handbag," he says. "And you can get back in your fancy buggy and get the hell out of here. You won't get any money from me."

Well, I was still green enough to say, "If money's a problem, don't worry about it." A regular Good Samaritan.

Next thing I knew, Virgil knocks me on my backside,

there's blood running out my mouth, and he kicks my bag toward me and says, "I don't need your charity." And he spits in the dirt at my feet.

I'm not a fighter. Never really hated anybody I know of. But that day I wanted to kill Virgil Bass.

Emma's baby weighed five or six pounds. About what I'd expect from Walter Bass. Weak, color no good, trouble breathing. If it was breeding stock we'd cull him out. She deserved better.

I delivered Emma Sinclair—Bass now—what was it, twenty-five, twenty-six years ago? I've delivered half the people in this county. I've sewed Emma up and put splints on her more than all the other girls combined. More than half the boys.

Emma's smart. And strong. Comes from good stock. I was just as surprised as everyone else when she married Walter Bass. Just couldn't see it.

I've heard the old saw about a mixed breed bringing strength to a line, but I don't buy it. Give me a purebred any day. Virgil Bass was a degenerate. Lilly was mentally unbalanced. Walter and Henry are just trouble waiting to happen. I expected them both to crawl off somewhere and sire a litter just like themselves. If I'd ever had any inkling that one of them would end up with Emma Sinclair, I'd have...But then, I'd never have had the chance, would I? I wasn't there when they were born, and the Basses never spent any money on a doctor.

Emma's fine. You can't tell from the way she acts that anything is wrong with the baby. She thinks she can pull the whole world right up into that glory land of hers. We'll see.

Walter was his usual self. Came slinking in like a whipped dog. Purity Morrison, who was helping me, nearly had to drag him in. Emma was good with him, of course. Just what you would expect. She's always been good with animals. Reached right out to him. He came to her like he was afraid of what she was holding in the blanket.

They named him Joshua Benjamin.

15

The Next Day
Purity

I CAN'T HELP THINKING about those miscarriages. Emma's just too small. Not enough pelvis. I've said it all along. She should have carried that baby another month. It could hardly breathe at all, even after Hamilton Blake cleared all the mucus out. Every breath like a sheet of paper slipping out of a satchel. Blue as a hardboiled egg.

Myself, I didn't want to be there in the first place. Most people would say what a wonderful thing it must be to deliver your best friend. But I don't know. With Walter moping around out front and Emma asking me about him, it just wasn't my idea of wonderful.

Hamilton Blake has started calling on me to help him with deliveries because Faith McCormick has the gout. Hamilton has never asked me do I want to do this kind of thing. It's just that with Mama and Sissy having so many babies, I've delivered more of them than anyone around here, except for Faith. Probably never occurred to Hamilton that I might not want to be the old maid midwife for all of Madison County. I doubt it's possible for a thought like that to enter into the brain of a man like him.

Father, of course, does not approve of just one more thing that takes me out of the house. Not because it has ever occurred to him that I might not want to be the midwife. God forbid the possibility of that thought ever crossing his mind. But he doesn't raise any objections because the work is, after all, maternal. He is convinced that I will never deliver him any fat grandbabies of my own, and I guess my being a midwife will somehow soothe our family conscience. And if I insist on working outside the home, peeling and coring at the cannery and delivering babies with Hamilton Blake are about the best he can hope for me. Very domestic.

And then there is the money. I share all my wages with Mama and Daddy, from the cannery and from Hamilton. Fifty, fifty. It isn't much, but it has certainly helped to quiet Daddy's fears, even though it creates an unspoken difficulty, I know, because he is not entirely comfortable with my increased independence.

It was nearly nine o'clock when I got home from Emma's last night. Daddy was sitting in the rocker by the fireplace reading his Bible, where he is every night at that time. Nine o'clock is bedtime at our house, and Daddy is as religious about bedtime as he is about everything else. But I could see Daddy was not happy. Things were not going according to schedule. Mama was lying on the sofa with a wet washcloth on her forehead and her mouth puckered up like a raisin, twitching every time one of the kids made a noise from the dining room.

Sarah June, who is sixteen and supposed to be helping

Mama when I am gone, and Samuel, who just turned fourteen two weeks ago and is supposed to be helping Sarah June, had both just gone off to bed without so much as cleaning up the supper dishes. But did Daddy say anything to stop them? Not on your life. And why not? Because I should have been there myself to see to it. I make my choices, he would say, if I cared to ask him, and I'll have to live with them.

The gravy was sitting out on the table, cold and thick as mud, and the biscuits were uncovered, getting hard. Of course, there was not one stitch of ham left. So much for my supper.

I could tell Mama had had one of her temper tantrums within the last hour by the way the young ones were whispering. Mary Grace, who is only twelve and bless her heart is already more dependable than Sarah June, was doing her best to keep the rest of them happy and quiet, which is no small order.

Well, it took me over an hour to get everything settled, even with Mary Grace and Philemon helping get the littlest ones to bed. And of course, Tennessee had to go to the outhouse. Nothing else would do. And she cannot possibly go by herself in the dark, and Philemon, who is almost ten, is scared to death to step outside after sunset and would not go with her. So I left Mary Grace and Philemon with Billy Boy and Jackson Lee and took Tennessee to the outhouse.

Tennessee would have nothing to do with me going inside the outhouse with her, just took the lantern and shut the door behind her and left me standing there in the dark. Middle of December, and I'm standing there in the dark, shut out of the outhouse. My life in a nutshell.

But really, when I think back on it, it was a blessing in disguise. It was one of those winter nights when the sky is clear and so full of stars it's like a quilt thrown over the world. My breath was steaming out in front of me, and I pulled my coat collar up around my chin and just looked up at that sky. Not a sound anywhere. It was a little bit of grace and mercy poured over me, and Lord knows I needed it right then. Needed that quiet with my skin tingling and the stars shining and my breath easing out in little clouds.

I took a deep breath and held it in for just a second before I let it out, and it felt like the tender hand of Jesus himself pulling all the hurt and worry and tiredness right up out of me. I felt warm, like everything would be alright.

Of course, the moment did not last. It's not easy to be spiritual at the door of an outhouse. Tennessee had begun to make sounds like a bed sheet popping in a stiff wind, and I began to feel a chill.

"Hurry up, Tennessee," I said, and she didn't answer me.

A minute later the door opened and out stepped Tennessee with this sanctimonious look on her face like she had been at her prayers. She marched right past me and on up to the house without even so much as a by your leave, let alone a thank you.

And that was just the beginning. Mama had dragged herself up off the sofa and into bed at some point, and while I was cleaning up the kitchen, Daddy had to make a last pass through on his own way to the outhouse, grumbling about the waste of fuel oil and the loss of sleep and breaking God's natural laws and the stress on Mama. Not a word about the stress on me. Never even crossed his mind. He didn't say anything to me directly, but it was clear what he meant. This was all my fault. If I wasn't working outside the home, none of these problems would exist. Never mind that Mama sucks on a bottle of Doctor Dromgoole's every waking hour and hardly lifts a finger to the housework. Never mind that Sarah June is the laziest sixteen-year-old in the state of Arkansas. Never mind that Horace and Sissy and Abraham and Moria Lynn, though I am the oldest, have all gone off and started their own families and left me here to put the young ones to bed and clean up the kitchen while everyone else sleeps in their beds. Never mind that I spent all evening delivering Emma Bass. Never mind that Walter Bass stood there in the mercantile five years ago staring at the shelf and couldn't say a word, even though he wanted to. I know he did. And never mind that Emma is just too small, that she will never make him as good a baby as I would if I ever got the chance. Which I never will now. It was as clear to me at that moment—as I stood there scrubbing the skillet, the split skin in my thumb burning—as clear to me as that big open sky full of stars outside.

Emma was so happy when Hamilton Blake laid that little blue baby on her stomach. Big tears of happiness running down her face.

When I opened the front door to tell Walter that it was all over, that he could come on in, he was standing at the top of the steps. He looked at me like he expected me to tell him everyone was dead.

I said, "Walter, you can come in now. It's a boy." But he

stood there staring like he didn't believe me. He is hopeless. I wanted to go get him by the ear and drag him in.

"Come in, Walter, the air is cold," I said. He crept in the door and stood there trying to get his breath before he went to the bedroom, his sister-in-law, Naomi, sitting at the wood stove, still green in the gills from coming in too soon and seeing the afterbirth. It makes you wonder what all her learning is good for.

I had to turn away and go to the kitchen before I said something I would regret.

I am thirty-one years old, and the chances are slim that I will ever have a husband and a child. Wasted fuel oil and lost sleep seemed like nothing at all compared to the waste and loss I felt as I stood at that sink after Daddy walked through. I just stood there and had a good cry while I finished the dishes. Then I put the scraps in a pan and covered them to feed the chickens this morning and went to bed.

16

January 1904
Naomi

JANUARY, FROM THE ROMAN GOD JANUS of beginnings, the god of doors and gates. The cold is bitter. The sky is gray and dull, and whatever false and temporary hope the Christmas season might have offered is ground out by winter.

I sat in the buggy in front of the depot, a wool blanket tucked around my legs, my hood pulled low over my forehead, my hands thrust into the muff on my lap, my toes beginning to ache from the cold. I was a fool to sit in the buggy and freeze waiting for Henry. He had stopped by the house on his way to the depot to see if I needed anything. And he asked me, impulsively, as if none of the past twelve years had happened, if I wanted to go along. Of course, I did not want to go. What in God's name would make me want to go? But I went. And I didn't know why.

His face, most likely. He looked at me somehow—I couldn't say exactly how—like a child that's been hurt, and it made my chest and my throat ache.

We stood there in the silence after he asked me to go. The skin around his eyes was turning fleshy from the drinking. As he held his hat in front of him like a schoolboy, I thought about the veins that stood out on his forearms under the coat. When he shifted his weight and looked away, the thin scar showed on his flushed temple. His eyes narrowed and he pushed his lips together. I used to like his anger, his hatred of Delaney. Our first year of marriage, I listened for the sound of him coming up the stairs to me each night, loved the sweet smell of whiskey on him, the taste of it when he kissed me.

But I could not throw off the weight of my uncle leaning down over me, eyes closed, muttering prayers, pressing closer, breathing all the air, leaving none for me. And my father at my lessons, sitting silent across the table, hands folded, looking at the wall behind me.

After the first year of marriage to Henry, I began to feel that I was drowning. A starvation for air wedged itself into the euphoria as I lay exhausted under him, with him barely breathing. And I bit my tongue to keep from gasping, to keep from fighting my way up from the bed. The suffocation was gone as quickly as it came, and I thought it was a passing thing, something that happened to everyone who was getting settled into marriage, but it came again, and then again and again, the need for more air, until it crept with his hand down the buttons of my blouse, and from his lips when we kissed, till I felt myself cringe at his touch.

And he never asked what the matter was. He pressed harder, straining for whatever it was that was gone, like a man dying of the cold, raking the wet match head across the granular surface harder and harder as the sulfur spreads impotent and red. And when I couldn't breathe, I bit my tongue to lie immobile until he sighed and rolled away.

And he began to stay longer in the kitchen at night before coming upstairs, and I blamed the drinking, and knew it wasn't the drinking. And I felt him tense when I turned my head away on the pillow. I wanted to get back the feeling we had when we spit in the face of Delaney. And I saw sometimes the look in his face of a dog begging.

And so when he came by and asked if I wanted to ride to town, as he turned to walk away, the color rising along his neck, I called to him, said wait, I'll go.

He said it was just brief business. But there I sat in the buggy waiting, the temperature below freezing, and a dry powdery snow spitting off and on from the thick clouds. I had expected him to be waiting for me when I finished at the store, but he wasn't, and I would not go into the depot and wait for him there, the good wife. He had to be nearly finished, but it was pure foolishness waiting out there in the cold. I decided to leave my basket in the buggy and walk back to the house.

The door to the depot opened, and I turned and opened my mouth to speak, but it was Hamilton Blake pulling the door shut behind himself with one hand, balancing a small crate in the other.

"Dr. Blake," I said, "is Henry still in there?"

"Afternoon, Mrs. Bass," he said. He stepped down to the side of the buggy. "Yes, he's there. I'm afraid he had to wait on me to check every one of the vials in this case for breakage before I signed for it."

He shifted the crate to the other arm. "You better go inside and get warm," he said, and he touched his hat and turned toward his office.

"Dr. Blake," I said, "have you been out to Emma's today?"

"No," he said, "but I was there yesterday," and he looked across the square at Job Delight's store.

"How is Joshua?" A crow cawed from beyond the depot, somewhere along the river.

Hamilton Blake stepped to the horse and patted its rump and said, "He should have been past all this by now. I'm afraid his lungs aren't developed."

"What are you doing for him?"

"Nothing," he said. He looked again at Job Delight's store. "Could be membranous croup, but I don't think so." He moved to the horse's head and ran his hand down across its nose. "There's nothing I can do."

"Afternoon, Mrs. Bass," he said and walked off across the square.

I should have gone to see Emma, but she always sat and patted and rubbed the baby and cooed to it like a mother dove, while the baby struggled to breathe. My chest ached at the sound of his rasping breaths.

And there was nothing Hamilton Blake could do. So much for modern medicine. The membranous croup. I refused to sit there any longer and wait for Henry.

I pushed the blanket down off my legs and laid it across the basket at my feet, swung my feet out the side of the buggy and stepped down onto the running board, wincing at the pinpricks of pain in my feet.

Across the square, the sycamore tree that rose behind Job Delight's house spread out against the gray sky, its trunk white, its bare limbs arching upward, sprinkled with seed balls, a few stubborn leaves hanging in the upper branches.

Nothing he could do. Nothing anybody could do. And Emma just kept praying to that god of hers, as if he'd done much for her in the past. Given her two miscarriages before torturing her with a baby that wouldn't live to see his first birthday.

I pulled my scarf up over my mouth and nose. When I stepped up onto the boardwalk in front of Roberts' Mercantile, Pauline Roberts looked up at me and waved from behind the counter, where she sat reading a magazine. The boardwalk ran west from the mercantile beyond the corner of the square and down Delaney Street past the bank and Solomon's Café and ended at the Fayetteville road. The street itself went on beyond the road, where it passed our house, then narrowed to one lane that curved north around the end of the valley before turning west again and following Delaney Creek back into the hills.

The sound of my heels on the wooden planks rapped sharply out into the empty square. As I passed the gap between the mercantile and the bank, a gust of wind swirled into me and I caught my breath.

His lungs weren't developed, and the air was so cold a healthy adult couldn't breathe. *Super te, mors suspendit,* little one. Death hangs over thee.

The crows clamored from the river behind me, making the woods sound like a great empty room, full of children yelling to hear an echo.

The river slipped past the low rock bluff just the other side of the tracks. Slow-moving, ice cold, it is the one sure thing in Delaney, the one absolute—quiet, clear, muddy, green, black— always moving, always whispering.

My first summer in Delaney, I stood on the loading dock of the depot, sent by Aunt Rose Eltha to pick up a package from Fayetteville. Just ready to turn fourteen, restless, I was thankful to be away from my father in Fayetteville. But the novelty of living in a different place had evaporated. Aunt Rose's relentless instruction on sewing, cleaning house, and cooking had worn me down. And my uncle's sermons. The only time, in fact, I missed my father was on Sunday morning—his sermons had always lasted about twenty minutes, Uncle Isaac Samuel's never lasted less than an hour.

Standing on the loading platform, waiting for the package to arrive on the train, I first saw Henry Bass. I was watching the river run below the tracks, down the steep bank, when a wagon, loaded high with posts, pulled up to the end of the platform. Two men rode hunkered on the sides of the pile of posts, leaning into the pile and bracing their feet against the side boards. Their pant legs were tucked into their boots and their shirts were open and one of them wiped his face with a bandanna. A small man with a thin blond beard sat on the seat up front beside Henry, who drove the wagon. When the wagon stopped, Henry leaned back against the posts and pulled a twisted rope of tobacco out of his hip pocket. As he tore a chew off the end of it, he looked over at me. His long face was handsome. His eyes were angry. He looked at me as he handed the tobacco to the man beside him, then he turned away. His shirt was dark with sweat, open in front, and his hat sat loosely on the back of his head. He sat there on the wagon seat, talking occasionally with the man beside him, for ten or fifteen minutes until the train arrived.

That was fourteen, fifteen years ago.

As I approached Solomon's Café, Able Solomon opened the door, swept a small heap of dust and dirt out onto the boardwalk and stepped outside, pulling the door closed behind him. His jowls lay over his shirt collar, which was buttoned to the top, and his apron hung straight down from his belly.

"Morning, Mrs. Bass," he said. "What you doing out walking on a day like this? Ought to be inside by the fire."

I stopped beside Able Solomon and pulled the scarf down from my mouth. "Tired of waiting for Henry at the depot, Mr. Solomon," I said. "I have things to do of my own. A good walk on a cold day never hurt anybody."

I like Able Solomon. I once asked him why he spelled Able with le instead of el, and he told me that he was not named after the biblical son of Adam and Eve, but was named Able because it was clear from the day he was born that he was just that. He played Santa Claus each year at the town Christmas celebration at the schoolhouse, and he always had one of the Morrison boys climb up on the schoolhouse and shake a set of Christmas bells and stomp around on the roof before Able made his entrance. And he always went afterward to the houses of several families who could not come to the celebration.

He went to Emma and Walter's house this year, and Emma cried later telling me how he came quietly in the front door to be sure not to wake Joshua, how he shook Walter's hand in both of his and wished him a merry Christmas, hugged and patted Emma, laid the small stuffed animal beside Joshua in the crib and touched Joshua's head.

Able swept his little pile of dirt off the boardwalk with a big swipe of the broom, and grunted when a gust of wind spread most of it back around his feet. I tried not to smile, and as I started down the walk, I said, "Goodbye, Able."

"Mrs. Bass," Able called after me, "how's Emma's little boy doing?"

I stopped and turned back to him. There was nothing he could do. "Not well."

Able poked at the boardwalk with his broom and shook his head. "It's a shame." He started for the door.

Yes, it was a shame. Almost a Christmas baby. What more could anyone want? Hamilton Blake and Purity Morrison were so matter-of-fact about Joshua's birth. But it was the first time I had been at a birth, and when the final contractions began, the look of fear on Emma's face made me giddy, and I left the bedroom. I stood by the wood stove in the living room and listened to Emma's grunting, Purity's firm responses, and Hamilton Blake's quiet instructions.

Then when I heard Emma's final high-pitched squeal and heard Purity say "It's all over now, Emma," I could not stay out.

I went to the bedside, my eyes brimming with tears, expecting to see Emma propped up in a nest of pillows with the baby nursing at her breast. But the bed was bloody, and the red and purple infant lay at Emma's feet. Hamilton Blake cleared the mucus from the infant's mouth and nose and then held it up by the feet and swatted it on the bottom, and I felt faint. And as I went back to the living room, a croaking cry came from the baby, and I sat in the rocker, light-headed, my ears ringing.

I crossed the frozen dirt and gravel of the Fayetteville road. Our house marked the western edge of the cluster of buildings that made up the town of Delaney. There were other houses further down the road and scattered all through the hills, but none of those people thought of themselves as living in town.

I turned back and looked east down Delaney Street to the square, where the buggy waited at the depot. To the north, the sky was gray, and the broken tree line of the hills across the river was a shade darker gray. Up the Fayetteville road, where it curved a little to the east with a bend in the river, a boy stood on the wooden bridge across Delaney Creek, dropping rocks into the water below. A collie dog sat beside him on the bridge and watched each move. The dog's long nose followed the boy's hand out into the air, followed the rock as it dropped down out of sight. The dog broke into a pant like a laugh as it looked back to the boy's face, waiting.

When I closed the door behind me, I turned and leaned against it, facing the dim foyer and the living room beyond. The house was silent, empty. My chest felt tight, and I breathed deeply. I had work to do. I went to the kitchen.

The newspaper lay open beside the half-empty coffee cup, where I had left it when Henry came. An ad for Castoria caught my eye—"Dr. Samuel Pritcher's Prescription for Infants and Children—No Opium, Morphine, or Other Harmful Substances—Cures Colic, Constipation, Sour Stomach, Eructation, Kills Worms, Gives Sleep, and Promotes Digestion."

And there was nothing Hamilton Blake could do.

I folded the paper and dropped it in the waste basket and headed upstairs.

17

That Night
Emma

I WAITED FOR THE LORD, waited for his salvation. Just as Abraham and Sarah waited for the son of promise, and God gave them Isaac. Now there was Joshua. Naomi told me that his name meant Jehovah is salvation. The Lord tested Abraham and brought back Isaac from the brink of death.

The owl called in the night. I lay awake and listened to it call as Walter slept, his breathing heavy, the short, scratchy breaths of Joshua rising from the dark crib next to the bed.

The owl called on and on. Soft and smooth as rabbit pelt, it floated through the darkness from the barn. Between the calls, the silence, Walter breathing steadily, Joshua moist, uneven.

18

February
Purity

SOME THINGS IN LIFE JUST DON'T MAKE SENSE. Example, in this house Scripture verses are quoted left and right—one for every occasion. "The fear of the Lord is the beginning of knowledge." I've heard that one all my life. "Hear the instruction of thy father and forsake not the law of thy mother." Daddy especially likes that one. "He that shutteth his lips is deemed a man of understanding." That one was useful in a house full of kids. The Bible rules the roost around here.

Here's the part I don't understand. The Bible forbids witchcraft and augury, and people around here put witches almost in the same league as the devil himself. But yet those same people outdo the devil in reading signs and omens into everything. Maybe I'm missing something here, but it just doesn't add up to me. And what's worse, it seems like the omens have more punch than the Proverbs.

That is certainly the case with Mama, especially since the advent of Dr. Dromgoole's. We are at the mercy of omens. For example, a strange dog following us means good luck. We all of us carry a rabbit's foot. When Daddy goes fishing, he has to promise Mama to spit on his bait to bring luck. And every New Year's Eve, right before midnight, Mama opens all the windows to let the bad luck out and the good luck in. We also nearly freeze to death.

Then Mama religiously sweeps the dirt out the back door because sweeping out the front door sweeps the good luck out and lets the bad luck in. And we are careful not to be photographed with a cat. More bad luck. And whatever we do, we don't step over a broom that has been dropped or knocked over.

And then, of course, with Emma's baby slipping away since the day it was born, Mama has seen death omens on all sides.

When I told Mama that the lamp in the living room at Walter's house went out because it was out of oil the night the baby was born, her lips puckered up and she shook her head, her eyes all watery, and said "Death in the house, sure as the world." It occurred to me that Walter might be excused for forgetting to refill the lamp, but there was no use saying any such thing to Mama. She looked at me like we were sharing this deep understanding of some tragic fate, so I just bit my lip.

A couple of weeks later, Martha Sinclair mentioned to Mama that she had broke a needle quilting, so Mama mopes around the rest of that day whispering there will be a death before the quilt is finished. And the last straw was when that red rooster of ours stood right there at the back door last Thursday morning and crowed. Mama just sets her coffee cup down like she has just realized I poisoned it, and she looks at me with that we've-got-a-secret look that is so irritating and says, "He's announcing a imminent death." And she looks at

Sarah June, and Samuel and Mary Grace and Philemon and Tennessee and Billy Boy and finally at Jackson Lee, who is sitting in my lap sucking on a sorghum biscuit—looks at them all like it may be the last time she ever sees them. And they are all looking back at her—Sarah June, Samuel, and Mary Grace real disgusted like, but the littler ones with their eyes about to pop. And I can see that tired look come over Daddy's face like "How long, oh Lord?"

But Mama fixes me with those watery eyes and says, "Emma's baby."

My eyes watered up, and I don't know if it was Emma and the baby and Walter, or Mama, or the way Daddy looked at me like "See what comes of working outside the home?" But I couldn't hold it back any longer.

Any fool with eyes could see that Emma's baby was in trouble from the start. And it didn't take empty oil lamps and broken needles and stubborn roosters to tell someone with half a brain that the baby was going to die. And whether it had lived six weeks or six months, or whether Martha Sinclair ever finished that quilt, none of it matters.

About a hundred blackbirds were gathered in the big oak tree outside the back window just beyond the chicken coop Thursday morning as we all sat there looking at each other. The tree was just full, all of them chucking and screeching so loud you could barely think a clear thought. Then all of a sudden they up and fly all at once with a big flutter and whoosh, one or two stragglers scuttling off at the last, and there is nothing but the gray and misty cold, and that big old bare oak skeleton sticking up over the coop into the gray sky. Just silence and emptiness and mist.

Nobody said a word after Mama's big pronouncement, and Joshua died that very night. I am going to take a platter of fried chicken over to Emma this afternoon. If that rooster wasn't so old and stringy, I would get a good deal of pleasure out of wringing his neck.

19

A Week Later
Walter

BEFORE JOSHUA WAS BORN, Emma miscarried twice. Both times she held onto me and cried until she fell asleep. And both times it happened so early in the pregnancy that she wasn't even showing. There was really nothing there to lose. It was just a mistake. And we went on afterwards like nothing had happened.

Not like this.

The day Joshua was born, Emma was starting labor pains when I got home from work. She came out on the porch and called to me so I wouldn't put the horses up. She couldn't stop smiling, but I took her back in the house and then headed for the Morrison place to get Purity.

The Morrisons were sitting down to dinner, of course, but Purity told me to go on and get Hamilton Blake and she would take care of Emma. I could tell she wasn't very happy about her dinner being cut short, because she wouldn't even look at me.

After I stopped at Dr. Blake's house, I went to tell Naomi. She and Henry were eating too, and Naomi told Henry not to bother with the buggy, that she would ride out with me and come home with Dr. Blake.

Purity Morrison had everything under control when we got back to the house.

Emma was only in labor for a couple of hours. Then a funny high-pitched cry came from the bedroom and the grunt of her bearing down and a kind of a heave. Then a few minutes later Purity, framed in the lamplight in the screen door, called me.

"It's over," she said. "It's a boy. Come on in." She pushed the screen door out toward me and held it open.

The shadows stretched across the floor and the far wall in the light from the lamp by the bed. People still called that house the old Sinclair place. I heard Emma clucking, like a hen, followed by a gurgle and meow from the baby. Purity said, "Come on in, Walter."

Just inside the door I stepped to the side and leaned back against the wall. Naomi rocked in the chair to the right, looking at the wood stove.

When I went to the bedroom, Emma looked up at me from a nest of pillows and quilts.

"Walter, come and see," she said, and she held out a hand. Dr. Blake, off to the side, finished drying his hands.

Death and sorrow are words, empty, as the house was empty after the long struggle of Joshua slipping away. Then came the bright morning at the grave, Emma dressed in black, a black veil covering her face, keening as the box was lowered into the ground, her voice a taut filament stretched thin across the open grave in the cold February air.

Brother Leery sat with us in the silent living room at the

house after Joshua died, and he spoke words of comfort as the dust rose and fell in slow motion in the afternoon light that slanted across the floor to the base of the wood stove. While Brother Leery sat and held Emma's hand, his words fit with all the other words he had spoken, fit with the rhythms, whispered prayers, the excitement I had felt in the little church house.

But even as Brother Leery spoke, the knot grew large in my throat. And for a crazy moment, as I stood and watched, I could see the words slip between Brother Leery's lips, black letters in block print like headlines on the air. THEY SHALL RISE UP WITH WINGS LIKE EAGLES. Emma nodded to each word as it passed. And then I imagined myself pitched from the bluff above Hidden Hollow, in the waterfall. Felt myself falling with the water, the rocks below rushing up at me.

I was surrounded by that thundering power, that same thundering power that pressed me down in the church, and I remembered Lilly's eyes, dark and hollow. Lilly wasn't gone, but waiting, and I looked over my shoulder there in the living room.

Brother Leery's lips moved, his eyes moist. My ears rang, but I forced myself to listen to Brother Leery's words.

"They shall rise up with wings like eagles." The words drifted across the room to me. "They shall run and not be weary. They shall walk and not faint."

Emma sniffled, her head leaning forward, and a tear hung from the ridge of her upper lip, like a drop of water suspended from the porch roof after a rain, then fell into her lap. She raised her handkerchief and blew her nose and said in a broken whisper, "He is come unto Mount Zion, unto the City of the Living God, the heavenly Jerusalem."

The wings of eagles. The city of God. Emma's pain hit me like a fist in the stomach, lodged in my belly. It was a bad job after all. Just like it had always been. And I couldn't do a thing. Couldn't think of a thing.

After Brother Leery left the house that day, I held Emma in the quiet as she cried against me, held her through the night as she slept while I followed each crack across the paper on the ceiling, and then followed them all again in the light of the lantern on the bedside table. They all ran off in so many ways but crossed and recrossed and led back to each other and away again in a maze.

20

March
Walter

I WAS A FATHER. Now I am not a father.

The headline in the *Fayetteville Democrat* this morning read, "Fair Nearly Ready: Activity Everywhere in Evidence at Greatest of World's Fairs." Robust optimism. Robust. That's a new word for me. Everything is, as President Roosevelt says, bully, and he predicts at year's end he will lead the Republicans in a landslide to a second term. It's a new age, a new century. It is robust.

On page three, another headline caught my attention: "Secretary of Confederate President Dead." Burton Norville Harrison, private secretary to Jefferson Davis for the duration of the war between the states, died of old age. The old world is dying out.

But the new world, the robust one, is dying too. Joshua's grave is a small mound of earth with a simple gravestone, gray and unpolished granite. The inscription reads "Joshua Benjamin Bass, Infant." Then a vine. Then, "Do not hinder the little ones from coming unto me." And at the bottom are the words "In the year of our Lord 1904."

He was in the world but not of it. He was a cough, a cry, a rattling breath. Two dark eyes. That which is sown in corruption shall be raised in incorruption.

I should pray, commend Joshua into Jehovah's hands. But the idea lies like a steel bar in my belly. And the weight of my tongue lodges in my throat. For the past six years I have prayed on my knees at the bedside with Emma, our hands touching, our heads touching, our breaths mixing. In church we have lifted up praise and called on the Name. And now I stand dumb by Joshua's grave.

After Emma and I married, her prayers scared me. They tumbled down her life like a stream down a hillside. In our prayers together, whenever she stopped talking, the silence swelled over me as she rocked forward and back, forward and back, and waited for me to speak. She was on such good terms with the awful God who struck me down in the blinding light and the pounding rhythms in the church house.

The weight of glory that pressed me down, slowly buried me in the flood of music and singing and prayer, as if I had walked into the waterfall at Hidden Hollow. First the spray, then random pellets of water, then the wavering stream, and finally the thunderous pressure of the heart of the falls, forcing me to my knees. I slid beneath the surface of the pool and surrendered.

And out of the darkness, Emma's voice like a rod of light that stilled the roar of the water. Her hand a buoy that lifted me. The church was hot and close before I fell that night. Rachel Hogan stood over Magin Wilson, both hands raised over her head, vibrating that tambourine like the warning sound of a fat rattlesnake. Then the flash of light. It happened to me as it happened to Magin before me. Struck down. Come through. Washed in the blood of the lamb. Magin yelled, "Jesus, oh Jesus."

Emma's fingertips moved over me, a breath that called up the fire. Like the lame beggar at the pool of Bethesda, I looked each night for the stirring of the waters by the angel of God, and I lowered myself into its healing warmth.

But the absence of Joshua Benjamin lodges now like a splinter in my intestines and festers and swells. The world was hardly disturbed by him.

Before Emma, what was there? I didn't give a damn when Virgil left. And Lilly, what was she? A moth, a spider, sucking the life out of everything around her. I thought she was gone. Thought she was pulled into the flame, lost, forgotten. But I have felt at times these last weeks as if she is only hiding.

The cemetery is shaded in the morning light by the scattered oak and elm trees, their trunks straight, supporting the high canopy of leaves, the green shifting in the occasional breeze. Redbud trees grow here and there, bent and spindly, reaching for the insufficient light that filters through the foliage above.

They look like old women stooping over the graves, sheltering them.

Patches of Easter lilies rise from the mixed grass that grows in the thin topsoil of this hillside. The faint odor of charred grass and leaves drifts to me from a blackened area at the east edge of the cemetery where someone has burned away last year's growth, and where the dead lower limbs of an elm tree bend toward the ground.

Near the cemetery gate lie the uneven lines of the oldest stones. They are small, some broken, leaning into the tall grass, covered with moss. Some just rocks with no names.

At Joshua's grave, I should say something to fill the emptiness. But there is nothing, and the absence of words, like a vacuum, pulls the air from me. The grass along the edge of the bare mound of earth moves in the breeze; the dew glints in the morning sun. A crow caws from the nearby woods, mournful and rebuking. The mockingbird's twitter comes steady from across the field.

The grave mound is barely three feet long, barely a dent in the world. Joshua was small. Small, weak, with dark eyes. He will rise up, Emma said again and again, as he lay panting in her lap. He will rise up.

Looking down at the small mound of earth, I say the name. Joshua. The shadow of the stone angles across the first few inches of the mound and then stretches into the grass to the right. The rounded top edge of the stone is bright in the sunlight. The surface of it, though not polished, is clean and new. Its face stands in the shadow.

Here beside the grave in the sunlight, the meadow and the woods smell moist and old, as they always have. The birds and the leaves sound the same. The breeze against my face feels the same. But here at my feet the small mound rises, with the stone at its head, "Joshua Benjamin Bass, Infant."

When I turn away from the grave and walk toward the

gate, I pass stones with names I recognize—Solomon, Farley, Wilkes. Perhaps there is a shadow world here where the shades still move and talk and carry on a commerce of their own. My skin crawls at the thought of Joshua living here, and as I open the wrought iron gate, I set my mind on the mill, on moving the logs through, on keeping the workers working.

21

July
Steeling the Heart

AT A DOLLAR PER ANNUM, the newspaper, delivered by train from Fayetteville every Thursday morning, provided practical, useful information. It listed the daily schedule of train departures and arrivals for all the towns along the forty miles of the Frisco Line, St. Paul Branch. And it lauded the miracles of the modern world available to the American consumer. The iron, tools, nails, barbed wire, plows, and Charter Oak stoves at the hardware store. The "Scientific Simplicity, Expert Service, Modern Methods, Pleasantness and Satisfaction" found at the dentist office. The cure for rheumatism in Hood's Sarsaparilla, the One True Blood Purifier.

The newspaper had value because it was useful, functional, carried its weight in the world. Its worth, like the worth of all things, was based on what it did.

The dark pupils that filled Henry Bass's eyes left only a touch of white visible on either side. His brown hair strayed down across his forehead to the thin scar that ran from the middle of his left eyebrow back across his temple. A candle burned on each side of the mirror in front of him. He pulled the leather strop up and slowly stroked the razor up and down its length, stopping once or twice to hold the blade up in the light and look at it.

He let the strop swing back to its place and raised his chin, moving his head back and forth, checking the lather. He lifted the razor to his Adam's apple, stretched the skin down taut from below, and drew the blade in a slow sweep up to his chin. An urgency gnawed at his insides, as it did each morning, a fear that he would not be the first to arrive at the mill. When he came down to breakfast, the coffee, eggs, and bacon would be ready. He wanted Ewing, Wheelin, and Isham—and Walter, especially Walter—to see him already there working when they arrived. And he was always the last one to leave.

The razor clinked against the basin in front of him when he rinsed the lather from the blade. The mill heaved and choked and belched grease and oil and dirt. It was inundated with scraps of wood and surrounded by piles of useless sawdust that had to be burned every year. Virgil Bass's running off was the best thing that had ever happened to Henry, a chance to get away from the filth and noise of the saws, away from the goddamn fools he worked with, away from his puling excuse for a brother. The chance to show all the half-assed monied men in Delaney that he could play their game, could speak their language, take their money and laugh at them as he put it in the bank.

He had never understood why some women, and sometimes the most unexpected women, would risk everything—family, tight social world, public disgrace—for him. Truly

Greenway was no surprise. After Tobias lost his arm at the mill, he wasn't worth much to her. But nothing could have prepared Henry for Miriam Martin. Her husband, Othell, a big wig in that holiness church, was Mr. Religious, and Miriam had always looked to Henry like she lived on green persimmons. She was forever promoting some charity or other. Carrying a Bible. He would be willing to bet good money that after the affair was over, what little there was of it, she was driven by that perverse mind of hers to tell her husband everything, to endure the wrath of her master Othell, to get it all off her chest, what little there was of that, and take her beating and be the fallen woman restored to her place. She was the type. Othell had always looked down his nose at Henry, and Henry couldn't tell any difference in the way Othell looked at him now. There was no way to know, and he didn't really give a damn.

He heard the clatter of a pan in the kitchen below him.

He turned his head a little to the right, pulled the skin down taut again, and shaved the left side of his neck. After feeling the skin and touching up in a couple of places, he did the same on the other side. His office, at the far end of the loading docks, was out of reach of the dirt and noise. Everything there was clean, in its place, his desk centered in the room, orders in one basket, invoices in another, each basket resting on an opposite corner of the surface. The inkwell, pen, and blotter lay neatly between the two baskets. Nothing was left unfinished on the deskop overnight. Each day when he entered the office, it offered indisputable evidence of order.

The only area of the mill Henry liked outside the office was the loading dock, where the ties were stacked in piles of fifty, waiting to be loaded onto the wagons that hauled them down to the depot, where they were transferred to the flat-cars and transported down the line. It was a system, a regulated system that operated according to schedules. Delaney was the fifth of nine towns along the forty-mile rail spur. At each of the towns, more ties were loaded onto the train and delivered back to Fayetteville. From Fayetteville they were sent all over the countryside, wherever new tracks were being constructed or old tracks being repaired. He felt satisfaction in seeing the finished product, trim and square and stacked, ready to go, ready to enter the system.

He reached across in front of his forehead, put his finger on his right sideburn and raised the skin of his cheek and worked the razor down to the edge of his jaw. The razor clinked again on the porcelain of the pan as he dipped the blade in the water. *The Fayetteville Democrat* had printed an article in the "Local Interest" section that described Delaney and the leading citizens of the town. He had read the paragraph on himself a dozen times: "The Henry Basses live in a two- story house built in the Victorian style, and they drive a black Springfield buggy with fine leather upholstery. Mr. Bass is the proprietor of a lumber mill just outside the town. The lumber business prospers in this area, feeding the railroad's appetite for hardwood ties, and producing mass quantities of posts, staves, and lumber. Mrs. Bass is a homemaker." The writer was obviously not from Delaney.

A homemaker. Naomi Bass the homemaker. When he first met Naomi, she was young, strung tight, like the high strings on a fiddle, and she was mad and was waiting for a chance to break down the door and walk out of that prim and proper little life she was caged up in. When he asked her to leave the Fourth of July picnic with him and go walk down by the river, she hesitated only long enough to blink once and glance over at that old prune Rose Eltha Belle Cravens, who was up to her neck in gossip and not paying any attention to anything else.

Their marriage was too easy, right from the beginning. But it didn't last long. By the end of the first year, some dark shape crept up on him and clung to him and grew in his chest like ice spreading across the surface of a pond, trapping him like a waterfowl on a winter morning, its webbed feet frozen tight.

So he drank Old Long Horn whiskey, which was also easy. He had it shipped direct to him by mail order from Fort Smith. He had been drinking most of his life. Now when his throat burned for a drink during the day at the mill, he focused on the papers that crossed the polished surface of the desk from the basket on the left to the basket on the right, and when the image of the smooth glass of the bottle, the smell of the whiskey, and the snug sound of the cork slipped over him in unguarded moments, like the mists rising from the river, he forced his eyes to focus on the papers, on the columns neatly filled in, on the stacks of fifty ties trimmed and squared, waiting on the dock to be loaded.

And occasionally he saw the invitation in the way a woman looked at him, and he found a way to accept. But always afterward he had to go home again. And he felt a nagging remorse every time, remorse that he could not see any reason for, felt it in his stomach. And he knew then the absurdity of his hang-dog desire for Naomi, in spite of the years of her apathy. And at night after the lanterns were extinguished, he sat in the kitchen at the table in the dark and drank.

Then when the old house at the mill burned down with Walter and the old woman living there, it was just what all the loose-lipped shits, all the stuffed-shirt storekeepers in Delaney needed to confirm their opinions of the Basses. Walter was spineless, bullied for years by an old woman so bent with arthritis she could barely move and hiding from the world and taking it out on her family, what was left of it after Virgil was gone.

For years Virgil Bass had worked in the steam and grease and scraps, himself a scrap, rotting and yellowed, cursing the men around him, and slinging the cut boards and ties away from him as if they were poisonous snakes, stopping frequently to drink from the pint bottle kept in one hip pocket, and occasionally gnawing a chew from the twist of tobacco kept in the other. Until he couldn't take it any more and slunk out of town like a weasel leaving the chicken coop.

And Walter had always been there, working like a horse beaten into submission, snorting and groaning, skittish.

Henry's reflection looked out of the mirror, the face still lathered on one side, like a scarecrow in blowing snow. He put his thumb on his sideburn and drew up the skin on the left side of his face, reaching across with the razor as he did so. He paused with the razor poised just below his ear and looked at the glass.

Lilly had always whined and fluttered and wilted, but with age and arthritis she had become more and more volatile and unpredictable. He remembered her face, contorted as she yelled at him. Saw it uncoil like a dropped rope, go flaccid, and stare at him, then snort as she turned and stalked out of the room. Pond scum. Like she was looking at pond scum, unavoidable.

He shaved the side of his face, then looked it over carefully.

He rinsed off the razor for the last time and wiped it on a towel and folded it and put it in the drawer. He splashed water on his face, dried it, and examined it. He touched the thin white line of the scar above his left eyebrow, one of Virgil Bass's lasting gifts, from seventeen years earlier when Henry was only seventeen. They were stacking ties on the docks, and Virgil had nearly emptied his flask and was snorting and belligerent. Henry dropped his end of a tie that he and Virgil were carrying.

"Sorry bastard!" Virgil yelled. "You nearly tore my fingers off. What did you think you were doing?"

Virgil picked up a short piece of slab and lunged at Henry, swinging the scrap at Henry's head. As Henry ducked, the slab glanced off his shoulder and struck him just above the eye, splitting the scalp and tumbling him over the tie at his feet and into the loose pile of slabs at the platform edge. Stunned, he looked up to see Virgil standing over him, his lips drawn back, bringing the wooden scrap down over his head like an ax aimed again at Henry's head. Henry rolled away just enough to take the blow across his back.

The pain ran down his legs, and he felt the loose slabs shift under Virgil's feet and heard Virgil yell "Damn it!" as he stumbled over Henry.

Henry was jolted by Virgil falling against him, and Virgil's face was thrust up next to his with a look of strained surprise. But when Virgil's eyes focused on Henry's, he spat into Henry's face, the tobacco juice spreading down Henry's cheek.

Henry looked into the mirror, holding the towel in his hands, then wiped his face and turned away.

He had thrust his right hand into Virgil's graying hair and his left hand up under Virgil's beard, grasped the throat just above the protruding Adam's apple, and ignoring Virgil's blows to his side and shoulders, pounded Virgil's head against the slabs. Virgil struck at him for a few seconds, then went limp.

Wheelin Combs, Isham Birkes, and Tobias Greenway, who had backed away at the first outbreak and had watched from a safe distance, pulled Henry away, forcing one of his hands from Virgil's throat and tearing away a fistful of Virgil's hair with the other. They laid Virgil and Henry both out on the platform and Wheelin Combs went for Dr. Blake.

The two men lay there for the twenty minutes it took Wheelin to find the doctor and bring him, Virgil groaning, half conscious, and Henry staring silently at the roof. The other men kept at a distance, talked quietly, glanced over at the two lying on the platform. Ewing McCracken was the only one to speak to either of them.

"Better hold your bandanna on that cut, Henry. It's bleedin' pretty good."

But Henry didn't look at him or say anything in return, and so Ewing went back to sit and wait with the others.

When the fight started, Walter, who was fourteen, had been ready with Ewing to lift the next tie. Through it all, he had hung back against the conveyor. He remained there in the aftermath, watching Henry with a look of intense interest, one hand resting on the shining rollers of the conveyors, the other hanging at his side.

Henry rolled his head to one side and looked at Walter, who looked away. As far as Henry could tell, Walter was no use in the world whatever, and he would never be otherwise. Four years earlier, when they had tried to run away together, when they had made a pact together to leave this sorry excuse for a life behind forever, Walter had panicked. As the train crept by, he had turned and run, and Henry had stood trying to swallow his heart, and watched the train roll by, reached out and touched it as it passed. Walter was chaff, hollow and useless, at the mercy of the wind.

Dr. Blake cleaned Henry's head wound and wrapped his head in gauze. Then he inspected Virgil's head, looked repeatedly into his eyes, opened and shut them with his thumb, then shook his own head in disgust.

"They'll both be moving again after awhile," he said. "Oughta stay in bed for a week, both of them. But the damn fools will be out here working tomorrow, probably trying to kill each other again. Serve them both right, and better for the rest of us if you ask me."

Ewing, Wheelin, and Tobias helped Walter move both men down to the house. Then they went back to work for the rest of the day.

"We'll see you in the morning, Walter," Ewing said as they left that evening.

"I guess so," Walter said. "I reckon even if they don't feel like working, Virgil will want us to go ahead with the ties."

From that day, until he deserted them seven years later, Virgil never laid a hand on either Henry or Walter. He showered his abuse over them like a waterfall of curses and threats, slinging words and lumber and any loose item at hand in an aggression of near misses. They worked with him in a dreamlike world of precarious security, watching their step, Henry sullen and grim, daring Virgil to touch him.

Henry looked through the washroom door into the darkness of the hall. He turned back and blew out the candles beside the mirror, then started for the bedroom, feeling more at ease in the dark. It was the dark that covered him every night, after the lanterns were put out, as he sat at the kitchen table of his two-story Victorian house and drank Old Long Horn whiskey, as he listened each night to the footsteps on the wooden floor of the room above him, as Naomi got ready for bed, the tap of her hard leather heels slow and tired as she moved about the room. And each time she crossed from the dresser to the closet or back past the foot of the bed, the boards creaked and Henry looked up at the ceiling and searched the empty air.

He buttoned up his white shirt, stiff with starch. Walter was a fool. Just like him to turn into a holy roller. What did he think he was doing? Who did he think he was fooling? All that business about the Holy Ghost, the power and the glory.

A load of bullshit.

He stopped in the middle of combing his hair, walked over to the window and looked out at the early morning darkness. He straightened the string tie at his neck.

And Walter and his pious little wife finally had a baby. And it was dead.

Henry had never even gone to see Joshua. Naomi had gone often and brought home descriptions smothered in nervous fluttering energy that reminded him of Lilly Bass. But when Joshua started to die, Naomi's nervous energy disappeared, and she and Henry spoke very little during the last days of Joshua's life.

At the funeral Henry stood beside Naomi and thought that Walter's god had failed him, that it had done no good to become a holy roller after all. But when four men dressed in black lowered the small wooden casket slowly, unevenly into the ground, letting the ropes slip through their hands as carefully as they could, Henry felt an urge to stop them and to open the casket so that he could see Joshua after all. He struggled with a clouded image of him from Naomi's descriptions, but he could picture only a dark form now lying nailed shut in the small box, disappearing into the grave. He had gripped the brim of his hat with both hands down in front of him, forcing in a deep breath to steady himself.

After the ropes were pulled up out of the grave, Walter and Emma stepped forward to the edge, and each lifted a handful of dirt and let it fall onto the casket below. It rattled on the wood. Naomi, who had been standing beside Henry without touching him, moved in beside Emma, placed her hand on Emma's arm, and dropped a handful of dirt into the shadow of the hole. As the hollow sound of it striking wood reached her, she wept openly.

Henry took his coat from the closet and slipped it on. Everyone had expected him to stand beside Walter. He knew that. To drop in his handful of dirt. But he had felt, as he stood there, separated from Walter and Emma and Naomi, in fact could still feel as he walked down the dark hallway on the runner of carpet, the people around him looking at him, and he had not been able to look up, had not been able to make himself step toward the grave. The sound of the dirt rattling down on the casket at the bottom of the hole froze him where he stood. He had stared at the hole and forced himself to breathe evenly. Somebody in the crowd behind him, all of them from the holiness church except Orval Anderson and the Farleys, began singing "Shall we gather at the river, where bright angel feet have trod." Someone blew her nose and someone else said softly "Hallelujah," followed by another's quiet "Yes Lord!"

As Henry started down the stairs to the living room, he tried to shake off the crawling of his skin. That old bastard Leery had railed on about eternal life and the comfort of the resurrection and the light overcoming the darkness.

As he walked across the dark living room toward the kitchen, thinking of bourbon whiskey, wishing the long hours at the mill were behind him, looking forward to the comforting darkness after the lanterns were out, he knew that the light was insufficient, that the world was cold and dark, and even the moon and stars looked down cold and careless at the pitiful world beneath them. That every man, woman, and child was finally alone, isolated in his or her own bleak life where blind passion fought to overcome reason, and the mind survived only by steeling itself against feeling and by force of will keeping the heart under control.

Part III

His Presence Is an Awful Fire

22

October 1904
Embracing the Dying

THE CORN AND THE TOMATOES HAD WILTED in the August sun, turned crisp and brown. The dust, two inches deep, rose up in clouds around the wagons and lay on everything, a brown powder skin on the landscape. It coated the trees, the grass, the dishes in the hutch. It turned to mud on sweaty skin, to grit between the teeth, and worked its way into the weave of the fabric of shirts, pants, and hats. Life in Delaney seemed to be on hold, waiting for the rain. People moved more slowly, spoke in tired tones, looked at the blue-white sky and shook their heads.

The rain came on a Thursday in early October. Walter and Isham were driving a wagon full of ties across the square to the loading dock of the depot. The raindrops, fat and cold, pelted the dust of the street, drummed into the dirt around them, rattled the brims of their hats, and rumbled down on the buildings and boardwalk around the square. Walter stopped the wagon and sat and listened. Muddy rivulets ran down the horses' rumps before their rumps turned dark and slick. Steam rose from the railroad tracks. He shivered.

"Well I'll be damned," Isham said.

Bill and Pauline Roberts came out onto the porch of the mercantile, and Bill reached out to let the water running off the porch roof splash onto his hand. The door of the mercantile stood open. Able Solomon came out onto the boardwalk in front of his café, where there was no awning, and stood with his face up, his eyes closed, his arms stretched out. The rain plastered his hair down onto his head and ran down his cheeks and jowls onto his shirt. It beat down onto the apron that covered his broad belly. He reminded Walter of Brother Leery standing on the dais praying, glistening with sweat, surrounded by the low muttering of the prayers of the people. And Walter shook the reins and started the horses toward the dock.

"Let's get this stuff unloaded," he said.

Through it all, through the dry months and the cooling of autumn, the demand for railroad ties and fence posts and barrel staves held steady, and the mill ran ten hours a day. And Walter kept Isham and the others working and the logs moving through the mill. During the drought, they wore bandannas over their faces to keep from choking on the dust, like highwaymen from one of the dime novels Ewing McCracken read. When the rains came, Walter was glad to get rid of the bandanna and breathe the cooler air. And the stacks of ties, fifty to a stack, stood on the loading dock, and the wagon loads of posts rolled away toward the depot.

It was nearly eight when Walter pulled the wagon up the lane beside the house, stepped down, and began unhitching the horses. The pale light of the lanterns showed in the windows of the dining room and the kitchen. The sky had cleared, and as he stood in the cool October night, the wide darkness over him, the stars scattered across it, he thrust his hand into the warmth of the horse's mane before unbuckling the harness. The horse shook its head and snorted, and the harness rattled, and afterward the faint sound of Emma humming drifted out to him.

He scratched the horse's ear and breathed the animal's sharp salt smell. The dark blue sky around the white half moon faded into star-flecked black. The chittering of the tree frogs stopped and started again. Somewhere off toward the Morrison place, a dog woofed half-heartedly. The horse's head bobbed up and down twice, and again it shook the harness. Walter turned back to unhitch both the animals, and when they were free, he led them through the back yard and down the hill to the barn.

He forked hay down from the loft and poured a bucket of grain in the trough, then walked up the hillside past the orchard that stood on the slope below the garden. The air was thick with the smell of rotted apples that lay on the ground around the trees. He and Emma had picked the Jonathans in September. He picked the tops of the trees from the ladder, the sack slung over his shoulder. Emma picked what she could reach from a stool. The pears still hung thick on the drooping branches of the pear trees and dropped every day to rot ungathered.

Walter's boots sounded heavy on the steps leading up to the small wooden porch that opened into the kitchen. The screen door closed with a pop behind him, and he slipped off his boots and left them inside the door. The room was warm. Emma came out of the pantry at the other end of the kitchen and put a pint jar of canned peaches down on the counter.

"Will you open these for me?" she said.

For months her voice had been bound up like a coil of tight new wire with no bends or kinks. It unrolled slow and even, as if a life depended on every word. It seemed like one more effect of the drought, something else that dried up in the heat. But when she spoke to him there in the kitchen, he remembered their first year of marriage, the motion of her head when she spoke, the same look and voice—but not the same, as if he held a lightly smoked glass between them, and her features had been darkened, as if her voice were coming now around the pane, altered by it.

That first year, Emma's mama and the other women at church had asked Emma probing questions, at least once a week, about when they could expect to hear the good news, and maybe they would look at her belly with those coy smiles. As one year stretched into two the questions came less frequently. Then they stopped. Then the false hope of the miscarriages. And her mama let him know, without ever saying a word, that it was his fault. Just the way she looked at him.

Emma stood in front of him, waiting, holding the jar of peaches out to him. The smell of baked bread and fried round steak hung in the heavy air. His hands were still dirty from the mill.

He stepped over to the counter, wiped his hands on his

pant legs, and twisted the lid of the jar, loosening it. When the lid gasped, he loosened it but did not lift it off. Emma reached out and touched his arm, and said, "I missed you today." Small lines spread from the corners of her eyes. Sun wrinkles she called them, because they came from working in the garden without a hat.

She looked out the window above the sink, out into the darkness, and said, "I love this time of year."

Then she turned away and picked up a bowl of mashed potatoes that lay on the counter across from them.

"I'm putting supper on, but you've got a few minutes to wash up a little." She went into the dining room. "Stay out of those peaches," she said. "They're for dessert."

He took the bar of soap from the dish on the window sill over the sink and stepped out onto the back porch. He slipped off his socks and his shirt and laid them across the porch rail, then went across the yard to the well. The grass was soft and cool, and the air chilly, and a shiver ran through him. He let the bucket down into the well until a hollow plosh sounded in the darkness below, then cranked it back up. As he set the full bucket on the edge of the well frame, the call of an owl drifted up from the barn loft and was answered by another, the voice rising and falling from the woods at the bottom of the gully.

Like everything else during the drought of summer, Walter's prayers had turned to dust. He wanted Joshua back from the grave, but the prayer, fragile, splintered on reality. Sometimes he was close enough to smell and feel that world full of spirits but couldn't reach out and take hold. He had begun to think that maybe Henry was right, that his religion was just a sugar-titty to keep the baby satisfied.

He splashed water from the bucket onto his face and neck and lathered himself.

Back at the house, he dropped his dirty clothes in the laundry room and went to the bedroom, put on a clean shirt and trousers. He slipped his suspenders up over his shoulders as he walked through the living room and into the dining room.

Emma sat at the table in the chair nearest the kitchen door, resting her chin on her hands, waiting for him. He ran his hands through his wet hair and sat down across from her.

The lantern, a little to one side on the table, cast a soft light onto a bowl in the center, where red and yellow leaves were mixed with dried corn shucks, which were nearly white from bleaching in the sun. Two ears of Indian corn, the kernels black, red, yellow, and white, nestled in the shucks. When Walter looked up from the bowl, Emma was watching him.

The yellow light from the lantern cast her shadow on the wall behind her, the sound of the tree frogs rose and fell outside the window to his right, and his own uneven breathing broke the silence between them.

She smiled. "How were things at the mill today?"

"Springfield up in Fayetteville had a rush order for lumber for floorboards for their wagons," he said. "Want them in Fayetteville Monday afternoon. We'll be pushing to make it."

For a few minutes they ate quietly, their knives and forks scraping on the plates.

When Walter finished eating, Emma picked up the plates

and took them into the kitchen. She returned with a pot of coffee and filled their cups, resting her hand on his shoulder and leaning lightly on him as she poured. He breathed the smell of the bread, of the coffee, and of the long braid of her hair, which she had pulled around to the side and swung now close to his face.

Emma took the coffeepot back to the kitchen, then sat down at the table. Walter cut a slice from the half loaf of bread that lay on the cutting board, handed it to her, then cut a slice for himself. The butter had warmed sitting out in the kitchen, and it spread easily.

"Papa stopped by this morning," she said.

"Need something?" he said. He didn't want to talk about her parents, about the fact that her mother couldn't stop blaming him.

"Just had the urge to see his little girl, I think," she said. "I was working in the garden, pulling up the corn stalks and stacking them." She took a bite of bread and chewed slowly. "Those stalks stand out there like skinny old women after harvest, turning brown, stooped, shuffling in the wind." She smiled. "Always made me think of somebody I know, like Mrs. Ivey."

She sipped her coffee. "This year it made me think of myself." She looked across her coffee cup at him. "Funny isn't it?"

Her eyes were gray beneath the dark eyebrows, and the shadow of the coffee cup just touched her lower lip.

"What I like best," she said, "is that when the stalks are gone, the pumpkin vines cover the garden, and the pumpkins look like fat little islands."

She seemed to be lost in her thoughts for a moment, and he took a drink of coffee. "I'll get to those stalks this weekend," he said.

"I think I noticed for the first time," she said, "how the skin is sagging under Papa's eyes."

She began to talk a little faster, as if she wanted to say something before she forgot it.

"Then I found myself talking about Joshua," she said, "telling Papa how we prayed so long to have him, and how helpless he was and how I couldn't do anything, couldn't pray him through, and how now it seemed like something more than Joshua was gone."

Outside the window, darkness had swallowed everything. The lane, the fence, the shed, the field. She would have to talk about Joshua, and as always, he would rise up between them, and every other possibility would be smothered in the wringing of hands and the tears.

"Papa said the strangest thing. He said that that old wagon, the hearse, rolls down through town and out to Patrick cemetery pretty often. Always carrying somebody, always leaving somebody behind. And problem is, we see how full that cemetery is of people we know, people not ready, not finished living. Worst of all how many stones stand over infant babies."

Her eyes watered. In the first months after Joshua's death, he had held her, shushed her, patted on her after he put out the lamp, as she cried herself to sleep.

"Then Papa said that it took him a long time, but he finally learned that the biggest part of faith is taking the world on its own terms. I wasn't sure what he meant. Taking the world on its own terms. And then he said, 'Emmy, sooner or later you got to embrace the dying.'"

She picked at the bread on her plate. "Embrace the dying. Now that's a new one. He told me to look at those autumn leaves, all that dying, falling back to earth, burning in the sun like fire from the Holy Ghost. He said it was the Good Lord's way of saying, 'Look at this dying here, it's a thing of beauty.'"

She picked up her cup and started to take a drink, but stopped and said, "I'm going to need some more coffee to finish this bread. How about you?"

Walter wanted to tell her that for once her father was right and not to talk any more about Joshua. He said "Sure."

She brought the coffeepot, and before she poured his coffee, she stopped and looked out the window into the dark and said, "Almost the last thing Papa said before he left was 'Emmy, you know what's hurting you most, don't you? It's never being able to touch Joshua again. That's what's hurting you.' Then he said 'But Emmy, you got a lot of living still to do. You can't quit touching now.'"

She leaned over and poured his coffee. "After Papa left," she said, "I kneaded the bread dough, and while it rose, I sat out on the front porch cutting up the Jonathans for a pie, thinking about what Papa said."

Walter made himself breathe slowly. The smell of her hair, the coffee, the bread. She poured her own coffee, set the pot on the table, and sat down.

She sipped the coffee. "And I kept thinking about those

corn stalks," she said, "drying out, rattling in the wind." The corners of her mouth started up and she looked away.

They ate the bread slowly, as if they were just killing time.

"Those starlings are pests, you know," she said. "I put scraps out on the feeder, and the starlings chase off the cardinals and the chickadees. Only thing meaner is a blue jay, I think."

He said, "I heard a couple of owls calling while I was out washing up."

They drank the coffee between bites of bread. When he finished his bread and swallowed the last of his coffee, she looked up at him, part of her bread in her hand. Her gaze dropped to her plate and her breath rose and fell and he could see a smile lift the corners of her mouth again, just as it had when they sat on the front porch of the Sinclair house before they were married. When she said Yes. She put the bread back down on her plate and stood up. He stood, stepped around to the side of the table, cupped his hand around the top of the lantern globe and blew out the flame, then held out his hand to her.

She took it as she came up to him, and he pulled her to him and kissed her before she turned and led the way to the bedroom. As they walked through the dark living room, she pulled the clasp from the braid of her hair and let it fall loose around her shoulders. Their footfalls were quiet, but the floorboards creaked just in front of the bedroom door, first as Emma crossed them and then again with Walter.

The bedroom was cool, both windows half open, and a breeze slid across the foot of the bed and lifted the lace curtains. They did not light the lantern. Emma pulled back the quilt and sheet and fluffed the pillows.

Then she knelt beside the bed and began to pray, her voice barely a whisper. He felt like a schoolboy asked to recite a lesson he did not know. But he knelt beside her. The curtain in the window lifted again toward him and eased back into place. And the lost words of his prayer for Joshua hung in the darkness, just out of reach, lighter than a whisper, fading.

Her voice was a murmur. He could not think of God with Emma there beside him, the warmth of her, the smell of her. She finished so quickly he was surprised. She pulled his face down to hers and kissed him, and as he reached up to slip his hand around behind her neck, she pushed his hands down in front of them and stood, pulling him up with her.

She unbuttoned the cuffs of her blouse and started working her way down the front as he stood watching, unbuttoning the cuffs of his shirt. When she dropped her blouse behind her, the white of her slip reflected the dim light bleeding in from the moon. The tree frogs sang outside the window, and a bobwhite whistled. She reached behind her and unhooked her skirt, letting it fall to the floor.

"Emma," he said.

She stepped up to him and slid his suspenders off his shoulders, then began loosening his shirt, and he pulled her to him and lifted her and stepped over onto the bed.

The jar of peaches sat on the kitchen counter, the lid loosened, unopened, in the light of the lantern, which was not extinguished until the middle of the night when Emma remembered and slid over Walter and padded into the kitchen to put it out. The floorboard at the door creaked when she returned, and his voice came from the darkness.

"What are you doing up?"

She lay down beside him and pulled his arm around her and said, "Having dessert."

23

February 1905
Emma

I WOKE IN THE COLD MORNING, in the gray light just before dawn (that in-between time when I first open my eyes and am not sure what I see, when I wonder, for the briefest moment, if I am alive or dead), and heard Walter breathing, almost snoring, the low moist stertor deep in his throat. Uncle Beau made that sound, lying on the porch where they brought him when his horse fell on him, the front porch of this house, where he died, just there outside the bedroom window, his breath bubbling up pink from the corner of his mouth, waiting for the doctor. Aunt Jean sat there, quiet, watching him, not able to reach out and touch him.

Walter's profile was pale in the half light, his mouth open, the Adam's apple like a stone lodged in the throat. I traced with my finger down the length of his nose, around his lips, over the small chin, and down to the raised cartilage in the neck. He swallowed and it moved under my finger.

I kissed his cheek, then slid out from under the heavy quilt, put on my housecoat and slippers, and went to the kitchen and started the fire in the stove and put on the kettle for coffee. Walter came in rubbing his eyes. He stretched and yawned. The sleeves of his long johns were not quite long enough, and his pants fit loosely, held up with suspenders. His scuffed boots were untied. He went out the back door and a few minutes later came back with a bucket of cold water from the well, poured some water into the metal basin beside the sink, and then set the bucket on the counter. He leaned down and tied his boots.

He kissed me on the cheek, half awake, and turned and walked out the back door, grabbing his coat off the hook, and headed for the barn to fork hay into the horses' stalls and feed and milk the moon-eyed Jersey cow waiting for him in her stall.

While he was gone, I washed myself from the basin. The cold water shocked me awake. In the field across the gully, the bermuda grass was brown, and the bare oak and hickory and elm and sweet gum covered the hillsides, their roots under a thick carpet of dead leaves. When we were girls, Ollie and I chewed the gobs of sweet gum sap that balled on the trunks.

The sunlight glinted on the windowpane, and the last dry leaves twisted in the breeze. I had awakened in the middle of the night, and out of the silence came the throaty mutter of the horses. They were standing at the gate to the south field just beyond the orchard, as if they were watching the moon, waiting for someone to turn them out.

Walter came back from the barn, and as we ate breakfast, as we talked idly while I cleaned up the breakfast things, and most of all when he came back into the house and kissed me goodbye after hitching up the wagon, standing in the front door, his hat pushed back on his head, I felt like those horses, waiting at the gate to be turned out.

I know how lightning jumps from the clouds to the charged and waiting earth, and I saw Ransom Todd on the stage, two years ago at the Fourth of July dance, crank the handle of his magneto and make electricity leap across the empty space between two rods. Walter and I, like charged cells, carry the current inside us, and it sparks and leaps across the space between us as we sit and eat, as we sit and talk in the gray dark, not lighting the lantern.

Just the night before, we had listened to the fire crackle and hiss in the potbelly of the stove, two charged and waiting bodies, and the air seemed to crackle with sparks as we brushed against each other, the hair rising on the back of my neck when he reached out to touch my hand. We sat next to each other on the couch in the living room, the heat of the stove just beyond our feet.

As I stood at the sink, I was not able to look at the scraps of my uneaten eggs from breakfast without feeling nausea, and I let myself believe what I had suspected for two weeks. I walked the half mile to the Morrison farm and asked Purity to take me to Dr. Blake. I don't know what I would do without Purity. She looked at me, and one eyebrow rose in a question mark for maybe two seconds. Then she knew, and I think her eyes watered, and her mouth puckered, and she said "Oh, Emma." And she wiped the flour from her hands onto her apron and came to me with her arms outstretched.

We went to the barn, and she hitched Ginger to the buggy

and drove me to town. I know she thinks it silly of me to need a doctor to tell me what I already know. She has so much experience with this kind of thing that I know she thinks I'm a fool. But she has always had too sweet a nature to tell me so. And I had a more particular reason for going that day.

I asked Dr. Blake if this baby would have weak lungs and die as Joshua did. I looked away from him at the eye chart hanging on the wall, at the giant F at the top of the chart. From the top shelf of his medicine cabinet, a skull stared out, but I kept my eyes on the chart. Dr. Blake held my hand, rubbed it and smiled and said that my baby was just as likely as any other baby to be perfectly healthy. That I should just take care of myself and put my fears out of my mind.

"I don't give guarantees," he said, "but you don't have any reason that I know of to worry."

No guarantees. I couldn't finish anything I started after I got home from Dr. Blake's. The dress I was making lay in pieces on the dining room table among scraps of the pattern. The apples from the root cellar lay on the counter unpeeled, with the flour, lard, and salt for the pie crust. I sat down at the table and cried. The scrubby limbs of the blackjack oaks that lined the field north of the house twisted back on themselves in a tangle, and I felt the weight of Joshua in my arms and shuddered at the memory of his nursing.

In the late afternoon, the wagon pulled into the lane. Walter was home early. I was sitting on the single bed in the second bedroom, beside Joshua's crib, which Walter had moved there after the funeral. I held the baby blanket Mama made, which was lying in my lap. The top drawer of the chest of drawers was open, tilted down, and several pieces of clothing lay on top—a small night shirt, the knitted booties I made such a mess of, a knitted head warmer from Faith McCormick. Two more blankets lay on the bed beside me.

The back screen door popped shut. Walter walked to the door of the bedroom and stopped, looked puzzled, filling the doorway, not moving into the room. A shaft of sunlight from the kitchen window crossed the dining room behind his shoulder. Dust floated up and swirled in the light, seemed to curl up over him, the only movement in the house. The clock ticked on top of the hutch in the dining room.

I wanted to jump off the bed and run to him, to tell him the news. But I just sat there, my body not responding to the urgency in my stomach. When I opened my mouth to speak, I expected to hear my words slur slowly across the space between us, as they would have in a dream.

But the whispered words came quickly. "I'm going to have another baby."

He stood there for a few seconds, still, then shook his head slowly. The falling flecks of dust that rose over his shoulder disappeared as the shadow of a cloud on the horizon cut off the light from the kitchen window.

"No," he said and looked surprised at his own word. He squinted as if he was trying to remember something. "That's not what I . . ." he said, but stopped.

He looked miserable, and I said, "What, Walter?"

During the past few months when I had seen the light in

his eyes fade, I had whisked away the fear that rose in my throat, had blown it away like a mustard seed in the palm of my hand. He looked away from me to the chest of drawers, then quickly down at the floor.

I kept my lips firm, but my eyes watered, and I asked, "Walter, don't you want another baby?"

"I was going to say I didn't mean to say no," he said. But he did not look back up at me. "I don't know what I meant," he said. He walked over to the bed and sat down beside me and put his arm around my shoulders and touched my cheek.

"I wasn't expecting..." he said. "It's just that when I saw you...another baby."

The clock in the dining room chimed five times.

In the quiet that followed the final chime, he looked down at me out of the corners of his eyes. His half-released breath sounded like the whine of a child. He stopped in the middle of it. I reached up with both my hands and pulled his face to me, and he hid his face in my neck. His weight carried us back onto the bed, and we lay there as I stroked his face, the blank ceiling over us.

I had never seen him cry before. He had not cried after Joshua's death, but I was on familiar ground. I whispered to him as if to a little child, stroking his head and face. His breathing steadied and slowed. He lay quiet, and then inhaled a long breath and exhaled, and it seemed to me that his breath carried with it out into the room the last of his misery.

The flowered pattern of the border separated the wall from the ceiling. He rolled onto his back and said, "What about this baby, Em? Maybe . . ."

"Dr. Blake says there's no reason to worry now just because of that."

"I don't know," he said and sat up on the side of the bed and held my hand in his lap. "I don't know." He ran his finger tip down the length of my fingers. "I'd better go take care of the animals," he said. "You milk yet?"

"No," I said.

"I'll do it," he said. He stood and reached out and touched the rail of the crib and then walked over and picked up the head warmer on the chest. He took another deep breath and exhaled. "I don't know. I just ..." He turned and walked out of the room.

I lay on the bed with my eyes closed and ran my hand slowly back and forth across my belly, then let it lie there.

There was a tapping at the front door and I sat up quickly, wiped my eyes, and stood up. I had the urge to shut the bedroom door and stay there, the urge to hide. I wanted to wrap myself in the shadows of this room for a while. I dropped the baby blanket on the bed and went to the living room. When I opened the door, Purity, bundled in a heavy coat and ear muffs, stood on the porch with a basket in her hand. The light outside was just turning dusk.

"I saw Walter taking the horses around back," she said. "I didn't think he'd be home yet. But I just wanted to bring you a little something after our trip to town today and all." She handed the basket in to me.

"Come on in here before you freeze," I said.

Purity shook her head. "No, you take this and enjoy it.

Maybe I've caught you so that you won't have to fix any supper tonight. I just had a feeling, you know."

She looked at me like she was trying to see how I was really doing without having to ask, then reached out and touched me on the arm. "Close the door before you get a chill," she said, and she turned and walked back out to her buggy, climbed in, and flicked the horse's rump with the long, thin whip.

As the buggy wheeled around in the road, I called out, "Thanks, Purity," and she raised her hand without looking. The buggy moved down the road toward the Morrison farm, the horse in a quick trot.

I stood with my back against the door, the house quiet, the basket in my hands in front of me. The sun had gone down behind the hill across the gully behind the house, and though the sky was still blue-gray there in the west, with a line of pink clouds on the horizon, the house was darkening fast. One of the steers bellowed from the gully, answered a few seconds later by another in the field on the hilltop beyond. The sound slid away into the distance, as if the world outside the darkening walls were sliding away with it. The silence afterward was deeper.

When I was growing up, the only child, sometimes in the evening, if Mama and Daddy were both still working outside, I would sit in the house and watch it grow dark around me, part of me enjoying the excitement of fear. Afraid to get up and go find them, I would sit wide-eyed and wait for the door to open and my mother's or father's voice to fill the darkness.

Walter hadn't been able to look at me when I told him about the baby. His first word was no, and he had almost said he didn't want a baby. He might as well have said it, as good as did.

He said No. There was simplicity and finality in that word. But we could not live by it.

After supper, after I cleaned up, we sat in the living room with the lamp lit, and he held my hand in his lap. We didn't talk, just watched the fire in the stove. When we went to bed, we lay together under the quilt, not speaking. The winter moon shined through the window onto one corner of the foot of the bed, where the quilt looked ghostly. I snuggled against his side, his arm around my neck and down across my breasts to where his hand lay on my stomach. The two of us, it seemed to me, were squeezed up in a tight fist, afraid of what would happen. Afraid we were still in the fiery furnace, that the chaff and stubble were still being burned away.

The tension in Walter was like a damp heaviness on his chest. He was gentle, held me, patted me. But I tasted the tautness when he kissed me, breathed it when he breathed on me.

It was no use talking. There was nothing I could say, nothing I could do.

Long after the slice of moonlight in the room had narrowed, slipped shut and disappeared and left behind the darkness of familiar shapes, Walter lay with his eyes open, his chest steadily rising and falling, his fingers moving lightly back and forth over my stomach.

24

The Next Day
Purity

ALL THIS FREEZING AND THAWING is just ruining this road. All these ruts and chuck holes are going to tear up my buggy. I know it. Wheels stuttering worse than that youngest Beasley boy.

We never have lost a baby at our house, so I can't say I know how it feels. But I can imagine. After Mama had Jackson Lee, she got down in the dumps something awful. Moped around all weepy like she thought she was going to die. And of course, I had to take over the house and the baby.

And I swan, talk? Mama talked like she was saying her last good byes. When a baby is born, she says, a woman feels deserted somehow, scared without knowing why. Then with her eyes all red and watery, looking like she could see right through me, she tells me all about the nursing. Right out of the blue. Something happens, she says, though she couldn't say exactly what it was. Like the baby was reaching clear back down into the womb and tying that cord back, invisible, but you could feel it.

I could not believe she was saying all this.

Like you were pouring yourself into them, she says. And they look up at you, like they're seeing into the deepest part of you that nobody has seen, not even your man, maybe especially not your man.

As if I had ever had a man. As if that was supposed to mean something to me.

How can a man ever know that far down in you? she says, finally focusing on me, like she had forgotten I was there. I could not believe she was asking me that. Thirty-one years old and living at home and never been with a man longer than it takes to pray him through in the middle of a crowd. How in the world could I possibly know?

Well, I hope Emma never loses another one. Not many folks get by without losing some, one way or another, somewhere down the line. And her with that small pelvis.

25

August
Walter

AT HIDDEN HOLLOW, Slater's Creek falls over a semi-circle of bluff, drops forty feet onto a pile of rocks, and tumbles into a large pool before winding through the woods to the White River a half-mile down the valley. The overhang of bluff makes it possible to walk behind the waterfall on dry shale, and the mist that rises from the water that pounds the boulders drifts up into the gully and keeps it pretty cool. I was surprised that nobody else was there on a hot Sunday afternoon.

We looked forward all week to going to the waterfall. It would probably be the last time Emma and me could get to Hidden Hollow before the baby came. When we got there we left the blanket and food at the falls and went for a walk. I decided to climb up the runnel that empties into Slater's Creek fifty yards below the falls.

The creek dropped down the head of the narrow gully through large rock formations and fallen tree trunks. The springwater was cold even in the heat. The gray trunks of fallen trees lined both sides of the stream, and a layer of dead leaves covered the ground. The woods were brittle and dusty. We'd had another dry July and August. Some of the springs were drying up.

Emma turned back as soon as the runnel got steep. She went back to the waterfall to lay out the blanket and get the food ready.

"I'm hungry, Walter," she said. "Let's go back and eat."

"Be right there," I said, but the words were lost in the sound of the water, and I kept climbing up the runnel.

I picked my way up the creek bank, glad not to worry any more about Emma slipping and falling. Broad patches of dark green moss covered the rocks and fallen tree trunks, and the climbing was slippery. Streaks of sunlight splotched everything. The water churned over rotten logs and swirled around the bases of large rocks and dropped sometimes a foot or two over short slate bluffs. The air seemed a little cooler there in the crotch of the gully. A place like this, and back at the waterfall, were probably the only cool air in the county.

It was about the only way to stay cool on a Sunday afternoon late in August, besides swimming in the cold water of the White River itself, which Emma refused to do in her condition. She didn't want to be around people much at all.

I had never seen her so edgy. She had gained a lot more weight this time and moved like a fat, old woman. And there were still two months to go. Dr. Blake had told her to slow down, get lots of rest, take it easy. But she was cantankerous, like she had to show everybody that she was her own boss. It wasn't like her. I was looking forward to getting it over with. For the time being, I was glad she had gone back to the falls. The narrow gully under the oak trees shut out the rest of the world, and the hushed sound of the water was soothing.

Just the Sunday before, she had exploded at me—the first time I had ever seen her lose control like that, at anyone. We were sitting on the front porch. It was hot and there was no breeze. Emma rocked herself in one of the cane rockers and fanned herself with the newspaper. A drop of sweat trickled down her neck. Large half-moons of sweat showed under her arms. The dress was too tight. Her eyes were puffy, and she looked drowsy, nervous.

I sat on the front edge of the porch, leaning against a post, one leg cocked up beside me, the other stretched out to the ground, the way I always like to sit. I was breaking some of last year's walnuts on a flat rock in front of me, tapping them with a hammer, then searching through the chunks of shell, picking out the pieces of meat and dropping them in one of those blue enamel bowls beside me.

I didn't notice when she stopped rocking, didn't know how long she had been staring at me, but the tears rolled down her cheeks and she pressed her lips tight together. She didn't look angry, at first, just hurt.

"What?" I said.

She closed her eyes and her breathing came in heaves and she stood up faster than I thought she could have.

"Damn it!" she said. It was like she spit the word onto the porch.

I'd never heard her swear before. Never.

"What?" I said again. I was too surprised to say anything else.

She opened her eyes and stamped her foot, then closed her

eyes and bit her bottom lip and stamped her foot three more times.

"You're driving me crazy!" she said, almost a screech, and the hair stood up on my neck. "Do you have to pick every little speck of meat out of those shell scraps?" she said, struggling to keep her voice down, short of crying.

Then, slowly, her voice rising a little on each syllable, she said, "Do you know how long it takes you to do a single walnut?" And she waited, breathing through her nose.

And I remembered the school teacher, Pleasant Tweedy, standing over me, that tired look in her eyes, asking me one more time, if it weren't too much trouble, to explain the motto "Fifty-four forty or fight." I just about always knew the answer when Miss Tweedy asked me a question, but something in me dug in its heels and wouldn't let me say it, no matter how much I wanted to. And there was always this lead weight in my stomach because I knew I was responsible for Miss Tweedy's frustration.

The problem here was that I didn't have the least idea how to answer Emma.

"Well?" she shouted, her voice cracking.

I didn't know what to do. I looked down at the flat rock in front of me, the pile of shell scraps off to the side, the crushed walnut I was working on in the middle. There was still meat to be picked out there. She liked walnuts. I was picking them out mostly for her. I felt that weight in my stomach.

She threw the newspaper into the rocker and stalked into the house, letting the screen door slam shut behind her, the spring humming to a stop. After a long time with no sound from the house, I began picking through the walnut shell.

Even after a week, I was still smarting over it. I pulled myself over the flat edge of a large sandstone boulder and stood up carefully in the thick moss there. To my right, beyond a mossy log, lay the bones of a deer. It lay head downhill on the rocks near the runnel, the four black hooves still in place at the end of the legs, an inch or two of hide starting up the ankles, like little booties, everything else picked clean and white. The scavengers must have been small, the bones all being so nearly in place and all. Nothing there to rot, no odor drifting on the wind, just clean, white bones on the bare rocks.

I had seen a story in the newspaper about a woman who witnessed a murder and waited five months to tell the sheriff. The body was down an abandoned well all that time, and nobody knew except the murderer and the woman. I don't know why that story has stayed with me, why I think of it every now and then. There was something, I don't know. It always gives me the creeps.

The spring came out of the hillside not far above me, but I turned and sat on the edge of the boulder and relaxed, listened to the water, the birds in the woods. Then I dropped down off it and started back down the runnel. Emma would be waiting, maybe not too upset since it was cool at the waterfall.

I walked up the path along Slater's Creek, switching the tall grass along the bank with a stick. Emma was sitting on the blanket a few feet from the pool and across from the falls. The pool was so clear that, though it was eight or ten feet deep in the middle, you could see every waterlogged stick on the bottom. A steady stream of cool air was pushed by the waterfall out across the pool and over our blanket.

"Wish we lived right here in this hollow," I said as I sat down on the blanket and tossed the stick out into the pool, where it plunged end-first into the water and then bobbed up to the surface. "But if we did," I said, "I doubt if I'd ever go to work." I glanced sideways at her, and she was smiling at me. I felt good. She looked rested. But the small dark areas under her eyes had not gone away.

I picked up a Mason jar and raised my eyebrows at Emma as I strained to loosen the lid. When the vacuum released with a sound like a gasp, I smiled at her and said, "Sweet sound to a hungry man," and we both laughed.

As we ate, we talked, and the drumming of the waterfall behind our conversation made me think of the underground river in Harper's Cave, and of the isolation I had felt as I sat beside it on the soft mud bank, the candle flame dipping and settling in the slight shifting of air as the water slid by in a murmur, black and reflective, and the shadows wavered on the uneven walls. I had gone there the day after Henry took me to Pearl Bear at the roadhouse when I was fifteen.

The memory of that night at the roadhouse always drew a line up tight in my belly. I had sat on the edge of Pearl Bear's bed with my face burning and my stomach twisting, and the sound of Pearl's voice as she called to Henry through the window stung me. The stillness seemed to last a long, long time after Henry opened the door and stood looking, before the odd mixture of anger and worry in his words—"What?" he had said, "What's going on?" And the faint sound of laughter came from the bar and dance floor on the other side of the thick log wall.

We had gone back into the roadhouse, and Henry had drunk several beers without saying anything. I sat there miserable, afraid to say anything, and finally Henry stood up and walked away and I followed. We rode toward home, but Henry, over the sounds of the horses, said, choking on the words, "Jesus, Walter, what the hell happened?"

And the answer was there, rehearsed, the words shaped and ready, buzzing like hornets in the moment before they swarm from a nest that's been disturbed. But I couldn't say them. My voice was lodged tight in my throat.

"Goddamn it, Walter," Henry said. "What's the matter with you? Are you a....well, Jesus, what the hell happened?"

And I said it. I hadn't meant to say it at all, but it just came out. I said that everything had been fine with Pearl until I had thought of Emma Sinclair. And Henry jerked his horse into a skidding stop and sat in his saddle and stared at me as I turned my horse and came back to where he waited. And he laughed, a real mean laugh that embarrassed me.

"Until you thought of Emma Sinclair," he said, his voice mocking. "That tight-assed little strumpet isn't half the woman Pearl Bear is."

When he said that, I jumped onto him across the space between the horses and dragged him to the ground, all the shame exploding into anger. And Henry, after the fight, both of us bloody but me beaten and on the ground, went back to Pearl Bear to, he said, save the family name. And I sat there and remembered Pearl's breasts, full and brown, swinging right there in front of me as she unbuttoned my shirt, remembered the gravelly chuckle of her voice as she joked about making a stud out of me, remembered the excitement, my hands trembling, then the sudden cold shot that went through me when the picture of Emma came into my mind, standing in the creek, naked, a rock in each hand, ordering me to come to her. The shame, the panic.

When Henry found me at the cave, he said they had been looking for me, that I had been gone more than a day and that Lilly Bass was down in bed distraught over it all, damn her anyway. But he had guessed that I might be at the cave, and he asked had I had any food and was I hungry, and I'd better come get something at home though it might not be a bad idea to wait till Lilly Bass had fluttered herself to death as far as he was concerned. And before we got on the horses outside the cave to go back home, Henry tried to say something to me but wasn't able, something about Pearl and Emma, but he couldn't, and he finally swore and kicked his horse in the sides and led the way without saying anything else.

And lying there beside that waterfall on a Sunday afternoon, where the sunlight was scattered on the water of the pool, on the blanket, on Emma's dress, on her bare arm as she laid it on mine while she talked, I felt cut off from the world again, as I had been in Harper's Cave, able to say anything for this little while. The lines that were drawn tight inside me slackened.

When we finished eating, we lay back on the blanket and listened to the waterfall and felt the cool air move across us and the sun warming our faces. It was enough for the time being. I would go back to the mill the next day, move the logs through, keep the crew working.

And Henry would sit in his nice, clean office and shuffle papers and step out onto the loading dock now and then and look over the mill like a prince surveying his kingdom. And maybe Wheelin or Isham would make some comment to the others about his majesty checking on the serfs.

I pushed the thought of Henry out of my mind and listened to the water splashing on the rocks. Emma lay on her side facing me, asleep. Her face was puffy. I closed my eyes and felt myself getting drowsy.

26

September
Naomi

EMMA SNAPPED A BEAN and threw it into the bowl held between her knees, just beyond the mass of her belly. "I hate canning green beans," she said. She grabbed the bowl and lowered it to the porch beside her chair, dropping it the last few inches. It bounced and flipped several of the beans out onto the porch. She ignored them. "I don't even have a lap," she said.

I moved my bowl and leaned down and picked up the beans from the porch and dropped them back into Emma's bowl. She chewed on the cuticle of her thumb and looked out to the yard. Her eyebrows moved as if she were working on a difficult arithmetic problem.

"I didn't want a second crop of beans," she said. "Walter's been falling all over himself to find something to do this summer, so he plants a second garden in July of all things. With just the two of us. We have canned goods left over from last year, and he plants a second garden." She bent over to get the bowl, grunted and sat back up without it. "I can't bend over, Naomi," she said, "I have to hold the bowl between my knees I'm so big." She turned her face away from me and wiped the tears off her cheeks with the back of her hand.

"It'll be okay, Em," I said. I didn't know what else to say. It was not okay—the puffiness, the dark eyes, the high pitch of her emotions. But what could I say? I have never been pregnant. I don't know how it feels.

Emma reached over and took my hand. "Naomi, you're the only one who seems to understand anything," she said. "Mama just keeps on telling me how it was for her when she was pregnant and how it seemed to last forever and how the whole thing seemed to be nothing after it was over. Like I was a child that needs shushing. Like Joshua never happened." She squeezed my hand. "Sometimes it makes me want to scream at her."

I said nothing. How could I be the only one to understand? Understand what? I didn't know what to say. I didn't know how it felt. I patted her hand, a small hand like a girl's, and rubbed it. It never seemed to occur to Emma that I could not possibly understand. She has always assumed that I did, that I understood why Emma Sinclair would marry Walter Bass, though it was as much a surprise to me as to everyone else in town. She assumed I understood the Pentecostal fervor of her relationship with Walter, though that has been the greatest mystery of all to me, who can find no way to square it with my own experience of religion and love in my father's house or the house of Henry Bass. She assumed I understood the betrayed emptiness, the sense of something lost, something never known when she miscarried, and the innocent but absolute self-centeredness of her pregnancy with Joshua, and of that day when she first wore the maternity dress to visit me, blushing through her smile. All these assumptions are so much a part of Emma that she could never do otherwise. All of it has baffled me from the beginning. But somehow it has forged a link between us. I think sometimes that Emma is my only friend. Except maybe for Aunt Rose.

"Naomi, he's driving me crazy," Emma said.

"What's he doing?" I said.

"Nothing," she said. "Everything. Anything that irritates me."

"Like what?" I said.

"Like every time I get a quiet minute and want to just sit down, he starts doing something right there beside me, so close I can't breathe. Cracking walnuts and picking through them until I want to scream. Cleaning his shotgun. The smell of the oil makes me sick at my stomach. And he runs that cleaning rag through the barrel over and over and over."

Emma pulled her hand away from me and shifted in the chair and grimaced and tried to take a deep breath. "And he is always trying to make small talk. Isham Birkes' mule's gone lame. Lem Carter's little boy had a patch on his eye when they came to the mill the other day."

She closed her eyes and tried to breathe deep again. "I know it's just me," she said, "that nothing's really any different. He's always cracked walnuts. He's always cleaned his gun. He's always polished his boots on Saturday night so they'll look good Sunday morning, and made small talk the whole time. But I've never felt so wound up tight like a clock spring ready to break."

"Has Dr. Blake given you anything?" I said.

"Oh," she almost snorted, "just Dr. Miles Nervine, which makes me sleepy and I hate it, and this ridiculous liniment he has me trying, called Mother's Friend. You rub it all over your stomach morning and evening. Supposed to relieve morning sickness, make childbirth painless, and shorten labor. Anybody who believes that deserves to spend the dollar for the bottle. I think Dr. Blake is getting desperate. He just keeps saying get lots of rest and be patient and it won't be long now."

She shifted her weight again in the chair. "But I know he's worried. He's told me I'm getting too big. Tries to be kind, but what do you say to a woman who's fatter than an old sow about to drop twenty piglets?"

She straightened her dress where it fell over the mound of her stomach. "Rest and be patient. How can I rest and be patient when I want to throw things. Sometimes I want to throw things right through the window. And how can I rest when I feel like there's a knot of energy wadded up in my chest that I've got to use up or it will burn right through me, but I'm too clumsy and too tired to do anything. I can't even keep a bowl on my lap to snap beans in."

She was crying. "I didn't even want a second crop of beans," she said.

She sniffled and wiped her nose on her sleeve. "And I never have a hankie when I need one." She tried to laugh.

I pulled a handkerchief from my sleeve and handed it to her.

"Thanks," she said and blew her nose. "Naomi, I wish Walter was more like Henry."

"What?" I said.

"You know," she said, "quiet, steady. Henry doesn't have to talk to prove he's there." She folded the handkerchief and blew her nose again. "When you and Henry are together, he hardly says a word, and he's not always driving you crazy doing things for you. But I can see the way he looks at you when you're talking to someone else. I know how much Walter loves me. I just wish he was more like Henry in the way he showed it. He really was more like Henry when we first married."

"No," I said. I was so surprised at what Emma had just said that I didn't know what to say next. I hadn't intended to say anything, and now Emma looked at me and waited, her eyes asking "no what?"

I wanted to say it's not what you think and your dreams would die and he'd come to you drunk every night and spend himself and leave you empty and you would finally pull away from him and steel yourself against it just to save yourself. I wanted to say you've been wrong all these years in what you thought you saw, no matter that you have always seen so much with those gray eyes and you have been right so many times with me. You have seen what you wanted to see and I have never understood all the things you assumed I understood and I can never understand because I've never lost a child and never had one to begin with and you can never understand because you have never felt yourself smothering, dying for a breath of air beneath the inert body of a man who has anesthetized himself against your touch.

"No, you don't really," I said. "You're just upset. And for

good reason maybe. I wish I could change something and make it better for you, make the pregnancy easier somehow, but I can't." There was only one thing in all of this that I really did understand, and that was the feeling of being trapped.

"Emma," I said, "I envy you."

"What in the world do you mean by that?" Emma said. "You want to be fat and ugly and not be able to do the dishes because you can't reach the sink?"

"No," I said. I wasn't sure how to say what was coming into my mind. "I never asked you why you married Walter. I married Henry to get away from my father and my aunt and uncle, to spit in the face of polite society. I had some crazy idea in my mind of him taking me away somewhere. I was sixteen."

Emma smiled. "I remember the talk," she said. "Henry Bass running off with the preacher's niece. All the girls in town worked real hard at being scandalized."

I hesitated. What I wanted to say was becoming confused. I wanted to tell Emma everything, to have Emma understand, but it didn't sound right. The suffocation I felt as I lay exhausted under Henry. Uncle Isaac Samuel bent over me praying that the Lord would gird up my loins, his eyes closed, his greasy breath pressing me into the pillow, using up all of the air, making me dizzy as I lay in my bed and hated him. My father Jeremiah Stotts sitting across the table from me with his hands folded in front of him, looking at the wall behind me, his face chalky, the clerical collar snug beneath his beard. If Henry looks at me now when I talk to someone else, saying nothing, doing nothing, it is not my fault. There is nothing I can do. I have to have air to breathe. And he has never asked me why it happened. Never asked what the problem is.

When Mama's coffin arrived at our house, I watched through the window of Mrs. Simms' high-ceilinged parlor next door, the silence of the big empty room, the dark red rug that covered all but the outside edge of the floor, the padded window seats, the occasional voice of someone coming or going at my father's house. It was not my fault. Things happen that cannot be explained. How could I tell Emma what I did not understand myself?

"It's when Walter talks to you," I said, "that I envy you most. Henry and I used to talk more."

I kept snapping beans. Henry and I used to talk, late at night just before we fell asleep. We talked about us, about what we wanted. Henry wanted to laugh in the face of Emma's father, Ben Sinclair, in the face of his condescension when he bought lumber. But I could hardly tell that to Emma.

What I wanted was simple. After escaping from my uncle Isaac Samuel's house, I wanted only one thing—for the Right Reverend Jeremiah Stotts, my exalted father, to acknowledge his sins against me and to ask my forgiveness. That would be the turning point, the crux, when the fulcrum of my life would tilt. And I would consider carefully, and forgive him, maybe, and allow him to die in peace.

But I had known from the beginning that it would never happen. And it was like a thorn in my foot.

And somewhere along the line I had begun to feel the suffocation. I had never been a drinker, but I began to envy

Henry the oblivion whiskey offered him. And I pretended to be asleep when he came to bed. And he said nothing. Did nothing. And the silence became heavy. And I wanted to tell Emma that it wasn't my fault, that none of it was my fault.

Emma blew her nose again. "I'll wash this and get it back to you," she said. She shifted in the chair. "The crazy thing is, I've always loved it when Walter and I talk. I know I'd hate it any other way. But lately when he says something to me, I get so mad I can't be civil. I can't be nice even when I want to."

"Yes," I said. I knew exactly what Emma meant in that particular. The two voices inside me, one a whisper, blown away on the storm wind of the other.

I heard myself, standing in front of the old schoolhouse, daring Henry to take me away and marry me, Henry sitting on the steps, his hat pushed back, a stem of fescue between his teeth. Who was I when I said those words? A mad sixteen-year-old girl sick of the narrow hallway of her life. Bravado, it had all been bravado. And now I am afraid of being alone. Plain, and alone. No children, no husband, no mother, no father.

I leaned down and got Emma's bowl of green beans and held it out to her. "You want to snap some more beans?" I said.

"No," Emma said, her voice tired. "Let's forget it. I'll throw the rest of them out."

"No you won't," I said. "There's not that many. I'll finish them up. You relax."

Emma leaned her head back against the rocker. I put her bowl down and began again to snap the beans.

27

October
The Valley of the Shadow

SHE FELT LIKE ONE OF HOMER BARTON'S FAT, OLD SOWS when they finally lie down and refuse to get up till the piglets are born. All fat and jowls and tits, and hardly any legs to carry it all. Afraid if she sat down, she wouldn't be able to get up again.

The late October leaves fell in a steady whisper of yellow, red, orange, and brown. Walter had left early for the mill. Emma wished it were Sunday so that Walter could stay home with her and she could rest all day.

She drank a cup of coffee at the dining room table, the newspaper lying open in front of her. She lumbered around the house, her breath heaving. She stopped frequently and stood with her eyes closed.

Along the bottom edge of the gully across the road, among the white oaks, red oaks, hickory, wild cherry and dogwood, the sun was bright, and the gully moved with color.

She stood beside the dining room table. On the front page of the newspaper an ad in bold letters stretched three columns wide down half the page. POSITIVELY THE ONLY

BIG SHOW COMING THIS SEASON. RINGLING BROTHERS, WORLD'S GREATEST SHOWS AND THE STUPENDOUS SPLENDOR, GLISTENING SPECTACLE.

The only circus this season, and she couldn't go to it even if she could convince Walter to take her on the train to Fayetteville and spend the night. Which she couldn't. Not in a thousand years. She would not be on the square in Fayetteville at ten o'clock in the morning next Tuesday for the "Grandest, Longest, Richest Street Parade Ever Seen." She had never seen a real live honest-to-goodness elephant.

The circus was just one more thing she couldn't do. She could look in the mirror instead.

She had left the front door open, and the breeze felt good on her neck. The night had been cold, and the morning was chilly. But she was hot and she wanted the air moving. She went to the kitchen. She scraped the leftover eggs from her plate into the pan of scraps, feeling bloated and clumsy. She had to stand sideways at the sink, and her back ached. Bending over the bed or trying to move the broom around her ponderous stomach made her shoulders and legs ache. She wanted to finish the tedious chores, sit on the porch, rock back and forth, breathe the cool air as deeply as her belly would allow, gather her strength for a walk in the gully, in the trees, the colors.

She tried to raise the kitchen window in front of her to get the breeze, but she could not even reach across the sink with both hands and lift. She dropped the plate and knife into the sink, where they clattered, and she turned away, gripped the counter edge on each side of her, and stamped her foot.

"I hate this," she said aloud, and her eyes watered. She looked up at the ceiling, but the answer was not written there, and she could not see into heaven.

With a shrug, she turned back to the sink and finished the dishes. After making the bed, she could not make herself pick up the broom. The house was hot, and her forehead felt clammy when she brushed back her hair. She would go to the woods, in spite of what Walter said.

She had not been having that much trouble getting back up the path from the gully, and Walter should not be feeding the chickens before he leaves for the mill. It was her job. He was just too cautious.

She shrugged again and swung back around to the sink. She took the pan of scraps out onto the front porch, let the screen door close behind her, but did not pull the door shut. She had not put any wood on the fire, so the door didn't matter. She was too hot, and a fire was just a waste of wood.

At the front edge of the porch she stopped, slid her left hand around to her lower back and tried to arch backwards. Her eyes closed in a grimace at the pain, and she grunted. Standing with her head back slightly, she waited for the pain in her back to ease, and she opened her eyes. A straight line of clouds stretched across the sky, the front edge of a dark cloud bank moving in from the west.

Maybe a little rain in the afternoon would cool things off.

She took the two steps down from the porch like the old women at the church, at a slight side angle, first one foot down, then the other, then one foot to the ground, then the other. She stood for a moment, catching her breath and ignoring the slight dizziness she felt.

"You'd better come soon," she said to her stomach, "or you'll be the one carrying me instead of the other way around."

She walked slowly toward the road, favoring her left side with a slight limp, the catch she felt there running down into her leg.

Didn't know anyone could feel so ugly, she thought. Didn't know anyone could be so slow.

She wanted to throw the pan of scraps across the road and let the chickens fend for themselves. But the wind gusted, and the treetops across the way shifted back and forth, scattering the mid-morning sun through their branches. The woods were where her life had turned back into its familiar channel after the death of Joshua, like the Damascus road to Saul of Tarsus, where he was struck down, blinded by the light that let him see. Another paradox in the great web of mystery under which the God of Glory shrouded the world. And that same God had touched her there in the woods, just as he had touched Saul. Not with a blinding brightness, but with light filtered through the dying colors of autumn.

She filled her lungs with the cool air, then exhaled and filled them again. It was raining back in the west. The breeze was loaded with the smell of dusty moisture. Her nostrils flared.

Oh well, she thought, and her pinched lips twisted. I should be back to the house before nightfall if I keep this pace up.

The path down into the gully was steep, and her weight shifted back and forth from one foot to the other in short steps, and she stopped every few steps to rest and catch her breath. Before she was halfway down the slope, the chickens rushed up to meet her and clustered around her, clucked and darted back and forth on the path, turned their heads from one side to the other, as one eye and then the other looked at the pan in her hand and searched the ground around them. She raised the pan and tried to kick the chickens away from her. Her breathing became quick and shallow, and she stopped again to rest. The chickens closed in on her in a tangle around her feet, clucking, their heads cocked first at her then at the ground in front of her. Her throat constricted, and she moaned softly, closing her eyes. Her mother had gone every morning to the chicken pen behind their house. Early morning sun lit her mother's face and hair, her apron clean white, the leghorns and reds scurrying to her from the coop. Her mother broadcast the feed with a wide sweep of her arm, and the grains as they fell became tiny stars that floated in the air and swirled around her, bright in the sun, dissolving her in a gold whirlwind.

The pan of scraps dropped from Emma's hand and clattered to the ground at her feet and slid a little way down the path, where the chickens clamored after it. She opened her eyes and squinted, trying to clear her vision and steady herself.

The colors spread out before her, flailed in the wind that gusted across the road behind her. Her body was becoming weightless, rising into the colors that swirled around her like the prism of light reflected on a drop of grease floating in a skillet when the afternoon sun slanted through the kitchen window. She smiled as she relaxed into the colors and let her head loll backwards.

The clean, straight line of dark clouds had moved farther east into the morning sunlight, and at that moment it moved across the sun itself, and the sun became a disc of gray, and the long edge of the cloud bank looked ethereal, bright with the last of the sun's light.

Emma staggered back a step or two and struggled to catch her balance. If she reached out in front of her, she thought she could grasp the porch rail and steady herself, maybe sit down in the rocker and rest. That was all she wanted, a little rest. But when she leaned forward, hands stretched out, she lurched down the path, staggered and lost her balance.

The colors spread out before her, muted like the colors of the quilt that covered the bed. She gave herself to the forward movement, raised her right knee to climb onto the bed, and closed her eyes.

The cluster of chickens at the pan scattered squawking and beating their wings as she fell into them.

She collapsed to the ground like a puppet dropped from the hand, and she rolled and slid down the path to its base, where the chickens again gathered round her, walked stiffly in the sudden silence, hesitating, their clucking subdued, their heads cocked as they searched the ground and pecked among the pebbles, scratched, backed up and looked, scratched again, and walked on.

The patter of raindrops began on the ground around them. The empty pan, which lay near her on the ground at the bottom of the path, echoed the pelting of the rain on its upturned base, and two of the chickens scuttled over to peck around it.

She lay sprawled over to one side of her stomach, with one leg bent at the knee in front of her, the other at an awkward angle behind, as if she were trying to run in spite of her stomach. One arm stretched out above her head, and the other hand lay lightly on her cheek. A thin line of blood edged its way slowly from her temple down across her closed eyelid just below the brow, paused at the bridge of her nose, then rolled forward again, and dripped steadily onto the taffeta of her dress splayed out under her face.

A low rumble of thunder rolled from behind the hillside toward the house. Only a thin line of blue sky remained in the east, and the woods around the coop faded in the dim light. The limbs of the trees pulsed in the wind. Leaves showered the clearing around her, and when lightning crackled across the sky to the south, the chickens moved toward the short ladder leading to the dark opening into the coop.

She breathed in short gasps punctuated by motionless pauses. As the rain increased, it matted the hair on the back of her neck and thinned the trickle of blood from her temple.

She opened her eyes. She felt cool at last. A few inches from her face, the stems of the wild fescue grass bent toward the ground under the weight of the rain, and water dripped from the tassels at their heads, which bobbed in the large raindrops that pelted the ground around them. She thought of the circus, of the acrobats in white tights, their hair greased back, their teeth polished white, their leather wrist bands. Thought of them swinging through the air on trapezes. Thought of trick riders circling the center ring, bobbing with knees flexed on the horses' haunches. Thought of the elephant lumbering in, on its upturned trunk a monkey dressed in blazing colors.

Her vision blurred, and she closed her eyes. Daddy would come outside and make her come in out of the rain in a minute. Mama would fret about lightning and the cold and would send him out to get her.

She saw herself and her father making a game of getting back to the house. He pretended to drop a penny, and they searched for it on their hands and knees in the grass, in the rain. He would say, "Here it is. No, no, that's a pebble. Here it is. No, no, that's a stick." And he would repeat the animated act, each object more ridiculous, until they doubled over with laughter and went to the house soaking wet, Emma riding on his shoulders and wearing his broad-brimmed hat.

The pain in her abdomen made her cry out.

When he came, he would pick her up and hold her lying across his arms, and he would coo, "Emmy-jemmy, what's the matter? All your bones are going clatter."

"Papa!" she cried, the pain striking through her abdomen and up her back. The thunder rumbled overhead, a hollow roll, then a heavy boom that vibrated through her.

"Walter, help me!" she said and held her breath and tried to concentrate. She pictured Walter at the door. He bent down to kiss her goodbye, then turned and walked away. As he dropped into the seat on the wagon, he turned and looked across the front yard at her. When he raised his hand into the air, the wires of the screen door seemed to run together, and she could not see him.

A rivulet of water ran down the path, dammed momentarily by her foot and ankle, and found its way around the toe of her shoe before spreading out into the clearing.

Dark clouds had covered the last line of blue in the east. The gully darkened, as if dusk were falling. The rain, whipping in sheets down the road above where Emma lay, slacked up, and the wind calmed to a breeze. The rain stopped. The storm left behind it, as quickly as it had arrived, a dusky, dripping world. In the gully, the dripping from the trees around the clearing, the trickling of the water down the path, and the soft clucking of the hens, roosting safely in the dark hen house, were the only sounds.

28

That Evening
Purity

MY GOD, MY GOD, Why hast thou forsaken me? Those were Jesus' very last words when he was dying on the cross.

Last night I had just put Jackson Lee to bed, Sarah June and Billy Boy were playing Slap Jack on the living room floor while the others watched, and Mama was cleaning up the supper dishes, which is a miracle. I've about quit asking for any help from her. Daddy was dozing in the rocking chair in front of the fireplace with his pipe hanging down from his mouth almost to his shirt. I swear he is going to set himself on fire one of these days.

I heard the horses coming at a dead run from down toward Walter and Emma's, and then Walter screaming "whoa" and the wagon pulling up with a clatter and his boots hitting the porch. The door almost came off the hinges with his pounding on it. Daddy's pipe dropped into his lap, and he lurched up slapping bright little coals off his overalls. Sarah June screamed, and I heard a dish crash into the bottom of the sink in the kitchen.

Walter yelled "Purity, please!"

I don't have to tell you I lunged for that door with my

heart clear up in my mouth. When I opened the door, I screamed worse than Sarah June. I thought Walter had been shot. There was blood all over his shirt and pants and his hands and a smudge of blood right next to my face on the door where Walter had pounded.

Walter had a wild look in his eyes like he had gone crazy, and I had this absolutely terrible thought that maybe he had murdered Emma in a passionate frenzy and had come here half crazed to finally speak his mind. My heart was just about to break at the tragedy of it, but I could barely say "Oh, Walter, no," before he started talking like a madman telling me to go get Hamilton Blake, that Emma had fallen down the gully and was bleeding to death and had lost the baby.

He didn't know the half of it yet, of course.

He didn't even give me time to answer, just turned and ran to the wagon and lashed those horses back down the road. Well, if there was anybody in my family but me that could drive a buggy faster than a trot, I would have gone with Walter. He couldn't have been much use to Emma in his state. But Daddy is just an old woman when it comes to driving a buggy and would never have broken a walk in the dark like that. And no one else in that house can handle the horse even in broad daylight.

Daddy was already hitching Ginger to the buggy when I got to the barn. Her eyes were skittish and she snorted. Animals have a sixth sense about human tragedy. When I climbed up into the seat, Daddy told me to drive careful.

It was awful, having to go rouse Hamilton Blake instead of going straight to Walter's house, but I made that trip in short order, my mind a jumble of pictures of what Emma would look like when I got back, all that blood on Walter and all.

People say that trouble is never as bad as you imagine it will be, but I have not found that to be true. Real trouble will win out over a person's imagination nine times out of ten, it seems to me. That was certainly true this time.

When I burst through Walter's front door, he was in their bedroom right there on the left, sitting beside Emma, who was stretched out on the bed. He was rubbing her hand and saying her name over and over. She was gray as a ghost. I thought sure she was already dead.

Then I saw it, just on the other side of her. The baby, just a blue and muddy lump on the bed spread. I had to close my eyes.

I said, "Walter, get up. Let me see if there's anything I can do."

He said, "Don't let her die, Purity. Don't let her die." But he didn't move.

I pulled him up off the bed and told him to get some water heating up. I could tell there wasn't a fire anywhere in the house and hadn't been all day. It was cold in there.

Emma's skin felt just like a fish when I touched her wrist, wet and clammy, but she had a pulse. Not much of one, but her heart was beating. I lifted an eyelid, but there was nobody there. I didn't see how she could live another minute. I was just sick.

Think, Purity, think, I said to myself. You have got to do something quick. She was covered in mud like she had been thrown around in the corral, and again I thought with this horrible feeling in my stomach that Walter might have killed her.

The lower part of her dress was soaked with blood, so I pulled it up to see about the bleeding. It still just makes me sick to think of it. Walter had stuffed a wadded-up pillow case there between her legs and had pulled her legs together on it to try and stop the bleeding. The pillow case was soaked through, and I wasn't sure I ought to take it off before Hamilton Blake got there. But I had to do something. I couldn't just stand there like a doorstop.

When I pulled her legs apart and eased that pillow case out of the way, my heart almost stopped. There was another baby trying to come.

Oh my God, I thought, oh my God, twins. Walter, I thought, what have you done?

I heard Hamilton Blake's buggy come thundering into the front yard. When he hurried in the front door I said, "There is one baby dead, but she's having another one, and she has lost a whole lot of blood but she still has a pulse."

I knew at that moment that I could have been a nurse, knew from the rush of excitement I felt as I said those words, that I could spend the rest of my life in the middle of a medical emergency. I stood there, ready to be Hamilton Blake's extra set of hands striving valiantly but hopelessly to save a life. Walter would see me in a whole new light, and I would say nothing about my suspicions.

I should have known better. At that very second Faith McCormick, who must be the oldest practicing midwife in Arkansas, came huffing and puffing through the door. All two hundred pounds of her.

The McCormick farm is just at the end of the rainbow curve between our place and town, and of course, I did not even consider stopping to see if Faith was available. Why would I? But Hamilton Blake is set in his ways, and he picked her up on his way out here. I was sure she was too old. She would get in the way. We didn't need her.

I could have been very helpful to Hamilton Blake there in that bedroom, in spite of having to work around Faith McCormick, which is not easy considering how much of her there is to work around. But the first thing out of his mouth was "Purity, go get some water heating."

"I had Walter do it first thing when I got here," I said, feeling a rush of pride in my forethought.

I could see Hamilton Blake would rather have had me there to help him than Faith, but it was one of those delicate situations. He was trapped.

"Then check and be sure he's done it," he said, "and then get a fire started in that wood stove." He never even looked up from the instruments he was spreading on the bed at Emma's feet.

What could I say? I didn't say a thing. Just walked out of that bedroom feeling how cruel the world could be. Faith McCormick was tearing strips off an old sheet.

Walter was standing in the kitchen watching that pot of water on the stove with a look in his eyes that made me want to cry. Like all of this could be washed away if that water would just boil, like everything in his life was depending on those first lonely bubbles coming swiveling up from the bottom of the pot.

I reached out and touched his arm, and it was all I could do not to say, "It's alright, Walter, I'll take care of you." And I pushed the thought of him murdering Emma right out of my mind.

When I touched him, he looked over at me and barely smiled, like he wanted to smile at me but just couldn't quite make it.

I told him it would be a big help if he could get a fire started in the living room. I could see he was grateful for something to do, anything to get away from that impossible water. A watched pot never boils.

I told him to wash his hands and I would get him a clean shirt. As he turned to leave, I said, "You haven't had any supper, have you?"

"No," he said and looked around the kitchen as if remembering what it was. "No," and he turned for the front room.

Well, it was what I could do under the circumstances. Banished from the real work of trying to save Emma, I would have to provide for those still with us. Faith's husband, Daniel, had gone off to tell Ben and Martha Sinclair. God only knew how many people would be tramping in here before long.

Ham and biscuits and flour gravy was the best I could do.

29

That Night
Walter

FROM WHERE I STOOD IN THE KITCHEN, I could see Dr. Blake come out of the bedroom. According to the clock over the kitchen stove, it was midnight. Faith McCormick, who sat in the rocker near the front door staring at the open grate of the wood stove, looked up when he came in. The dim light from the lantern on the table beside Faith faded the flower pattern on the wall behind her to gray and brown. She filled the rocker, her excess seeping over the arm rests, but her feet barely reached the floor. Her eyes were bloodshot and watery in a face that sagged like melting putty, and she held a white handkerchief wadded in her lap as she rocked slowly back and forth, her feet lifting and settling with each rock. Ben Sinclair was asleep on the couch.

Hamilton Blake spoke quietly as he pulled his coat from the hat tree by the door and put it on. I had to listen real hard to hear him. "Faith, it's late," he said. "Martha can handle things here. Your Daniel will be worrying about you."

"Oh, Daniel quit worryin' about me years ago," she said. "And besides, he thinks I'm too mean to get into any trouble."

Her voice was tired.

They spoke to each other as if I didn't exist. As if it weren't my house. They hadn't let me in to see Emma since Dr. Blake arrived.

Dr. Blake put on his hat, pushed his glasses up on his nose, and looked through the dining room at me in the kitchen door. I went back to the sink, to cleaning up after the supper Purity Morrison had fixed earlier in the evening. I was the child sent off to do busywork just to get me out from underfoot.

Faith McCormick said, "I'll be stayin' for a while to take care of the bed linens. They'll need a soaking in cold water and a good, hard washing if we're gonna save them. Ben will drop me by the house." And then she said, as if I wasn't there, as if it were not my house, "That poor lost calf will be wandering the house all night, doing more harm than good if somebody doesn't see to him."

More harm than good. What more harm could I do than was already done?

"Just check before you leave to be sure she's not bleeding again," Hamilton Blake said. "Martha's going to stay the night. I'll stop by Henry and Naomi's when I get back to town. Somebody ought to tell them. And I'll be back first thing in the morning to see about Emma."

I put down the plate and the towel and went back to the kitchen door. Dr. Blake walked to the front door, and as his hand turned the knob, Mrs. McCormick spoke.

"What in heaven's name could have come over the child to crawl off into the woods like that?"

He pulled the door open and turned to her as he pushed open the screen. He shook his head. "She's strong," he said. He shifted his bag to the other hand. "If we could have saved the babies. At least one of them. Left her something." He pushed his hat down snug on his head.

She said, "I hate to think of Walter finding her there," (as if I were not standing there), "one of the babies on the ground."

She hated to think of me finding her there. She hated to think of me. "Don't worry," I wanted to say.

"Good night, Faith," Hamilton Blake said and went out the door.

I tried to think, to remember, to understand what he had said. Martha would stay. Maybe Ben would go back to the farm. Hamilton Blake would stop by Henry and Naomi's. They should be told. He wishes he could leave her something. There was something lying on the bed in the spare bedroom. One of them already on the ground. What could have made her do it? Made her. What could have made her?

I went back to the sink, picked up a plate and the towel, started drying the plate, though it was already dry.

Faith would take care of the sheets. Faith would help. I had to grit my teeth and stifle a laugh. It was almost a joke. Faith would help. The plate slipped from my hand and clattered in the sink, but didn't break.

She lay in the bedroom, and they hadn't let me see her since Hamilton Blake arrived. And in the other bedroom, what Dr. Blake couldn't leave her.

I dropped the towel in the sink and went in the dining

room. The clopping hoof-fall of Hamilton Blake's horse moved slowly up the road. I went to the window. Dr. Blake leaned forward in his buggy in the moonlight, leaned on his knees, and the lines drooped slack. The bowl of his pipe glowed as he drew in a long lungful of smoke, making a sharp silhouette of his face and a strange orange reflection on the lens of his glasses.

I would go see Emma. She would need time.

He would tell Henry and Naomi.

Faith would help. Faith would help.

The buggy eased into the shadows at the far end of the field.

30

That Night
Faith McCormick

BABIES BORN DEAD OR DYING SOON AFTER are not new to me. I have been helping deliver babies in Madison County for a good thirty years. And I am aptly named. Faith. I have faith, a heart as strong as a post oak. And I am faithful, with a will as pliant as a willow sapling, bending always to the subtle currents of God's will. I have developed an ear sensitive to His voice. I can always offer some comfort to a grieving young mother. Always. Chapter and verse. Submission to the mysteries of His will. Faith.

And I am not, praise Him, as some are, who are drawn away of their own lusts and enticed. Then when lust hath conceived, it bringeth forth sin; and sin, when it is finished, bringeth forth death. Wherefore put away all filthiness and overflowing of wickedness and receive with meekness the engrafted word, which is able to save your souls. Book of James, first chapter, verses 15 and 25.

The Basses, for instance. Virgil Bass and his brood. Or the Farleys. Tommy Farley. Trouble from day one. All of them drawn away of their own lusts. All of them bringing forth sin, bringing forth death.

After Hamilton Blake left Emma's house, I sat there by the fire trying to get warm. The bedsprings creaked in the bedroom, and I leaned forward and listened, but it was quiet, and I was plum wore out, so I sat back again. That old rocker groaned like a dungeon door every time I shifted my weight. Made my lips twitch forward, which is a habit I've had most of my life, whenever I'm unsettled.

A dish clattered in the kitchen, and I got up and walked over to where I could see through the dining room to the back of the house. Walter was still standing at the sink rubbing the plates with a towel. That was a good supper Purity Morrison fixed, though Hamilton and I are the only ones who stopped to eat a little when we could. I don't understand why a girl like Purity gets passed over. Good looks aren't everything.

I looked into the bedroom while I was up. Emma, not much more color than the sheets, breathed shallow. Martha Sinclair was sleeping in a chair at the side of the bed. I went back to the living room stove. It's hard to stay warm at my age.

Trials and tribulations. We all fall into them. We must count it all joy when we fall, knowing this, that the trying of your faith worketh patience. James, chapter one, verses two and three. For every good and perfect gift is from above and cometh down from the Father of lights. Verse seventeen.

Ask and ye shall receive. But ye ask and receive not because ye ask amiss, that ye may consume it upon your lusts. Chapter four, verse three.

Lust is the root of all evil.

Lord Jesus, how did Emma end up married to Walter Bass? Men like that have always lusted after the daughters of the saints. It's the gospel truth. The Basses have never been anything but pure poison from the day they came to Delaney. Able Solomon saw them arrive, says it was a sight to see, Virgil and Lilly Bass rolling into town in a rickety wagon. Says it was clear enough right away that something was wrong with Lilly Bass. Sat there in the wagon with that bonnet covering her face, hunkered down like she was dead sorry to be alive. Pregnant he said. That would have been Henry, I reckon.

I never did see Lilly myself. Not once. She never even let anyone attend the birth of her children except some relation of hers from up toward Crosses.

With Hamilton Blake and myself ready and willing. It was an insult in a way. And so I never did see her. Never. But you can tell a tree by its fruit the Bible says, and both those boys are misfits. Bad blood if you ask me. Blood always tells.

I picked up the poker and dug into the coals under the burning logs. Sparks swirled up the draft. Then I laid the poker on the metal pad beneath the stove and squatted in front of the door, my arms resting on my knees, comfortable like, and watched the fire. It's my favorite position to think in. Daniel laughs at me, says I look like one of them booda statues.

As I watched the fire, I was glad, in a way, that Emma wasn't conscious, wasn't able to ask where her baby was, and wasn't able, before she got the answer, to look at Faith McCormick with that horrible look of fear hanging onto the edge of trust, knowing the worst but trusting me to change it, to deny it. It's a terrible burden to speak those words and watch the soul behind the eyes of a young mother fall over that edge into the darkness of the truth. It was all the worse with Emma, who seemed to me still to be a child herself.

The fire in the wood stove burned warm as I rocked slowly back and forth and looked past the flames and into the heart of the kingdom, the white hot heart of the glory of God.

Emma was the only pregnancy Martha ever had, and I was there thank you Jesus to assist at the birth. When Emma was a little girl, Ben just sat back in wonder and watched, leaving Martha to try and keep control. I prayed for Jesus' mercy and his grace to bring her back from that dark edge.

A pan scraped in the sink in the kitchen. I pushed myself up, grunted as I straightened my legs, and went to the bedroom where Emma lay asleep. The lantern was turned down low, the room a shadow world. Martha Sinclair, leaning over onto the edge of the bed, was asleep, her head resting on the crook of her arm.

I decided to get Walter to go draw the water for me, get him out of the house, out of the kitchen before he broke half of Emma's dishes.

As I bent down to pick up the pile of sheets by the bed, I looked at Emma, pale from the loss of blood, gray in the lamplight. She looked like a picture lying there, like one of those pictures of the Virgin Mary forgive me Jesus.

But there was no child. It was a lonesome picture without the child.

31

The Next Day
Henry

THIS IS WHAT I DID.

I was in the kitchen. My eyes adjusted to the darkness, but even those things I could see were slipping, blurring slightly as the whiskey beat down the dull ache in my temples. My nostrils spread as I sucked in air, staring down at the glass I held loosely in my hand. My arms rested on the table. From the darkness beyond the screen door, the low voice of a bullfrog rolled across the pasture.

Jug-o-rum, jug-o-rum, jug-o-rum.

I knew it was getting late.

My head moved back and forth to his rhythm, like it was pushed by the sound, like when I sat in a rocker on the porch. Through the open door, the chilly air drifted in, moist with the dew that weighted it. The sound of Naomi's footsteps in the room above me broke through the fog in my mind. She didn't know. She was blissfully ignorant. It would hurt her when I told her, maybe in the morning. For the moment I would stay there in the dark, in the easy dark. It felt good there. Every breath was good there, good all the way down into my belly, and when I exhaled I felt good. Good just to breathe.

I would sing if I could. Jug-o-rum.

Glad you're still up, Dr. Blake had said. But he had hesitated, looked past me toward the dark living room. Then watching me real close, he told me about Emma, slowly, as if he spoke to a child. Do you understand? he had said. And I, the tumbler half empty in my hand, already feeling each breath good in my belly, had almost laughed. Understand. Did I understand? The babies were dead. Emma would live. What was there to understand? Hamilton Blake looked into my eyes, started to say more, then turned and left without speaking.

I breathed again through the nostrils, lifting my head up straight, and exhaled slowly, my lips pushed out. The skin on my cheeks and neck came alive, tingling. I looked up at the ceiling. It was late. The floor creaked as Naomi passed the foot of the bed. She must have sat up later than usual reading. Just like her not even to notice when Doctor Blake stopped by. I closed my eyes and imagined her loose hair falling down around her shoulders, the shrug of her shoulders as she slipped off the housecoat, the way she leaned her head back and shook out her hair and pulled it together with her free hand and draped it down around one side of her neck.

She would lay the housecoat on the chair at the head of the bed and turn back the covers. She would lift her nightgown, baring her legs above the knees, and slip forward onto the bed and sit back on her heels, her knees still uncovered as she fluffed the pillows.

I had seen it all, night after night in the first year of our marriage, before it went wrong, before separate rooms became more comfortable. Back then I poured only one glass and put the bottle back in the cabinet, squeaking the snug cork back into place, my breath quickening as I sat in the dark with the tumbler on the table in front of me, feeling its thick smoothness against my palm and fingers, the sweet smell of the bourbon drifting to my nostrils. I would think of Naomi as I sat there, and I would picture her slipping off her shoes, dropping the dress to the floor around her, unpinning her hair and shaking it loose. And as the first sip of bourbon burned along the edges of my tongue, the heat of it sliding down my throat, warming my stomach, I would breathe deeply.

Then the slow steps to the sink and the careful rinsing of the glass and the placing of the glass top-down on the folded towel at the sink's edge. I would walk slowly out through the living room, carefully avoiding in the dark the sofa in front of the fireplace, my steps knocking on the hardwood, then thumping lightly on the rug behind the sofa, then knocking on the hardwood again before I reached the stairs. The routine had always been the same.

In the dark of the kitchen, I lifted the tumbler to my lips, tilted my head back, and let the last of the whiskey slide into my mouth, let the glass rest for a few seconds on my upturned face before letting my head fall forward. I closed my eyes, my chin rested on my chest. The aroma from the empty glass, resting just below my face, roused me, and I raised it to my nose and breathed in.

I looked again at the ceiling, listened to the silence. I set the glass on the table and pushed it away from me, pushed hard at its indistinct outline, at the small, accusing face of it staring up at me. It slid part way across the table top, turned on its side, and rolled off the edge, clattering on the chair seat and then the floor. It rolled, slow, gritty, on the wood surface, and stopped with a quiet bump on the cabinet base.

The outline of the screen door separated the darkness of the room from the darkness outside. My stomach tightened at the darkness that surrounded me, at my marriage, at the blind, mad providence that gave Walter children, then killed them, that gave me and Naomi no children at all. And finally at Naomi, who in public laid her hand on my arm like any other wife, who as we stood in a circle of people, laughed with a knowing look and shook her head as if we shared in the common mysteries of married life, while in our home she was silent as a stone, distant, and empty in her denial.

When I stood, the chair grated on the wooden floor, and I leaned forward on my clenched fists, my eyes shut tight. I didn't care what happened to Walter and his crazy wife Emma. I had nothing to do with them, nothing to do with their children dying.

As a boy, I leaned over the table that same way, feeling the sting of the long hickory switch across my back and legs, hearing the words of Lilly Bass hissing through clenched teeth, grunting with the exertion, striking with each forced word.

"Wretched, stubborn, bone-headed stupidity. I am your mother. I am your mother. Do you understand me?"

And I, even as a child, had understood that it was my silence that enraged her. And I had gritted my teeth and breathed slowly. Silence had become my weapon. It had worn her down, left her impotent, left her each time weeping, and each time she had thrown the hickory stick aside and hovered over me, reached out to me, unable to touch me. And pushing the strands of hair away from her own face she would leave me.

And now I knew the other side of silence. I could not remember when it began—did not know when Naomi's whispers had ceased in the darkness in which we clutched at each other, or when she stopped calling my name as we finished. But I had felt a cold lump in my stomach when our heat was spent in a silence that left me hollow, afraid, and angry at the emptiness I felt as I lay staring at the ceiling. At her silence.

And the silence spread, like oil on water, suffocating, from the bedroom into every room of the house until the house rang like a mausoleum with our footsteps.

I turned from the table and steadied myself with my right hand. Leaving the uncorked bottle standing near the table's edge, I started for the living room. I reached out to the doorframe as I passed through it, unable to focus on anything in the darker room ahead of me. My boot heel caught on the edge of the rug, and I stumbled forward, righted myself on the back of the sofa, and stopped there to regain my balance before going on to the stairs.

A long time ago, Lily and Walter and me sat in a darkened room, a fire burning low in the hearth, the lantern on the table turned low. The clicking of the knitting needles chirped like a cricket from the dark corner, over the steady creaking of the rocker. Then the creaking of the rocker and the clicking of the needles stopped.

Lilly rose and started for the bedroom, stopped by me, pushed the hair off my forehead, licked her thumb and rubbed my cheek, pulled the top of my shirt together. Then she gripped my cheeks between her thumb and fingers and pulled my head around to face her. Her eyes shifted from one of my eyes to the other, her lips working.

"I do everything I can," she said, the words fluttering around me like her hands on my face and shoulders.

Gripping the banister with my right hand, pulling and balancing, I moved up the stairs, fumbling with the buttons of my shirt.

When I stopped at the landing, where the stairs turned back to my right and rose to the second story hallway above me, I turned and leaned against the wall in the corner. From the landing window beside me, the vague light from a sliver of moon filtered in, lighting the newel post in front of me. My eyes followed the banister into the darkness above. At the top, to the right, Naomi's bedroom door would be shut and my own, across the hall from hers, would be open.

I leaned away from the wall and stood swaying, looking up the stairs. I slid my jacket off my shoulders and let it fall behind me on the landing. Then I pulled my shirt out of my trousers and finished unbuttoning it before peeling it back and letting it fall. My suspenders hung down at the sides of my legs.

I stepped forward and took hold of the banister. My ears rang with a high-pitched hum. The surge in my belly was held in check by the slow steps, one foot at a time, each moving me nearer Naomi's room. The runner of carpet down the center of the stairs absorbed the sound of my boots. The wisp of my hand slid up the banister. Each slow breath brought the faint smells of Naomi, hanging in the air at the top of the stairs outside her room, the perfume, her clothes, her hair.

When I reached the top, I turned and sat with my feet on the steps. On the middle landing below me, the newel post stood dim, at its peak the polished wooden ball, and lying at its base, hardly visible, the jumble of clothes I had dropped. I took off my boots, then my socks, slowly, deliberately.

When I stood, I leaned back against the wall, the broad hallway between me and the door to Naomi's room. From the newel post at the top of the stairs, a short banister ran across the open front of the landing to the far wall, where it ended just a few inches from her door knob.

I drew in a deep breath, leaned my upper body, and grasped the newel post to pull myself forward. Holding onto the banister I balanced myself in the darkness and stood in front of her door, listening. Hearing nothing, I said quietly, "Naomi." My voice sounded out of place, like it came from somewhere else. I reached up with my left hand and held the door frame, reached down with my right and slowly turned the knob and pushed the door open and let it go. It swung three quarters of the way around to the wall and stopped without a sound. The faint traces of Naomi that I had breathed coming up the stairs were stronger when I stepped into the room.

Naomi said nothing, and I heard no movement from the bed. The shades were raised on both the windows, which stood open, and the sheer curtains on the window straight across from the door lifted slightly inward and settled back in the dim light.

The outline of the bed and of Naomi's form under the quilt took shape. I walked, my steps unsteady, padding softly on the cool hardwood floor, to the rug at the side of the bed. She breathed slow and steady. She was sleeping on her back, the quilt pulled up snug under her chin, her hair splayed out to the left of her face, her right hand showing above the quilt at the end of her pillow.

I leaned down to her, till my face stopped a few inches from hers. She had always fallen asleep easily, had always been a heavy sleeper. She had not awakened with the clanging bell and galloping horses of the volunteer fire crew the night the old house had burned at the mill. The noise had startled me awake, and I had thrown back the thin sheet under which we always slept in summer and stepped to the window to see which direction they were going. I saw the orange glow on the hillside in the direction of the mill and lit the lamp, dressed, and hurried out of the house to follow.

During all the excitement, Naomi had only rolled over and muttered in her sleep, pulling up the sheet. I had thought of it later, when I returned to the house, as I stood shaving, struggling to control the shaking of my hands as I remembered Walter standing in the glare of the fire, staring like a statue into the flames, the fire crew, too late, watching silently.

I had paused in my shaving and looked at my hands, at their trembling, and had in that moment despised Naomi's escape from the world, that deep refuge into which she retreated each night and from which she seemed to return each morning untouched by the awful possibilities that lay before her. Later, after I moved to the other room, I lay each night across the hall, stared at the ceiling, turned from side to side, listening to the silence from her room.

I reached down and jerked the covers back from her in one sweeping movement. She stirred, rolling her head to one side and laying her right arm across her abdomen. She had never in our first years slept without a nightgown. Her nakedness now, like a bull snake coiled in the hen's nest, stunned me. It would haunt me as I sat in the dark kitchen night after night during the following months. The whiteness of her skin, the dark circles of her breasts.

Why am I telling this? Talking won't make any difference. The lead weight of what I did will still lay like a fistful of bird shot in my stomach.

Her eyes fluttered, then opened wide. Her arms jerked up across her breasts and she screamed. My open hand shot out like a snake striking, snapping her head away from me on the pillow, cutting the scream short. Before she could scream again, my left hand covered her mouth, and my right grabbed the back of her neck. I shook her head back and forth and sprawled across her, my right leg hanging off the side of the bed.

"Damn you, shut up!" I said. "If you scream again, I'll break your neck, you hear?" My words, half whispered, rasped from a tight throat.

I struggled to force myself onto her, and as I raised

myself, lifting my weight to my knees, her arms came free. They struck blindly at my sides. She clutched my hair and pushed me away. I let go of her mouth and struck out at her arm, knocking it away from me, and before she could scream again, hit her again hard with my open hand on the side of her face. The loud crack of the blow to her cheek right in front of my own, and the grunt that wrenched from her, stopped me, afraid that I had killed her. But her head turned back to face me, and her body relaxed.

Holding myself above her, I felt the rise and fall of her breathing, smelled her hair and the faint tinge of my own sweat. She stared right at me, looked at me as if I were a lump of dirt on the side of the road. As if I had nothing to do with her. As if I were a thing that existed in the same world but had no value. And then I said it, not knowing I would, like it came out of nowhere, said to her, "Doctor Blake stopped by. I came up to tell you. Thought you might be interested in what he had to say."

Her expression didn't change. I was still just dirt by the road.

"He just came from Walter and Emma's," I said. Her eyes focused on me, a flicker of interest, but she said nothing.

"Emma fell, she's hurt pretty bad," I said and waited just long enough to drive the next part in like a nail with a single blow of the hammer, "lost a pair of twin boys."

Her eyes widened, and her lips trembled, and her mouth opened like she was going to speak. I felt a rush like when I lay out a full house with a pile of money on the table. But she saw something in my face that cut off her response, and her eyes watered, but she didn't cry. Her face just settled like melted wax into a pool. Nothing. And she looked right through me like I didn't even exist.

I gritted my teeth and dropped onto her. She made no sound, just stared at the ceiling, and when I was finished, I rolled away from her, unable to hold up my head. I felt empty, cheated, too dizzy to keep my eyes open.

Fighting to stay awake, I turned my head on the pillow to look at her again. She hadn't moved. Her eyes were fixed on the ceiling. Loose strands of her hair lay down across her mouth, dropping below her chin and twisting back over her shoulder at the base of her neck. She was still not crying.

As my head rolled away from her and my mind clouded, I thought that at least she would not find refuge in sleep that night and that for once I would leave her lying there impotent to change the world, defeated, while I would myself escape, slipping into the darkness of anesthetic sleep.

When I opened my eyes, pain throbbed at the base of my skull. I was still lying on my back. I turned my head slowly to the left and looked at the bed beside me. She was not there, and I listened carefully, barely breathing. I could hear the distant shuffling sounds of her movement in the kitchen, as I heard her every morning when I got up.

The cool air brought me awake, and I slid my legs off the side of the bed and sat up. My head pounded each time my heart beat. I opened and closed my mouth on the cottony dryness and the thick heaviness of my tongue. From the darkness outside the window, a mockingbird chattered. I got up, and dragging my bare feet across the cold wood floor, moved out into the hallway and down the runner of carpet toward the washroom at the end of the hall.

I stood before the mirror. My eyes were sunk deep in the skin hanging loose around them and my jowls sagged, like an old bloodhound.

Beside the sink stood the pitcher of warm water left by Naomi. In the flickering candlelight, my implements lay on the small shelf below the mirror. As I worked the brush into the shaving soap, I thought about going downstairs. Naomi and I seldom spoke in the mornings anyway. I always ate breakfast as she served the food and cleaned up. Running the straight razor back and forth over the leather strop beside the sink, I remembered Virgil Bass standing beside me in the pig-pen, the knife in his hand.

"You watch, boy, hear?" Virgil said. "It's gotta be done right, or you ruin the meat."

He stepped out quickly, pinned the pig to the fence with his leg, reached down and pulled up the pig's snout with his left hand and slid his right hand, holding the knife, around under the pig's throat. The pig squealed and struggled.

"Nice and clean, boy," he said and drew the knife back across the animal's throat, "and not too deep. Want 'em to bleed good but not die too quick." The pig screeched and struggled as Virgil held up its snout, lifting its front legs slightly off the ground.

He looked over at me, his eyes narrow and intense. "Just like when we jumped a Yankee picket," he said, "but we'd go plenty deep then, cut the windpipe quick like. Didn't want 'em to squeal and have 'em crawlin' all over us." He smiled. "I wasn't much older than you are now."

As the pig's cries weakened and its struggles subsided, Virgil wiped the knife blade on his pantleg and looked at it closely.

"Takes some practice," he said, then spit on the blade and wiped it again across the side of his leg.

My hands trembled as I looked at my lathered face and raised the razor to the base of my throat. With my other hand I touched the skin just below the Adam's apple and pulled down, stretching it taut. A pan clattered in the kitchen downstairs.

32

Three Days Later
Walter

A BLACK CRICKET crawled out from under the sofa, moved across the floor toward the stove, stopped every few inches, moved on again, its antennae testing the air around it. When I leaned forward and reached down for it, it leapt away with a twitch so quick that it seemed to disappear. It was there. Then it was gone. Like Joshua. There, then gone. Like the twins.

In autumn the crickets know they are going to die. The chill in the air seeps into them, and they know. The cicadas are already gone. The crickets try to put off what has to happen. And they come in out of the cold, hide in the cracks and crevices, rub their wings together for warmth, and the ringing of them fills every room.

The door of the potbellied stove stood open, and the fire made a low sizzling noise. I wondered if she heard the crickets, if the sound of them bothered her. For three days she had lain in the bed without speaking, sometimes asleep, sometimes propped up slightly on pillows, looking out the window to the woods across the road, as if she were still there, deep in the trees, crawling toward some place deeper still.

That was where I found her the night she fell. I followed the trail she dragged through the wet grass and mud, nearly a hundred yards down the gully from the coop. There was blood along the way, like she'd been dragged by a bear. I ran bent over, calling her name. There wasn't light left when I went down to the coop to begin with. The wood stove was cold, the front door open.

For three days afterward she didn't ask about the babies.

Purity Morrison came by every day to check in on her and help Martha take care of her. I didn't like the way Martha looked at me. The old look. It was all my fault again.

Emma didn't eat much. I tried to feed her, the eggs and toast I fried for breakfast, the lunches Purity brought, and in the evenings the suppers Martha fixed before going home to cook for Ben. When Emma did eat, she didn't respond to the food, and she seldom took her eyes from the window.

In the stove, the small blue flames of the fire licked around the edges of the short pieces of wood, and from one of the logs the heated sap oozed out and ran down and dripped into the bed of orange coals. The room smelled like hickory smoke. The firewood was from a big hickory tree that died during the summer on the hillside behind the house. It hissed and popped. If I could have stayed there and not moved, I might have rested for the first time since Emma fell.

I dreamed about Virgil one night. I woke up troubled in the dark. I struggled to go back to sleep, but the dream was too real, and I lay with open eyes and listened, and the clock in the dining room ticked. In the dream I stood on a creek bank open and grassy that stretched down to still water, a wide, deep hole that ran for fifty yards or so along a short bluff on the far side beneath the woods, all sycamore and cottonwood, with the sunlight angling toward me through the trees, glimmering on the water. I stood back up on a slight rise of ground, thirty or forty feet from the creek, looking at the sun that filtered through the leaves across the way, and Virgil stood between me and the creek, short and stocky, wearing loose work trousers held up by suspenders, a loose gray shirt with long sleeves and no collar, buttoned all the way up to his neck, and a broad-brimmed hat with a flat crown. He stood in profile, turned slightly toward the creek, and looked down at the water.

What bothered me most in the dream was that dragonflies filled the air around us. The air was heavy with the wet green smells of the water, and a hint of honeysuckle. It was my birthday, and Virgil had brought me there to teach me to fly. Dumb as it sounds, it seemed natural as could be in the dream. He turned toward me. The dragonflies filled the air around us.

I woke up from the dream and sat up. I was sleeping in the second bedroom so I wouldn't disturb Emma, and I got up and went to check on her, the floor cold on my bare feet. Then I lay in the dark with my eyes closed and tried to get the dream back, to look back up the creek bank, the image of Virgil Bass still fresh in my memory. I tried to burn away the mist that surrounded the face. But it remained veiled.

Sitting in the warm living room, the fire whispering to me, my head resting against the back of the rocker, I drifted into that easy place between awake and asleep. The memory of the dream—the image of Virgil standing on the bank, dragonflies hovering in the strange light— wavered in the mist of sleep that moved over me, and I thought for a moment I was dreaming it all again. I was surprised by the sound of my name being called out. In the confusion before my eyes opened, I thought Virgil had called out to me in a fearful, high voice. I sat up in the rocker, wide awake, my heart pounding, and listened.

The voice of Emma, soft and calm, came from the bedroom. "Walter."

I hurried to the side of the bed. She looked up at me as if she was waiting for me to answer a question.

"Your daddy's been here to see you every day," I said. "Sits right here on the side of the bed." I sat beside her and picked up her hand. Emma's mother had been here every day too. She was there most of that very day, straightening up after me, sitting in the cane chair by the bed praying and reading scripture.

"I know," Emma said. "I've seen him and Mama coming and going. And Purity and Doctor Blake." She looked straight at me. My eyes felt dry from lack of sleep.

"You look tired," she said. "You've been taking care of me like I was a child." She turned away from me back to the window, to the dark beyond it.

"Why didn't you say something to them? They were worried half to death about you," I said. The base of the lamp on the small stand at the head of the bed was white, with a farm scene painted on it, a boy holding out grass through a board fence toward a cow that grazed in lush meadow and ignored the boy. In the background a red barn rose at the other end of the field, a white frame house flanked by spreading shade trees. The flame in the lamp wavered, and the shadow of the curving iron bedstead danced on the wall. Her hand in mine was small, smaller than any grown woman's that I knew.

"Walter," she said, her voice like the slip of a knife on a whetstone, whispery but distinct. "Out there in the dark that night I saw it, saw it all," she said. "The angels' voices led me to the place. A pillar of fire that moved like a whirlwind—but slow. And around it the angels worshiping."

Her eyes watered and her lips trembled.

"And one stepped forward," she said, "his golden hands covering his face, and stood before the fire, and when he took his hands away his face was too bright to see but hidden as if in a mist."

She looked at me like a child looking down the steps into a dark cellar. The hair rose on the back of my neck, but I was so relieved to hear her voice, to have her look at me at all, that I said nothing, just looked down at her hands and ran the tips of my fingers over the surface of her knuckles, tracing their shape over and over.

She said, "And the Lord said to the angel 'Where have you come from?' And the angel said 'From going to and fro in the earth, and from walking up and down in it.' And the Lord said 'My servant Emma Bass is upright and faithful. She fears God and shuns evil.' And the angel said to him 'Is she faithful for nothing? Have you not made a hedge about her and her house?'"

She lifted her hand and covered her mouth, and tears slid

down both sides of her face. I didn't know what to say. This was crazy. She thought she was Job. I could understand that, all the suffering, the losing of children. I put my hand on her forehead to see if she had a fever.

"It was Lucifer, the angel of light," she said, "prince of darkness, so beautiful it made me ache to see him there, but I was so afraid I couldn't cry out. Then the Lord said, in a terrible whisper, 'All that she has is yours but do not raise your hand against herself.' And Lucifer turned and disappeared into the air, and the song of the angels grew so loud it hurt my ears and the light so bright I had to cover my face, and the pain of it ran through me till I cried out but couldn't hear my own cry."

She squeezed my hand and searched over my face again.

"Emma," I said. I wanted to tell her about the twins, but I could not say it. The burial was the next morning. How could I tell her?

She closed her eyes and relaxed. "I have come out of the darkness," she said, "into the twilight, and I am waiting on the Lord." Her eyes opened slowly, and she turned away from me and searched over the wall. "I am on the verge of seeing a great light," she said, "but a veil has been cast over my sight." Her gaze stopped at the window again, and a calm settled over her face. "I am the handmaiden of the Lord," she said, "and He will not turn away from me again. I know it."

"It was twins," I said and heard the fear in my voice. "Boys, both of them. Hamilton Blake and Faith McCormick tried to save them, but it was too late. It's a miracle we still got you." And I almost said that Doctor Blake wanted to leave her something, wanted her to have something out of her suffering, but she had nothing. Nothing at all. And I said nothing. I pulled her hand to me and rubbed her knuckles.

"A miracle, yes," she said in the whispery voice that made the hair stand again on my neck. "Walter, we must be prepared for the word of the Lord. For it's coming, and his presence is an awful fire. None that have seen it have lived."

"Emma," I said, "I don't want to hear the word of the Lord." How could I want to hear the word of the Lord. Hadn't he spoken already with a resounding crash? Hadn't his words lain there all that night in the second bedroom under a blanket, cold and unmistakable? "Emma," I said, "I want to hear you. I want you to talk to me."

Her eyebrows drew together, and her gray eyes looked into mine, back and forth from one to the other.

"It is to me then that the word must come," she said and closed her eyes. When she opened them again, she stared out the window, across the road, into the darkness. A lack of focus, a distant look settled over her.

"No, Emma," I said. "Listen to me. I want to talk to you." She didn't respond, and I reached out as if to pinch her cheek between my thumb and forefinger, turn her face toward me, put my face close to hers and shout.

But I sat silent, holding her hand, rocking a little back and forth, staring at the lamp. The flame burned so steadily that it seemed to be painted on the inside of the globe.

Part IV

The Unclouded Day

33

December
Walter

ALL THE PEWS in the Word of Holiness Church are full, and maybe a dozen people stand with me at the back of the sanctuary. It is cold and damp outside, but the glut of people warms the building and the woodstove halfway up the center aisle burns low. The congregation has just sung "The Unclouded Day," and the pews rustle and squeak as people settle into them, and Otis Hogan leaves the piano and goes back to his seat on the front pew, and the images from the song still hover in my mind—that home far beyond the skies, where He smiles on His children and His smile drives their sorrows away, where no tears ever come again in that lovely land of unclouded day.

The first time I came into this building seven or eight years ago, it was scary. I stood right about here when I came in. Emma stood against the wall near the front up there on the left, the light in her eyes.

Now she stands beside the podium on the dais, her face thin, gray as death, her eyes dark and shadowed.

Joshua was born two years ago this week. The ground in

front of the gray stone in the cemetery is still mostly bare, but settled now, near level.

Emma is giving her testimony tonight. Some of these folks don't come to church all that often, but word got around and they came to hear her. Everyone in Delaney knows all the details by now.

Only a week till Christmas, but the only decoration Brother Leery allows is a wreath hung outside the front door.

Four weeks ago Emma attended services for the first time since she fell in the gully. And all along I have heard the talk, the whispering. Rumor said that she never spoke at home, to me or Purity or Martha or Ben, that maybe the loss of the twins had left her touched, that she would never be the same. And I didn't know what to say to people, so I said nothing, though it was mostly untrue, or half true at best.

While she was confined at home, the congregation prayed for her at the services, speaking in tongues, calling on the Name on her behalf. And I listened to their prayers but could not pray with them because the words caught in my throat. Even as I sat in the pew and rocked back and forth, my head bowed and my eyes closed, I could not pray the words everyone else prayed so easily.

We weren't thinking of the same person. They prayed for a woman mourning for her dead young, suffering the loss, crying out for comfort. But that was not Emma. Emma was gone, and in her place a stranger walked the house, shuffling across the wood floors, her slippers whispering like the spirit that spoke to her, that called her to follow.

They prayed for her in the spirit, calling on the Lord of Glory to free her from bondage. They had no business calling on that awful power, that Holy Ghost who seemed bent on our destruction. Who had struck me down with his mighty fist. Who had taken Joshua, then the twins. Who now dangled Emma by a thread.

When she came back to church with me, quiet and withdrawn, they shook their heads and whispered together. "The Lord's will be done," they said, and "He giveth and He taketh away."

She stands on the dais now, just to the side of the lectern, and waits for the sanctuary to become quiet. Someone coughs. A pew creaks. Everyone looks at Emma, and she raises her chin a little.

(They cannot know where I am going. They will think I am just quoting scripture, just using scripture to make my testimony. They think they know where I have been. They think they know.)

"In the fifth day, in the twelfth month," she says, "in the year of our Lord nineteen hundred five, the word of the Lord came to me. In the fire and the whirlwind it swept over me, the least of his handmaidens, and He lifted me up in the spirit and showed me the things that I was to do."

She stops and looks around the room. She raises her hand to the front of the lectern beside her and grips it to steady herself. Her dark hair is drawn back tight into a knot at the base of her skull, and a spare black bonnet covers her head. Her gray eyes, sunken, look out of her round, gray face, her eyebrows slanted, her lips parted and relaxed.

Men and women lean forward, waiting, interested, wondering. They recognize the shape of her words, the long tradition of the prophets of God rebuking Israel. Children look up at their parents, sense the currents of emotion moving in the air, and crane their necks to see Emma, afraid to break into the stillness of the room. Only the shuffle of someone's feet and the creak of another pew break the silence. The people standing beside me look over at me. My face burns, but I keep my eyes on Emma, waiting like everyone else to see what will come next.

When Emma speaks again, she looks from face to face as if she is speaking to each person in private.

"I was a child here in this room," she says, "sitting between my mama and papa, listening to Brother Hamish, and then later Brother Leery, preaching in the spirit, feeling the Presence, as the Holy Ghost descended on us all. Many of you were the loving hands that helped and guided me, as I grew up here."

Faith McCormick sits on the right side of the sanctuary near the front, her face streaked with tears, her lips trembling as she stares at Emma, her eyes large with ecstacy. She sat in the rocker the night Emma fell, staring at the fire, as if I were not there.

Emma's mama leans forward as she wipes the tears from her cheeks with a handkerchief. Ben Sinclair sits straight and still, looking directly at Emma, and his erect posture and full gray beard make me think of the photographs of confederate officers in profile, their penetrating gaze fixed on something off to the side.

Magin Wilson and Owen Dempsey stand on each side of me at the back. Everyone in the room, it seems, is looking at Emma. For the last three days—since that moment when we sat together in front of the fire and she pushed the poker into the coals and the mound of embers and smoking remnants of wood burst into flame, lighting her face and reflecting in her eyes— she has been trying to tell me where she is going, but it has made no sense to me, something to do with the smoking remnants and the flame, and I tried each time to talk about something else. And a little while ago I didn't want Brother Leery to take Emma to the front of the sanctuary before the service began, leading her like she was a child in a room full of strangers.

I wish that I had listened more carefully to what she was saying, to that prophetic voice, wish that I had tried to understand what she meant. She has not looked at me since she went to the front of the room.

The congregation looks at her as if she were one of the prophets of old come to life before their eyes, familiar, almost intimate, yet remote and inaccessible. But she shouldn't be up there. I told Brother Leery she wasn't ready to testify, but he wouldn't listen. He prayed with her, and she said all the right things, all the words he wanted to hear, and he told me that testifying was the work of the Spirit, not subject to mortal scrutiny.

"The Lord chasteneth whom he loveth," she says, and her soft voice carries easily across the silence of the room, "and withholds not the rod from his children." She closes her eyes for a moment, then opens them and says, "My sins have been as scarlet."

Emma, I think, what would the Lord ever have to chasten you for? I shake my head slowly, denying the possibility.

(The cowlick of hair that rises from the crown of his head, about which we have laughed so many times, which I

have wet and combed down for him Sunday morning after Sunday morning, stands up now outlined against the bare boards of the wall behind him, and moves in a slow rhythmic arc with each turn of his head. Like the arm of the metronome on Mama's piano, its insistent clacking breaking the silence as it marked its time, as Papa sat at the table reading, the lamp close at his side, and Mama put my unwilling fingers on the piano keys in the yellow light of the lantern on the piano top. The pendulum weights of the cuckoo clock hung down nearly to the piano top. The room smelled musty.)

Emma looks past me without focus, and something passes over her face, a shadow, a doubt. Her eyes come into focus and she looks over at Purity Morrison, who sits by the center aisle at the end of the second pew, her family filling the pew to the far end, the youngest boy in her lap. A look of tragic comprehension holds Purity's face, and her eyes water.

(If only you knew, Purity, if only you knew, you would not feel this grief for me.)

Brother Leery sits in his chair on the dais behind Emma, on his face a look of sympathy and blessing, waiting for Emma to speak again. He told her, in spite of my hesitation, to speak whatever the Lord put on her heart. I wonder what Brother Leery will do, what the Lord will put on his heart.

Emma looks at her father and says, "The spirit of the Lord is upon me because he hath anointed me to preach the gospel to the poor."

Faith McCormick's eyes are small pools of contentment in the wrinkled wasteland of her face.

Brother Leery's face shifts almost imperceptibly. I see the controlled beginnings of surprise, the effort to maintain the mask of sympathy.

Ben Sinclair sits still, returning Emma's gaze. I can't tell what Ben feels or thinks, there is no outward sign at all. I wonder what he will do, and what the Lord has put on his heart.

Martha Sinclair's eyes are closed, and her lips move in silent prayer. And your heart, Martha, what has God put there?

There is a stirring in the pews, and Emma looks out over the faces in the congregation, looks hard, her eyes narrowing. The faces reflect curiosity, embarrassment, and anger.

Why would anyone be angry at Emma? The prophetic voice has descended on various people in this congregation. In times of need. And though some voices have had a clearer ring of truth than others, none has stung the brothers and sisters here with the anger I see in some of them now.

Is it her claim that she is anointed to preach the gospel that has offended them? Such an anointing, even in women and children, is not unheard of. Would not call up that anger.

And this is Emma.

And knowledge, like the unhatched chick, grown too big for the shell that confines it, begins to break on me, though I cannot yet see it clearly. It pushes through with its beak, a small rupture that reveals at first little of the clumsy, grotesque and featherless creature within. And so I know that the revulsion people feel grows out of the fact that Emma, no matter who she was through twenty years of her life among them, is now and will always be a Bass.

"We are the poor," Emma says. "We were raised in these hills in houses that we mostly built with our own hands. We don't have much education, don't know much about the world. Our days are spent doing what we can to keep body and soul together."

There is a simplicity, an intimacy in her voice that makes me think of the two of us sitting in front of the woodstove in the dark of the living room before all this happened. Around the sanctuary at that moment everyone is listening carefully to what she says. The smile is still fixed on Brother Leery's face, but his eyes are wary.

"The gospel is the good news," she says, "and we are the sort that are hungry for good news. Jesus fed the hungry. He cured the lame, the sick, and gave sight to the blind. He raised up the dead. We have come here hungry and thirsty for righteousness, and we have been fed. We have come here sick in heart, our minds blinded by the temptations of the world, and we have been healed. We have come here spiritually dead, the servants of Mammon, and we have been raised up in the power of the Holy Ghost and given new life in Jesus Christ."

The room is silent except for scattered sniffling and the sudden hiss of a dying log in the fire. Those who are sympathetic sit in a rapture of attention, the puzzled wait, the angry have retreated into silence. Brother Leery's face goes through a series of transformations. The mask of blessing is gone. The sympathy is crumbling. His eyes move quickly. He is trying, I am sure, to decide what has to be done.

It was so easy for you yesterday, Brother Leery. Just say what the Lord has put on your heart.

I would go to the dais and get Emma, take her home, get

her away from this. But I can't. The voice of God has led her here, and she will shut me out and turn away from me before she will betray that call.

Emma's gaze lifts and she seems for a moment lost in thought. "I hid myself away from God as if on a ship bound for a far country," she says. "God sent a storm, and in order to save that ship, I was cast over the side and sank into the sea. And in the belly of Leviathan I raised up my eyes to God, and He heard my prayer. I have become refuse cast upon the shore."

And I want to say "No, Emma, I would never cast you into the sea." I take a breath to say it, but knowledge pushes in on me again, and the blind chick thrusts its ugly head through the shell, and a more terrible knowledge is revealed in its lidded eye. That I am not her refuge, not the ship on which she sails, that buoys her up over the darkness. That I am instead Leviathan, the great cold fish that has swallowed her, and through the horror of losing the babies she has been vomited onto the shore, cast up.

And the uncanny rightness of being a Bass hits me like a blow to the stomach, and the air rushes from my nose and I am afraid to look at the people beside me. I am the great fish, the Bass that has swallowed her.

Emma's eyes close, and we all wait. In the silence, the voice of Elvira Parks, who sits toward the back of the row of pews to my right, breaks out in its pure alto tones, in the first line of the chorus from the book of Isaiah that the congregation has turned to time after time, its rolling melody and solemn rhythm drawing everyone into harmony.

"I see the Lord..." she sings, drawing out the vowels of the first and last syllables of the line.

From long habit, with what seems to me like a collective sigh, releasing the tension and perplexity, the congregation responds in mass, "I see Jesus..." They dwell on the syllables of the Name as if they are reluctant to let it go.

"I see the Lord..." Elvira Parks sings out again, holding onto the final word, tasting its sweetness, calling everyone to enter into the house with thanksgiving.

Then most of us raise our voices, some of us raising hands into the air, some standing and swaying gently, "He is high and lifted up, and his train fills the temple."

The rhythm becomes steady as Sister Hogan raps the tambourine on the heel of her hand. The tones rise and fall in a slow wail, the sound of the children lost in the wilderness, borne along by faith, children of the whirlwind and the pillar of fire. Emma's face is still turned to the ceiling, eyes open. The blessing rolls over her. We sing the chorus, drawn into the almost painful tension between the slow, undulating rhythm and the ecstacy of the vision.

The volume rises with the climactic final lines, "The angels cry holy...the angels cry holy...the angels cry holy is our God!" A collective sigh follows the drawn-out, triumphant final word. Whispered prayers and murmured hallelujahs trail off into a silence pent up with expectation. As I sing the last lines, the peace fills me, my eyes closed, face uplifted, my right hand raised over my head.

I'm not sure what is true. The things I want to believe are

not as clear to me now as they were six months ago. I don't know what's possible, but I know that Emma is real and that she stands at the front of the sanctuary and speaks with a voice that is awful. And I feel myself moved by her words, by the singing, by the spirit that is beyond my understanding, and I want to go with her to that land of unclouded day.

At the front of the sanctuary, Brother Leery sits leaning forward with his elbows on the arms of his chair, one hand over his eyes, the other gripping his Bible.

Emma sways slightly, and with one hand still holding the front of the podium, and her face still tilted upward, she raises her left hand, palm forward, fingers spread. Her eyes, open wide, are glazed and look through the ceiling to a far, distant place. She speaks in a quavering drone that seems driven forward, barely pausing to draw in breath to continue.

"Out of the midst of the whirlwind came a brightness like amber," she says, "and out of the brightness the four living creatures of old, every one with four faces, every one with four wings. And their feet were straight and sparkled like bronze, and they turned not when they went. They went every one straight forward."

The people recognize the words of the prophet Ezekiel, but a few seem troubled, uncertain how to hear the words, how Emma means them to be heard in her testimony.

But Emma pushes on, "And the likeness of their faces were the face of a man and the face of a lion and the face of an ox and the face of an eagle. And two wings stretched upward and two spread down to cover their bodies. And they went straight forward every one; they turned not when they went. And a light moved among them like a burning coal of fire, and I lifted up my eyes, and on the surface of the earth and on the surface of the heavens, the likeness of a wheel, and the creatures within the wheel, with all one likeness, as a wheel within a wheel."

Around the congregation there seem to me to be the faces of men and of lions and of oxen and of eagles straining toward her, all responding to the secret nature of their own hearts.

"And they were dreadful," Emma says, her eyes still looking far beyond the ceiling, "filled with eyes round about. And they turned not when they went; they went every one straight forward. And the noise of their wings was the noise of great waters, and they stood, and they lowered their wings. And the heavens above them shone like a stone of sapphire. And there appeared above them the likeness of a throne, and above the throne the likeness of a man, and the brightness of the amber round about him. From his loins even upward the appearance of fire; from his loins even downward the appearance of fire. The brightness round about him; the appearance of the likeness of the glory of the Lord. And I fell on my face and heard the voice of one that spoke."

She pauses, holds her breath. Everyone is mesmerized by the words of the prophet Ezekiel. But the vision is no longer his. Clearly it has become Emma's own. And I hold my breath and wait for something to break the silence, and I think of her standing in front of the house on our wedding night, waiting for me as I approached her, the wedding veil that covered her face lit up by the moonlight.

When she begins again, her voice has an edge of urgency, and the rhythm quickens as she rocks back and forth.

"And he said unto me, 'Handmaiden of the Lord, stand upon thy feet, and I will speak unto thee.' And the Spirit entered into me when he spoke unto me, and set me upon my feet. And he said, 'Be not afraid, either of word or deed, though briers and thorns be with thee, and thou dost dwell among scorpions. But hear what I say unto thee. Be not thou rebellious like that rebellious house of Israel. Open thy mouth, and eat what I give thee.' And when I looked, behold, a hand was sent unto me; and, lo, a scroll was in it. And he spread it out before me, and it was written within and without; and there was written in it lamentations, and mourning, and woe."

A rustle of movement creeps over the congregation. My heart beats against my chest. Othell Martin stands up with a stricken look on his face, as if he has just been slapped by his sweet wife, Miriam. It is clear now even to Othell that Emma is not just quoting scripture but sharing her own vision. The word of the Lord that came to her. Othell is by the aisle and in full view. His hands grip the pew in front of him, the skin stretched taut from the strain. Emma's gaze moves over the sanctuary.

(You do not know where I have been, but you are afraid of where I am going.)

She looks directly at Othell and says, as if it is a personal message, "And he said to me, 'Handmaiden of the Lord, eat what thou findest; eat this scroll and go speak unto the house of Israel.' So I opened my mouth, and he caused me to eat that scroll. And he said unto me, 'Eat, and fill thy stomach with this scroll that I gave thee.' Then did I eat it, and it was in my mouth like honey for sweetness."

Othell, his face pinched with anger, steps into the aisle and motions with a tight jerk of his head for his family to move toward the door. The three children file out wide-eyed, looking at their father as they pass him. Miriam hesitates and looks over her shoulder at Emma. She is crying.

(Her heart is full of charity, and she wants to go where I am going, but she cannot.)

I take a step toward Othell. I want to stop him, to tell him to ride it out, to wait and see where it is going. But Othell does not see me, and he takes Miriam by the arm, and they walk out the door behind the children.

The knowledge that has been breaking on me now lies open before me. The chick has wallowed out of the shell and lies wet and helpless in the pieces.

How do I say this? Emma was much more to these people than they are willing to admit. Much more than just Emma. Then one day she was a Bass. And it was personal for most of them. And it would have been easy for the Othell Martins in the congregation to turn away, horrified, but God had betrayed them. Because I had been, after all, before Emma chose me, struck down on the church floor and prayed through. It was a sign. They had no choice, but take me in.

But their god did not forget them in their distress. The miscarriages. Joshua. The twins. Emma was fallen. The vindication of the righteous. Emma and I were in our place, broken, rebuked. And they were in theirs. Benefactors. Praying for us.

They came here tonight to hear her confession. To forgive her. To lift her up. And she made a good start of it—her sins like scarlet, the words of the prophet Ezekiel.

But in the blink of an eye their compassion has turned into anger. She has raised herself up without them and claimed that God has made her a judge over them. A bitter pill they refuse to swallow. One that Othell Martin, elder of the church, could never swallow.

The little boy in Purity Morrison's arms begins to cry, and she bounces him gently and whispers to him while the six-year-old beside her pulls at her dress.

(Everyone knows where you are going, Purity. You would never go with me.)

Emma looks over to where her parents sit. Her mother's head is still bowed. Martha and I are on familiar ground these last few weeks. This is all my fault. Ben's eyes, though still on Emma, are vacant, as if he is lost in thought.

Emma says, "And he said to me, 'Get thee unto them of the captivity, unto the children of thy people, and speak unto them, and tell them. Thus saith the Lord God.' Then the Spirit lifted me up, and I heard behind me a voice of a great rushing, saying, 'Blessed be the glory of the Lord from his place.' And I heard the noise of the wings of the living creatures that touched one another, and the noise of the wheels beside them, and a noise of great rushing. So the Spirit lifted me up, and took me away, and I went in bitterness, in the heat of my spirit, but the hand of the Lord was strong upon me."

The hair rises on the back of my neck, and the skin of my face tingles. Three of the women stand and spread their arms, palms up, faces lifted, eyes closed. "Oh, Jesus, in thy glory," calls out a woman's voice from somewhere in the back. Some of the people flick sideways glances at people near them, not wanting to make eye contact. The whole thing is perched on a fulcrum, I think, and ready to slide either way.

(I must say it all. I must finish.)

Brother Leery has sat through it all, motionless except for the movement of his lips. In the pause, the people begin to look at him. They are waiting for Brother Leery to do something. He is the shepherd. Abruptly, he stands and holds up his Bible open on his palm before him. "Open our eyes that we may see," he says, looking up at the ceiling, "and our ears that we may hear thy voice, oh Lord." More people stand, and some of them turn again to Emma.

Brother Leery looks over at Emma, calculating, judging his next move, still uncertain. You cannot stop it now, shepherd. We are almost there.

Emma closes her eyes and lifts her other arm so that both hands are raised in front of her. "And the hand of the Lord was there upon me," she says, her voice rising, "and he said unto me, 'Arise, go forth into the valley, and I will talk with thee there.' And I arose, and went forth, and the glory of the Lord stood there, and I fell on my face. And the Spirit entered into me, and set me upon my feet, and spoke with me, and said unto me, 'Go, shut thyself within thine house. And behold they shall put cords upon thee, and shall bind thee with them, and thou shalt not go out among them. And I will make thy tongue cling to the roof of thy mouth, that thou shalt be dumb, and shalt not be to them a reprover, for they are a rebellious house. But when I speak with thee, I will open thy mouth, and thou shalt say unto them, Thus saith the Lord God. He that heareth, let him hear; and he that forbeareth, let him forbear."

The congregation hangs in the balance, held in the collective urge for movement, for relief. Brother Leery steps up to the podium, and as he does so, he looks at Otis Hogan and draws his eyebrows sharply together.

I know what he is doing, and I feel as if the sanctuary floor tilts under me and the ringing in my ears rises to a pitch.

Brother Leery speaks, "Thy word, oh Lord, is a lamp unto my feet, and a light unto my way. And I will ever lift up my voice in praise of thee." As he speaks, Otis moves to the piano and sits watching closely. Emma opens her eyes and looks at Otis, and she lowers her hands, the right one coming to rest on the podium beside her. Brother Leery grips the front of the podium, and his left hand covers Emma's hand there. "Lift us now, oh Lord," he says, "by your sweet Holy Spirit."

Otis Hogan strikes the chords of "I Have Found a Friend in Jesus," and everyone who is still seated stands and joins in the clapping and singing that follow, allowing all the tension to pour out into the song.

Emma stands beside the podium, calm, and looks first at Otis, then at Brother Leery, then out over the people. And she knows. Knows that the balance has shifted away from her.

The faces of the people are upturned, the eyes of some

closed as they clap their hands and shift their weight with the rhythm. None of them looks at her now. None but Ben Sinclair, who looks at her steadily, focused, curious. The two of them look at each other without moving in the jubilant chorus that surrounds them.

Then she turns her eyes toward the back of the sanctuary where I stand, and for a moment she looks at me, then through me and beyond me, but not to that home beyond the skies where His smile drives all sorrows away. Her eyes just lose focus, go empty, as if the light in them was turned out and her spirit has scuttled back out of sight like a muskrat into its hole on the riverbank. And the face of Lilly Bass rises up in my mind as it was when I pulled away the shawl that covered it in the light from the fireplace ten years ago, just before the house burned. My skin crawls.

Brother Leery sings beside Emma. I want to go to her, get her away from him, take her home and hide her and not let anyone near her again. But how can I now? I am, after all, Leviathan, the monster that has swallowed her in her sins. I press my hands against the wall behind me.

Magin Wilson and Owen Dempsey have moved gradually a little away from me during the song. It is only right that they should. They don't want to end up in the belly of Leviathan. And I am alone and feel like any moment all the congregation will turn and look at me.

I start toward the door, but I stop in front of Owen Dempsey and look at him. Owen stops clapping and stands with his mouth open. No one else responds to my movement.

I leave Owen gaping and hurry out onto the porch and close the door behind me. The sky is dark and starless. And I think about the home far beyond the darkness, in the land of unclouded day. I think of Emma standing at the podium looking at me with her empty eyes. The porch vibrates, just as it did the first time I stood here years ago. I was afraid then, just as I am now. I had no idea then, ignorant as I was, what I was walking into, led by that vague desire for a woman I hardly knew.

My chest begins to shiver and I tighten my stomach muscles but it doesn't stop. My breath steams out of my mouth in the cold. I turn and start down the lane toward the square.

On the dark road south of town I pass the little Riverside Church of Christ, a small, white clapboard building without a steeple. From inside, the somber voice of Isaac Samuel Cravens barks out exhortations to the silent congregation.

34

**Later That Night
Purity**

WELL NOW I'VE SEEN EVERYTHING. I knew from the minute Walter helped her down off that wagon and I went up to greet her—we had just arrived at church ourselves and Daddy was tying the team at one of those small oaks just off the alley—I knew that something wasn't right, that it was a mistake Emma giving her testimony tonight. Could have told Walter right out if he had asked me, which of course he didn't, and never would.

Later, when Brother Leery took Emma up front, her floating along beside him, hanging on his arm like a paper doll. I told Sarah June, who was sitting on the other side of Billy Boy, that I had a bad feeling about the whole thing.

Jackson Lee, of course, was in my lap. He always comes to me instead of Sarah June. Wants me to hold him all the time. Just goes to show that a child wants discipline. Sarah June didn't pay any mind to what I said, which didn't surprise me. She's about as good at listening as she is at taking care of little ones.

It just broke my heart to see Emma go to pieces like that right there in front of God and everybody. I don't know. It just seems like some people have no end of trouble. But yet here's my mama with twelve healthy children and four healthy grandchildren and never lost a one.

Of course, Sarah June will run off and get married any time now, and God only knows what will happen. It really will be a miracle if she can keep from losing half of hers.

But then you know the Bible says the rain falls on the just and the unjust. The Morrisons have just been blessed, that's all.

Of course, Mama's change of life could have been a little smoother. Her mouth stays puckered up all the time now from taking Doctor Dromgoole's, like she just bit into a green persimmon, her eyes all squinty. But I will say one thing. Even though she spends a lot more time lying down than she ever did before, and I seem to be doing all of the housework in addition to working at the cannery, still and all her general temper is about as pleasant as I've ever seen it.

Well, the mood in church was a little tense, to say the least, after Othell Martin made a fool of himself and stormed out with his family in tow. And then Emma just stood there and lost her mind again right before my eyes, with the whole congregation singing, their hands up in the air, just about killing themselves trying to look anywhere but at Emma. I felt so sorry for her I couldn't help crying. Jackson Lee pulled on my lip and said over and over "Why cry, Puree? Why cry, Puree?" He is doing real well with his speech, but my name is simply too much for a four-year-old who has been spoiled rotten since the day he was born. The fact that he still sucks his thumb does not help one bit, I assure you. He is the only

Morrison child to suck his thumb. If it had been Sissy or me raising him, things would have been different.

Anyway, it was real sweet the way Brother Leery stood there beside Emma with his hand laid on hers, trying to carry her through.

Then it happened. After we sang three or four hymns, everybody praying, I'm sure, that this whole thing would just go away, with her standing there like she was in a trance staring at the back wall, she made another stab at it. It was just tragic. Her face flushed and her eyes lit up like a candle flaring before it gutters out, and things got quiet and she announced that she would hold a revival meeting right there in the church. A Holy Ghost revival with signs and wonders, tongues and healings, casting out demons, taking up serpents. It never occurred to her in her state of mind that this time of year there wouldn't be any serpents to be had.

But it didn't really matter anyway. The Word of Holiness Church has never handled snakes or drank poison. She pretty well scared everybody off with that. The condition she was in and all.

I still had my wits about me enough to see that she was in trouble. But what could I do with a four-year-old insisting on sitting in my lap the whole living time, sucking his thumb, and his six-year-old brother sitting beside me and pinching him?

But something had to be done about Emma, especially after that little cannon shot about picking up snakes, and I had just about decided to do something myself, even though it was, of course, Walter's responsibility as her husband. I turned and looked back to where he had been skulking on the back wall to see if he was going to do anything to help his wife, and I almost dropped Jackson Lee off my lap. Walter was nowhere to be found. There was just this empty space between Magin Wilson and Owen Dempsey.

That is when Ben Sinclair slipped out of his pew and went up to the front and took Emma's arm and put his arm around her. I smiled at Ben with every bit of human sympathy I could as they passed me, just to encourage him, but I don't think he saw me. He was staring pretty hard at the back door. And of course Emma was not even really there. I didn't expect her to respond.

That empty space on the back wall between Magin Wilson and Owen Dempsey will stay with me for the rest of my life. It just makes me shiver to think that I came within a hair's breadth of being wed to that empty space myself. The Lord works in mysterious ways to preserve his children. What I thought was my cross to bear has become my deliverance, a song in my heart.

And I wonder. For years the words "old maid" have fallen on me like a curse, and I have had to swallow them like bitter cud that keeps rising in my throat. And I have to say that there are times when that cannery is a hell to me. Half burned alive from the fires under those big kettles, and half deaf from the noise.

But I see now things could be worse. And after all, I'm good at the things I do. Not everybody can say that. Peeling and coring. Delivering babies. Faith McCormick is getting too old to be dragged around the countryside to deliver babies. I have heard her say, I don't know how many times, that she feels like the mother of half the people in this valley.

The advantage, of course, is she doesn't have to raise them, to wash their clothes, change their diapers, cook for them. That is something to think about. I would have that to look forward to.

35

January 1906
The Eye of the Owl

HENRY'S GLOVES MUTED THE SOUND of his knocking on the heavy wooden door at the back of the roadhouse. When he looked away and waited, his breath steamed out toward the woods, and a gust of wind bit at his face. The horse huffed and turned her head toward the woods, her ears erect, reins lying loose on her neck. Snow, broken by clumps of fescue around the cabin, exaggerated the moonlight.

He didn't know what he would say, and when Pearl Bear opened the door he turned to her and said nothing. He shifted his weight, and the snow creaked under his boots, and she said, "I've got to admit I'm surprised." She waited and leaned into the edge of the door. "So what do you want?" she said.

"You gonna let your place get cold while we talk?" he said.

She stepped back to give him room to pass, but she said nothing and her face showed nothing. He walked past her and stomped his boots on a braided rug just inside as she closed the door. Nothing in the room had changed—the smell of leather, of sage, of lilac.

"Go ahead," she said, "take off your coat. You know

where it goes."

He took off his coat and hat and hung them on the pegs beside the door. When she passed him, he smelled the perfume, the same perfume she had always worn. She walked away from him, over to the cookstove that stood against the wall. Two large posts, heavy pine trunks with short stubs of limbs left for pegs, supported the ridge pole that ran the length of the ceiling. Three woven baskets hung from the pegs of one pole, a shawl, and a long strip of braided leather hung on the pegs of the other.

"You'd never guess what I'm cooking," she said. "A gift from my little brother Paul." She stirred the pan on the stove, moving her hand in a slow circle, and shook her head.

It was just like her, he thought, to begin a conversation as if the last twelve years hadn't happened.

He walked over to the small woodstove in the opposite corner of the room at the foot of the bed. The smell of lilac was strong there from the bowl she kept on the stove. Lilac and the musky smell of the bed. The pistol would still be under the pillow. The woodstove was hot. She had always kept the room so warm he had to go outside to cool off.

"No, I'd never guess," he said.

"The eyes of an owl," she said, and she stopped stirring and looked up at him. "Fresh killed. Paul just dropped them off a little while ago. Eating the eyes restores lost eyesight. He says I'm lost, says it will help me find my way. He's being his sister's keeper." She turned back to the pan and stirred again.

She put the lid on the pan and came over to the woodstove. "You're supposed to swallow them whole, raw," she said, "but not me. No way I'm eating an eye without cooking it in a broth." She backed up to the woodstove beside him. "It's bad enough I'm eating them at all, but he'd never let me alone if I didn't. Amazing, the things we do for the people we love."

Henry stood beside her, facing the stove, felt the warmth through his pantlegs, his hands in his pockets. He didn't want to talk about her brother Paul. The years showed in her face. Lines creased the corners of her eyes and her forehead. The muscles in her cheek twitched once.

At home Naomi sat across the table from him every evening, the desire to talk snuffed out like a fire when you kick snow on it, when it goes from crackling flame, to sizzle and smoke and steam, to cold, wet ashes. And now he was always guessing what it was he was supposed to do, and always guessing wrong, always watching her face tighten up in response to what he said or did, always feeling the heave in his stomach when he said or did anything. A blind mole digging, the thing he wanted always just out of reach.

He was sick of prying into the omissions, the crevices between sounds, where everything seemed to be at risk. Ambition, love, everything.

And now the warm water she left for him in the washroom made his skin crawl, the food she put on the table stuck in his throat.

And he had come back here.

"Want something to drink?" Pearl said.

"Sure," he said.

She opened the cabinet above the sink and pulled down a half-empty bottle and two metal cups. "Not as fancy as you're used to now." She poured some whiskey into the cups and gave him one. "Those eyes need to simmer in that broth a little longer."

Her long hair, thick and black, was tied back with a piece of leather. The thick eyebrows and long lashes, the sharp nose and full lips that pouted even when she relaxed, the body that moved without a sound—twelve years, gone, and none of that had changed. And his response to her was the same when he looked at her, when he smelled the faint perfume.

He tried to imagine that the last twelve years had not happened, that he was still twenty- six, that he had laughed when Naomi dared him to marry her there in front of the schoolhouse that hot Sunday afternoon.

"I almost believed you," Pearl said.

"What?" he said.

She took a drink. "Nothing," she said. "It doesn't matter."

She went to the counter and got the bottle and refilled the cups. "Drink up," she said. "I guess we ought to drink to old times." She drank. "You remember the old times, don't you, Henry?"

"Some of them," he said. "The waterfall."

She was lifting her cup, but it stopped short of her mouth and she looked at him before she drank.

"The waterfall," she said. "I was thinking of the time you took me to Fayetteville, the weekend in the Ozark Hotel. That minstrel at the opera house. That weekend cost you a lot of money. Only time I've ever been to Fayetteville."

"No," he said, "the waterfall." He finished the whiskey in his cup and held it out to her. She poured again for both of them.

"At midnight in July," he said. "The moon shining through the trees, the water hitting those rocks. Nothing will ever get close to that."

"Okay," she said, "the waterfall." She rubbed her finger along the lip of her cup.

When she looked down into her cup, her hair shined, and her long lashes extended from beneath her eyebrows. Her nose was straight and narrow. Not at all like Naomi's. And Naomi kept her lips drawn in a tight line, always in check.

"That's as good as it got alright," she said, "but it didn't happen that often, Henry." She swirled the whiskey around in her cup in quick, small circles.

"I wish it was July," he said.

She held the bottle up and checked it, then filled both the cups again. "It's January, Henry. A foot of snow. You'd freeze it off for nothing."

She started across the room toward the cookstove. "Those eyes ought to be about boiled away by now," she said. She put the bottle on the counter and lifted the lid from the pan. "Nope, they're ready to go."

She brought the pan back to the woodstove. "Hold out your cup," she said. "You may want to leave a little whiskey in the bottom, I don't know. Cool the broth a little, maybe hide the taste."

He held out his cup.

"Don't know why I'm doing this," he said. "It's your little brother thinks you're blind."

She poured broth into both their cups, shaking the pan around to get an eye to drop into each cup. A wisp of steam rose, and Henry swirled his around and blew on it. She put the pan on the woodstove. "Maybe you need it worse than I do," she said.

They both stood without doing anything. "Go ahead, Henry," she said. "Toss it off. Let's see if it's true. Maybe it'll help us both find our way."

He drank it without looking into the cup and felt the eye, like a peeled grape, slide past the back of his tongue. The broth was bitter and hot. The whiskey did little to cover it.

"What the hell did you put in that?" he said.

"Nothing special," she said. "Salt, pepper, a little ground-up yellow root." She raised her eyebrows. "Did I put too much yellow root? Maybe it's the eye, Henry. Maybe you can't hide the eye. Too strong to cover up with a little seasoning."

He reached out and pulled her to him with his hand at the back of her neck, and he kissed her and dropped his cup and pulled her up against him with the other hand. She pushed against his shoulders, her cup still clenched in one hand, but he held her to him, and her free hand moved to the back of his head and her fingers threaded into his hair and for a moment she held it there, but then she balled her fist in his hair and pushed hard, pushed his head away.

Broth from her cup spilled on his shoulder and steamed there, and he let her go and opened his mouth but didn't say anything.

She stepped back and spit on the floor. "Bitter, isn't it?" she said. She held her cup up between them and slowly poured what was left of the broth onto the floor. The soft pulp of the eye dropped over the lip of the cup and fell with a wet sound at their feet. The lilac in the bowl on the woodstove smelled sweet, the wood hissed in the stove.

"What the hell are you doing?" he said.

"I can see okay now without it," she said. "I see you. Me. Especially me, sitting here waiting twelve years ago."

She shook her head and picked up his cup and went to the sink and dropped the cups in. They rattled against the metal sink bottom. She grabbed a damp rag from the edge of the sink and came back to the woodstove and dropped the rag on the mess on the floor and got the pan off the stove.

"You're a son of a bitch, Henry. You didn't even bother to tell me." Steam rose from the pan in her hand. "One night you're here, the next day you're a married man. And I don't hear another word." She took the pan to the sink and shoved it in and it clattered. "I kept waiting for you to come and explain it to me, to tell me how it was that I got caught so off guard."

She came back to him, took the strip of braided leather off the post as she passed by and tied it around her waist. Her face was relaxed, but the lines around her eyes and in her forehead were more distinct. "Screw you, Henry Bass," she said, her voice soft, a little louder than the hissing of the wood in the stove. "Go on back to the little tart from Fayetteville."

She walked over and sat on the bed, leaned over on one hand, her fingers sliding just up under the pillow. "I'm going to bed now," she said. "Alone."

When he walked out the door, the cold air hit him. The

horse had turned with its rump to the wind, its head down, its tail blowing up under it's belly. The leather crackled when he untied the reins, and the saddle groaned when he mounted.

Naomi was probably getting ready for bed, probably angry at not knowing where he was. The bitter taste rose in his mouth. The eye of the owl.

He pulled the horse up to a stop. The wind whispered in the trees. The river, on the other side of the field along the tree line, whispered like the wind, but deeper. From beyond the river in the deep woods came the low, throaty hoot of an owl.

He leaned over in the saddle and vomited, and the snow darkened beneath him in the moonlight. He spit and wiped his mouth on his sleeve. His eyes had watered, and the water in his lashes had begun to freeze, and he brushed it out of his eyes and put his hands on the saddle horn and shivered.

The horse nickered and started forward at a walk, then broke into a trot. He left his hands on the horn, let them ride there, the reins lying loose on the horse's neck. It was two miles to Delaney. There was nowhere else to go.

36

That Same Night
Naomi

SOMETIMES WHEN I GO TO BED now the quiet keeps me awake. It's the same silence that I woke up to that night three months ago. A sudden movement, a rush of cold air over me, then Henry's face thrust up to mine, his breath heavy with whiskey.

I lock my bedroom door now, and I don't sleep until I hear his footsteps come up the stairs and go into his room. When I hear his bedroom door close, I relax and close my eyes, and it does not take long to fall asleep. But the slightest sound in the night wakes me. This is my life now. Adapt thyself to the things with which thy lot has been cast, says Marcus Aurelius. I have done that.

Henry did not sit in the kitchen and drink tonight as he usually does. About the time I expected to hear his kitchen chair drag on the floor, he left the house. There is a foot of snow on the ground, and he rode off in the night without a word. He is a fool. A fool who is tired of drinking alone.

I fell asleep not long after he left, but I was awakened by the soft pressure of boots on the carpet runner of the stairs. Just for a second I didn't know I had fallen asleep, and I opened my mouth to scream, my heart thudding in my chest because someone was coming up the stairs slowly, trying not to make any noise. But then I knew that it was Henry coming home, and I felt lightheaded and almost called his name to be sure it was him. His name caught in my throat. My face burned and my stomach felt like a beehive knocked off its stand.

The sound of his boots reached the top of the stairs, and the bed creaked as I sat up. He stopped on the landing, stood there in the dark between his room and mine. I reached over and got the clock on the bedside table and held it out in the moonlight from the window. It was midnight. The house was losing its heat, the fire in the woodstove dying down, and the cold seeped through my gown. I lay back down slowly, and the bed creaked again, and I pulled the quilt up around my throat and listened. After a minute, maybe two, the seconds drawn out in the silence with him standing there on the dark landing, he went into his room and closed the door.

I couldn't sleep. The empty gray of the ceiling hung above me. At the age of sixteen I chose to run off and marry Henry in the flush of what I thought was love and what I knew would get me out of the house of my uncle, and since that time nothing has gone the way I wanted it to go. Aurelius says the universe is either confusion or ordered providence. The odds are not that good, it seems to me.

I lay there and thought about the many violent ways people died in the Bible. The knife plunged into the stomach till the hilt was buried in the fat, the nail driven into the head, stoning, burning alive, heads smashed on the rocks. And, of course, crucifixion.

It occurred to me that I could go to Henry, or call to him across the hallway, unlock my door and lie down and wait. He would come. I could offer myself, the sacrificial lamb, humbled and contrite. In spite of everything, in spite of the fact that he has not been able to look me in the eye for more than a glance, in spite of the fact that we have not spoken more than a word or two at any one time for the past two months, in spite of the fact that our daily routine during that time has persisted like a thread by which we hang, a thread which cannot hold—in spite of all that, he would come to me here in my bed if I called. He would not be able not to come. He would not have the sense, would not have the capability in his warped narcissistic mind to see the danger.

And as he lay with me, I would whisper into his ear, *mea culpa, mea culpa,* I am guilty of your suffering. And as he pressed himself onto me, into me, his breathing loud, his eyes full of moist reconciliation, his throat there close to mine, I would do it, become the grim reaper. And I would be washed in the blood of the bull, of the goat. And if there were a god in heaven, he, or she—yes, especially if it were she—would appreciate the irony and forgive me all my sins.

Emma thinks she is God's messenger. Aunt Rose prods me about her every Monday morning, trying to pry loose a few scraps she can take with her to the other gossips around town, but I cannot bring myself to talk to Rose about Emma. It frustrates Aunt Rose to death. I am her inside source, but I am recalcitrant. I give her nothing with which to enlarge her holdings among the other women.

But what could I say? Emma has suffered great violence at the hands of her god and has become the servant of the very one who thrust the violence on her, the dark angel who threw her down the hillside and took her children from her. What choice has she got? Her universe will be either confusion or providence. She has made the only choice she can—declare God righteous and become his handmaiden. And she has declared herself the savior of the town.

37

Two Weeks Later
Walter

THE LANTERN THAT HUNG from a wrought iron arm at the back of the dais burned in the silence. Beneath it, in Brother Leery's oak chair, Emma sat with her hands folded in her lap. I sat alone in the front row pew by the aisle. No one had come. Not even Ben and Martha. Brother Leery had seen to that. No one except Elias Oatman, who had staggered in about seven-thirty and floundered into a pew at the rear. His head rested on his hands on the back of the pew in front of him, as if he was praying.

He was dead drunk.

His head jerked up, nodded forward, then jerked back up. He opened his eyes and squinted at Emma, then turned his squint on me. He looked around him as if he had no idea where he was. Then his eyes closed, and his head nodded again. I thought he would pass out, but he stood up, holding onto the pew in front of him to keep his balance. He eased himself out into the aisle and carefully walked up front to me. He gripped the end of a pew with one hand and my shoulder with the other and leaned down until his face was two inches from mine.

"What day is it?" he whispered.

I flinched at the rank breath. "Thursday," I said.

"The hell you doin' here on a Thursday?" Elias whispered.

I said nothing.

Elias stood up, swayed, held onto the pew. He sniffed. He turned and started toward the doors at the back, helping himself down the aisle with the end of each pew. "Hell they doin' here on a Thursday," he muttered. He snorted and shook his head and careened across the aisle to the other row of pews. When the door closed behind him, the sanctuary was silent. Then Emma's soft voice drifted down from the stage. The song was barely audible: "Rock of Ages, cleft for me; let me hide myself in thee."

The week had been warm, with temperatures of fifty and sixty degrees. One of those weeks you love to see happen in January. Just a couple of weeks earlier snow had fallen on New Year's Day nearly a foot deep and temperatures dropped near zero. But it had rained all afternoon before we came to the church, a slow drizzle that felt like spring and raised the rich dark smell of the rotting leaves. I raised the windows of the church when we got there, and water dripped from the eaves in the darkness outside.

Ben Sinclair had ridden over to the mill the day after Emma testified to tell me what she'd said after I left the church. He and Martha took her home from the service that night. When Ben was telling me, standing off to the side there on the loading dock at the mill, he didn't ask me where I'd run off to. Never said a word about it. Acted like it never happened. But it burned in my chest and face. Wheelin Combs kept looking over at us from where he was working at the conveyor belt.

As Ben turned to leave, he reached out and touched me on the arm, just the way Emma does so often.

Emma hadn't said a word to me at home about her revival. But then, she didn't speak to me at all. She didn't seem mad about it, just went about doing everything like normal except she didn't look me in the eyes or say anything.

Brother Leery had waited two days after Emma's testimony at the church to show up with three of the elders. It was a week before Christmas, and I had put up a tree and decorated it, but Emma never noticed it. She had finished washing the dishes that day and was drying her hands when we heard the buggy pull up outside. She looked out the window, then looked at me and said, "They have come to anoint me."

I have to admit that Brother Leery, his hair compressed around the side of his head where his hat had sat, tried to be gentle with Emma. The elders sat awkward, fiddling with their hats, afraid to look her in the eyes. They glanced at me with pinched, sympathetic smiles that showed the wrinkles around their eyes. Their chewing tobacco smelled sweet when I shook their hands. The rain was good, we needed it. It was a dry winter. The damp cold cut through me that day, but the fire felt good, and I put another log on while the elders talked between themselves about the weather.

I guess I knew what was coming. The long and short of it was that Brother Leery asked Emma not to preach until she had a chance to get well. He hesitated for about a heartbeat before the words "get well."

To tell the truth, I was glad to see Brother Leery come to the house. I thought maybe he could help somehow. Then I saw Emma's face when he told her she couldn't preach—like a child who expects praise and gets rebuke, all the life going right out of her eyes.

But I have to hand it to her. She never backed off an inch. She told him there in the living room, sitting right by that potbellied stove, that she would follow Jesus, that she had been called and would obey the call. And Brother Leery told her, solemn—and the mole on his temple, large and dark, stood out like a bullet hole—that he was the shepherd of the flock, called by God, and that he forbid her to preach. And she was silent after that, and I told them that she was tired and that they had better go.

The elders fled in their relief, but Brother Leery stood up heavily and looked down at Emma, then shook my hand, looked at me in that silent way of communication that says "you are my ally in this, you must do something here" and turned and went. And Christmas came and went like a train in the night when the whistle calls out of the darkness, and half awake at the sound I listen to the clacking of the wheels and the murmur of the engine.

And then the snow came. And the bitter cold. Then the warm week. And finally the night of the revival. Nobody came. Except Elias.

"It is clear to me now what the angel meant," she said, her voice clear and firm. "He said to me 'Be not afraid, either of word or deed, though briers and thorns be with thee, and thou dost dwell among scorpions.'" She looked right at me.

"Emma," I said, but didn't know what else to say. I didn't have the right to say anything. I remember wanting to go to the podium the night of her testimony and rescue her, like the hero in a school play would untie the heroine from the tracks and rescue her from the train bearing down on her. But I didn't. I was a goat, not a hero. A scorpion. Leviathan.

She didn't blink, and the hair at the back of my neck rose.

"He commanded me to speak to the house of Israel," she said, "and I did, and he gave me the words, and they were like honey in my mouth." She smiled, the smile of one who had lost everything and found her strength in the loss, and said, "The angel told me to shut myself in my house. That they would put cords upon me and bind me with them. That I would not be able to go out among them, and my tongue would cling to the roof of my mouth. That I would be dumb. For they are a stiff-necked, rebellious house."

I stood and walked onto the dais and knelt down in front of her and took her hands. Her eyes closed and her lips quivered, then pressed tight. She opened her eyes, her face a little above mine, in the shadow of the lamp, the darkness under her eyes made darker. I felt like a penitent kneeling at the altar. Just for a second I saw Lilly's face leaning in toward mine in the shadows, and the hair stood up on my neck and arms.

"They cannot go where I am going," Emma whispered, "none of them." She squeezed my hands and looked back and forth from one of my eyes to the other. Her face relaxed again. "I must wear sackcloth and ashes," she said. "I must go into the wilderness. And my tongue will cleave to the roof of my mouth."

I stood up and pulled her up and put my arm around her, and we walked out of the church. I lifted her up into the wagon, then went back into the church and put out the lanterns and closed the windows. I climbed up beside her, and she did not speak, and I thought again of Lilly Bass. I wondered what Lilly was like before the weight of the world squeezed the life from her. What she was like before Virgil Bass.

I swore to myself that I would never tell anyone about that night. I would look straight at people in town without flinching. I would never deny Emma.

But they would all know, for Elias Oatman, drunk as he was, would remember, would tell them all. And they would tell each other, would pity Emma, and me. Justified by their charity.

But I would ignore their pity, and she would come back to me sooner or later.

I slapped the lines on the horses' backs, and the wagon lurched forward into the dark toward home.

38

February
Emma

I HAVE SHUT MYSELF UP, as the angel commanded me, here in my house, and I am waiting. The world, stiff-necked, stumbles toward its own destruction.

The sound of footsteps comes from the living room. Othell Martin's wife, Miriam, stands in the doorway as Walter turns away behind her and leaves us. She comes to the table, stands across from me. Her face is full of sympathy, as it was the night she left in the middle of my testimony, when she looked back at me as she passed her husband, Othell, standing rigid with his back to me, herding his family out the door in his outrage.

"I hesitate to speak in a person's misery," she says, "and Lord knows I'd be the last one to involve myself in the affairs of others, but how can anyone with a heart beating in her breast stand here and not say something when it's weighing on her like this?"

She pauses, and I try to understand what she has said, but she goes on. "Ain't a soul in this community that doesn't know you're a good and decent person. I'm sure, in a way, your goodness makes it worse for you. But, Emma, you know in your heart as well as I do that ain't none of us innocent. Each and every one of us is plowing iniquity, sowing wickedness, and reaping the same."

I believe for a moment, briefer than the single, bleak call of the crow in the distance, that she has come to confess her sin and receive the Lord's anointing from my hands.

Then she leans over the table, her eyes wide. "Despise not the chastisement of the Lord," she says, "for happy is the man whom the Almighty corrects for He will raise him up. The time of trial has come upon you, Emma, and you must own up to your sins, confess them with your mouth while there is yet time to receive his blessing."

After her words, a cow bawls in the north pasture. It bawls again. My tongue cleaves to the roof of my mouth. The silence holds everything in the room in place, and I let my eyes close. Miriam wheezes slightly as she waits. And I yearn in the silence for everything to pass away. The peace that comes of the absence of words holds me, and I wonder what manner of thing I must be that I would cause Miriam Martin to come and torment me.

"Emma?" Miriam's voice tears the soft curtain of silence that hangs between us. I cling to the fragment of silence that follows my name. Then her footsteps fade as she leaves the room, and the front door opens and shuts. The silence settles against my skin like the soft warmth of Joshua snuggling into the crook of my neck.

A day passes. Two days. Maybe three. I sit at the dining room table in the late winter afternoon, and someone knocks at the front door and Walter walks to the door and opens it. Katherine Morrison, Purity's mama, comes into the dining room and walks around the table to me and stands there, not speaking at first, holding a small white handkerchief to her mouth, which moves oddly beneath it. She is alone, and it is striking to see her without any of her children hanging onto her. Their absence fills the silence between the two of us like the emptiness of a schoolyard after the last bell sounds, the swings still warm, still swinging, but almost stopped. Katherine sits in the chair beside me, the corners of her mouth drawn down, her lips scrunched as if pulled by a drawstring, and her eyes wide with sympathy.

"It's the children, isn't it?" she says. "The little babies dead and gone. No one knows better than I do the power they wield over a mother's heart. And God knows I'm thankful beyond words that in bearing twelve I haven't lost a one and God willing they'll all grow to decent men and women like Horace and Sissy did. But I know your silence is born out of suffering, as the loss of them babies in the way you did would break any mother's heart, and I know just how I would feel if I lost any of my own, God forbid."

She reaches out and holds my forearm, grips it, and looks into my eyes as if she were trying to read the words that I will not say.

"I'm sure I'm no more deserving of the riches of his blessings than anyone else," she says. "We are each and every one of us after all born into sin and in sin we live out the days of our lives, under the curse, all of us alike."

And I think yes, you are so close. Say the words, ask, and

receive the blessing.

She pats my arm and sits back in her chair dramatically and says, "But I ask myself again and again whose fault can it be? And there is only one answer. God is a righteous god, and his nature is unchanging, though the world be fallen. He is just, and therefore in this world below we reap what we sow and the wages of sin is death."

She leans forward again and puts both hands on my arm. "Oh, but He is merciful," she says, "and if you would but turn back to him, turn away from your sin and make supplication, though your sin be as scarlet He will make it white as snow." As she finishes speaking, her head leans forward and she rocks back and forth, whispering for a moment. Then, her lips bunching and working, she is quiet.

My tongue cleaves to the roof of my mouth. The snow falls silent beyond the window pane. Katherine's chair creaks each time she rocks forward. The world is white with snow. The snow is so fine that the flakes move in a horizontal line across the landscape in the wind. The flakes are small and look like mist, but in the swirl of wind around the side of the house vagrant flakes rise and fall in slow motion at the window pane, appearing and disappearing as the wind comes and goes.

The wild cherry tree across the yard stands straight, rises from the brown grass, passes through the dark gray line of trees along the horizon in the distance, and stretches its thin, bare limbs into the gray sky. Snow lines the top sides of the big lower limbs, the white line of it sharp against the dark wood.

A dusting of snow covers the ground, uneven, like rippling white water in the field, and like a thin sheet of ice over a pond in the yard. Scattered leaves, left from the autumn, stick up through the ripples. The lane beside the house is white, broken only in spots by the slight rise of ground between the wheel rows.

I feel as if I am looking at it all from behind a thin veil.

Along the fence that borders the road, the snow in the field is broken by two dark, wet patches a short distance apart, the stations where the old horse stands every day in a kind of ritual of watching the woods. A dark line marks the path walked by the horse between the two scars, not a straight line down the fence, but a sweeping arc that drops away from the road fifteen feet or so at its furthest point. A dog crosses the road and enters the field, stops at the path and sniffs the ground, then moves on at a trot. The horse is nowhere in sight.

The dog disappears across the pasture. The snow turns at the window screen into a whirlwind that spreads and engulfs the yard, the woods, the house, the room, and finally me. It is silent and warm. I wait.

I wait for what I know will come. The word of the Lord that will come like a pillar of fire, that will consume hay, straw, and stubble. That will melt the earth and float the dross and leave only pure gold, precious silver.

I wait for two days, three, maybe four. And finally, out of the silence, the sound of boots as someone crosses the living room and enters the dining room. It is cold and raining, and Walter is at the mill and I sit at the table in a chair by the window waiting. And Isaac Samuel Cravens, Naomi's reverend uncle, walks around the table and pulls a chair up facing me just out of reach.

I do not believe, even for a moment, that he has come to ask forgiveness for his sins or to receive the anointing from my hand.

"Mrs. Bass, you will have to forgive me," he says. I turn to look at him, at something in his voice, a mixture of humility and rebuke that begs my attention. "You are not one of my flock, I know," he says, "but I am like the shepherd in the Master's parable, who having safe in the fold the ninety and nine, leaves them there and goes into the night to find the one that is lost. For I have always had a burden for this town—every man, woman and child of it—for which I intercede daily with tears of compassion, just as our Lord wept over the sins of Jerusalem, praying that all the lost and wandering souls would turn away from their sins."

His words push against me, folding over me layer upon layer.

He says, "But the wrath of God burns in my breast against the wickedness of this generation, and like all of the prophets before me sent by Jehovah to speak a word to the people, I call down his judgment upon them."

He draws himself up straight as he speaks, and he lowers his voice and says, "You must know, Mrs. Bass, if what people say of you is true and you have indeed read the Good Book for yourself, that the truth is this: We deserve worse than we get—all of us. Our sins are an offense to the holiness of God. They are the dark underbelly of our lusts which, though hidden from our neighbors, yet will be brought into the light of day."

Our sins, he says, but it is my sins he means. His eyes are

the eyes of a wolf, staring down its prey. The rain falls on the windowsill and freezes along its edge. Ice coats the upwind side of the fence posts, and small icicles hang from the wires between posts, all the wires, from post to post. At the tip of each icicle a drop of water reflects the light that seeps from the gray sky. All down the lane, on all of the wires, the short, pencil-thin icicles tipped with light. They drip the rain, and with each drip the light falls to the ground yet remains, suspended. The rain is falling everywhere, on everyone, falling on the just and the unjust. And the sins of everyone are brought into the light of day.

And I understand, finally, what it is I must do. Understand that my humiliation, is not yet complete. I am to be made perfect in suffering. I must give up everything, lay the final, most precious gift on the altar. For the Word of God is living and powerful and sharper than any two-edged sword, piercing even to the dividing asunder of soul and spirit, and of the joints and marrow, and all things are naked and opened unto the eyes of the Lord.

I have kept from him, hidden in a most secret place, that gift, my last possession. Emma. The apple of her father's eye. She must be offered up.

"Emma Bass," Isaac Samuel Cravens' voice rises slightly, becomes agitated, "the Lord God has sanctified and ordained me to speak his Word among the lost. For you must know this day that he sees into the darkness of your life and that he sees the iniquity there and that the hand of retribution will not be lifted until you repent of the wickedness that besets you and confess your sins and humble yourself before him."

His jaw is set, his beard juts forward, his eyes narrow, intense. One of his eyebrows rises slightly as he looks at me, and the level stare does not waver, but looks down on the vanquished.

"Emma Bass," he says, and his voice is stern but fading beneath the sound of the water dripping from the icicles along all the wires up the lane and down the road as far as I can see, the sound growing like the cascading of a stream down the steep side of a gully, drowning out everything else in its clamor. It grows louder and I close my eyes and let the roaring of it cover me, and I see again the whirlwind of snow swirling about me, turning me in its power, whiting out the world in its suffocating purity. And the sound of the wind of it roars in my ears, and I clutch my shawl to me and cover my face.

39

March
Walter

WHEN EMMA TOLD ME SHE WANTED TO GO into town with me, I didn't know what to say. After what she did three weeks ago—after she shaved every hair off her head like that—I didn't let anyone but family in the house. Because nobody in Delaney had ever seen anything like that, except for Jim Beasley, who had gone to the Ringling Brothers' Circus in Fayetteville last fall. He said they had a bald lady there in a side show, head slicker than a cue ball. But that was in the circus.

I had come to think things couldn't get any worse for Emma and me. But I was about to learn better. She sounded like she was asking me to do the simplest thing in the world, like help her with a button she couldn't reach, just a little bit of tease in her voice, and she offered, turning away just a little, to cover her head so it wouldn't draw attention. How could I tell her no?

When we got to town, Emma stayed in the wagon while I went into the mercantile. I asked her to go in with me, but she looked down at her hands in her lap and shook her head. That was natural. Even with her head covered by a scarf, she might be embarrassed. That was a good sign. She was aware of the effect she had on other people. So I left her in the wagon. By herself. I felt just a little tug in my chest as I walked away. Not enough to make me change my mind.

I was paying Pauline Roberts for the groceries I'd got, when we noticed people stopping on the boardwalk out front and looking out onto the square. My hair stood up on the back of my neck. I knew it was Emma.

I made myself take my change from Pauline, and I put it in my wallet slow and easy, then picked the sack up off the counter and snugged it up against me before I turned toward the door and started out, saying, "Think I'll take a look."

Pauline followed right behind me. And when we got out on the porch and saw Emma sitting there in the dirt of the square, her dress spread nice and neat around her, a big clump of hair on a saucer in front of her, the scarf gone from her head, I didn't look at anybody. I knew they were all looking at me. Pauline was real quiet behind me.

I walked across the open square to the wagon, forcing my feet into a slow rhythm, and put the sack of groceries behind the seat. There were little groups of people collecting around the square—at the mercantile, the bank, the hotel, the loading dock at the depot. I didn't look at anybody.

When I got back over to where Emma was sitting, she was just striking the match to light the hair. I stood and watched without saying anything. That hair went up like dry pine needles.

Then she did it. I've gone over it a hundred times in my mind. Two hundred times. And every time it has the same effect on me. Like jumping off a high place. When you first step off, the flutter runs through your groin and stomach, and then that real clear concentration, the excitement and fear before landing.

That hair in the saucer blazed up and then was gone, and she looked up at me with a look I'll never forget. The hair on her head was barely long enough to lay down by then, and it made her ears distinct. Her gray eyes were wide and calm like nothing else existed in the world but me at that moment, and a kind of shock ran up my back and my scalp prickled because I recognized that look.

It was Joshua. Helpless, lost, not of this world, eyes fixed on mine. And I couldn't move to save myself. Couldn't move to save Joshua. To stop Emma.

And she raised that paring knife in one slow easy motion and put it to her cheek right at the high cheekbone and drew it down toward her jaw. And the bright red line followed the point of the knife across her cheek and then spilled over and spread uneven at a tight angle down her face. And the look in her gray eyes never changed one bit. Never wavered, never blinked.

A woman gasped from somewhere on the boardwalk, but nobody spoke and everything was still.

Emma looked back down at the saucer. I took out my bandanna, squatted down beside her, and covered her head, tied the bandanna under her chin. The whole time she just kept looking at the saucer. Then I helped her up and walked her over to the wagon and lifted her up into the seat. She looked like she was about to fall asleep. The bandanna was turning dark on her cheek from the blood.

I don't know how she brought the saucer, the clump of hair, the paring knife with her. We left that saucer out in the square. I never even thought about it until a long time later. I wonder now whatever became of it.

40

That Same Day
Purity

I SWEAR MAMA HASN'T MOVED that fast since before she had Jackson Lee. I knew it was something real important when she just came storming in that front door like a steam engine and of course she couldn't help but see me right there in the middle of the room and she gave me that look with her eyes narrowed, looking at me off to the side like she does, and of course her mouth all puckered up just making it worse—that look that says I have got something to tell you that will shake your apples.

And of course I know better than to try and rush her because it would not do one bit of good. Some people just cannot be rushed, and Mama is one of them. And the first thing out of her mouth was "Didn't I tell you to get up off your lazy duff and go to town with me? Didn't I?"

"Why, Mama," I said, "what has gotten into you?" As if I could just drop everything and run off to town at the drop of a hat with Jackson Lee and Billy Boy to take care of and not a smidgen of help from Sarah June.

So she just stands there looking at me for about ten slow

seconds, her mouth all puckered, knowing exactly what she was doing to me and then says, "Emma Bass, right there in the middle of the square, shaved head bared to the world, burned a saucer full of hair, pretty as you please."

"Mama," I said, "you have got to be kidding me."

Ever since the word got out a couple of weeks ago that Emma shaved her head, right down to the skin with a straight razor, it has of course been the main topic of conversation in Delaney. Charlotte James and Miriam Martin have made it their personal mission in life to see that there is not one soul in the town that hasn't heard the story. And up until now the whole thing has been a matter of some debate, since most people didn't believe it. After all, Mama and Miriam both visited Emma the end of February, and she had her hair then.

Well, when Mama said that about Emma burning her hair, I just felt this awful thing in my stomach because I haven't gone to see Emma at all since she gave her testimony in church at Christmas. Over two months. Not that I didn't have plenty to do at home. But she just lives down the road, and I know for a fact that if I was sick Emma would be here every living day.

"Must have been twenty or thirty people stopped to watch," Mama said in that kind of smug I-told-you-so voice she has.

It was bad enough I had to stay home and sweep and dust the house while Mama ran off wherever she pleased, but to be mending Jackson Lee's flannel jumper while half of Delaney stood on the square and watched Emma Bass set fire to a saucer full of her hair was just more than I could bear. Me, her best friend, who hadn't been to see her in two months, who lives barely a half mile down the road.

I tried not to cry. I really did. But the next thing I knew Mama had her arm around me, patting on me, saying "Oh, Honey, don't cry. I should of known it would break your heart. I should of had more sense than to blurt it out that way."

Well, what could I say after that? It just made it worse. Mama sat me on the couch and patted me and started telling me the story, but right after she told me how Emma's hair just went poof in a little ball of flame with Walter standing right there in front of her and half of Delaney watching, she stopped and looked at me like she was afraid.

I just had this dreadful premonition that something awful was coming, but I would never, not in a hundred years, have been prepared for what came next. I said, "Mama, tell me what happened."

When Mama told me about Emma cutting her own face half off with a paring knife, I stopped crying. I have read about people who survive a train wreck and go into shock, not able to understand the simplest things that are said to them. Now I know how they feel. I was sitting there with my mouth hanging open like Abram Clement's little boy who is not quite right, and all I could think was a paring knife, good Lord, a paring knife. Peeling and coring will never be the same as long as I live. I will be thinking about this every day of the world I spend in that cannery.

Mama was saying how sad it was when Walter covered Emma's head with his bandanna and lifted her like a little child up into the wagon, still holding that paring knife in her hand and her face bleeding into the bandanna.

What she did not tell me was that the talk had already started about Emma being a witch. But I would hear plenty of that the next day at church. Miriam Martin of course was leading the pack. She stood right there on the church porch at the top of the steps and said the stupidest things. Trying to make it out like some Bass family curse had been visited on Emma because of Lilly Bass being a witch and dying in the mysterious way she did.

My God, you would think they would let Lilly Bass lie.

I'm just sick about not going to see Emma all that time. I may never have the courage to show my face at the Bass house again.

41

November
Naomi

THERE WERE TIMES DURING THE SUMMER and early fall when I thought maybe I really would leave Henry and go to Kansas City. I'm not sure why I stayed. Maybe it was Walter, the way he hovered around Emma, nursed her along.

Or maybe it was Emma herself, sitting there in that dark dining room at their house looking out the window the way she did day after day, and nobody to sit with her. Walter did all he could, but he couldn't do that.

Ben and Martha were scared to death of Emma staying by herself at the farm while Walter was at the mill every day, but Walter wouldn't hear of moving her. She wasn't helpless, he said. She would be alright. He could take care of her.

I sat with her off and on, when I could. She spent most of the winter in that chair at the table, her Bible open in front of her, whispering about the cords that were binding her. About her tongue clinging to the roof of her mouth.

I understood her better than she knew. Understood that sometimes a woman has got to do things. But of course I couldn't tell her that. Other women might do what Emma did and be able to start over. If it really was that easy.

Still, it is hard to imagine a woman sitting in the town square and cutting her face like that. Like something out of a nightmare.

I went over to see Emma the next day, as soon as I heard about what she did. She sat there at the dining room table looking at me like a spaniel, her face bandaged, and told me that she was carrying the iniquity of the people on her shoulders.

The fine new hair coming in on her head reminded me of the down on a quail's face.

I'll never forget the day she shaved her head. Henry came in for lunch fuming that Walter hadn't shown up for work. Said Walter hadn't been worth a damn at the mill since Emma lost those twins, ranted about how a man's got to put something like that behind him and go on. Then he headed for Walter's place after lunch to straighten things out.

What happened that afternoon was funny in a pitiful sort of way. Henry came home looking like he had seen a ghost and told me to get out there and see what I could do. Walter was sitting out in the wagon looking like someone who's just been dragged out of a mine cave-in. Henry's horse was tied to the back of the wagon. He'd driven Walter in with him, was taking him on out to the mill. They had work to do, and they were by god going to do it. When I asked him what in the world had happened, he couldn't even say it. His face flushed red, the white scar a slash across his temple. Men can be so helpless.

What is it that makes a woman's hair so sacred? I confess that when I got to Emma's house that day I was shocked. I had never seen a woman that way, shorn of every strand of hair.

But as the dust particles circled in the sunlight around her, I had the crazy thought that she was beautiful. That I had never seen anything so beautiful. Like the mannequins in the window of J. T. Wilson's in Fayetteville, without their wigs. She seemed perfect somehow. Her head smooth. Her gray eyes large. Her brows dark.

Then she sat at the dining room table and told me, in the simplest way, like a child, that she was being obedient. She pushed the Bible across the table to me with her finger planted on the fifth chapter of Ezekiel. Then she sat like a stone and watched me read every word. The Lord told Ezekiel to shave his head with a barber's razor, to weigh his hair and divide it, burn a third of it in the middle of the town, smite all around a third of it with a sword, and scatter the last third in the wind. That's a recipe for success if I ever heard one. I had never cared for the prophet Ezekiel. Too much of a circus act for me. The only reading I cared much for from the many long and dreary readings assigned by my father from the Old Testament prophets was Jeremiah, the weeping prophet, thrown in the miry pit and left to starve. Nothing flashy about that. Jeremiah would have liked Marcus Aurelius.

Emma's hair was piled on a clean white pillow case, beside it the basin, the foam of the shaving soap specked with hair floating in it, the handle of the razor showing from behind the basin. The oval mirror that lay on the table reflected the gray paper on the ceiling.

After I finished reading, she nodded as if there could be no doubt now that I understood. She separated part of her hair out and held it in one hand. Then she took me by the other hand and led me out to the orchard, telling me the whole time about the throne of fire. My heart was beating hard.

But I think I was as much afraid of her beauty as of her madness, that unearthly purity of her just-shaved head above those gray eyes. I wanted to comfort her, but she took that handful of hair and flung it up into the chilly wind, and it scattered into the trees all spotted with the red tips of the early apple blossoms.

She thought she was carrying the iniquity of the people on her shoulders. I wonder what she sees now in that crusty old preacher at that cracker-box little church, now that her mind has come back right. After all he has done. To go from sackcloth and ashes to the singing and dancing. I wonder if it is the same Holy Ghost that moves her now as moved her then. I wonder if she is carrying my iniquities.

During all the time that Emma's mind was lost in the Old Testament prophets, she was the daughter of Zion who wept bitterly in the night, and all her friends dealt treacherously with her. There was no sorrow like hers. Her god had sent fire into her bones and spread a net for her feet and made her desolate, and there were none to comfort her.

All I could do was sit with her. She cried about how the elders kept silence. She said that everyone who passed by clapped their hands at her, hissed and wagged their heads at the daughter of Zion. Her god had made her flesh and skin old and had broken her bones, and she was in a dark place like the dead of old.

It was madness, but still, it was beautiful.

The day Emma burned her hair in the square and cut her face, Miriam Martin came straight from the square to my house. She had not been to my house more than two or three times in all those years.

"My God, Naomi Bass, my God," she said as she brushed past me at the door. "Let me sit down before I faint."

She plopped down in a chair at the kitchen table and said, catching her breath, "I didn't know who else to come to. It was a nightmare. I have to tell someone."

And she told me what Emma had done. The burning of the hair, the knife drawn down across her face.

"Walter Bass stood right there in front of her," Miriam said, "not three feet from her, and didn't do a thing to stop her. Just stood there. It was awful."

Miriam Martin is a prig and a gossip. I have never liked her, and never less so than when she sat there relishing the moment, in the kitchen of the sister-in-law, in the house of the other Bass. She would go from my house straight to Charlotte James or one of the other gossips and tell the tale. I was now part of the story. Coming to me was a master stroke for her, and she could barely contain herself in the flush of her excitement.

I would like to tell Emma that if I could shave my head with a barber's razor and burn my hair in the middle of the town, even cut my face with a paring knife, and make my life turn out right, I would do it.

In the bottom of my bottom dresser drawer, hidden away, I keep a small cardboard box. On the front in bold letters it says "Dr. Dromgoole's English Female Bitters," and in smaller type below "Cures all female complaints." Inside the box, a lock of Emma's hair, taken from the table that day. I have not opened it since I hid it away, but I know it's there. And someday, when the image of Emma shorn and helpless begins to fade from my memory, the fragile image of that stricken beauty, the box will be there, and the lock of hair, and I'll open it then and restore everything that has been lost in the interval.

42

November
Emma

WALTER HAS GROWN OLD IN HIS EYES. A dark line trails down from the corners of them, and they are fleshy, the skin above the eyelid making a soft flap down onto his lashes. He looked so sad yesterday that I said "Walter!" and was going to say what happened to your eyes, what could have changed them like that. Then I felt like someone poured a bucket of cold water over me, moving down my body from my head to my breasts to my stomach. And in that moment I saw again everything that had happened over the past year.

I saw the church and the testimony and the call to preach and the weeks of sitting at the window waiting for the angel of God to come and point the way. I saw Walter nursing me along, his eyes averted. I saw Miriam Martin, Kate Morrison, Isaac Samuel Cravens, all three clustered in my memory as if they were lined up waiting to get to me. I saw my hair in a pile on the table in front of me. Saw the look of wonder on Naomi's face as she sat across from me. Saw Walter walking across the square toward me with a soft smile, as if I was a child that had gotten into something she shouldn't have. But I wasn't a child, and my hair burned there in front of me in a dish, and I did what I did to my face, and Walter covered my head and lifted me up and put me in the wagon.

And yesterday as I stood there, it was as if a line divided the world in two, or I had just stepped through a door, and both rooms were right there with me, and I could still smell the room behind me and feel the air of it, but would never go there again.

And I reached up without thinking and touched my hair, which was long enough to comb again by then and wavy and I wasn't wearing a scarf over my head anymore, and then I touched the thin scar that ran down my face from my cheekbone to near the jaw line. And Walter was standing there waiting for me to say something else.

He said, "What?" And I couldn't have made any sense of it to save my life, but started crying and saying it's okay it's going to be okay now. And his dark eyes seemed to sink under the soft skin of the lids, unsure, but we hugged each other.

And something else happened then, like a small window opening up into a house that is boarded up, left just as it was when the last of the family, after years of living alone, dies. The light comes through the window, the only opening into the dark, and reveals in its small square of illumination a chair beside a table and a lamp. On the table, a book. Beside the book the reading glasses. And I knew it was good, in that moment of recognition, seeing Walter's eyes and seeing my life and knowing, even if only for a moment, who I was. Completely apart from babies, alive or dead. Apart from Walter. Apart from the whole world around me. On our wedding night, I stood in front of the house in the moonlight looking through the veil and thinking that the world was something separate, something that I looked out on from myself. I had never been more alive than at that moment in the moonlight. Our marriage was like a thimble full of gunpowder thrown onto the fire. An explosion of sparks and color and surprise and laughter.

And somewhere I got lost. I could blame the deaths. That would be easy. But it was something else, something more subtle, more dangerous. I don't know how to say it. I started believing a lie. I don't know where the lie came from. Walter, my parents, Brother Leery, myself—somehow the world, everything in it, told me, tells us all, that we have not done enough, that there's something more we have to do. Make a farm, make a home, speak in tongues, make a baby. But if we listen to the lie, no farm or home or baby is enough, and even if they're good, we will always hear a voice down in us somewhere that accuses us, tells us we're not enough, tells us we have to do something more. Like Lucifer tempted Jesus in the desert.

It's the worst kind of lie.

And gunpowder can put a fire out. Can leave it a scattered mound of smoldering sticks that must be breathed on, blown back to life. We are flames that burn for a little, and life is gunpowder, and every time it truly touches us we explode with the sparks and color, and then we hear the lie, the most beautiful lie ever told, and we listen to it every day and take it in and love it and begin to believe that we are not enough, that we must have more, do more. And all the time we're dying, but something is there to breathe life into us if we just push away the lie, turn our backs on it.

I run my finger down the scar on my cheek again. My hair will grow back, and it will be as if I had never cut it off, but the scar will never go away. It will always be there, and I will always have done it. I cannot take it back, and I cannot hide it. And that is its beauty. I am not what I was. Am not even sure what I was, but know it grew out of the lie. It has gone through the fire, and the dross has been melted away. What is left is true. And the scar is the sign of grace. I am not what I was, but I am this, and this is true. It's beyond what I can say, but I live in a peace beyond understanding.

Cain killed Abel, and when Cain pleaded for mercy, God set a mark on him. The mark of Cain.

People look away from the scar when I talk to them now. Pauline Roberts at the mercantile, Jim Beasly at the depot. Except Able Solomon, who reaches out and touches it now and then.

Mama and Papa are uneasy with it, especially Mama. How could she have known when she tried to warn me off from marrying Walter that it would not be his violence that would touch me, but my own? I would change the way she and Papa feel if I could. But I cannot.

My only fear, really, has been that the scar would always hurt Walter. That it would be a reminder of all that went with it. That he would find a way to blame himself. But from the moment he reached down to me there in the square, the knife in my hand, the burning sting in my cheek, the tickle of warm blood crawling down to my chin—from that moment there has been no sign that he sees the scar, that he even knows it is there.

It is the surest sign of grace.

And I am pregnant. But I'm not afraid. How can I be afraid, now that I am not what I was? I bear the mark of grace.

Part V

A Late Flooding Thaw

43

December 1909
Emma

A COLD MIST DRIFTED DOWN THE GRAY SKY moving slow like a cloud settling down onto the earth. When I reached the front porch steps at the head of the gravel path, I turned and looked all around into the mist at the wet world. I was warm in Walter's heavy coat and gloves. Walter's hats have always fit me. They are not the least bit big on me, even with my hair pulled back snug out of the way.

We have a photograph in an oval frame hanging on the living room wall above the lamp. It's easy to see in the picture why we can wear the same hat. Walter's head, like the rest of him, is long and narrow, and with the short cut of his hair, his ears look large. The slope of his shoulders and the long straight nose make his head seem even smaller in the picture. He holds little Reuben, not quite a year old, in his left arm between us. With my hair pulled back and covering my ears, my wide forehead and round face make my head look larger than Walter's. He is more than a foot taller than me, and our three heads in the photograph descend from left to right.

The cold air brushed across my face, and the light fog of

my breath spread into the mist. I turned my face upward to let the mist fall on it. Reuben was asleep on the front room floor in the middle of his blocks. I had gathered the eggs while I had the chance to do it without having to rein him in or answer the steady stream of questions he always asks. He likes to run wild among the chickens. He can empty a henhouse faster than a fox, and he usually scatters the hens off into the woods.

The world was at that moment quiet under the mist. I haven't always, but I have grown to love it like that. Two hundred yards away from me everything disappeared. The farthest trees were vague outlines with rounded, uneven edges. The trees closest to me, on the near side of the road at the edge of the yard, stood distinct, their bare limbs, wet and black, clean against the mist and the brown grass beyond. The steady drip of water from the rain gutter into the water barrel at the corner of the porch was the only sound. Except maybe for a fluttery patter, not as loud as raindrops, of the mist on the leaves.

In the open field just beyond the garden, one of the horses stood at the fence, his neck stretched out over the wire. Like a brown statue, he stared across the road toward the gully that falls away into the woods, his legs, tail, and mane black with the moisture. His great figure seemed to droop. All his lines swept and curved around each other downward, and he seemed attached to the earth through the black lines of his lower legs and his long black tail dropping thick and straight to the ground.

I opened the front door real quiet, not to wake up Reuben. He was still asleep, so I took the eggs to the kitchen. When I went back into the living room, I stepped on that board in front of the bedroom door, and it creaked and woke up Reuben. He rolled over onto his side, his head resting on his outstretched arm, and began playing with the blocks as if he had never fallen asleep, his eyebrows furrowed and his dark eyes focused on the blocks. I stopped to watch him. Walter says Reuben gets that serious look from me.

It was so easy giving birth to Reuben. Like he didn't want to waste any time getting started. He let out a squall when Hamilton Blake swatted him, and I don't think he's stopped talking since. He is nearly three, and when he talks, he is like a cat with a ball of yarn. He plays with words, knocks them every direction. You never know where he is going next, but it's never boring. After the birth, it was a long time before Walter stopped lying awake at night listening for sounds from Reuben's room.

As I watched him play with the blocks, an image crouched at the edge of my memory, shuffling now and then like the quiet child at the back of the school room. Naomi sitting across the table from me during that winter after we lost the twins, her face lit up by the soft light of the lantern. She crouched there in the chair in the dining room every day for a week, maybe two, like a wounded rabbit in a thicket, absolutely still, its heart beating five hundred beats a minute. I remember thinking she had come to me for refuge. But it was just my confusion.

Naomi whispered to me, once, when we were sitting at the table one of those winter afternoons, her crouched in the bundle of her heavy coat and muffler. I didn't respond to her. She probably thought I didn't hear her. But I was struck by it, even through the hushed whispers of that great crowd of witnesses who murmured to me day and night during those months, and it is one of the few clear memories that have survived that darkness. The way she looked down at her hands on the table after she said I was beautiful, as if she was afraid of the words.

Another thing about that time after the twins. Beyond Naomi, in the background, almost out of focus, Walter. He came and went, stopped now and then, reached out and almost touched my shoulder, then moved on to the next room. Like an animal lingering near the dead body of its mate, passing it again and again, testing the air, unwilling to leave.

44

December
Henry

I HAVE TO SPEAK THIS ONE LAST TIME. Not because it will make any difference. I have never tried to defend myself. I don't really give a damn what people think. There was something, when I married Naomi, like a light to a man lost in a cave. I scrambled toward it, not caring about the pitfalls in the darkness. What it was I can't say because it wasn't until it was lost that I stopped to look close, wasn't until the darkness swallowed it up that I thought to give it a name. I'm not trying to give it a name now, but still it's there and it's the reason, somehow, I have to speak.

It's a half hour before first light. I open my eyes to the dark and quiet. I have been dreaming about Virgil, and I listen carefully for the sound of his voice, the low, gravelly singing, the Irish in it barely noticeable. The blankets lie crumpled beside me, and I feel the cold on my bare arms and chest. I remember the old man, years ago when I was a kid, as he sat at the table, crying drunk in the firelight.

In my dream, I was at Joshua's funeral. I have dreamed about the funeral again and again over the past five years. I was alone at the edge of the empty hole dug for his grave. On the other side, the rounded mound of dirt rose, and a little ways beyond it, maybe twenty yards, a clump of people stood, dry eyed and silent, looking at me. Behind me Virgil's voice sang "Shall We Gather at the River" slow and quiet. He sounded sober, which surprised me as much as the fact that he was singing a hymn. The words were clear, but even though I don't know anything about hymns, I thought the song was somehow wrong. I turned and saw him a few feet away, staring at me, his face yellowed and limp, the skin waxy. His lips barely moved with the words of the song. I couldn't look away and felt like I was slipping off a tree limb hanging over a deep pool of water. Virgil's features began to darken, and the corners of his mouth turned slowly upward, and he nodded toward the grave.

I turned back, and Joshua's coffin, three feet long, a foot wide, a foot deep, lay on top of the mound of dirt beside the grave, leaning toward the dark opening. There were no handles on it, no ropes, and I wondered how I was supposed to let it down into the grave. The clump of people stood and watched. The only sound was Virgil's voice behind me singing. I wanted to say something. I wanted to open the coffin, but there was no seam in the smooth wood grain, nowhere a sign of a nail, a screw, or a peg. And I thought it might really be a big brown egg and if we buried it, it would never hatch. Or maybe it would hatch down in the ground and suffocate there.

I started to speak to someone in that little knot of people, but Naomi stood there by herself, and the other folks, barely visible, stood clustered at the top of a rise about fifty yards further on. Naomi's eyes were empty, her dark hair pulled tight in a knot at the back of her head. She turned real slow toward the head of the grave, toward the stone. I wanted to look at the stone, but couldn't. The grave was small. Too small. I turned to Virgil behind me, still singing real slow, and he nodded. The grave was too small. When I turned back to it, Naomi was gone. The rise of ground in the distance was empty.

I let myself down into the grave, the ground level at my chest, and reached up and pulled the coffin down to me. The wood sighed on the fresh dirt, then hissed on the gravel at the edge of the pile. The grave was narrow, but I took the wooden box in my arms and wedged myself down into the damp shadow. The hole wasn't long enough for me to stretch out, so I wrapped myself around the coffin as well as I could and rested my head on top of it. Virgil's voice still sang above me, the words clear but almost a whisper, "On the bosom of the river, we shall meet and sorrow never."

Dirt trickled down onto my shoulder and neck. My stomach tightened and the air blowing out of my nostrils moved the thin layer of dirt that spread on the coffin lid in front of my face. Someone stood beside the grave and, outlined against the gray sky, began to shovel dirt down on me. I held my hand up in front of my eyes to look. Naomi, her black shawl swinging loose from her shoulders as she worked, wore a bridal veil, old and torn, dirty like she had been digging graves a long time in it. Her lips moved slowly. Virgil's voice sang from them.

I pulled the coffin up tight against me. The dirt rattled as it hit the wood. Dirt landed on my arm and bounced onto my face. Virgil's voice sang from Naomi's mouth, something about reaching a shining river and laying every burden down.

I lie on the bed in the dark and take a deep breath. Every time my heart beats, it shakes me like someone has bumped the bed. A pan rattles on the stove, hollow and metallic, in the kitchen down below. A chair scrapes on the floor. Then it is quiet. I sit up and swing my legs over the side of the bed. I have never really been afraid of the dark. But I shiver in the morning chill. The dark seems heavy. I take another deep breath but can't get enough air. Pans rattle in the kitchen.

I slide my feet into the slippers, pull on my housecoat, and start for the bathroom at the end of the hall. The carpet runner in the hall absorbs the sound of my footsteps, and I feel like I am dreaming again as I walk. The candle that lights the bathroom wavers and the shadows there move on the wall.

The heat rising up from the kitchen through the floor grate just to the left of the wash table has warmed the bathroom. As I take the candle that Naomi left beside the basin and light the candles at each side of the mirror, the sound of movement in the kitchen below me echoes, out of sight beyond the grating. I could get down on my hands and knees and look through the grate, maybe even speak to Naomi, but I don't.

The pitcher of warm water stands to the right of the sink. Naomi was there only a few minutes ago. I breathe in carefully, nostrils opening to the warm air, feeling for her. But there is no trace of her. I pour warm water into the basin and wet my face, then wet the brush and begin working the lather in the shaving mug. When the lather is ready, I begin to brush it onto my chin. My eyes are moist, rheumy, and the skin around them sags.

I pick up the razor, carefully unfold it, and begin drawing it up and down the leather strop. The kitchen is quiet below, and over the silky sliding of the blade on the leather my ears are ringing.

Then the low gravelly voice of Virgil comes to me again, singing "Shall we gather at the river, where bright angel feet have trod." I do not turn and look, afraid he'll be standing there with his waxy face.

I stood by the rail fence as a boy and watched Virgil draw the knife blade across the neck of a squealing pig. My first slaughter. When I cried, he turned his head to one side and spat into the dirt beside him, then yelled at me to get away, to go back to the kitchen with the women where I belonged. I stood there sniffling, trying to stifle the hiccup in my chest. He snarled like a dog over a piece of scrap meat and with a whispery quick motion, like a buggy whip flicking over a horse's ears, threw the knife. It stuck in the post in front of my face with a thud, inert and black handled, and I turned and ran.

The shaving soap smells sweet, and I think of Pearl Bear looking up at me with that strained look in her eyes, part hatred, part desire. The smell of leather, lilac heating on the stove, the bed. The cup she held out to me with the owl's eye in it. To help me find my way. To help me see in the dark.

Walter stood in front of the burning house. The volunteer firemen stood in a loose clump by the fire wagon, watching.

The house was too far gone to do anything about it. Engulfed in flames. The horses sidestepped in harness, snorted and squealed. Walter stood just at the edge of the circle of light off to the left.

I told the fire crew to leave, to get off my land since they couldn't do me any good. I thought then that I was hiding the humiliation of Walter. But I see now it was something more. It was only what I had always wanted to do. But had never done.

The flat mask of shaving soap in the mirror looks out at me. Behind the mask, a weak, stumbling baby. Go back to the kitchen with the women where you belong.

Naomi's eyes looked up from the bed past my face, empty, apathetic. Her hair splayed out crazy, part of it across her mouth. The scrape of a pan on the stove echoes up through the grate, and Naomi's voice barely audible. I strain to hear what she says. She sings, but I can't quite hear the words. I get down on my hands and knees at the grate and put my ear close to the metal. It sounds like one of the old songs she sometimes plays at the piano. Her voice is feathery, sad.

I hold my breath and listen, but I cannot catch the words, only the rise and fall of her voice, interrupted by the movement of metal on the stove. Then the noises stop, and her voice rises just a little. I rest my ear against the grate and listen, my eyes closed, but the kitchen is silent. Neither movement nor singing for what seems like a long time. Then the sound of a spoon scraping against metal.

The sizzling of bacon in the frying pan intrudes, and the thick smell drifts up through the grate. I push myself back up, stand at the wash table, and look again in the mirror. My eyes have retreated even further into the mask. Naomi's face in the dream, skin white, eyes empty, was framed by the opening of the grave. I can't go back to the kitchen; I could never go back to the kitchen where I belong.

Virgil's voice, low, soft, lilting, wrong, all wrong, comes to me—"Soon we'll reach the shining river, soon our pilgrimage will cease, soon our happy hearts will quiver with the melody of peace."

45

January 1910
Walter

I HAD WORKED LATE. It was after dark, and I needed to get home before Emma started to worry. But as I was leaving the toolshed at the mill in the cold of early nightfall, I remembered all those nights I had leaned against that doorframe drunk, the town below like lights reflected on a pond when someone throws a stone in.

On winter evenings, just after sunset when the valley was dark, the line of sky beyond the hills sometimes flamed red, and long into the night the white stars hung above, out of reach, silent.

A quarter moon hung over the hills, and the stars were half hidden behind high, thin clouds. The pump handle rose in the darkness, barely visible in the clearing, like a claw reaching out of the ground, waiting to snatch whatever wandered blindly into it. The stones of the chimney and the scattered dark foundation of the house still stood beyond it.

Once when I was twelve or so, Lilly stood by a fire in the yard out behind the house, a big kettle of water steaming beside her. She poked a stick into the kettle and raised a pair of work pants up and looked at them. I stood with my feet planted and my hands raw and burning as I gripped one end of the pants while she twisted the other end, wringing the hot water out of them.

She shook the pants out and turned away toward the valley. "I've got no strength for work like this," she said. "My hands are ruined."

She looked down at the town, her eyes open wide, searching for something, just like the white-tailed doe that had wandered into Yancy Rany's back yard, that tried to stand up after Yancy shot it. It got up and staggered and fell and tried again, but only got up to its knees before it lurched over onto its side, pushed by its back legs, like they were trying to jump a fence. The whole time, it never stopped looking at Yancy. Big eyes, dark, looking straight at him. Like Lilly's when she looked at Delaney. And she turned her eyes and looked back on me, like that deer in Yancy's back yard. And she said, "I was pretty."

Then her eyes nearly closed, like she might fall asleep standing there with her arms down in front of her, the ends of the pantlegs touching the ground. I thought she was going to cry, but her nostrils spread, and her lips tightened. She lifted the pants and looked at them like she was trying to remember why she was holding them. She closed her eyes and her head nodded, and then she looked up at me like I was a stranger who had just walked into her house without knocking, and her face screwed up and I stepped back. Then she flung those pants at me, and I shied away as they flopped over my shoulder and neck. I jerked them away from my face and stood ready to drop them and run.

"Throw those over the line," she said and turned away from me and picked up the stick and stirred the clothes in the steaming kettle. She bent over the black pot, the steam rising around her, like one of the haunts Henry had always told me about, to scare me when we couldn't go to sleep. One of the witches that stole babies from their cribs and cooked them deep in the woods. Thanks to Henry, Lilly was a witch to me.

I took a deep breath of cold night air and walked down the steps of the shed and out across the bare ground to the well pump. It didn't matter now what Henry said. As they would say at the Word of Holiness Church, Henry had gone to his reward. If Brother Leery was right, Henry was with Lilly, and they were both burning in hell. I thought of him floating on a lake of fire and brimstone, his boots polished, his string tie snugged up beneath his Adam's apple. And on the broken shale shoreline of that lake a big black pot stands boiling and steaming and beside it a bent old crone, Lilly the witch, stirs the water with a long stick, her face covered by a dusky brown rag draped over her head. She stops stirring and dips into the broth with the stick and pries down with it on the edge of the pot, and slowly up out of the boil, like the insides of a minnow bucket with water gushing in all directions, Henry rises. His eyes are boiled away and his neck is laid open, like it was when I found him in the washroom at his house the week before Christmas.

I shook off the thought and stepped up onto the cement slab and took hold of the pump handle. The metal was cold, and my breath clouded in front of me and disappeared. The first floor windows of the hotel, as usual, offered the only weak light in Delaney.

When I found Henry lying dead on the bathroom floor, Naomi slumped in the hallway staring at him, I tried to get her up but she wouldn't let me. I sent Dr. Blake over there and went straight to get Emma. In the few seconds before I spoke to Emma, standing between the living room and the dining room, trying to get my breath, and trying all of a sudden to keep my gorge from rising, I thought that if maybe I could keep the words down, swallow them before they passed my lips, I could keep it all inside, keep it away from Emma.

The sky was a clear blue wall beyond the trees that day, and the sunlight made all the winter edges—the fence posts, wagon ruts, and brown grass—stand clear. The tangled web of bare trees stood out against the sky on the horizon, and the white trunks of the sycamores shined. Emma sat at the dining room table while Reuben slept, a cup of coffee on the table in front of her, light brown from the milk she always used in it, and her Bible lying open beside it.

During the dark winter after the twins died, Emma sat there at the dining room table, looking out the window, not responding to anything I said or did. Then one morning I came in from feeding and milking and there she sat, with her hair piled up in front of her on the table. The scissors and basin and shaving mug sitting there beside it. You might say I wasn't prepared. My knees got weak and I had to steady myself against the door frame. She looked like a starving dog, her eyes big and watery, her head not yet shaved but her hair cut off with the scissors, a scruffy patchwork like she had the mange. She looked at me like she was trying to read my mind, and I opened my mouth but nothing came out, and I went to the living room and sat in the rocker and rocked, not able to leave her but not able to go back in there.

And it was dead quiet. Just the faint creak of the rocker. Then it began, the click of the shaving brush handle on the side of the mug and the clink of the razor on the basin. I stopped rocking and listened. It was eerie, those little sounds out of the silence in the dining room.

I'll never forget the look on Henry's face after he stormed up on the porch and pounded on the door and then walked right in like he owned the place and asked me what the hell I thought I was doing sitting around the fire like an old woman instead of working at the mill. Then when I just looked at the dining room without saying anything, he snorted and said what the hell's the matter with you and marched into the dining room, and when he got to the doorway he jumped like he'd seen a rattlesnake ready to strike and yelled God damn and then stood stock still as a statue with his mouth open and his eyes moving from Emma to the table and back again two or three times. Just like the time Henry and I stood by the railroad tracks, the freight train groaning past in front of us, and I turned and looked up into Henry's face and his eyes were scary, wild, like someone I'd never known, and I was scared to death of running off with this stranger.

Henry hitched the wagon, threw my coat at me, and took

me to the mill. On the way we stopped at his house, and he sent Naomi out to do something about Emma.

So the day I found Henry dead, I stood in front of Emma in our dining room and tried to find the words to tell her.

"Walter, what is it?" she said and rose from the chair and started toward me.

"Henry's dead," I said. Too late to stop it. The words were out in the air with a life of their own.

"What?" she said and stopped where she was, covering her mouth. "Walter, what do you mean? What happened?"

And then I couldn't speak. The scuffed toes of my boots shifted on the cracks in the linoleum under my feet. Henry was crumpled down on the washroom floor, like he'd passed out while he was shaving. The candles were still burning and were getting short, and the wax from one of them had run down and hung from the holder like the stalactites on the ceiling in Harper's Cave. The razor lay on the floor in front of the wash stand at Henry's feet, along its edge a dark line of blood dried almost black. He was face-down on the floor grate, and so I didn't see the blood on him until I rolled him back. It hadn't pooled around him but had run down through the grate.

"Naomi," Emma said. "What about Naomi?"

"She was sitting in the hallway on the floor," I said, "leaning sideways against the wall, staring at him."

"Oh Jesus," Emma said, closing her eyes. "What was it, Walter? What happened?"

"Killed himself. Must have," I said in a whisper. "Cut his own throat with his razor."

She groaned, and I was afraid she was going to be sick, but she breathed deep. "Naomi," she said.

"I closed the bathroom door," I said. "The blood, down in the kitchen, was how she knew. I tried to help her up, but she pushed me away."

Emma stood there with her arms folded across her abdomen and cried. She'd be the one later that day who cleaned the blood up in the kitchen while Naomi slept. She'd take the grate out, clean it, put it back.

"Henry didn't show up at the mill," I said. "I went to check on him," remembering how he'd come to my house like Roosevelt charging San Juan Hill. "I ran and got Dr. Blake and then came here." I stood there in front of her, tired, waiting.

She wiped her eyes and nose and put her handkerchief back in her apron pocket. "We've got to get over there," she said. "You okay?"

I nodded. The sunlight fixed the cup of coffee and the Bible on the table like a painting.

And so they were gone, all of them. Virgil, Lilly, Henry. And a lot of other things needed to go too. The mill, the farm, everything. We had to start over.

Standing on the concrete slab, I levered the pump handle a couple of times. One star was real bright, just off the moon's lower point. A bright, hard beauty in the darkness. And somewhere the sun, beyond the top of the world, circled, lighting some other place, moving toward morning, pushing the darkness away.

I levered the pump handle again and shivered when the water surged out onto the slab. All those easy prayers I had prayed in the flush of the good times were like water bugs skimming across the surface of a pond.

Just up the hillside from me, the heap of stones that used to be the chimney of the house crouched in the dark. The night the house burned, I scrambled out the door and down the steps on my hands and knees. I lay in the dirt out front and watched the outline of the door in the light from the hearth. I lay there a good long time, till there was no light at all inside.

There's a reason why I did what I did after that. It has taken me a long time to understand it, to be able to say it right. But it needs to be said. If I'm really going to start over now that they are all gone, the first thing I need to do is say it right.

That night of the fire, as I lay there in the dark and sobered up, all I understood was what had to be done. I was clear on that.

And so I pushed myself up from the ground and walked, drained and unsteady, to the mill shed. I fumbled with the lock on the door and groped along the wall until I found the can of coal oil and felt on the shelf above the worktable for the box of matches. I went back to the house, poured coal oil across the front porch, and then doused the outside of the walls all around the building.

Earlier that night, Lilly had sat in her rocker in the dark corner, pushing herself back and forth in short rhythm, her heels hardly lifting from the floor. Her dry cough punctuated the steady rasp of the runners on the floor.

I was halfway through a bottle of Old Longhorn at the table, drunk enough not to bother lighting a lamp. The shadows cast by the fire in the fireplace, jumping on the walls, were enough to pass the time.

The next thing I know, Lilly taps me on the shoulder, and when I turned to look at her, her hands started in on me. Fluttering around my face, pushing the hair off my forehead, messing with my shirt collar. The look in her eyes scared the hell out of me. She used to do that kind of thing all the time, but had left me alone for a couple of years, maybe since Henry and Naomi had moved out.

"Leave me be," I said and slapped one of her hands away from me.

Both hands dropped out of the air like shot quail and worried their way into the folds of her dress. She breathed hard, dry and rasping, and hacked two or three times, a small dry cough.

Then it happened. She lashed out with one arm, knocking the whiskey bottle over. It bounced and rolled and spun around one full circle and then lay there, whiskey gurgling onto the table. Then she went for my eyes.

One of her fingernails laid open my eyebrow, and she flailed at my face, lunging as if she was going to bite, like a stray dog trapped in a corner. Her hands, after years of frustration at being held at bay, hammered at my face.

"What the hell are you doing?" I yelled and pushed her away. She was dried up and light as a bundle of corn stalks in August, and she lurched backwards and stumbled and fell. Her head hit the stone hearth. After the mute thud, she groaned and rolled slowly onto her side.

I shook my head, trying to clear my vision. "Mama?" I

said. "Mama, are you all right?"

She dragged herself around toward me, clumsy like her arms and legs weren't working right. She struggled up onto her hands and knees and reached out to a table leg to steady herself. Her hands were desperate now in a different way, clutching the table leg and pressing her weight up off the floor.

Then she reached up to the edge of the table and pulled herself up and got her feet under her and stood up, holding onto the table with both hands and swaying.

"Damn you," she said and fell forward, dropping into my lap like a sack of old bones. I jerked away from her, pushing her off onto the floor, and the chair tumbled backwards.

I scrambled to my hands and knees and waited for her to come at me again, not believing for a second that she would die that way. But she lay there in a heap with one arm stretched out toward me, her shawl covering her head.

I crawled to her, cautious and ready to scramble away again. I spread my own hands to steady myself on the floor that reeled under me, and I lowered my face to her outstretched hand. It was like a tarantula squatting and ready to jump, and the hair stood up on my arms and neck. The dark veins in the hand coiled under the transparent skin drawn up between tendons and bones. It was barely visible in the poor light from the fire.

I struggled to keep my balance, but I couldn't stop looking at her hand. I don't know how long I hung there over it, but finally I lowered my face closer, and then let my face rest on it, cool and dry. A fishy odor rose from it. The wood in the fireplace popped and hissed, and I pushed myself away and crawled out the door.

Later, as the fire gathered up the planks of the house, slowly at first and then spreading through the inside and finally pulling down the roof, I stood and watched, half expecting her to crawl from the flames, herself a lump of flames inching her way toward me.

I told myself that it was the only way.

She had always hidden when anyone came to the house. Once when Virgil, out of pure meanness, threatened to take her to town, she prowled the house like a caged cat and threatened to kill him if he did. I could not tell anyone how she died. There would have been an inquest. A circus. Dead, she would have been on display for the very people she had spent so much of her life hiding from. They would have come in droves to see the invisible Lilly Bass, the witch of Delaney. And she could never have met their expectations, a withered old crone in a pine box.

It would have been just what she deserved. Exposed and at the mercy of those people. But I couldn't shake the memory of the doe that Yancy Raney shot. On her knees struggling to rise, those big eyes trained on Yancy the whole time. And the memory of Lilly looking down on Delaney. Besides, it wouldn't have been Lilly lying there in the pine box. Not really. Not with her hands lying still on her stomach.

So you might say I turned her loose. And nobody, not Yancy Raney or Pauline Roberts or Othell Martin, would get their chance.

And I thought I had set myself free too. But it didn't take long to see how wrong I was. And in the years since that night, I have learned it takes more than fire.

I raised the pump handle and levered it one more time. I needed to get home. Emma would be worried. I walked down the hill to the wagon in front of the mill office, climbed up into the seat and picked up the lines. The lights of Delaney shined in the dark below me. I slapped the horses' rumps with the lines and turned the wagon down the hill.

46

June
Making Bread

NAOMI STOOD AT THE KITCHEN COUNTER with the heels of her hands pressed deep into the bread dough. Out across the field, beyond the barbed wire fence at the back of the yard, a quarter of a mile to the west, the brown line of the road ran north along the base of the hillside till it turned away up the valley toward the Sinclair farm. She brushed a loose strand of hair out of her face and spread flour across her cheek.

The hills across the valley were dark green in the late June sun, with shades of gray.

The thumping sound the dough made as she worked soothed her. A wagon moved at a slow walk along the base of the hill in the distance, like a spider edging along the window sill, the shadow of the hillside behind it a dark bruise.

She picked up the mass of dough, dropped it back down on the counter, and folded it in on itself, then turned and leaned against the counter and wiped her hands on a towel. In the living room the round cap of the polished newel post shined at the base of the stairway.

Money would not be a problem. Henry would not be a

problem.

In the long stretches of quiet, she focused her thoughts on the things at her fingertips. On the bread, the kitchen, the house.

She turned back to the dough and worked it hard, then stopped to get her breath. She brushed the strand of hair out of her face again. A dozen cows walked in a slow line across the field, and she went to the stove and got the coffeepot, brought it to the table, and filled her cup. The black coffee tumbled over itself, a slight wisp of steam rose.

She took the coffeepot back over to the stove, got a piece of wood out of the wood box, opened the door to the fire chamber and threw the wood in. She shaped the dough into three loaves, dropped them into three bread pans, took the pans over to the stove, lined them up and covered them with a dish towel.

She came back to the table and sat down. A dog barked in the field out back.

She put two teaspoons of sugar in the coffee and stirred it, then poured in cream and watched as it swirled into the vortex, black and tan, turning to brown. She stirred it again.

Fayetteville was a possibility. But her father, the Right Reverend Jeremiah Stotts, to whom she had not spoken in twenty years, lived there. Kansas City? All those nameless faces. Even in Delaney, Miriam Martin kept watch, ready to pounce at a moment's notice. And Isaac Samuel Cravens prayed over the city and would, no doubt, fold it under his wings, if only it would come.

But then, Aunt Rose Eltha came every Monday morning to drink coffee and gossip.

And Walter and Emma were accessible now. And Reuben. She was Aunt Naomi. And Emma was due again in just a few weeks. And they were moving into town.

Delaney then.

The cup and saucer clattered when she put them in the sink.

The smell of the bread dough was sweet, and the kitchen was warm. It was mid-afternoon, and bright sun slanted in through the window across the sink and counter and onto the floor at the foot of the table, making a bright square on the kitchen floor with crisp lines at the shadow's edge.

She sat in the chair beside the table and ran her finger along the smooth surface of the line that divided the two halves of the table. She reached out and moved her hand through the dust particles in the light, and they whisked through her fingers in a flurry, circling.

She ran her finger down the straight edge of the table, then reached up and took the strands of her hair that had come loose from the tight bun on the back of her head and pulled them down in front of her face. She looked through them at her feet in the square of sunlight, bright on the polished wood, so bright that the light seemed to come from the floor rather than the window. The strands of hair made indistinct lines running down across her vision, opaque and insubstantial. She brushed them back.

She toyed with the bow at the front of her apron, watched the dust particles circle.

She lifted her foot a few inches in the sunlight. The black laces criss-crossed the polished brown leather in a pattern that disappeared just above her ankle under the hem of her dress.

Delaney.

She went to the stove, picked up the big water kettle, and took it to the sink and poured out enough hot water to wash the dishes that were there. In the field beyond the fence a small boy walked, carrying a stick taller than himself, followed by a long-haired dog that stopped, raised his nose into the tentative air, turned his head slowly, and looked out over the field toward the house.

47

August
10:00 p.m.
Emma

THE CONTRACTION DRAWS MY STOMACH into a tight ball of pain that reaches through me until even the roots of my hair pull against it. When it seems as if the muscles in my stomach will snap, and when light streaks across the darkness at the back of my eyes and my ears ring so that the sounds of the room fade like voices behind a waterfall, I feel the child push against the impossible opening, and I am afraid. Afraid of being torn apart, afraid of the power that grips me at that moment, which is not the child, nor me, but some other thing, bigger, beyond me, that overwhelms me and thrusts itself into the world, blind to the heart of either of us, to me, to the child. Like rocks and old bones caught in the underbelly of a glacier, we are locked under the weight of it, pressed against the granite surface of the earth, and will be ground into dust.

Unto the woman He greatly multiplied sorrow and conception that in sorrow she should bring forth children. For we have eaten of the tree, and He has cursed the ground for our sake, and in the sweat of our faces shall we eat our bread until we return unto the ground.

The voices of Hamilton Blake and Purity beside the bed are calm, unhurried. "It won't be long now," Hamilton says.

It cannot be, or we will be ground into nothing by its power. Then the pain slides away, slips slowly into the bed beneath me, and I lie in the peace of its absence. I open my eyes, and the ceiling blurs. I roll my head to the side and, blinking my eyes to clear them, look at the oval photograph that rests on top of the dresser, leaning against the wall. We have not yet hung it, though we have lived in the new house for nearly two months.

The pain of the next contraction seems to seep up from the mattress, slide into my back and spread through me, like the muscles of my abdomen are sewed to ropes that go down through the mattress and somebody under the bed is starting to pull. I close my eyes and breathe heavily, the fear returning with the pain. I am sure I am going to die. I will be crushed here under the weight of it, torn in two, left empty with nothing that is me, no spark of life, just the dry bones and flesh, alone. I am hot, and I hate the sheet that covers me, hate the touch of it on my skin and the clumsiness of it as I push it away.

As the contraction strains to its peak then turns and eases, a moist rag touches my forehead and moves down the side of my face onto my neck and up the other cheek, where it rests for a moment before moving again to my forehead. Then a hand, cool and dry, takes mine and holds it, and Naomi's voice, calm, barely audible, says "I'm here, Emma. It's going to be fine, everything is fine."

And I remember sitting at the dining room table in darkness, after the death of the twins, in the overwhelming darkness, hearing her voice from the doorway, small and quiet. "Emma," it said, and she moved to the table and a spark jumped from the match she scratched on the side of the matchbox, and she lit the lantern on the table and sat in the chair across from me in the soft glow of the light and pulled her hood back off of her head and let it drop down onto her shoulders.

The memory fades with the contraction as it coils away into the mattress beneath me. I breathe easily and let my head relax into the pillow.

"I'm not leaving this time when the baby's born, Emma." Naomi's voice is close to my ear, almost whispering. "When this child is growing up, I'm going to tell him that I was there when he drew his first breath and let out his first squall."

"Naomi," I say, "I'm afraid."

"It's okay," she says, "Dr. Blake says everything's going just fine."

"Where's Walter?"

"We sent him and Reuben out of the house," she says. "Reuben's probably taking Walter on the daily rounds in the middle of the night."

The muscles of my stomach contract again. And again I feel the fear of the power that possesses me, my muscles not my own but doing the bidding of some other invisible thing. I remember the labor when Joshua was born, and I remember, barely, the pain as it got stronger. The funeral, the emptiness, the hollow echoing house when Walter went back to work.

Then, as if it were a nightmare mostly forgotten, the fall and the loss of the twins, the pain I felt as I lay on the wet ground, the branches of the trees, brilliant with autumn colors, waving above me, and the sound of water dripping all around, and the pain that made me dizzy as I crawled down the wet path following the sound of the music, of the voices of angels singing deep in the woods.

And I remember, months later, sitting at the dining room table.

"Emma?" It is Naomi, still close to my ear. The contraction eases and I open my eyes. I am tired and want to sleep, so I let them close again.

"I'm so hot," I say. "Is Mama still here?"

"I'll get something to fan you," she says and lets go of my hand. "Martha's in the kitchen."

"Don't go, Naomi," I say. I am afraid the contraction will come again while she is gone.

"I'll just be a second, Emma," she says. "Be right back."

I try to relax, but I can't. I wait for the first signs that the contraction is returning. I hold my breath and listen for Naomi but hear only Purity humming as she brings an armload of linens into the room. I look around for Hamilton Blake but do not see him. I lay my head back, close my eyes, and try to imagine Walter and Reuben walking around the Delaney square in the warm summer night. I wonder if there is any moon. I can't remember if there was any moon before the contractions started. I can't remember the town square or where the house sits on it.

"Emma?" Naomi's voice is quiet and close. The fanned air cools my throat and face, and Naomi's hand takes mine and holds it. "Emma," she says, "Dr. Blake says everything looks fine. He's gone out to the front porch to stretch and smoke a pipe."

The contraction begins again, and I breathe deep and grip her hand. The screen door pops shut, and the sound of Hamilton Blake's boots grows louder as he enters the room.

"Emma." It is him, speaking from a distance through the roaring in my ears. "You've got to push, Emma. It won't be long now." The voice fades, says something else I cannot understand in the tightening grip in which I am suffocating. I open my mouth to speak, to call for help, but cannot speak for the gasping for air, and cannot hear the scream I force in a slow arc through the wind and roar of water that is the only sound.

48

10:14 p.m.
Walter

ME AND REUBEN WALK ALONG the loading dock by the depot under a black sky thick with stars. Mud and algae and fish smells rise from the river, and sometimes honeysuckle. When we stop and stand with our hands in our pockets, water gurgles along the rock ledge down below the railroad tracks. The town is quiet. Then sudden laughter from the lobby of the hotel drifts across the square.

Probably a drummer from Fayetteville, come in on the afternoon train to pitch the stores tomorrow, telling stories to the Nielsons. Somebody inside the hotel lobby walks past the open window. The short, plump figure of Mrs. Nielson, whose husband owns the hotel, steps into the light and is framed by the window. She looks out into the dark, then moves away. She was a Sinclair, Emma's aunt, but I have seen very little of her during most of our marriage. Other than Emma's parents, I have not been close to any of the Sinclairs. Maybe that will change now that we are living in town.

Moving was the right thing to do. I first thought about selling the mill the day after Henry's suicide, when I went to the office and faced the awful possibility of running the mill without him. Ewing, Wheelin, and Isham ran the big saws that moaned and screamed in the background as I sat in the chair at Henry's desk, everything around me in perfect order, the desk polished and tidy. I forced myself to open the file drawers and try to make sense of what I found there.

But the files were stuffed with hand-written notes, reminders of things to do, bills of sale, orders for lumber. And there was a ledger—a maze of numbers in which I was quickly lost, with notes on payroll, inventory of raw lumber, and contracts with the railroad. All of the clean red and green lines on the white pages kept the numbers in place, formed neat patterns, smug, confident. I closed the ledger, laid it on the desk top, and covered it with my hands.

All those years I had avoided learning anything more than I absolutely had to know about what Henry did. The gully between our lives had grown so steep and rocky that we no longer bothered to cross it. I was half owner of the mill, but you couldn't tell it by looking. I was one of the hands—foreman, maybe, and paid better than the others—but I wanted nothing more to do with Henry and his polished surfaces. His obsession with order and his string ties. And he was more than happy to keep me in my place and act like a tycoon.

There had been a time when Henry and I were close to each other, like any helpless people are close to each other, our anger and fear focused on the same threat. When I was ten we tried to run away together. And there were times, later, that even though he could never have said any of the things one brother might say to another, he would act impulsively to do something for me. Like the time he took me to Pearl Bear to make a man of me. But by the time he died, whatever thin strand of sympathy had connected us had long since withered away.

Running the mill had appeared easy as Henry came and went between the office and the loading docks. All the neatly printed forms he waved in front of us as he filled in numbers on the clipboard, brandishing the pen in a flurry of authority, standing just beyond the reach of the sawdust and the sweat and the steam.

Laughter again drifts across the square from the hotel, and Reuben looks in that direction, scratching his nose absent-mindedly.

"What are you looking at, Reuben?" I ask.

He shrugs his shoulders. "The hotel, Papa. What are they laughing at?"

"Drummer telling some story from Fayetteville, probably," I say.

The bank building beyond the mercantile is a dark squat shape. I went there the day after I searched through Henry's files, went with my stomach churning, feeling helpless and stupid, carrying the ledger like a ten-pound stone fresh and dripping from the river. John Struthers, the branch manager, in his dark suit and gold tie pin, came out of the office to talk to me, expressed his condolences and shock at Henry's death, avoiding the details, and showed me the accounts for the mill. He was very helpful. Henry had made regular deposits and paid his bills. There were no debts. It was an easy sell.

Turning loose of the farm was more difficult. A dozen

years of marriage, love making and sorrow, birth and death, soaked into the woodwork, the creaking floor boards, the soil. Emma struggled. The memories of Joshua and the twins would not let her go, as if the pain had hallowed the ground, or the farm become a monument that somehow made sense of their dying. She cried as she gathered the eggs from the hen house and as she walked in the orchard when the apple trees bloomed. In the end, it was Reuben who made it possible, his excitement at living near the depot, being able every day to meet the train, visit the hotel, watch the blacksmith work, and talk to Able Solomon at the café. He chattered about it for weeks and finally wore Emma down. And then there was the pregnancy. So she agreed.

With my part of the money from the sale of the mill, I bought a half interest in Roberts' Mercantile. Bill and Pauline are getting close to retirement, and I've got a couple of years to learn the business. If things work out, I'll buy them out when the time comes. Change the name to Bass Mercantile. Redeem the name at last.

It was awkward the first time Ewing and Isham came to the mercantile, with me standing there in an apron, stocking the shelves. But Ewing just laughed and said I was cut out to be a storekeeper. Now whenever they come in, they keep me posted on how things are going with the new owner at the mill. Man named Sikes. Moved here from Illinois.

The one-story frame house we bought from Job Delight sits on the square next door to Owen Dempsey's post office and general store, catercornered from the hotel, and in sight of the depot, all of which Reuben approved of. He leaves the house each day promptly after lunch and makes the rounds. Emma worried at first, followed him all over town, but it soon became clear that she didn't need to bother. The Nielsons let Reuben sit behind the counter at the hotel and pretend to check in guests. Jim Beasly let him wear his railway cap at the depot and stamp discarded tickets. And Able Solomon always seemed to have an extra piece of apple pie for him. He'd sometimes end up at the mercantile stacking cans into pyramids until they fell. Emma forbid him going to the blacksmith shop without her, said it was too far off the square and a dangerous place for little people, and he was satisfied to go with me when I had business there.

When we reach the end of the loading dock, the silence seems strange, not filled with his chatter. He has said almost nothing since the two of us were shooed out of the house by Purity when Dr. Blake arrived. Naomi has been at the house since mid-afternoon, when Emma's pains started. Martha came after dinner. She and I have struck an uneasy truce over Reuben.

Across the square at the small, white frame house, a dim light fills the windows and the screen door. The shades are pulled down in the bedroom, where Emma lies and where Dr. Blake and Purity work to deliver her. My throat tightens when I think of it.

The evening is pleasant for August. Late summer on the river can be awful, so muggy your skin stays damp, clothes stick to you, and the mosquitos whine around your head, persistent, and bite through your shirt.

"There's the dipper and Orion," I say. I recognize them from Emma's showing them to Reuben so often. They are the only constellations I know.

"Why does the train track smell funny?" Reuben says. He has climbed down from the loading dock and is standing on the sloped gravel of the track bed, throwing rocks across the tracks toward the river.

"Creosote," I say, looking down at him.

"Like Gran makes in the kettle," he says.

I smile but don't answer.

"I like Aunt Naomi," he says. "She talks to me a lot. I like it when she laughs." He tries to balance on one of the rails, his arms outstretched, tilting back and forth. He bends at the waist, then pitches over onto the bank again. The track stretches into the darkness and bends slowly with the river as it moves south toward the town of Patrick.

The lane leading to the cemetery curves like that, up and away from the road, two parallel wagon tracks passing under the arched gate. The day of Henry's funeral was overcast, the temperature in the twenties, a dusting of snow. Miserable weather. The ground in the cemetery was a patchwork of white and brown, the snow gathering in the slight depressions, surrounded by the dry winter grass. Brown leaves piled against the base of some of the stones and all along the fence of the south end of the cemetery.

Naomi stood rigid during the service, her face composed behind a thin black veil, staring ahead, across the grave and beyond the cemetery into the woods. Emma stood beside her, the soft hood of her cloak hiding her face, quietly raising her handkerchief to her eyes throughout the brief eulogy, one arm locked with Naomi's. A large crowd attended the service. Another Bass scandal. I was sure people were thinking about Lilly and the burning of the house. It made me uncomfortable. We shifted our weight in the cold and hunched our shoulders, and our breaths clouded white before fading away.

Emma and I had offered to take care of the funeral arrangements for Naomi, intending to use her uncle, Isaac Samuel Cravens, but Naomi surprised us. She requested the service be done by Brother Leery. Insisted on it. I went to Brother Leery at his cabin up on Foster's Mountain just the other side of the river, told him what she said, and asked if he'd be willing. The old man looked down at the worn boards of the porch, shook his head slowly, and ran his fingers through his beard.

"It's a hard thing," he said, "preaching over a man like Henry Bass." His voice was not cold or judgmental, but pondering. He looked at the porch in silence. "Can't make a silk purse out of a sow's ear," he said. "Supposed to comfort the family, pay a man his due." He shook his head again.

He pulled his fingers through his beard, reaching up to his chin each time as if he were picking an apple. It was a soothing motion, and as we stood there on the front porch of the cabin, the town below us in the distance, the air cold, the trees bare, the river a bright band curving through the trees, the old man deep in thought, crows called in the woods up the ravine behind the house.

"He's burning in Hell and that's a fact," Brother Leery said, "and I'm supposed to be speaking the true word." He was quiet again for a few seconds, then sighed at his own decision. "I guess I'll tell a little truth, leave a little out, like always."

The service was short. Brother Leery preached about the suffering of life, about the rain falling on the just and the unjust, about the death that comes to all men alike, great and small, and about the resurrection to eternal life. The people from The Word of Holiness Church offered an occasional amen, but it was otherwise pretty quiet. Naomi had requested that only one hymn be sung, after the eulogy. So we sang "Amazing Grace," but it was unconvincing, drifting out into the cold air and, like the vapor from our mouths, disappearing quickly.

It occurred to me, standing there listening to Brother Leery, that Henry would have understood none of it, as he had understood nothing at the funeral of Joshua or the twins. Me and Henry had buried the charred bones of Lilly Bass without a preacher, without friends, without any fuss whatsoever, just Orville Waite's burial crew sliding the casket into the ground, covering it up, and setting a small stone. I wished it could have been that way for Henry, too.

He had always scoffed at religion. The idea of him burning in Hell made my skin crawl as I stood beside Emma, holding my hat in front of me. And the question came to me over and over: Why had he killed himself? The mill was making money, he had a good wife, good home. I looked at the casket resting on the poles laid across the clean cut sides of the grave. I still don't know why he did it. He was the strong one who knew exactly what to do. He had no patience for weakness. But I can't say that I ever knew what was going on inside him.

"Papa, I'm going over to the hotel," Reuben says. "You coming? Aunt Mary likes me to check people in for her. Will anybody check in this time of night?"

"No, Reuben, it's mostly just when the train arrives," I say, and I jump down from the platform and follow him.

He reaches up and takes my hand as we angle across the square toward the hotel. An empty wagon stands off to one side of the lane that runs in front of the hotel and leads to the cannery, a dark outline in the moonlight a hundred yards down the tracks. The tip of the wagon tongue lies on the ground, joined there by its shadow. It reminds me of the head of a fox. Reuben stomps his feet to make the dust rise and kicks at a rock.

"I'm gonna be an engineer some day and live in the hotel," he says, "and check people in when they get off the train."

"Aunt Mary will like that," I say.

We stop on the porch of the hotel, which faces the railroad tracks fifty yards away. Reuben looks back at the tracks, his eyes moving as he imagines all the hustle and bustle of people disembarking and following him over to the hotel to be checked in. He smiles and looks up at me, raising and lowering his eyebrows as if to affirm what a grand thing it will be. He lets go of my hand and goes to the door, reaches up and opens it. The bell jingles and he goes in.

Around the square, the loading dock, the tracks, the buildings are gray in the moonlight. The smell of honeysuckle comes strong from the fence along the south side of the building. If I could warn Reuben, put into words some secret, some answer that would always be ready, that would carry him through the pain and confusion, I would do it. Sometimes it seems close, the knowledge that has been forming slowly over the years, but it is like the mist that rises from the sloughs along the river in the early hours of morning, between the night and the day, that disappears quickly, burned away by the heat.

The crickets and tree frogs sing all around me, and up from the river comes the bellowing voice of a bullfrog, three times, deep and rhythmic. I turn and go inside, and the bell jingles loudly as I open and close the door.

Philemon Morrison, who works for the Nielsons around the hotel, sixteen years old and the middle boy in the dozen Morrison children, sits at the counter to the left of the door with Reuben. They are looking through the register from an earlier month, laughing at some of the names they find there. The lobby of the hotel is a cozy place, with a couch and two parlor chairs around a coffee table in the center of the room on a large brown and blue rug with a dark red border. On the coffee table, a tall lamp with a half globe lights the room. A stairway just beyond the counter leads upstairs to the half-dozen guest rooms. At the rear of the ground floor a door with bookshelves on each side leads to the living quarters of Edward and Mary Nielson.

"Francis Frankfurter," Philemon says, turning to Reuben with his eyebrows raised and his mouth open. Reuben giggles and points at another name.

"What's this one, Philemon?" He looks up at Philemon, eyes wide, ready to laugh.

"I can't hardly read the handwriting," Philemon says, squinting. "It looks like Snipes."

Rueben grins and nods approval, looking down at the name. "That's a good one, isn't it?" he says.

Philemon turns the register page, looks down the column of names, and feigns surprise. "Here's one you'll recognize," he says. "Man by the name of Samson."

Reuben's face moves in on the name until he hangs over it, staring at the end of Philemon's finger. He looks up at Philemon and says in a high-pitched whisper, "Samson stayed here?" He searches Philemon's eyes with the open curiosity of a child ready to believe.

The corners of Philemon's mouth creep up as he tries to keep a straight face. "Sure enough," he says. "I wonder if he pushed down the pillars on the front porch while he was here!" He laughs and grabs Reuben in the ribs. Reuben squeals and struggles to get away, finally slipping to the floor and running to me.

"Hi, Mr. Bass," Philemon says. "If you're looking for Mrs. Nielson, she's just gone to bed. I'll be leaving in a few minutes myself." He looks at the clock on the wall behind the counter. "Nearly ten-thirty. Can I do anything for you?"

"No," I say, "thanks. We're just staying out of the way. Emma's in labor." I grin nervously as I say it. Philemon is likable, and I feel a twinge of jealousy at the easy way he relates to Reuben.

Philemon chuckles. "I sure know how that goes. Pa and me been chased off enough times." He closes the registration book and slips it onto a shelf under the counter.

"You're here late," I say.

"I'm fixing to do a little night fishing up by the mill dam," he says. "Just stopped in here to see if Mrs. Nielson would need me tomorrow morning."

Reuben leans against my leg and rubs his eyes. I pick him up and settle him onto one arm, and his head drops onto my shoulder. I regret the bell over the door when Reuben raises his head at the sound as we leave.

"Let's go back to the railroad tracks, Papa," he says, his voice tired.

Standing between the rails of the tracks, we both pick up stones from the road bed and throw them toward the river. We can hear the plop of the rocks I throw as they reach the water, and Reuben doesn't mind that his own fall short, though he listens each time before picking up another.

"Let's go see the cannery," he says and starts off down the track toward the dark outline of the building, stepping with each long stride on a cross tie.

I hesitate, wonder how things are going at the house across the dirt square, not wanting to go far in case word comes.

"Okay," I say and start after Reuben.

At the cannery we sit on the loading dock while Reuben swings his feet back and forth, saying nothing.

"You're quiet tonight," I say.

"Can we go see Mama?" Reuben says without looking up.

My stomach lurches. "Maybe in a little while," I say. "A man's gotta be patient at times like this."

He looks up at me, his feet still swinging steadily back and forth, one slightly ahead of the other. When he searches my face, I look away at the woods across the river.

A bullfrog bellows from the river, answered by another, then another. He looks in the direction of the sound and says, "Why do we have to wait?"

I open my mouth to answer, to tell him these things take time, but can't. I can't tell Reuben what he needs to know to stave off the pain. I have no talisman. There may be some secret out there in the dark woods, or up there in the stars. At that moment I don't know. It seemed so simple back there in the Word of Holiness Church, the music pounding and Emma beside me, praying like the voice of God. Watching people being struck down by the Holy Ghost. That same fire burned in our marriage. It had all burned with life and swept us along.

Then Joshua died. The twins, Emma, the church. And since Reuben came, I feel as if I live waiting for the next blow, trying to stay prepared, not letting anybody know, not saying anything, in case I bring it on myself.

Reuben's head leans against my side and his eyes close, and I think he will fall asleep, but his eyes open at the call of an owl from Yancy Raney's place just beyond the cannery behind us. The sound slides through the night and wraps around us as it calls again, then again. Reuben sits up straight and says, "Let's go find the owl, Papa."

"Alright," I say, though I'm sure we won't find it. A disembodied voice, soothing, reassuring, out of the darkness of the woods, or the shadows of a barn or abandoned building. Never seen, but always there.

Hand in hand we walk down the dock of the cannery and around the front end of the building, and just as we are about to walk out of the shadow into the bright moonlight of the wagon lane, I stop and Reuben looks up at me and I put my finger to my lips to quiet him. There across the lane, in the full moonlight, not twenty feet away, on the corner post of Yancy Raney's field stands a big barn owl, his body toward us, but his head turned up the lane in the direction of the schoolhouse. We watch without moving, hardly breathing.

The owl's head rotates back to us like something mechanical, and stops, looking straight ahead, straight at the shadows where we stand, and everything seems to stop, even our breathing. The white of the owl's breast and face are lit up by the moon. The heart shape of the face is exaggerated by the half light, and his dark eyes fixed there in the center staring out of the darkness inside him, unblinking. Like the heart of the world, so deep the night itself could fall in and disappear. So still that the rushing wind, even the thundering rhythms of the Word of Holiness Church, would be absorbed, silenced.

I could fall into those eyes. The crickets have stopped, and the tree frogs and the bullfrogs have stopped, and not even a hint of a breeze touches our skin, and I can't feel Rueben's hand in mine. The owl's eyes are all I can see, there in the heart-shaped face. Everything else slides away into gray nothing, at the center of which the eyes look back into mine, and

I must give myself up, fall into the mystery, the experience beyond memory, beyond knowledge, beyond time. Or turn away, turn back to all those things that have consumed me every day of my life—Virgil, Lilly, Henry, Emma, the church, Joshua and the twins, Reuben, Delaney.

They are all just out of reach, like the images of a dream just after I wake—an impression, a sure sense that something is there, something that made a difference, that I need to see. But only the impression remains, and I feel as if I am standing on the edge of a bluff looking out over the empty space before me.

And I lean toward the face in the moonlight, toward the dark unblinking eyes, and the smell of honeysuckle slips over me sweet and thick, and I want to fall forward, fall into the eyes. And the word rises up from my belly like sudden laughter, like honey sweet on my tongue. Yes. And I open my mouth, and the word washes over me like those moments with Emma in the moonlight, when life pours into life and there are no words, only surrender. And I want to reach out to the face in the moonlight, and at that moment, before I lift my hand, the eyes sweep toward me, and Rueben yells "Papa!" and I hear the wings beat whump whump in the thick sweet air, and I feel the warmth and the rush of movement and Reuben's arms clinging round my legs and his voice excited "Papa, did you see it? It flew right over us. I thought it was after us. Wait till I tell Mama." And he laughs and jumps up and down and runs back to the dock of the cannery where the owl has disappeared.

And the word unlocked breaks into the night, and I say "Yes!" I say "Yes, I saw it," the words lost in laughter. I run after Reuben, out onto the cannery dock, out into the moonlight, run after him on up to the end of the dock where we stop and look out over the river to the woods that rise up on Foster's Mountain.

"Golly, Papa," he says, reaching out for my hand, "I thought he was gonna get us. Will he come back, Papa? Where is he now?"

"Yes," I say, "Yes," and I laugh again, and then we are silent, watching over the river. The night sings around us, the crickets and tree frogs in their rolling chorus.

I sit again on the edge of the dock, breathe the smell of the moss and the mud and the railroad tracks and the honeysuckle. Reuben sits beside me, leans against me, yawns and snuggles under my arm. He will sleep now, and all I want is to hold him there to me.

But my name is shouted nearby. "Mr. Bass!" It's Philemon, walking quickly down the track toward us, waving his hand above his head. My heart heaves in my chest.

"Mr. Bass," Philemon says as he reaches us, "I reckon your waiting is over. Looks like you got yourself another baby boy, and your wife wants to see the two of you. Purity caught me crossing the square and told me to find you all." He reaches to shake my hand and says "Congratulations" and stands waiting, good natured.

I reach out to Philemon and almost lose Reuben off my lap, then scoop him up onto my shoulder. I slip down off the dock and shake Philemon's hand, then start down the tracks toward the square with Philemon behind me in a rambling tale about the birth of his little brother Billy.

His name will be Caleb. The stars hang in the heat of the sky, and the deep burrump of the bullfrog comes from the river.

As we come out onto the square, the gray light on the dirt there, and on the roofs of the buildings, and on the picket fence along the side of the hotel yard surrounds the dark shadows beneath the oak and elm and sycamore trees in the yards and beneath the porches of the storefronts. As I stride toward the house, toward the light of the bedroom window and the screen door, Reuben snugged up against me like a half-full gunny sack, Philemon gives his goodbyes behind me, and a bolt of energy rises up from my stomach through my chest and I want to shout.

Emma is waiting, and I imagine Caleb on the bed beside her, red-faced and sleeping or cooing or crying. I laugh out loud and Reuben's head moves on my shoulder, and I walk faster.

49

Two Days Later
Purity

IT IS A FEARFUL THING TO FALL into the hands of the living God. That is what the Bible says. Mama says it means unrepentant sinners. But I'm not so sure. My life, for instance. It's scary to think about growing old in this house. The Bible also says "Be strong, do not fear. Your God will come and save you." But I've been waiting a long time. I am thirty-seven years old. By the time Mama was thirty-seven, she had eight kids.

The doors of my life are closing right before my eyes. That surely is a fearful thing in the hands of the living God.

I sweat a lot. Always have. The one and only way for me to get any relief at all in August is to sneak out onto the front porch in my slip late at night, after Mama and Daddy have gone to sleep. Sit back in that rocker and put my feet up in the cane chair and pull my slip up over my thighs. Sip a little cool tea and make a little breeze by rocking. Daddy would have a fit. But I can't tell you how good it feels, and I might even fall asleep and wake up I don't know what time of a night and have to get myself inside and to bed before Daddy gets up at the god-awful hour of four in the morning to go milk the cows.

Some day he will come walking out that door, and there I will be, sound asleep, exposed in my slip, and he will have a heart attack.

I cut my hair yesterday. I had those long braids since I was ten, I guess. But I was sitting there in front of the mirror yesterday morning, after being up late delivering Walter and Emma's baby Caleb the night before, and I realized that I had wasted part of nearly every day of the last three decades messing with that long hair. That was fine and dandy when all I had to do was the housework and help raise little brothers and sisters. Maybe a little garden work on the side. But I am way beyond that now. I still do most of the housework around here, thanks to Doctor Dromgoole's, but I also work a regular shift at the cannery and in my spare time deliver babies. And since Faith McCormick died in her sleep nearly two years ago, delivering babies around here has become a good-sized chaw, as Uncle Ebert would always say about anything that was more work than he wanted to do.

At least I am not raising any more kids for Mama and Daddy. Moria Lynn and Sarah June are both married and have kids of their own. I deliver their kids, but I will not raise them. Though it might be a good idea if somebody did. Sarah June's youngest is spoiled rotten already. He pitched a fit at the dinner table last Tuesday because I put green beans on his plate. He had already fallen on the floor and cried earlier that afternoon when Sarah June was ready to leave the house. He just couldn't live if he couldn't spend the night with Meemee and Peepee, which are ridiculous names for grandparents if you ask me, but of course Sarah June would never ask me, and those are exactly the kinds of names Sarah June would think were cute.

And of course all he wanted on his plate at dinner, after Sarah June was gone, was mashed potatoes, not a speck of anything else. And the first thing he does is start playing in the mashed potatoes, not putting a single bite in his mouth, with Meemee and Peepee sitting there smiling like it was the cutest thing they had ever seen. Well, I saw no reason at all for little Teddy—Sarah June named him Theodore Roosevelt Beasley, a name he will suffer under all his life, but of course that never once occurred to Sarah June, who thinks that Teddy Roosevelt is Jesus reincarnated and that the country is going to the dogs under Taft—anyway, I saw no reason for Theodore Roosevelt to waste the mashed potatoes and not get any vitamins to boot. So I put a helping of green beans down and told him, just as sweet as I know how, to eat them so he would grow up big and strong like Peepee.

That's when he pitched the fit. Started screaming at the top of his lungs "No geen beans!" After three or four times, he stopped and looked at me with his bottom lip stuck out like someone from darkest Africa.

"Then stop playing in the mashed potatoes and eat them," I said, still just as pleasant as you please.

He threw his table spoon at me. I could have been permanently blinded in one eye. If he was my child, the next step would have been easy—across my lap and tan his little bottom.

"I want Mama, I want Mama," he started screaming, turning red in the face, then putting his head down on his arms and bawling. A big put-on, plain as day.

"Now look what you've done," Mama says, looking at me and scrunching up her lips, and Teddy Roosevelt runs and gets in her lap.

Like I said, I will not be raising my nephews and nieces.

My little brother Samuel is all grown and gone. Mary Grace is eighteen and won't last another year. Not that we will notice when she is gone, since she hasn't lifted a finger to help since she got breasts and the boys suddenly noticed her.

Philemon is sixteen, strong as an ox, and a good hand for Daddy around the farm. Tennessee is fourteen, and to my surprise has turned out just as sweet as she can be, and a good worker. She takes care of Billy and Jackson Lee, who are old enough now to help out a little bit and don't need much watching.

All in all, if Mama could see fit to spend less time visiting around town, this house would be about ready to run without me.

That would shake the foundations.

I talked to Walter night before last, after Caleb was born. It was after midnight, and Emma and the baby had gone to sleep. Reuben had fallen asleep on the bed with Emma, and Walter put him in his own bed and then came into the kitchen where I was cleaning up Hamilton Blake's instruments.

He stood behind me for a minute like he didn't think I had heard him come in. But I knew he was there. Looking at me.

"Purity," he says, his voice quiet, and I couldn't help thinking that that was all it would have taken, twelve years ago, standing there in the mercantile, when I told him to speak his mind. It would have changed everything. But that is water under the bridge.

Walter sighed loud enough for me to hear and said, "I don't know what Emma and me would have done without you."

I was rinsing a pair of tweezers, opening and closing them as I poured water over them. Now it was me that couldn't say anything. Not that anything I could say would make any difference now. It is too late.

"I just wanted to be sure you knew," he said. "Wanted to say thank you. For Emma and for me."

I laid the tweezers on the dry towel with the other instruments. It was so quiet I could hear the clock ticking in the dining room. Then a floorboard creaked just beyond the kitchen door, and Hamilton Blake's footsteps moved into the kitchen.

Hamilton stopped halfway across the room and rubbed his eyes. His hair and mustache are turning gray. All of these babies coming in the middle of the night are taking a bigger toll on him than they used to.

"Don't worry about those, Purity," he said. "I'll take care of them in the morning."

"All done," I said, and I started putting things back in his bag.

Walter said "Excuse me" and walked past Hamilton out of the kitchen. His footsteps faded away toward the living room, and he said something to Naomi.

Hamilton stepped over to the counter and took his bag and started for the door.

"You don't like Walter, do you?" I said.

He stopped in the doorway but didn't look back. Just stared toward the living room.

Naomi laughed, and Walter said something else to her.

"Was my stethoscope in the bag, Purity?" Hamilton said.

Well, I'm not stupid. I know when I'm being ignored.

"No," I said. "It's hanging around your neck."

He looked down at the drum of the stethoscope against his shirt and shook his head. He looked back toward the living room. The clock in the dining room ticked steady.

"Funny how something can be hanging around your neck all the time," he said, "and you don't even know it's there."

Still ignoring me. I wasn't born yesterday. And I know which side my bread is buttered on. So I turned back to the sink and washed my hands.

"Good night, Purity," he said and headed for the living room.

I stayed in the kitchen until Hamilton Blake and Naomi Bass were gone.

Walter was sitting in the rocker with his eyes closed when I walked into the living room. He looked up and smiled.

I sat on the sofa and leaned back and looked up at the ceiling. I was dog tired, and I wanted to get on home because I had to work at the cannery the next morning. But I couldn't make myself move.

There was a time when I thought I would never be able to sit in the Bass living room again, back when Emma lost her mind and holed up in her house all winter and I was so afraid of going to see her. I have never been good with crazy people, and this was not just any crazy person. It was Emma. My best friend. What was I supposed to do?

I knew the whole time that I should go over there and do something. But I was scared to death she wouldn't even know me. Or worse, that she would know me and be real hateful and say awful things to me, the way those people do sometimes. I just didn't think I could stand that.

There wasn't a day went by that I didn't worry about it, and I felt just terrible. But I could not go over there.

And the next thing I knew it's been three months, and there was no way in the world I could knock on that door. And not one word from Walter the whole time. Not a word. At first everybody in Delaney was asking me, Emma's best friend, how she was doing. And when people finally quit asking me, because it became painfully clear that I didn't know anything, it was the worst feeling in the world. I would stand there when the gossip started, not able to say a word, with a great big rock lying in my stomach because I had not lifted a finger to help Emma. And there was no way I could tell anybody why. I didn't know myself.

Then one Saturday afternoon in the early summer it was over. I was dusting in the living room when there was a knock on the door. And there stood Emma. I was so shocked I just stood there like a big lump. Then I was so ashamed I wanted to run and hide. But before I could do anything, Emma was crying and put her arms around my waist and hugged me, and then I was hugging her and crying and saying I was sorry. And she just kept saying "I know, I know, it's all right."

Well, it wasn't all right, really. I was just sick about the way I had acted. And over the next few months it bothered me all the time. Emma was quieter, a little more withdrawn than she had been before that winter, as anyone would be after what she went through. But she never once said anything about me never coming. She didn't have to. It was on my mind all the time.

But when Reuben was born the next spring and Emma told Hamilton Blake she especially wanted me to be the midwife, well everything changed after that. I delivered Reuben myself, before Hamilton Blake got there, and when I handed Reuben to Emma wrapped in a bath towel, I was crying and Emma was crying and Reuben was crying and Naomi Bass, who was waiting in the living room, came running in and started crying. Walter came in from the front porch looking like a lost puppy, afraid Emma was dead, I'm sure, and I had to shoo him right back out so I could finish up with Emma. I felt sorry for him because I was blubbering and I'm sure I made no sense.

But I've been one of the family again ever since. Like a second mother to Reuben.

So I sat there night before last on the sofa in the Bass living room, the rocker creaking as Walter rocked real slow. I knew I was trying to say something that I couldn't even think of the words to say. Something that would make it all right that he didn't say anything in the mercantile twelve years ago. Something that would make it all right that I will never bear him a house full of strong children, children that would redeem his name and make him proud to be a Bass.

It has taken a long time, but I think I know now, after the

birth of Caleb, what it means to be in the hands of the living God. It is indeed a fearful thing.

Mama and Daddy will need someone to take care of them when the little ones leave, and there is, I guess, a good deal to be said for being needed. I look forward every day to peeling and coring with my friends at the cannery. I minister by the laying on of hands at the Word of Holiness Church, ushering weary souls into the Kingdom of God. I deliver babies with Hamilton Blake all over the county. I guess you could say I am a midwife of the soul and of the body. And I have Walter and Emma and Reuben, and now Caleb.

My hair looks good this length, and it will be a lot less trouble.

So I just sat there on that sofa in Walter's living room, feeling right at home, not in any hurry to leave, listening to the creaking of the rocker. And I didn't say anything. There was nothing left to say.